"Has everything a reader could desire: adventure, humor, mystery, romance, and a very naughty rake. I was absorbed form the first page and entertained throughout the story. A warning to readers: If you have anything on your schedule for the day, clear it. You won't be able to put *To Sin with a Scoundrel* down once you start reading."

—SingleTitles.com

"Steamy . . . intriguing."

—*Publishers Weekly*

"Fast-paced . . . a fun tale . . . fans will appreciate Lady Ciara as she challenges her in-laws, the Ton, and love with the incorrigible Mad Bad Hadley at her side."

—*Midwest Book Review*

"Delightful . . . filled with fun and some suspense and lots and lots of sexual attraction."

—RomanceReviewsMag.com

Also by Cara Elliott

To Sin with a Scoundrel
To Surrender to a Rogue

TO TEMPT A RAKE

CARA ELLIOTT

FOREVER

NEW YORK BOSTON

Book design by Giorgetta Bell McRee

Forever
Hachette Book Group
237 Park Avenue
New York, NY 10017
Visit our website at www.HachetteBookGroup.com.

Forever is an imprint of Grand Central Publishing. The Forever name and logo is a trademark of Hachette Book Group, Inc.

Printed in the United States of America

First Printing: February 2011

10 9 8 7 6 5 4 3 2 1

For CSSY 222
(You know who you are)
Our class discussions were the best inspiration
any writer could wish for.

And for my incredible co-teacher, Lauren Willig—
Your talents put me to blush.

TO TEMPT A RAKE

Chapter One

Ah, a naked lady. How lovely.”

Katharine Kylie Woodbridge felt a whisper of breath tease against her neck, its gossamer touch warm and wicked on her bare flesh.

“A naked *statue*,” she corrected. Ignoring the sardonic smile reflected in the diamond-paned glass, she carefully turned to the next painting in the portfolio.

The Conte of Como strolled a step closer and perched a hip on the edge of the library table. “It appears that Lord Giacomo has quite a talent for painting the female form,” he drawled, leaning his well-tailored shoulder a little closer.

A little *too* close.

As heat speared through the thin layers of silk and wool, like a hot blade melting butter, Kate tried to quell the liquid quickening of her pulse. *Don’t*, she warned herself. Oh, don’t react. It would be flirting with danger—nay, utter disgrace—to encourage the attentions of Giovanni Marco Musto della Ghiradelli.

Of all the men in London, he was the only one who might recognize the truth....

"Do you not agree?" The conte—who preferred Marco to his more formal string of names—traced a fingertip along the deckled edge of the watercolor.

Perhaps if she were rude enough, she could make him go away.

"Indeed," replied Kate, keeping her voice deliberately cool. "Lord James is a highly accomplished artist." She paused a fraction. "How nice to see a gentleman apply himself to mastering a laudable skill. So many aristocrats idle away their lives in debauched revelries."

"I, too, have devoted a great deal of time to the serious study of feminine shape and proportion," replied Marco, a flutter of amusement shading his gaze.

No man ought to have such long, luxurious lashes. Or, for that matter, such exquisite brandy-gold eyes, or such a supremely sensual mouth. Kate quickly looked back at the painting. And it was *most* unfair of the Almighty to bless a rakehell rogue with beautiful bones and hair that tumbled in sin-black curls to kiss the ridge of his shoulders.

No wonder he was said to be the very devil with women.

"And I would say that Lord Giacomo could use a little work on sketching the shape of a lady's breast, *si*?" went on Marco. Lowering his aquiline nose to within inches of the textured paper, he made a show of studying the painting from several angles. "It's not quite perfect. Perhaps he should draw from life instead of inanimate stone." The indecently long lashes gave another silky swoosh. "After all, he now has a lovely model close at hand."

"What a *very* vulgar suggestion, sir," replied Kate,

pinching back the urge to laugh with a thin-lipped frown. "Especially as the lady in question is your cousin."

"You don't think Lord Giacomo will be tempted to sketch his new bride in the nude?" asked Marco with a provocative smile. "As a connoisseur of Italian art, he seems to appreciate seeing the principles of symmetry and proportion stripped to their bare essentials."

The mention of body parts, clothed or otherwise, was absolutely forbidden in Polite Society, but as usual the conte seemed to take obscene delight in making a mockery of English manners. Which, in truth, was rather refreshing. She, too, found all the complex rituals and rules of the *ton* horribly constricting.

However, as she could never, ever admit that to Marco, Kate snapped the portfolio shut with an exaggerated grimace. "You are outrageously lewd, sir. And crude."

"So is Lord Byron," murmured Marco. "Yet women find him...intriguing, do they not?"

"That's because Lord Byron *is* intriguing. He writes wildly romantic poetry when he's not misbehaving. While you—I shudder to think what you do when you're not flirting or drinking."

Marco rose and smoothed a wrinkle from his elegant trousers. "I might surprise you, *bella*."

Her eyes flared in alarm at the whisper of Italian. Dear God, surely he didn't suspect that there was any connection between a long-ago night in Naples and the present....

No. Impossible.

But all the more reason to keep him at arm's length.

Quickly masking her reaction with a mocking laugh, Kate hastened to add, "Ha! And pigs may fly."

"Have I made you angry?" His sensual mouth slid into a lazy smile. "Come, let us cry *pax*. I was merely trying to tease a touch of color to your cheeks with my banter."

"Your mere presence is enough to do that," retorted Kate. "Your arrogance is really quite intolerable."

Marco clapped a hand to his heart.

Assuming that he had one, thought Kate. The gossip among the ladies of London was that the conte possessed only one sensitive organ—and it was *not* located in the proximity of his chest.

"You wound me, Miss Kate-Katharine."

"Actually, I've only insulted you," she replied. "You are lucky I am wielding only my tongue and not a rapier. Else your voice would be an octave higher."

A casual flick of his wrist set the fobs on his watch chain to dancing against the silk of his waistcoat. "Trust me, Miss Kate-Katharine. If we were to cross blades, you would not come out on top."

To Kate's chagrin, she felt a fresh flush of heat rise to her face.

Marco slid a step closer and flashed a lascivious wink. "I am considered one of the best swordsmen in all of Europe."

Much as she wished to riposte with a clever retort, she found herself momentarily at a loss for words. For all his braggadocio, he wasn't exaggerating his skills with sharpened steel. Even if she hadn't known for a fact that he routinely bested Angelo, the premier fencing master in London, she would have guessed at his physical prowess. In her former life, she had learned to assess a man's strengths and weaknesses in one glance.

And Marco? His gestures were deceptively lazy, but

beneath the pose of an indolent idler, the conte moved with a predatory grace. *Like a lean, lithe panther.* A sleek wild animal, all whipcord muscle and coiled quickness.

But that was not the only reason he was dangerous....

Recovering her voice, Kate stepped back and slowly drew on her kidskin gloves. "What a pity we cannot put such a claim to the test." He was not the only one who could employ theatrics.

Marco watched the soft leather slide over her skin. "You could use one of those to slap me across the face and challenge me to a duel." The hint of laughter in his voice—a rumble redolent of aged brandy and smoky boudoirs—sent a tiny shiver prickling down her spine.

"Tempting," she said. "But I mustn't forget that I am a lady."

"There is no danger that such a fact will ever escape *my* mind, *cara*."

Danger. The word stirred another whispered warning inside her head. Kate averted her eyes, reminding herself that she mustn't encourage him to look too carefully at her features. The chances were razor-thin, but he just might remember...

"No doubt because you rarely think of anything but sex," she said tartly, trying to deflect his attention. "Do you never tire of the subject?"

At that, Marco laughed aloud. "On rare occasions, I do think of other things."

"Now you *have* shocked me, sir."

"Not as much as you interest me, Miss Kate-Katharine—"

"Do stop calling me by that ridiculous moniker," she interrupted.

"Izzz wrong?" he asked, greatly exaggerating his accent. "My cousin Alessandra calls you Kate and your maid calls you Katharine. Knowing the English fondness for double names, I assumed—"

"Please spare me the long-winded explanations." As she preferred a more informal name to 'Katharine,' she was called 'Kate' by her close friends. Among whom the Conte of Como did not number. "And please address me properly. To you, I am 'Miss Woodbridge.'"

"Propriety is so boring," he murmured. "I should think that a lady of your intellectual inquisitiveness would agree."

Ignoring the remark, Kate stepped away from the display table. "If you will excuse me, I must find the bride and groom and take my leave."

"Why the rush back to London? Most of the wedding guests are staying until tomorrow."

"Charlotte has a lecture on medieval metallurgy to prepare for the Mayfair Institute of History and Science." The elderly scholar was, like herself, a member of the Circle of Scientific Sibyls, a small group of intellectual females who met each week to share their knowledge. And their friendship.

Given that the *ton* did not approve of serious learning for ladies, the five members had taken to calling themselves by a more informal moniker—the Circle of Sin. Kate felt a small smile twitch at the corners of her mouth. Without the stalwart support of the 'Sinners' over the past year, she wasn't quite sure how she would have navigated the uncharted waters of Polite Society.

"Sounds fascinating," drawled Marco.

"Yes. It is." She raised her forefinger and crooked it up

and down. "After all, without science, your steel might bend at an inopportune moment."

He was suddenly blocking her way. "I have heard of the phenomenon, but having never experienced it, I am not sure what could cause such a malfunction. Perhaps you would care to explain it to me?"

She gasped as his coat brushed against her breasts, the heat of him singeing through the silk. "*Nemernic*."

The dark laugh sounded again, far too close for comfort. "I speak enough Romanian to know that I have just been called a *very* bad name." His wide, wicked mouth was now only a hairsbreadth from hers. "I thought you weren't going to forget that you are a lady."

"I—" Her words were cut off as his lips came down on hers. Their touch was shockingly sensual, like sun-warmed velvet stroking the most sensitive spot of flesh.

The sensation held her in thrall, but only for a heartbeat. Recovering her wits, Kate struck a sharp uppercut to his jaw, her knuckles landing with a good deal more force than his teasing kiss.

Marco fell back a step. His nostrils flared as he drew in a taut breath and then he let it out slowly, looking oddly bemused. "Where did a gently bred female learn to punch like that?"

"Never mind," she muttered, surreptitiously flexing her fist. He had a *very* solid chin.

His nose quivered, like a bird dog on the hunt. "You smell like oranges and... something else."

Damn.

Before Marco could go on, a shadow slanted over the alcove.

"Oh, there you are, Kate." Alessandra della Giamatti—

now Lady James Jacquehart Pierson, wife of the Duke of Ledyard's youngest son—paused in the oak-framed doorway, her new husband by her side. "Excuse me, are we interrupting a private conversation?"

"*Ciao*, Alessa," answered Marco. "No, your learned friend and I were just having a very stimulating discussion on fencing."

A tiny furrow formed between her brows as Alessandra spotted the lingering red welt on his jaw. "Fencing," she repeated softly.

"*Si*, and had I known science was such a provocative field of study, I would have asked to join your little group ages ago." He moved quickly to kiss her on both cheeks and added a rapid-fire volley of Italian. "You are more beautiful than ever this morning, *cara*. Marriage must agree with you."

"And you are more incorrigible than ever," murmured Alessandra, deflecting the sly innuendos with a wry smile. Turning to Kate, she said, "If my cousin is annoying you, feel free to tell him to *va' all' inferno*."

Go to hell.

Kate made a face. "He's probably been there and back several times over."

"Aye." James Jacquehart Pierson chuckled. With his midnight locks, olive complexion, and muscled military bearing, he was known throughout London as "Black Jack." But Alessandra had assured Kate that he had a heart of gold. "I imagine that the devil booted him back to our world, after finding him far too obnoxious to tolerate for any length of time."

Marco contrived to look hurt. "And here I thought we were *amicos*, Lord Giacomo."

"Friends?" Jack arched a dark brow. "Don't press your luck, Ghiradelli. Your presence here is tolerable. Barely. In fact..."

Leaving the men to their verbal sparring, Kate drew Alessandra into one of the arched alcoves and brushed a kiss to her cheek. "Much as I hate to agree with your cousin on anything, you do look glorious. And happy."

"I am," replied Alessandra. Which for her was a notable display of emotion. Of all the 'Sinners,' she was the most reserved about her feelings and her past, even with her closest friends.

With good reason, acknowledged Kate. Alessandra had a dark secret from her past life in Italy that had recently come to light and threatened to destroy both her and her young daughter. But Black Jack Pierson, a highly decorated veteran of the Peninsular campaign, had proved his mettle in love as well as war by vanquishing a cunning enemy and winning her heart.

Glancing at the rows of leather-bound books, Kate felt her lips quirk. *Just like a storybook hero*. What a pity that a noble knight could not transform from ink and paper to flesh and blood.

Not that any mortal man could slay her dragon. Some secrets were worse than others...

Forcing a smile, Kate gave a light laugh. "We are all so delighted for you."

Alessandra squeezed her hand. "I am so grateful for my friendship with all of the 'Sinners.' I would never have survived the last few months without it."

"That is what friends are for." She paused, feeling a little pang of regret that she would be leaving Ledyard Manor that afternoon. "Speaking of which, I was just coming to tell you that Charlotte is anxious to return to London, on account of her upcoming lecture."

"Of course." Alessandra slanted a look at Jack and Marco, who were still exchanging barbs. "Come, let us fetch Ciara and Ariel from the conservatory, and visit her room while she finishes her packing."

The idea of circling their little group, if only for a short while, lifted Kate's spirits. "What an excellent suggestion. You don't mind leaving Jack to fend for himself?"

"Oh, once he and Marco stop needling each other, they will actually enjoy conversing on Roman art and antiquities. For all of my cousin's frivolous teasing, he is very knowledgeable on the subject."

"I never would have guessed that the conte had any interest in intellectual subjects," she replied slowly.

"Marco has a number of unexpected facets to his character, which he takes great pains to hide." Alessandra's voice took on a wry note. "But then, who am I to talk?"

Kate hesitated for a moment before answering. "I daresay we all have things that we keep to ourselves."

Let her go.

Assuming an expression of bored indifference, Marco slowly looked away from watching the two ladies walk off.

"Set your sights elsewhere," murmured Jack, as if reading his mind. "You may be her cousin, but Alessandra will chop off your *testicolos* and feed them to the Tower ravens if you try to play your usual wicked games with Miss Woodbridge."

Though he was thinking much the same thing, Marco reacted with a cynical smirk. "What makes you think she wouldn't welcome my attentions?"

"The fact that you are a conceited coxcomb and your arrogance is insufferable at times."

"*Si.*" Marco widened his mouth to a wolfish grin. "But most females find that intriguing."

"Alessandra's friends are not like most females," pointed out Jack. "Their intellect sets them apart, so you can't expect to charm them with your usual approach." He paused. "I imagine that Miss Woodbridge is smart enough to see that you are an arse."

"Trust me, Lord Giacomo, I don't need advice on flirting from you."

"No? Well, from what I have observed, you don't appear to be making much progress on your own."

Leaning a shoulder on the fluted molding, Marco watched the last little flutter of sea-green silk disappear down the corridor. To be sure, Kate Woodbridge was no ordinary young lady. But it was not just her brains that set her apart. There was an unexpected glint of grittiness shading her lovely aquamarine eyes. As if she had seen the grim realities of the world outside of the gilded confines of Mayfair's mansions.

Which was, of course, highly unlikely. Kate was the granddaughter of the Duke of Cluyne, one of the highest sticklers of Polite Society. She had been born into a life of wealth and privilege and was surrounded by an army of servants ready to do her bidding.

Such coddled innocence bored him to perdition. *So why did the sway of her shapely hips provoke the urge to follow?*

"Perhaps I haven't tried very hard," drawled Marco, turning his attention to the folds of his cravat. Smoothing a finger over the starched linen, he added, "It's hardly a fair match of skills. And contrary to what you may think, I do not deliberately toy with an innocent young lady's affections."

Jack gave a mock grimace. "Good God, you mean to say that you have a conscience?"

Marco straightened from his slouch. "You military heroes are not the only ones with a code of honor."

"Well, you need not wage any great moral battle with your self-proclaimed noble scruples. According to Alessandra, her friend can look out for herself."

Marco let out a grunt of laughter. "Miss Woodbridge may be clever and possess a cutting tongue, but that does not mean she is equipped to deal with the darker side of life." He curled a lip. "Rapscallion roués, jaded fortune hunters. Or rakehell rogues like me."

"Don't be so sure of that," countered Jack. "From what I gather, Miss Woodbridge has had a rather eccentric upbringing. Her mother tossed away title and fortune to elope with an American sea captain. She's spent most of her life sailing around the world."

He felt his sardonic smile thin ever so slightly. His cousin had not talked much about her friends with him. No doubt feeling that he couldn't quite be trusted with the intimate details of their lives.

"The fact is, I think she had a rather rough time of it these last few years," continued Jack. "Her parents died of a fever within days of each other, and only a deathbed promise to them brought Miss Woodbridge here to seek a reconciliation with her grandfather." He shrugged. "Apparently the waters at Cluyne House are anything but calm. She's fiercely independent, which tends to make waves with the duke."

"That begins to explain her salty language," murmured Marco thoughtfully. Today was not the first time she had let fly with a very unladylike word.

Jack chuckled. "Alessandra says she can swear like a sailor in nearly a dozen different dialects."

"Interesting."

"Yes, but not nearly as interesting as the collection of rare books I have here on classical architecture." For Jack, ancient Rome was a far more fascinating topic of conversation than Katharine Kylie Woodbridge. "Come, there is a seventeenth-century volume of engravings on the Temple of Jupiter that I want to show you...."

Marco reluctantly pushed aside all thoughts about ladies—naked or otherwise—to follow Jack to one of the display tables set by the bank of leaded-glass windows. Yet somehow the tantalizing scent of Sicilian *neroli* and wild thyme stayed with him, teasing at his nostrils.

Strange, it seemed hauntingly familiar, but he just couldn't place it.

And no wonder, he thought, dismissing the notion with a sardonic shrug. He had inhaled too many perfumes in his wicked, wanton life to recall them all. In truth, none of the women had been very memorable.

Save for one clever whore in Naples who had dared...

"Pay attention, Ghiradelli. If you drool on that Doric column, I swear I shall cut off your tongue."

Chapter Two

"What is that horrible smell?"

"Fish guts and dried cow manure." Kate shifted the inkwell on her desk and kept on writing up her notes, intent on catching up with her botanical work now that she was back home in London. "Sorry, I thought I had washed all of it off my hands."

Her maid eyed the streak of slime on the hem of Kate's work dress, which was slowly oozing onto the priceless Aubusson carpet. "Perhaps you might want to consider a change of clothing."

Kate glanced down. "Shite," she muttered under her breath.

"That's another way of putting it," replied Alice, who now was very used to her charge's peculiar quirks. Unlike the half-dozen or so predecessors, none of whom had lasted more than a month, the maid was not intimidated by noxious stains or foul language. "However, it does sound a trifle more ladylike when you say it in French."

"Yes, but I keep telling you, I am—"

"Not a real lady," chorused Alice. "Thank heavens. Otherwise this position would be awfully boring."

Kate grinned. "It was certainly a stroke of luck that Simpson found you. None of the others sent by the employment agency had any sense of humor." She tapped the tip of her pen to her chin. "It wasn't as if I deliberately put the dissected frog's leg in my sash to terrify poor Susan. I simply forgot it was there."

"It wasn't luck," said Alice. "After that incident, he gave up trying to find respectable candidates through an agency. I am acquainted with his cousin—don't ask how—and as the poor man was at his wit's end, he was willing to overlook the rather sketchy explanation of my past positions in return for me promising that I didn't faint at the sight of dissected reptiles."

"That doesn't happen often. I was merely trying to duplicate a lecture I heard at the Royal Zoological Institute." Kate brushed a leaf from her sleeve. "As you know, my specialty is botany."

"Is a fish now considered a plant?" asked Alice, giving another exaggerated sniff.

"I was just experimenting with a new formula for fertilizer. My friend Ariel and her new husband are working on developing a new strain of *Papaver somniferum*—that is a type of poppy from the East—but the seedlings are quite delicate."

Alice pinched at her nose. "Maybe your next project could be on formulating botanical oils for perfume."

The mention of fragrance caused Kate to suck in a slow breath and hold it in her lungs. She had always made up her own scent, a unique mixture of sweet spices and earthy herbs. The ingredients came from a tiny shop in Sicily that overlooked the Tyrrhenian Sea. It was, she supposed, a signature of sorts. Something that was hers, and hers alone.

Exhale, she told herself. Men were not subtle creatures. *Neroli* and wild thyme were used in myriad feminine fragrances. Marco had sniffed around far too many women to remember a fleeting encounter in Naples.

"An excellent suggestion," said Kate casually. "We could open a shop on Bond Street to earn extra pin money."

Alice pulled a face. "Can you imagine his reaction if the duke heard that his granddaughter was going into trade?"

"Yes, as a matter of fact, I can," answered Kate, unable to keep the edge of resentment from her voice. "Cluyne turned my mother out on her ear without a farthing when she dared to marry an American merchant sea captain against his lordly wishes."

Alice, who had heard a brief overview of her employer's history, clucked in sympathy. "Some people are just very rigid in their thinking, especially when they are surrounded by toad-eaters and flatterers who tell them from birth that they are always right." The maid thought for a moment. "No one defies a duke. So it must be hard for him to know when he is right or wrong."

Kate sighed. "That is a very wise observation, Alice." She took up her inkwell and set the thick, viscous liquid to swirling against the cut crystal. "But it's hard to forgive him all the same. His pride is so... so bloody unyielding." The ink spun faster and faster, creating a vortex that seemed to suck her mood into its black depth.

"I'm only here because I made a deathbed promise to my parents that I would seek a reconciliation with my grandfather," she continued. *But things were not sailing along very smoothly.* "To be honest, if I had my choice, I would book passage on the first merchant ship sailing from the East India docks and never look back."

"There is something to be said for a life free from worry and want," murmured Alice. "Here you are surrounded by luxury and people anxious to do your bidding."

"Yes, and most of the time it makes me feel like a bird trapped in a gilded cage. I'm used to my freedom, my independence, and I prefer to exercise my own judgment, rather than be treated as if I had naught but feathers stuffed between my ears."

Her maid smothered a snort. "That is for sure."

Kate tried to look offended, but a telltale smile curled the corners of her mouth. "Am I really that bad?"

"Well, let us just say that next time you wish to exercise your independence, try not to do it in front of Angelo's fencing salon. I'm not sure those two young gentlemen have yet recovered from having you threaten to cut off their cods."

"I didn't!" she protested. "Not precisely."

The incident *had* been a touch flamboyant, even for her. But Kate had thought Alessandra was in imminent danger and needed to speak with the infamous Giovanni Marco Musto della Ghiradelli without delay. It wasn't entirely her fault that the conte had chosen to saunter out into the street clad in a sweat-damp shirt, skintight buckskins, and bare feet.

"You may not have mentioned a specific anatomical appendage, but they weren't taking any chances." Alice primly smoothed at her skirts. "In the future, please try to be more discreet. I like this job, but the duke will have my guts for garters if I let you stir up a whiff of scandal."

"Hmmph," she huffed under her breath. "Had he been more circumspect with his own daughter, I would not be such a black blot on his precious ducal dignity."

"Society may remember the old scandal of your mother's elopement, but in their eyes, you are a perfectly respectable young lady who has grown up in Boston." Coals crackled in the hearth, speckling the ashes with a shower of orange sparks. "Let us try not to upset their assumptions."

Kate went back to her writing.

Moving to the delicate pearwood escritoire, Alice began sorting through the pile of invitations. "Shall you be wearing the indigo-figured silk gown to Lady Hamden's soiree tonight?"

"Drat, I had forgotten all about that." She slapped down her pen. "The dowager is dull as dishwater, and her musical programs usually sound like a sackful of wet cats trying to claw their way loose. I think I shall cry off."

"You've squirmed out of the last three engagements," pointed out Alice. "And the lady is a very good friend of your grandfather."

"Whose side are you on?" groused Kate.

"I've merely been listening to your little lectures on how a female must be practical and pragmatic," said her maid. "Attending tonight's soiree will please the duke—a fact that may prove useful the next time he frowns on something you wish to do."

"Lud, you would put Machiavelli to blush."

"Macky-who?"

"Never mind," said Kate. "He's an Italian gentleman known for his scheming mind."

"Italian, eh? Like that dark-haired devil with the divine legs? The one who looks like he was sculpted by Macky...Macky—"

"Angelo," finished Kate. "*Si,* like that one."

"Are all the men from that country handsome as sin?"

Sin. Recalling the tempting curl of Marco's mouth, Kate shifted on her chair, uncomfortably aware that somewhere deep inside her, a serpent stirred, slowly uncurling its sinuous scales. Damnably cold-blooded creatures, snakes sought any source of warmth—even the hellfire kiss of an unrepentant rake.

No. She would not—could not—let it rear its ugly head. She had been a bad girl in her youth, a wild, passionate creature, unbound by corsets or conventional rules. But she had promised her parents to reform. To abandon a vagabond life, fraught with danger and uncertainty. Kate knew that they regretted exposing their only child to such an unstable existence. Home had been a sleek wooden hull, and the roof over her head...

She stared up at the weighty rosettes carved into the ornate plaster ceiling. The roof over her head had been a flutter of sun-bleached canvas and an infinite stretch of ever-changing sky. The slap of the wind on her cheeks, the tang of the salty seas, the raucous shrieks of the soaring gulls—no wonder she so often felt constricted, confined here in London.

A small cough from Alice brought her musings back to *terra firma.* "Sorry," murmured Kate. "I—I was daydreaming."

"I don't blame you." The maid made a wry face. "And I've seen enough good-looking rogues to know better."

So have I, thought Kate. "Trust me, I'm smart enough not to be seduced by a scamp like Ghiradelli."

Alice didn't look convinced. "You know more about the real world than most young ladies, but men can be dangerous creatures. You know, Eve always gets the blame for giving Adam the apple. But I'll wager you that the cursed serpent was a male."

Kate laughed. "Seeing as the conte is also known as *Il Serpenti*, I would agree with you." She screwed the silver cap onto her inkwell, careful to keep the dregs from blackening her fingertips. "Don't worry, I'll be on guard against his fangs."

"But what lovely fangs," murmured Alice. "And that mouth...I suppose a woman could die happy from its bite."

Kate felt another little slither of heat in her belly. It was bad—*very bad*—to feel the slightest twinge of attraction for Marco. And she must try her best to be good.

"If I am to attend Horrible Hamden's soiree, I suppose you had better order up a bath," she replied with a sigh.

Preferably an ice-cold one.

She was here.

Marco edged forward and took up a position in one of the colonnaded archways of the music room. The movement must have caught her wandering attention, for Kate glanced around.

Their eyes locked.

His heart lurched and thudded up against his ribs. Her honey-colored hair was piled high on her head, revealing the elegant arch of her neck. Simple pearl studs highlighted her shapely shell-pink ears. The effect was entrancing.

Unnerving. Here he was—a jaded libertine, a notorious rake—staring like a spotty-faced schoolboy.

Masking his confusion with a sardonic smile, he flashed her a rakish wink.

Her lips thinned and Kate quickly looked back at the stage.

"*Ah, chi mi dice mai quel barbaro dov'è.*" Marco winced as the singer struggled through an aria from Mozart's opera *Don Juan.*

He had come here on a whim. His friend hadn't even been certain that Kate Woodbridge would show up at his great-aunt's soiree. The young lady often ignored the gilt-edged invitations to be part of Mayfair's exclusive social circle. As did he, but for opposite reasons.

She buried herself in serious studies, while he drowned himself in dissolute pleasures.

Glancing around, he saw several people slanting furtive looks his way. By morning, the drawing rooms would be abuzz with speculation on why he had appeared at a staid musicale. *Let them wonder.* It was a game to keep the *ton* guessing what his next dark and dangerous exploit would be.

Dangerous. He let his eyes be drawn back to Kate. She looked so solemn, sitting at rigid attention in her chair. On one side of her was a plump matron attired in flounces and feathers. On the other was a heavyset silver-haired gentleman whose patrician profile bore subtle similarities to hers. The imperious grandfather, no doubt.

"*Deh vieni a consolar il pianto mio...*" *Come to console my lament.* The tenor clasped his beefy hands over his heart, and while Marco could vaguely understand the mispronounced Italian, his own inner thoughts were proving impossible to translate. He didn't listen to emotions very often.

The soprano finally warbled to the end of the aria, and the hostess announced an intermission.

Chairs scraped on the parquet as the audience rose and lost no time in heading for the refreshment room. Marco remained where he was, watching as the Duke of Cluyne lingered to talk with another gentleman. After a moment, Kate murmured something to him and moved away with the others. But rather than seek a glass of tepid punch, she slipped out onto the balcony.

Marco waited until the crowd had thinned and then stepped through the set of French doors. A number of the male guests were lighting up cigars. No one seemed to notice Kate's presence. She floated along like a wraith to the back corner, silent, stealthy, as if experienced in stealing unseen through the night.

But he was acutely aware of her. Her expression, her shape. *Her scent.*

A breeze wafted through the thick ivy, twining faint traces of *neroli* and wild thyme with the sharp tang of the greenery. Standing behind one of the decorative urns, Marco felt the dampness of the London night seep into his skin. Even the fog and coal smoke couldn't overpower the delicate fragrance. It stirred...a longing.

For what? His youth and an innocence that could never be recaptured? Things like carefree laughter. Simple pleasures. Peaceful dreams.

God, what a maudlin mood. He shouldn't have come here.

A mizzle of moonlight angled off the walls of pale

Portland stone, the soft light catching Kate's upturned face. She seemed to be watching the stars play hide-and-seek with the scudding clouds. In the unguarded moment, she looked achingly young and vulnerable.

Much as he knew he should leave, Marco couldn't drag his gaze away. Luna, the Goddess of the Moon, had him ensnared in her silvery spell. Shadows flickered in and out of Kate's hiding place, forcing him to move a step closer in order to keep her in view.

Strange, but her beauty was hard to define. Her nose was not quite straight, her eyes had an exotic slant, and her mouth was a little too wide, a little too strong. Yet the effect on him was impossible to shake off. She was unique. Individual.

So...*alive.* Passion seemed to radiate from every pore.

He knew she cared deeply about her intellectual pursuits, and he envied her that sense of purpose. His own covert work with the British government was a source of some satisfaction. But for the most part, he wasted his time in idle dissolution.

Damn her for reminding him of the void. It made him uncertain. Angry.

But at least he understood anger. It stirred a spark of heat to his blood, helping to drown far more chilling emotions. Dragging his gaze down the shapely curves of her silhouette, he told himself that provoking her was just another idle game. A way to keep his inner demons occupied.

Marco looked around, and seeing that no one was near, he quickly crossed the marble tiles. "Enjoying the evening, *bella*?"

Startled, Kate fell back a step.

"Don Juan is a very wicked man, is he not?" he murmured, making reference to the Mozart opera arias. "He should be a lesson to all young ladies that the world is fraught with danger." Sidling closer, he added, "So you ought not venture into dark corners at night. Especially when you are alone and unprotected."

"Thank you for your concern, sir," she replied slowly. "But I can take care of myself."

"Ah, yes, the iron fist in the velvet glove." Marco brushed the back of his knuckles along her jawline. "You throw a very pretty punch, *cara*. However, I must warn you that it wouldn't prevent a true cad from having his way with you."

Kate recoiled. "There are other ways to stop a man in his tracks."

"There are," he agreed, edging closer. "For example, if you were to hook your finger in your bodice and inch it down to give me a peek at your perfectly shaped curves, I would find myself riveted to the stones."

Kate touched her tongue to her lower lip.

"Ah, do that again," he murmured. "It's incredibly provocative."

"As if you need any provocation for playing your wicked games," she rasped.

"This is only light foreplay, *bella*. If I chose to be truly wicked, you wouldn't still be wearing your clothes."

A muscle jumped on her jaw.

"Though it is a lovely gown," he went on in a whisper. "The fabric is exquisite and the cut flatters your figure. I particularly like the way the bodice accentuates your beautiful breasts and creates an enticing cleavage."

"Stop it." Though she tried to sound firm, her voice was a little ragged around the edges.

"Why? Because it is making your nipples harden?" Marco dropped his voice a notch. "Do I arouse your innermost naughty instincts?"

Kate quickly crossed her arms over her chest and slid a step deeper into the shadows. "You are an uncivilized beast."

"And yet you respond to me. What does that make you, Miss Woodbridge?"

Her mouth parted in shock, then quickly thinned to a prim line. "Don't flatter yourself, sir. There is a simple scientific explanation for the phenomenon you have just observed. Cold air makes skin pucker."

"So does heat," he replied. It was evil to tease her. Truly evil to taunt her with his dark, debauched thoughts. And yet he couldn't help adding, "Are you feeling a lick of fire between your legs?"

A swirl of the night air ruffled through the overhanging ivy.

"The intermission is almost over." Her hands clenched. "I must be going back inside to my grandfather."

Marco slowly stepped aside. "Yes, run on back to the bosom of your family, *bella*. As I said, it's not safe for young ladies to wander around alone at night."

"And as *I* said, sir, you might be surprised to find that some ladies know how to defend themselves," she replied.

"You wouldn't have a chance," he said softly.

She moved past him, but not before leaving a last word hanging in the air.

"Don't be so sure of that."

Chapter Three

Repressing a sigh, Kate settled herself into the plush velvet seat of her grandfather's carriage. Like all his possessions, it was of exquisite quality, but rather oppressive in its opulence. She preferred simpler things—all the gilding and gold-threaded draperies made her eyes ache.

Which matched the dull throbbing at her temples. The musical program had been even worse than she had anticipated. *Lud, where did Lady Hamden find such egregiously awful singers?* Opera was an art form, but she had heard a more melodic baritone from the rattle of rusty anchor chain.

And then, of course, there was the intimate interlude with Marco. Dear God, how dare he keep bedeviling her with his presence. She squeezed her eyes shut. How dare he tease such terrible longings to life inside her! Even now, a moist heat was lingering between her legs, an uncomfortable reminder of how little she had in common with the innocent young ladies of London.

The iron step shivered and a moment later the Duke of Cluyne eased his broad shoulders through the doorway. A liveried footman quickly fastened the latches and signaled the driver to set the team of matched grays in motion. The harness jingled, the wheels rolled.

Like clockwork, thought Kate. The duke's servants functioned like a well-oiled machine.

"It was good of you to come tonight, Katharine."

Kate looked up in surprise. Cluyne took obedience for granted. He expected people to bow to his wishes.

Unsure how else to respond, she merely murmured, "Of course, Your Grace." Not 'Grandfather,' not 'Cluyne,' but the far more formal 'Your Grace.' His knees were just inches from hers, but in her mind he was distant, detached. A stranger in spite of their shared blood.

"Not that I imagine you enjoyed it," he said gruffly. "Dreadful singers, dull conversation. But Lady Hamden is an old friend."

"Of course," repeated Kate.

"Her grandson and several of his friends were supposed to be in attendance. The fellows all belong to some sort of scientific society, so you might have found their company interesting. But I suppose the music scared them off."

"That says something in favor of their intelligence." She usually tried to temper her tart humor in the presence of her grandfather. However, the fact that he was taking it upon himself to find her a husband set her teeth on edge. Until now, Great Aunt Hermione had been in charge of finding a suitable match. But the poor lady must have thrown up her hands in despair.

"Be that as it may, Your Grace," she went on. "Please

do not feel obliged to act as matchmaker for me. I fear you will only be wasting your time." *And mine*, she added to herself.

"*Harumph.*" The duke cleared his throat, as if trying to dislodge an irritant, and folded his arms across his girth. But rather than speak again right away, he turned his gaze to watch the moonlit mansions of Grosvenor Square roll by.

Lowering her lashes, Kate studied his profile. *Austere. Autocratic. Arrogant.* Those were the first adjectives that came to mind. Despite his advanced years, Cluyne was still a very imposing figure. His silvery hair was thick and showed no signs of retreating from the broad plane of his forehead. His brows were bushy, accentuating piercing green eyes and an aquiline nose. And though his mouth was usually set in a grim line, his lips were full and well-shaped. As for the jaw, its square shape and stubborn jut were all too familiar a sight—Kate saw them reflected each morning in the looking glass.

"*Harumph.*" This time the sound was followed by speech. "Aye, it's clear you have a mind of your own, gel."

"Which clearly drives you to distraction," she said none too softly.

"I am only trying to do what is best for you," countered Cluyne. "It is my familial duty to see you well settled."

To Kate's ears, the words were eerily similar to what he had said to her mother so many years ago. Anne Woodbridge had not been bitter, merely sad when she had repeated them.

"We clearly have very different notions as to family and duty," replied Kate.

His eyes flashed, but in the shifting lamplight it was impossible to tell whether it was in anger or some other emotion.

Kate sighed. "I don't want to quarrel with you, sir. As you have pointed out, I have spent a good deal of my life studying science. So perhaps I should have known from the start that this experiment was not going to work out well. Like oil and water, certain elements just don't mix."

His brows drew together. "What are you saying?"

"That maybe it would be best for both of us if I leave England," she replied slowly.

"And go where?" he demanded in a thunderous voice. "Back to living on naught but a wing and a prayer?"

She waited for his imperious ire to stop echoing off the polished paneling. "I have not yet decided. However, you need not worry that I will make any demands on you to fund my future plans. I have enough money of my own to live quite comfortably." That was a gross exaggeration, but pride would not allow her to admit otherwise.

"Now see here, missy—"

"I'm not a schoolgirl, Your Grace," she interrupted hotly. "Please remember that I don't need your permission—or your blessing—to live my life as I please. I have been in London long enough to see that most people of the *ton* allow themselves to be controlled by family money and influence. I am not one of them."

A muscle twitched along the line of Cluyne's clenched jaw.

She looked down at her fisted hands, feeling torn between guilt and resentment that they often ended up arguing. "Forgive me for shrieking like a fishwife. As you have noticed, I have an unfortunate tendency to let my temper get the best of me."

The seat slats creaked as the duke shifted his bulky body.

"I am not ungrateful for your hospitality, sir," she added. "There are things I do like about London. I have made some very good friends, and the scientific societies offer a wealth of interesting lectures." Cluyne was not overly happy with her intellectual pursuits or her botanical studies, though he himself was quite knowledgeable on the subject. He would much rather she chase after some Tulip of the *ton*.

But she wouldn't pretend to be someone she was not, simply to curry his favor.

"Then perhaps you should not be so hasty to leave Town," he said tightly. "No need to kick up your heels and run off to some far corner of the globe at this moment."

It was as close to an apology as the duke would ever make. Kate decided to accept it.

"Very well."

She thought she heard him exhale a pent-up breath. But maybe it was just the whisper of her silk skirts or a hiss of wind blowing up against the windowpanes.

They rode on in uneasy silence for several moments, the sounds of the jingling harness and the hooves clattering over the cobblestones filling the void between them.

"I was hoping you would consent to come to the country next week," said the duke after smoothing out his cravat. "At the request of the Foreign Office, I am hosting a house party at the Kent estate in honor of the upcoming peace conference in Vienna. If you recall, Lord Tappan, one of the junior ministers, lives on the estate adjoining mine, but his house is not large enough to accommodate such a distinguished group. The guests will include a number of visiting European intellectuals and diplomats."

Kate couldn't help but be cynical—several of them must be unmarried and under the age of eighty.

"Lord Tappan also expressed a hope that you would consider the invitation."

"*Me?*" Her head came up in surprise. "I can't imagine why."

"To begin with, he mentioned that he has met you at a ball and is aware of your scholarly pursuits. He feels that your presence would add a nice touch to the gathering."

Kate did not recall ever meeting Lord Tappan. Was this just one of her grandfather's ploys?

"Seeing as a number of foreign military attachés are in London, Tappan is working with the War Office on making up the guest list," he went on. "And apparently Lord Lynsley mentioned to him that you might find the interlude enjoyable, given your scientific interests." Cluyne made an odd face. "I was not aware that you had met the marquess."

Several times in the last year, Lynsley had consulted with her scientific circle on some very odd questions. But as Kate was sworn to secrecy on the matter, it was not something she could reveal to him. She thought quickly. "I believe that my friends Ciara and Alessandra have a passing acquaintance with him."

"Well, I have known Lynsley for years. He's a capital fellow. Both he and Tappan add that you would be doing the government a service. The presence of ladies will help keep the gentlemen from arguing too much." Cluyne cleared his throat. "But lest you think it is just the ministers who wish you to be there, let me repeat that I, too, think you might find it interesting."

More likely, Cluyne was trying to avoid the embarrassment of having his granddaughter absent from the affair, thought Kate. He didn't care about her "interests." Only his cursed ducal pride. *God forbid that another female of his family stir up scandalous gossip.*

All her resentments came flooding back, and for an instant, Kate was tempted to tell him to go to the devil. But she forced herself to consider the matter dispassionately. Aside from doing Lord Lynsley a favor, there were personal reasons to consider. The estate conservatory was renowned for its fascinating array of exotic plants, and a new shipment of specimens had just arrived from the Far East. And her good friend Charlotte had recently remarked that a dip in her finances was not going to allow her to leave London for a sojourn in the country.

Recalling the earlier mention of Machiavelli, Kate gave a cool smile. "I will consider coming—that is, if the invitation includes my fellow scientist, Lady Charlotte Fenimore."

Cluyne's lips compressed to a grim line. After a long moment, he gave a curt nod. "I have no objection to that, I suppose. She is of respectable birth, even if she is considered a trifle eccentric by the *ton*."

"So am I," muttered Kate under her breath.

Whether he heard her or not, he ignored the comment.

"Then I may count on your presence?" asked the duke.

"Yes, Your Grace," she answered. Deciding it would

be churlish to needle him with a reference to her merchant father, who had taught her the art of negotiating a business deal, she left it at that. But the irony of it provoked a sardonic smile.

No, Cluyne would not understand. Nor would he be remotely amused if he did. And that, she admitted, was the essence of their estrangement. He was a man who could not laugh at himself. While she, on the other hand, was all too aware of her own follies and foibles.

Lord, what fools we mortals be…

Her education had been exceedingly eccentric, but Shakespeare had been part of her early reading.

Perhaps she should leave a copy of the Bard's plays on her grandfather's bedside table.

The brandy burned a trail of fire down his throat. Marco tilted the bottle for another swig, only to come up empty.

Hell, was the bottle really empty?

A slow shake confirmed his suspicions. Letting it slip through his fingers, he fell back against the plump eiderdown bed pillows, only to wince at the brittle *clink, clink, clink* of glass hitting glass. Strange, he didn't remember draining more than two other ones.

Usually his mind—as well as the rest of his body—could soak up a prodigious quantity of spirits without suffering any impairment. However, at present he wasn't feeling quite his usual self.

"*Ciao*, Marco! I'm back." The mattress bounced as a shapely bum dropped down beside him. "This is your lucky night—Madame Erato found one last bottle of your favorite Barolo wine stashed away in the cellars."

Prying one eyelid open, he saw only a hazy blur of slim, dexterous hands twisting a corkscrew. The Grotto of Venus spared no expense in keeping its customers satisfied. It could well afford to, he thought wryly, considering the obscenely high prices that were charged for the pleasure of passing an evening with one of its beauties.

Pop. A splash of liquid spilled into a crystal glass.

"Grrrrr," mouthed Marco, making no move to take the glass. "Maybe I've had enough to drink for now." The brandy had unaccountably left a sour taste on his tongue. It took another moment or two for his fuzzed brain to realize why.

Damn. Was he really still stewing over his encounter with Alessandra's friend?

What the devil did it matter whether he had shocked Miss Kate-Katharine Woodbridge? He had, he told himself, likely done her a favor. She might fancy herself a woman of the world on account of her travels outside the rarefied realm of the English aristocracy. But in truth she had no real knowledge of human nature. *Good and evil.* Light and dark.

Someone needed to illuminate for her how truly black a soul could be.

Averting his gaze from the golden glare of the candles, Marco made another rough sound in the back of his throat. "It feels like a red-hot pitchfork is jabbing into my skull."

"In a foul humor?" Paloma slipped her hand beneath the satin sheets. "Seeing as you are not in the mood for drinking, let's discover if we can find another way to elevate your spirits," she said coyly.

His growl softened—and his body hardened.

Her smooth fingers danced lightly along his stiffening length. "Your head might not feel up to it, but *Il Serpenti* is always in a playful mood."

True. On the rare occasions when he couldn't drown himself in drink, he was always able to submerge himself in lust.

Paloma straddled his thighs, teasing her touch through the nest of coarse curls between his legs. "Ah, Marco, you are the very picture of masculine beauty." She leaned back admiringly, watching the firelight flicker over his naked body. "A flame-gilded god."

"Who will likely roast in hell," he murmured.

"You are a *very* wicked man," she agreed. Dipping her fingertips in the wine, she circled his shaft and began a slow, rhythmic stroking. "But Lucifer and his glowing coals lie far in the future. For the present, you are here with me, so why not enjoy it?"

"Why not, indeed." Marco slid his hands to the warm, willing curves of her bottom and lifted her into the air.

A throaty laugh floated through the faint swirls of smoke thrown up by the scented candles. She hovered for an instant above his arousal, a dark angel casting shadows across his face, then gave a deep moan as their flesh joined and their bodies became one.

Pleasure. For a fleeting interlude, it was enough to keep his inner devils at bay.

Chapter Four

"A late night?"

Marco waved away the offer of tea. "Coffee, if you please," he said to the hovering footman. "Black and strong."

The Marquess of Lynsley went back to buttering his toast and reading the newspaper. "You look like dung."

"I feel like shite."

"Perhaps you ought to consider tempering your carousing."

Marco brushed a hand over his disheveled coat and cravat. He had found the note requesting his presence waiting for him when he returned to his lodgings an hour ago. As it had sounded urgent, he hadn't bothered to change his clothing or to shave. "Why would I want to do that?"

Lynsley shrugged his well-tailored shoulders. "So you don't end up a bloated, pox-ridden carcass by the age of thirty. But, of course, your life is entirely your own affair."

Shoving a tangle of hair back from his brow, Marco

curled a cocky smile. "I'll have you know, my carcass was just a few hours ago compared to the body of a Roman god."

Lynsley refilled his teacup. "Ah, I'm impressed that your latest whore knows the difference between Roman and Greek deities. I take it you have moved to the Grotto of Venus."

In spite of his muzzy head and a mouth that felt filled with dried horse droppings, Marco managed a laugh. "Madame Erato charges enough that she could hire the whole damn faculty from Oxford to teach her girls the nuances of ancient history."

"Somehow I think she would choose to spend her money on other sorts of instruction," said Lynsley dryly. "Now, do you mind if we switch the subject from your pego to politics? Or do you need another few moments for the coffee to move from your belly to your brain?" A pause. "Assuming you haven't left it behind in some bordello."

"*Madre mio*, have you never misbehaved?" Marco pressed his palms to his throbbing temples. "No, don't answer that. Your nobility will only make me feel worse."

Lynsley chuckled. "Come along to my study."

Marco quickly drained his cup and rose to follow him. The prospect of an assignment had already piqued his interest. A new challenge was just what he needed to pull himself out a blue-deviled mood.

For the last few years he had been working as a clandestine agent for Lynsley. The marquess's position as a minor minister at Whitehall disguised his true role as head of a secret government intelligence force. Most people thought him a bland bureaucrat, but Marco knew better. Some of the stories he had heard about Lynsley's youthful exploits were...impressive, to say the least.

"Have a seat," said the marquess, indicating one of the comfortable leather chairs set near a bank of arched leaded-glass windows. He took up a portfolio of papers from his desk and perched a hip on the polished oak. "I assume you haven't been so busy with your personal affairs that you are unaware of the upcoming Congress of European powers that is scheduled to take place in Vienna. Some of the delegations are already in place."

"Yes, I'm aware of the Congress," said Marco, repressing a yawn. "But the whores at the Grotto of Venus make Vienna and a gathering of pompous aristocrats seem very far away."

The marquess regarded him over the top of his gold-rimmed reading spectacles. "Shall I ask McDuffy to undertake this assignment? Your European title and connections would be extremely useful, but the job is going to require discretion, diplomacy, and a sharp eye for observing the nuances of behavior. None of which seems to be your strong points of late."

Marco straightened from his slouch. "You think I can't rise to the occasion?"

One well-groomed brow arched. "If I were asking you to infiltrate a brothel, there would be little question about whether you could function effectively."

"What *is* the blasted mission?" he asked. "It must be damn important, seeing as you summoned me here at the crack of dawn."

Lynsley took a handful of documents out of the case, but made no move to pass them over. "The Foreign Office has arranged for a lavish house party to be held at a country estate in Kent. The guests will include a number of diplomats from the various foreign embassies here in London, as well as some influential noblemen from the Continent."

He pursed his lips in thought. "It may turn out to be a purely social gathering, but with the Congress of Vienna slated to convene in short order, I think it prudent to know what is being said and done among the various European powers. If some intrigue is afoot, we need to know about it."

"A damn house party." Marco sank back against the soft leather, feeling disappointed. He was restless and bored. What he needed was action to distract him from mindless revelries.

Paper crackled as the marquess started to return the documents to the portfolio. "I had asked that your name be added to the guest list." Lynsley's voice was unruffled, but Marco thought he detected a note of reproach.

But perhaps it was just his own conscience speaking. Lynsley did not ask a favor lightly. To balk was churlish.

"However," continued Lynsley, "I shall request that the Duke of Cluyne replace it with that of McDuffy."

Cluyne. Despite the brandy still pickling his brain, Marco recognized the name. "Isn't he the grandfather of Kate Woodbridge, who is part of my cousin Alessandra's circle of scientific friends?"

"Yes."

The prospect of a house party no longer seemed quite so bland.

He held out his hand. "Let me have a look at your bloody notes. McDuffy is as clumsy as a Highland ox when it comes to understanding the nuances of Continental manners. He'll make a muck of the job."

The marquess fixed him with a penetrating stare. "If you are looking for bed sport, stay here in London. This assignment isn't about playing with your bat and balls. I need someone who will not be distracted from the task at hand." His expression hardened. "Not to speak of the fact that Miss Woodbridge is not fair game. The duke would have your guts for garters. And I'd be lending him my tailor to sew the stitches."

Marco felt the sting of Lynsley's words. "Granted, I haven't been acting very professionally of late," he admitted. "But you can count on me to…come up to scratch, so to speak."

The marquess regarded him for a long moment before slowly handing over the papers. "Here are the dossiers on the guests whom I wish to watch." His gaze was as cold as slivered ice. "I trust you won't make me regret this decision."

Marco felt its chill penetrate through his usual cocksure banter. The marquess was in no mood for joking. "Have I ever let you down, *amico*?" he asked softly.

"No," replied Lynsley. "Which is the reason I am going against my better judgment now." He rose and took up the Sicilian stiletto that served as his letter opener. "I won't say it again, but I need you to stay sharp. Your last job was successful, but you were a little sloppy. A little reckless."

Marco could think of no clever comment.

"I'll leave you to read over the papers." Flipping the razored blade into the air, Lynsley caught it by the jeweled hilt and placed it back on his blotter. "I will return in an hour. If you're still of a mind to take the assignment, we'll go over the other details."

"How nice to have us all together, even if it's only for a very short while." The scholarly part of their meeting completed, Charlotte began to pour tea. "I think we can be forgiven for rushing through the scientific agenda in order to indulge in a comfortable coze."

"I do feel a little guilty about not going over Ratherson's essay on mercury fulminite more carefully," said Ciara, the chemistry expert of the group. "I promise to draft a rebuttal as soon as Lucas and I return from our visit to Sir Henry's estate."

"You have had other responsibilities, my dear," murmured Charlotte. "As has Ariel."

Kate glanced at the two—no, make that three—newly wed members of their group. "Thank God we have heard the last chime of wedding bells. My ears were beginning to ring."

Alessandra broke off a bit of shortbread. "Don't be so smug. You are still single."

"And plan to stay that way," she replied forcefully.

"Ha, that's what I said." Ariel, who at age sixty-five was two years younger than her sister Charlotte, chuckled.

"Better late than never," quipped Ciara. Ariel had recently married for the first time and was the subject of some good-natured teasing from her friends.

"I admit that you look no worse for the experience," said Kate dryly. "But trust me, marriage is not in my future plans."

"As a scientist, you ought to know that sometimes

things simply happen in nature," pointed out Alessandra. She winked at the others. "You know, like spontaneous combustion."

"Ha, ha, ha," said Kate, echoing the merry laughter with considerably less mirth. She made a face. "You are welcome to your little jokes. But in all seriousness, I don't think marriage would suit me at all."

The truth was, after all her nomadic travels, she couldn't picture herself settling down to a normal English life with a husband and a household. However, she did not wish to throw a splash of cold water in the face of her friends by sounding sardonic, so she left it at that. They were clearly happy with their choice in life.

As she was with hers.

As the laughter died away, Ariel cleared her throat. "Are you sure you don't want to join us in the country?" She and her husband, Sir Henry Phelps, had invited Alessandra and Black Jack Pierson to stop for a visit before heading on for a wedding trip to Italy. It promised to be a lively gathering, for Ciara and Lucas would also be present, along with her young son and Alessandra's daughter, who were the best of friends.

Yet somehow Kate was a little relieved at having an excuse to demur. Given her current unsettled mood, the prospect of being surrounded by familial bliss wasn't overly appealing at the moment. "I'm sorry, but I promised Cluyne that I would attend his house party. We haven't been getting on terribly well of late, so I ought not rock the boat by changing my mind." She looked at Ariel's sister. "But really, Charlotte, you need not feel compelled to join me. I wouldn't blame you in the least for withdrawing."

Charlotte waved off the suggestion. "I think that this first wave of marital merriment is best left to newlyweds," she said with her usual blunt frankness. "Besides, I know things are not overly comfortable between you and your grandfather, so I wouldn't want to leave you alone to face a houseful of strangers."

"I am perfectly capable of fending for myself," replied Kate.

"That goes without saying. However, my offer isn't entirely altruistic. I am very curious to see the duke's famous conservatory, and look forward to spending some time examining its treasures."

"I confess, it's one of the reasons I said yes to Cluyne," admitted Kate. "I haven't spent as much time there as I would like."

"You still call him 'Cluyne,' not 'Grandfather'?" asked Ciara softly. "For all your differences, you are still family."

Kate felt her jaw tighten. "A fact that no doubt pains him every time he sees me enter one of the rooms of his gilded mansions. A wild weed among all his carefully cultivated blooms."

"A shared interest in botany gives you some common ground," pointed out Alessandra. "Perhaps if you tried to dig beneath the old resentments..."

"Yes, we, of all people, understand how difficult family relationships can be," added Ciara.

"Thank you for the advice," said Kate softly. "But I am afraid that just because you all have solved your own problems doesn't mean you can solve mine." Expelling a long sigh, she stared down at the dregs in her cup, wishing the dark tea leaves might provide some hint of her future. "The truth is, I have been contemplating whether to leave England. For good."

"That is a very serious decision, my dear," said Charlotte after a fraction of a pause.

"Yes. And not one that I have rushed into," replied Kate. "I have been here for over a year." She pushed her cup away. "And have never felt more like an outsider. None of you are forced to mingle with the other unmarried young ladies of the *ton* and listen to their silly schoolgirl prattle. They know of naught but the schoolroom and the pristine polished ballrooms of Mayfair, while I have sailed to some of the roughest hellholes in the world and experienced things they can't even dream about."

"I don't blame you for finding the balls and soirees boring." Ciara smiled in sympathy. "However, look at the rays of sunshine among the dark clouds. You met us, and you are a member of several other Societies that offer intelligent conversation and discuss interesting ideas."

"I—I would miss all of you very much," said Kate. "With all my family's wanderings..." She let her voice trail off, suddenly afraid of revealing too much. Her nomadic life had been painfully lonely at times, and so the wit and warmth and wisdom of her fellow 'Sinners' was special beyond words. But she had learned from years of hardscrabble experience to keep her feelings hidden. *Only the strong survived.* She was tough, and self-reliant. She didn't need to burden her friends with maudlin reminiscences.

"With all my family's wanderings," she resumed, taking care to sound nonchalant, "I've seen how very big the world is, and how many possibilities there are for an adventurous spirit."

"Of course we shall support you in whatever you decide to do," said Charlotte. "But I hope you will give it some more thought."

"Yes," chimed in Ariel. "Why not at least wait until the end of the year before coming to any final decision. Remember, the Amsterdam Tulip Society is presenting a symposium here in London on the history of the flower, which promises to be quite fascinating."

Alessandra couldn't help but laugh. "Only our little group would use science as an enticement, rather than men or fashion."

"Thank God for that," murmured Kate.

"Really, Ariel has an excellent point," said Ciara.

"Very well." Kate surveyed her close-knit circle of friends, realizing with a pang how much she would miss their company. "I'm in no hurry to spread my sails, so to speak. So I'll weather the present squall at anchor. Perhaps, as you say, brighter days lie beyond the horizon."

But she wouldn't count on it.

The papers slid across the polished desktop with a whispery sigh.

Lynsley looked up from reading a set of reports from the English embassy in St. Petersburg. "Are you in or out—metaphorically speaking, of course. If you take the assignment, I expect that the only rigid element of your person will be your sense of decorum."

"No seducing another man's wife?" said Marco. He set his mouth in a slight sneer. "*You* may be impervious to fleshly desires, *amico*, but to expect *me* to go without female company for over a fortnight is asking a lot."

The marquess drew the documents across his blotter. "As I said, I can assign—"

"However, considering the circumstances, I shall put business before pleasure," drawled Marco. "Though God knows why."

Lynsley's well-groomed brows quirked up. "Your better nature usually rises to the occasion, in spite of yourself."

Answering with a growled obscenity, Marco turned away and went to stand by the mullioned windows. Outside, a gardener was busy pruning a row of rose bushes. *Snip, snip, snip*. The withered blooms disappeared into a burlap bag.

If only it were so easy to cut off the dried, dead bits of one's life, mused Marco. Perhaps, then, fresh greenery might grow from the scars.

Turn over a new leaf?

His self-mocking smile was reflected in the glass. "I assume it's Von Seilig, Vronskov, and Rochambert that you wish to watch most closely."

"Precisely," replied Lynsley. "But that does not mean I have ruled out the others. Someone else may also be intent on making mischief."

"I rather hope so," said Marco. "Otherwise the assignment is going to be a dead bore." Rising, he gave a lazy stretch. "Well, seeing as I have to depart on the day after tomorrow, I had better sate myself with London's pleasures while I still have the chance."

"Marco—"

"Yes, yes, *amico*, I know." He gave a martyred sigh. "I must be good while I am in Kent. But in the meantime, allow me a last little fling at being bad."

Chapter Five

Kate hurried across the street, anxious to purchase several newly published reference books for the trip to Kent before the tiny shop closed for its midday break.

"Sort of like carrying coals to Newcastle," said her maid, looking around at the crowded cases and leather-bound volumes stacked on the floor. "I mean, it seems a mite odd that ye need to buy any books. Your grandfather's library in the country looks like it holds every word ever printed."

"The particular ones I want have just arrived from the university at St. Andrews. Charlotte is most anxious to see them." After making her selections, Kate consulted her list of other errands. "We must fetch a package at the milliner and then make a stop at the mantua maker."

Alice nodded. "You forgot about Madame Celeste's shop. She has made up three new evening gowns for your grandfather's house party."

"Right." Kate made a face. "I'd be happy enough to pass the time in my work smock and wooden clogs."

"I doubt His Nibs would approve of sitting down with his fancy company dressed in dirt."

"Right," repeated Kate tightly. "I'm already a stain on his name."

Her maid shot her a reproving look.

Heaving a sigh, Kate tucked the paper back into her reticule. "Don't worry, I will be a dutiful granddaughter and behave spotlessly in Kent. But if I am to be cooped up with a houseful of boring diplomats for a fortnight, I would like to use my last afternoon in London to get a breath of fresh air."

"Miss Katharine," began Alice, a note of warning shading her voice.

"I have hours before His Grace requires my presence for supper."

Alice frowned. "But you—"

"Yes, yes, I know—I must be very careful. And I am!" replied Kate. "I am always well-shrouded when we leave the duke's residence, and we always take a hansom cab, so I don't see that the risk is very great."

"I suppose not," said Alice grudgingly. "But I still say you are taking a risk."

"Yes, well, without an occasional risk to spice things up, life would be dreadfully bland here in England."

Marco stood on the edge of a crumbling walkway, staring down at the dark, swirling water. The tide had just shifted, turning the currents treacherous along this stretch of the river. Clouds scudded overhead, and as the gusting wind shifted, a damp chill slapped against his face.

Turning up his collar, he felt his mood sinking, sucked

into the murky depths by a potent vortex of brandy, boudoirs, and brooding.

Perhaps Lynsley was right—of late, he had been teetering on a razor's edge, his thoughts and his actions threatening to spin out of control. *One wild risk after another.* That was dangerous—both for himself and for others. With a clench of self-loathing, he flexed his bruised shoulder and winced. On the recent mission to Scotland, he had nearly lost an arm, escaping the explosion of gunpowder by the skin of his teeth. He had set the fuse a hair too short. Next time...

"*A diavolo*," muttered Marco. Perhaps next time—the next real assignment, not a damnable house party—he would lose his head. Few would mourn the passing of the arrogant, abrasive Conte of Como. Hell, he annoyed everyone.

Including himself.

Pressing his fingertips to his temples, he tried to massage away the dull ache in his head. He had spent the night at one of the seamier gaming haunts in the nearby slums, winning and then losing a great deal of blunt. Come morning...he winced, vaguely remembering a room draped in red silk and a lady draped in nothing at all. Save for a cloud of expensive French perfume.

The musky floral scent still clinging to his coat was making his stomach feel a little queasy. Its sweetness seemed even more cloying as he suddenly recalled the subtle fragrance that spiced Kate Woodbridge's skin. Her essence teased and tantalized. It didn't bludgeon a man in the gut.

Another lurch of his brandy-logged insides reminded him that he ought to be moving. His boots were already half-submerged in the vile-looking ooze. Squinting up at the sky, Marco judged that it must be midafternoon. A squall looked to be blowing in, so he started walking, hoping to spot a hansom among the cluster of warehouses up ahead.

Out in the middle of the river, several small wherries bobbed in the ebbing waters, their white sails silhouetted against the gray waves as they followed the flow down toward the Greenwich docks. Closer to shore, a lone lad was rowing a dory, his oars cutting in and out of the rippling eddies with a natural rhythm that seemed in perfect harmony with the river.

Marco found himself admiring the scene. It wasn't muscle—the youth was slender as a reed—that propelled the dory, rather a supple, sinuous grace...

As the wind gusted, the brim of the lad's floppy cap blew up, giving a glimpse of his profile.

Marco blinked, wondering if his bleary eyes and cupshot brain were playing tricks on him. Quickening his steps to keep pace with the dory, he watched for a few more moments before uttering a low oath.

"Well, I'll be damned."

It had been a stroke of luck that her father's old bosun had decided to settle in London, thought Kate as she gave another hard pull on the oars, reveling in the smooth feel of the blades cutting through the water. Eli Welch now worked along the Thames, overseeing a small flotilla of vessels that ferried cargo to and from the East India docks. He was always happy to lend her his little dory for an hour or two while Alice waited in a side alley with the hansom. And his quarters by the stone landing where his boats were moored provided a safe harbor in which to change from her gown to the set of boy's clothing that she kept stowed in his cupboard.

Her secret was safe with Eli, she mused, which allowed her a short interlude of freedom, a chance to escape from the gilded formality of Mayfair and experience the old familiar touch of vanished wood against her palms and a salty breeze on her cheeks.

Ebb and flow. Life was so much simpler as a vagabond sailor. *Wind, water, sky.* The rough-hewn timbers of a merchant ship rather than the perfectly polished parquet of a ducal ballroom.

Expelling a long breath, Kate admitted to herself that she was having a hard time navigating the uncharted waters of Polite Society. There seemed to be hidden shoals at every turn and treacherous crosscurrents ready to sink an unwary vessel. She much preferred the open sea and a limitless horizon. *Follow the sun.* Glancing up, she made a face. Here in London the heavens seemed perpetually covered by clouds, shrouding the city in dull, depressing shades of gray.

The only bright spot was the Circle of Sin. Her friends were kindred souls who dared to be different. Kate gripped the oars a touch tighter and quickened her strokes. Unlike the perfectly polished young ladies of the *ton*, who would faint if a hair drifted out of place or a bead of sweat defiled their brows. *Pattern cards of propriety.* While she was...cut from a different cloth. Salt-stained sail canvas and sun-bleached cotton, fluttering wild and free. Which of course violated every rule of Polite Society.

Rules. There was only one person she knew who

seemed to dislike rules as much as she did. The Conte of Como was unrepentantly arrogant, deliberately outrageous—and she rather liked that. As for his smoldering sensuality...

She felt her cheeks turn a trifle hot. His tawny eyes were lush with a liquid fire. Like fine brandy, they were potent with the promise of wild nights and forbidden pleasures. He reminded her of the jungle felines she had seen in her travels. Untamed. Unpredictable.

Dangerous.

Her mouth quirked. But then, she had always been attracted to danger. It set her pulse to pounding and made her feel alive.

A loud splash jerked her out of her reveries. Looking up, she saw a pair of ragged urchins running away from the riverbank. Mudlarks disposing of some detritus, she decided. The Thames was a graveyard of unwanted...

She suddenly spotted a small tiger-striped head swirling in the leaden currents—a cat, struggling to stay afloat.

Damn. A flurry of hard, quick strokes turned the dory and sent it skimming through the foam-flecked water. The eddies were tricky, and if she did not judge the drift just right, she wouldn't get another chance.

"Hold on, tabby," she muttered, maneuvering the oars to bring her in at just the right angle. The choppy water made the going hard work, and her hands were fast rubbing raw. Ignoring the pain, she fought against the racing current.

Steady, steady.

With a quick lunge, Kate grabbed the waterlogged feline just as it was about to be swept under by a cresting wave.

Plopping the bedraggled ball of fur into her lap, she let out a relieved laugh. "I daresay you've just used up eight of your nine lives."

The cat arched and let out an angry *meow*.

"Aye, let's get you back to dry land," she murmured, regripping the oars and turning for shore.

As the dory nosed up against the barnacled pilings, Kate scrambled out onto the landing, awkwardly cradling the still-dripping animal.

"Do you always go out of your way to save mangy strays?"

Kate stumbled at the sound of the slurred voice, and then quickly ducked to hide her face. The sudden jerk spooked the cat, and with a spitting hiss, it clawed free of her arms and darted off into the nearby maze of darkened alleyways.

"As you see, the ungrateful beast didn't bother to thank you for your efforts."

Of all the cursed luck. But as the Conte of Como sounded cupshot, perhaps he would move on if she remained silent.

Hunching low, she merely shrugged in answer and made a show of knotting the dory's hawser through the iron ring.

"Cat got your tongue, laddie?" continued Marco in a sardonic drawl. "Or should I say *lady*." He stepped out from beneath the brink archway. "The baggy shirt and threadbare trousers don't do your lovely body justice, Miss Woodbridge."

For a man four sheets to the wind, his gaze was still awfully sharp.

Deciding to ignore his last comment, Kate set a hand on her hip and fixed him with a defiant look. "One doesn't always require thanks for doing the right thing. Would you have just sat there and let the poor animal drown?"

Marco quirked a mirthless smile. "Perhaps it would have preferred to sink and be put out of its misery."

Kate was taken aback by the bleakness undercutting his sarcasm. "Life can seem awfully grim at times, but it's still worth fighting for," she replied slowly.

"Sometimes I wonder."

It was said so softly that Kate wasn't sure whether it was merely a whisper of wind rasping against the weathered stone. Uncertain of how to respond, she turned and grabbed up her jacket from the dory. "I have to be going," she said, scrabbling up the slippery steps.

Marco remained firmly planted between her and the narrow archway. "Which begs the question of what you are doing here in the first place?" he said.

To refuse an answer might only raise other unsettling questions. "I am used to more vigorous exercise than a sedate walk along Rotten Row," she replied grudgingly. "So I occasionally come here to visit an old crewman from my father's ship, who allows me the use of his dory." Seeking to distract him from further thoughts on her actions, Kate was quick to add, "I don't need to inquire how *you* have been whiling away the day."

His clothing was rumpled and his hair uncombed, the tangle of black locks accentuating the dark stubbling of whiskers on his unshaven jaw. Drawing in a breath, Kate caught the reek of cigar smoke and sex through the pungent smells of the river.

"Or night," she finished.

"*Si*," he answered with a laugh. "I've been engaged in all sorts of evil activities." He paused. "As were you."

"I was *rowing*," she protested. "As opposed to pumping my limbs between the sheets."

"There is also a simple verb for what I was doing," he said softly. "Shall I tell you what it is?" His mouth slid into a silky smile. "Would you like to enlarge your vocabulary on physical... arousal, Miss Woodbridge?"

"No, keep your depraved thoughts to yourself," she muttered. And yet his rumbled chuckle stirred a tingle of heat deep inside her. To her dismay, she felt it spreading.... In another instant her flesh would be afire.

"Both disciplines require a great deal of physical exertion," went on Marco. "And both work up a sheen of sweat. Ladies, of course, aren't supposed to sweat, but I daresay you are moist all over, aren't you?"

Thank God the light was turning murky. The angled shadows and dancing dust motes would hopefully hide her unwilling response. He seemed to take an ungentlemanly pleasure in teasing her to anger. She wasn't sure why.

But then, the Lord of Lechery seemed to take pleasure in a good many naughty things.

"You are welcome to enjoy a laugh at my expense, sir," she replied. "As long as you do me the courtesy of staying quiet about what you've seen."

His lashes gave a lazy flutter. "Well, now, if it were a more scandalous transgression, I might be tempted to turn it to my advantage."

Fear squeezed at her throat. She was right to think him dangerous. *Oh so dangerous.*

"But there is nothing depraved about strenuous exercise, Miss Woodbridge, so you need not look so stricken." A suggestive flex of his shoulders emphasized his words.

"Indeed, the ancient Greek intellectuals considered it essential for both body and spirit."

"Thank you for the history lesson," she replied in a rush of relief, then couldn't help adding, "Or was it biology?"

He laughed again, but a shadow seemed to darken his beautiful eyes. "Let me offer another fact of life. As you just witnessed, this is a dangerous area, where bad things can happen in the blink of an eye. It's not safe for you to be here all alone."

His wine-roughened voice teased a tingling down her spine. "As I told you the other evening, sir, I can take care of myself."

Marco watched her lashes flutter, a wink of gold against the encroaching gray as she pulled the brim of her hat a little lower. "So you say. And yet it appears that you are hurt," he replied. Capturing her hand, he held it up for inspection.

She flinched and tried to pull away. "It's naught but a scratch."

In answer, he lowered his lips and blotted a bead of blood from her wrist.

"Don't."

Ignoring her whispered protest, Marco ran his tongue along the line of claw marks and slowly drew the tip of her forefinger into his mouth. She tasted of salt and a sweetness he couldn't describe.

Rain started to fall, spattering her skin with silvery droplets. Yet neither of them moved.

Strange, thought Marco, suddenly mesmerized by the moment. She was a beguiling mix of strength and softness—something he had never encountered in a woman before. He suckled her skin, savoring the rough and smooth textures.

"Don't!" Her voice was louder, and a little ragged around the edges. Wrenching free of his grasp, she clenched her hands into fists and shoved him back a step.

"If you are trying to discourage a man from pawing over your body, allowing him a glimpse of it clad in a rain-soaked shirt is not a good idea." He lowered his gaze. "White linen is nearly transparent when wet, especially when the fabric is clinging to every shapely curve of your breasts. The effect leaves little to the imagination."

Uttering an oath, Kate quickly tugged on her jacket. "You've had your fun, sir, now kindly step aside. My grandfather is very strict about the supper hour and I must not be late."

"And if I don't, are you going to challenge me to a bout of fisticuffs?" Marco waggled a brow.

"Don't be so sure that I couldn't hold my own in a fight," she countered.

"You seem to enjoy flaunting your physical prowess, but rather than throwing punches, I could suggest a far more delicious way of engaging our limbs."

"Go to the devil," she muttered.

"As a matter of fact, I am about to embark on a journey," he replied. "So I, too, ought to be returning to my townhouse. I have a great deal of packing to do." With a flourishing bow, he stepped aside to let her pass. "Have a safe trip back to Mayfair, Miss Woodbridge."

"Enjoy your travels, Lord Ghiradelli," replied Kate as she brushed by him. "I hear that Hades is quite hot at this time of year."

Chapter Six

"A country house party?" Alessandra lifted a brow in surprise. "That is not your usual choice of diversions." She poured herself a cup of tea and gestured for Marco to help himself to the spirits on the sideboard. "I take it there will be some willing widow in attendance."

He shrugged. "Not that I know of. Though it would, of course, make the affair a good deal more pleasurable."

"Do you never think of aught but pleasure?"

"Very rarely."

Alessandra rolled her eyes. "*Dio Madre*, do try to be serious."

"Why?" he shot back.

Her heavy sigh stirred the sheaf of watercolor sketches lying on the library table. The deckled edges fluttered against the polished wood. "No wonder Jack is so often tempted to flatten that aristocratic nose of yours."

"*Va bene*—very well, I shall cease teasing." Swirling his brandy, Marco lifted the glass to his lips. Sunlight refracted off the faceted crystal, casting a wink of dancing amber patterns across the wainscoting. "In fact, I do have a serious question or two to ask you."

"*Si?*" She cocked her head, waiting for him to go on.

"What do you know of the Duke of Cluyne?"

"To begin with, he is Kate's grandfather. But somehow I think you are already aware of that."

Marco took a sip before nodding. "Which is why I thought you might be able to tell me something about him." Keeping his tone deliberately nonchalant, he went on. "What sort of man is he?"

Her lips compressed ever so slightly. "Why the interest in Cluyne? It is not as if the two of you move in the same circles."

"And yet our paths will soon be crossing. It is to his estate in Kent that I am invited."

"Why, Kate will be there as well," exclaimed his cousin. A tiny frown furrowed her brow. "Though she is not very happy about it. She only agreed to go when the duke consented to invite Charlotte."

He ran a finger along the edges of the watercolors, careful to avoid meeting her gaze.

"What is *your* reason?" she asked slowly.

"Perhaps I'm tired of Town life and wish to partake in a little country rest and relaxation."

Her reply was a very unladylike expression in Italian. "Since when have you ever tired of drinking and wenching?" she added.

"I can, on occasion, contrive to appear in civilized society without causing a scandal, *cara*." Marco moved away to refill his glass. "The guests include a number of European diplomats and noblemen, so it's not such a shock that my name was put on the list. In case you have forgotten, I do have a rather impressive pedigree."

"I am well aware of your lineage, Marco. It's *you* who I sometimes fear have forgotten your heritage."

Her words touched a raw nerve, but he brushed them aside with a sardonic laugh. "Oh, come now, it's a new century, and time to leave old-fashioned notions behind us. You possess a rational mind, so don't you agree that the idea of hereditary titles is absurd? They are naught but a string of fancy gilt letters strung together."

Conte of Como. Marco tried not to picture the name of his older brother, penned in as the heir apparent in the *Libro d'Oro della Nobiltà Italiana*, the large, handwritten registers maintained at the offices of the *Consulta Araldica.* His own, which now appeared in flowing script on the line just below the carefully crossed-out lettering, seemed liked a blot on the ancient parchment. If not for his own rash, reckless plan to save a neighbor's old horse from the slaughterhouse, Daniello would not be dead, his neck broken in a fall from the mountain trail.

"Democratic ideals make far more sense," he went on, after a long swallow of the amber spirits. "A man should be judged just on his merits, not some accident of birth."

"Ideas and philosophies may alter over the centuries, but some things never change," replied Alessandra softly. "A family name is more than a fancy gold crest. It's in the blood, an elemental bond flowing from one generation to the next."

The trickle of brandy burned a trail of fire down his throat. "*A diavolo*—women!" he muttered. "Even the most intelligent ones of your sex are hopeless romantics."

"While you flaunt your disdain for any sort of sentimental feelings by drowning them in drink and mindless debauchery."

"Please spare me the lecture on morality, Alessa. However shocking my life might appear to you, it suits me just fine."

"Even if it is digging you an early grave?" asked his cousin. "I swear, I am not sure what will kill you first—the wine or a cuckolded husband."

"It won't be a husband." Marco curled his lip. "My expertise with a pistol or a sword is as finely honed as my skills in the bedchamber."

"*A diavolo*—men!" she exclaimed, throwing his own exasperated words back in his face. "Hubris is far more dangerous than bullets or blades."

Tilting back his glass, Marco deliberately drained the rest of his drink in one flourish. "I'll take my chances. Without risk, life would have few rewards."

Alessandra's mouth compressed in concern.

"Now, might we return to my earlier question regarding the Duke of Cluyne," he went on. "Is there anything you might tell me about his character?"

She didn't answer right away but rather took a few moments to place her new husband's paintings back in the leather portfolio. "It still strikes me as such an odd request."

"As you have taken pains to point out, my actions often defy logic or reason. That I should choose to attend a staid country house party is simply a quirk of fancy."

Her eyes suddenly narrowed. "A party with European diplomats and noblemen... Has this anything to do with Lord Lynsley?"

"If it did, *cara*, I should not be at liberty to say so."

As he had hoped, his cousin did not press the point. Though she had never been officially informed as to the true nature of Lynsley's work, she suspected there was more to his minor government position than met the eye. On several occasions, the marquess had consulted with the 'Sinners' on some very arcane—and lethal—scientific questions.

Alessandra sighed. "I've only seen Cluyne from afar, so I cannot offer my own impressions. But Kate says the duke is a bit of a tyrant. He is very regimented in his thinking, and does not take kindly to having his authority questioned."

"The clash of wills between your fellow 'Sinner' and His Grace must put the Battle of Borodino to blush," quipped Marco. "From what I have witnessed, Miss Woodbridge has very firm opinions of her own, and she is not afraid to voice them."

"She had to be strong," said Alessandra somewhat defensively. "Her parents were both free spirits, so someone had to handle the practical details, lest the family finances sink in the River Tick. So yes, she is used to making her own decisions in life, and does not fear to defy convention. Nor does she shrink away from a challenge. But I sense that beneath the hard shell, Kate is not quite so tough as she appears." Light glinted off her rings as she toyed with the ties of the portfolio. "It is a pity that the duke cannot seem to understand that, and try to reach out just a little."

Recalling the intriguing depth of Kate's aquamarine eyes, and the defiant tilt of her chin, Marco felt a strange little tingle in his fingertips. "I will be happy to extend a comforting hand while I am at Cluyne Close," he teased. "Maybe two."

"*You?*" His cousin made a rude noise. "*Santa Cielo*, I shudder at the thought," she added. "Do me a great favor and stay away from her. She is not one of your doxies or jaded widows."

Given his rakehell reputation, he supposed he deserved the scold, and yet Marco found himself nettled by her tone. Flicking a mote of dust from his sleeve, he flashed a wolfish wink. "You've just taken great pains to tell me that Miss Woodbridge can look out for herself. So why not let *her* tell me if my advances are unwelcome?"

"She's only agreed to attend the party so that she and Charlotte may spend some time studying the exotic plant specimens in Cluyne's conservatory," explained Alessandra. "Fending off your flirtations will only be an unwelcome distraction."

"Most ladies don't find my attentions so onerous."

His cousin slapped a palm to the tabletop, signaling an end to the discussion. "Kate isn't like most ladies—a fact that you would do well to remember unless you want—"

"Want my *testicolos* fed to the Tower lion," finished Marco. "Or was it the ravens?"

Alessandra wagged a finger.

"Don't worry, *cara*. Your friend has nothing to fear from me during the coming fortnight."

"What a magnificent vista." As the entrance drive took a last turn and emerged from a copse of beech trees, Charlotte craned her neck to peer out of the carriage window.

"Isn't it," murmured Kate, reluctantly allowing her gaze to take in the view. "Cluyne engaged Capability Brown to redesign this section of the grounds. The woods were opened up, the gardens shifted to create a better symmetry, and a number of evergreen hedges were planted to add texture and color."

"Your grandfather has excellent taste. Brown's genius in landscape design is legendary."

"The duke can afford the very best," replied Kate, hoping her words didn't sound too waspish. She drew in a deep breath and tried to dispel the twinge of resentment she felt every time she entered the manicured grounds of Cluyne Close. The money spent on just one of the ornamental statues that graced the lush gardens would have paid for the physicians and medicines needed in Naples...

However, it was hard not to be impressed with the duke's country estate. Sunlight played over the lake at the bottom of the long, sloping lawns, looking like myriad tiny diamonds shimmering on a surface of azure blue velvet. Set in its center was a small island with a pale, perfectly proportioned marble folly built in the form of a classical Greek temple.

Kate shifted her gaze from the water's edge, up through the manicured grass, the profusion of muted colors and graveled walkways to the manor house situated on the crest of the hill. 'Castle' was perhaps a better description, she decided, given the turreted towers and crenellated battlements that crowned the massive stone structure. Over the centuries, a succession of architects had somehow managed to make the additions and elaborations to the original Norman building work in harmony with each other. Seen from afar, with the afternoon sun setting the local honey-hued limestone aglow, the effect was dazzling.

"Perhaps I should have brought a pair of tinted spectacles," said Charlotte dryly. "I might need them inside as well, so as not to be blinded by all the opulence."

Knowing that her friend's finances were stretched thin on account of her late husband's gambling habits, Kate tactfully tried to put her at ease. Charlotte had a very sharp sense of pride, and Kate had a feeling that she was loath to accept any money from Ariel, even though her sister's new spouse, Sir Henry Phelps, had a tidy fortune of his own.

"The diplomats of the party will all likely be trying to outshine one another. Thank God we can ignore them and spend our time here in more intelligent pursuits."

Charlotte's expression turned pensive as the manor house loomed larger and larger. "I knew your grandfather was wealthy, but I didn't quite visualize *how* wealthy." She made a wry face. "As you know, my gowns are all quite outdated, not that I give a fig for appearances. However, I do not wish to embarrass you."

Kate made a rude noise. "I think you know me better than that."

"You can always send up a tray to my rooms."

"A far better idea is having our supper served in the conservatory, where we can dine in our work clothes while we scrabble around in the dirt."

"I am looking forward to a tour of the glass pavilion," said Charlotte, after venturing another look at the imposing bulk of Cluyne Close. "And the outer hothouses."

"It will be light for several more hours, so I will show

you around as soon as we are settled." Gathering up the books and papers that the two of them had been reading during the drive, Kate tucked them into a small satchel. "We will be quartered in the west wing, which is close to the conservatory."

"Do most guests need a ball of string to find their way around?" quipped Charlotte.

"No, they have no need to copy Theseus in finding their way through the Minotaur's labyrinth," replied Kate sardonically. "The duke has servants enough to provide a private escort for anyone who needs one. He would probably have a fit of apoplexy if he saw a twist of twine sullying his perfect parquet floors and expensive—"

A discreet cough cut off any further sarcasm. "Now, my dear, do try to approach this visit as a pleasant interlude—"

"Rather than as a penance for my past sins?" she muttered.

Charlotte's brows rose slightly. "You've done nothing to be ashamed of."

Kate felt herself go pale.

Her friend appeared not to notice. "Sailing the seven seas was, to be sure, a rather unusual upbringing for a young lady," went on Charlotte. "But you've acquired an admirable knowledge and understanding of the world. I should think that would make any grandfather proud."

"Tell that to Cluyne," retorted Kate. Seeing her fellow 'Sinner' frown, she quickly added, "Sorry—you are right, of course. I shall try to leave my petty resentments in Town and have a more...positive attitude."

"You might surprise yourself and actually have a good time. Considering that a number of foreign diplomats are among your grandfather's guests, the discussions about the peace conference in Vienna promise to be quite fascinating."

"True," conceded Kate. "Assuming we ladies are allowed to be present when they speak of serious subjects. Most of the really interesting conversation takes place after the ladies are asked to withdraw from the dining room, leaving the gentlemen to linger over their port and cigars."

"Actually, that is usually the time they tell bawdy jokes and brag about their mistresses," said Charlotte dryly. "So we really aren't missing much."

A laugh welled up in Kate's throat. "Now who is being cynical?" she asked.

"That's better," observed her friend with an answering smile. "Let's not start off our stay with a scowl."

The carriage wheels crunched over the freshly raked gravel and came to a halt by the entrance portico. Charlotte looked up at the classical columns gleaming a mellow gold hue in the slanting sunlight, and then lowered her gaze to the procession of liveried servants coming to meet their arrival.

"Allow me, Miss Woodbridge." The duke's majordomo immediately reached for the bag.

Swallowing an inward sigh, she passed it over. She hated feeling coddled, but she had learned that argument only upset the servants. They had a very strict notion of propriety.

"Thank you, Simpson."

"The baggage carriage arrived an hour ago and your maid is overseeing the unpacking for you and your guest."

"Thank you," she repeated.

"And His Grace is in the west study, awaiting your arrival."

Another sigh, this one audible.

"William will escort you."

"William is to be our twine, so to speak," murmured Kate as the heavy oak-paneled door swung silently open and she and her friend fell in step behind the footman.

They passed through the elegant entrance foyer, the clicking of their shoes on the highly polished marble tiles echoing off the ornate plasterwork and gilt-framed paintings.

"This part of the house is only fifty years old," said Kate as they proceeded down a long corridor. "The original Norman keep is part of the west tower. The east tower was added for symmetry in the seventeenth century..."

She continued the architectural history through what felt like an endless series of turns. Finally, the footman paused before a closed door and knocked discreetly.

A gruff voice bade them to enter.

Kate inhaled, trying to loosen the tightness in her chest. *Would there ever come a day when she felt comfortable around Cluyne?* Shaking off such musings, she angled a quick look at her friend. She had warned her of the duke's imperious manner, but in the flesh, he was a formidable figure.

But then, Charlotte was not easily intimidated. Arthritic knees had slowed her step, yet she still carried herself with a regal grace. Tall and full-figured, she wore her hair wound in a severe chignon. The silvery strands framed an oval face dominated by a pair of piercing gray eyes and a long, thin nose. With such strong features, she would not be called beautiful, but rather handsome.

"Don't just stand there, come in, come in," barked the duke. He rose from his desk and clasped his big hands behind his back. "I trust you had a comfortable ride down from Town."

"Yes, Your Grace," replied Kate, quickly performing the introductions.

Her grandfather fixed Charlotte with a long, icy stare before inclining a curt nod. "Welcome to Cluyne Close, Lady Fenimore."

"Thank you for the most gracious invitation, sir," replied the widowed scholar with equal frost.

Cluyne's eyes narrowed, as if he was wondering whether her words held a faint trace of mockery.

Kate repressed a smile. If the duke expected Charlotte to be cowed by his title and wealth, he was in for a rude awakening.

"I have heard a great deal about your collection of botanical specimens," Charlotte went on. "And look forward to seeing them."

"Hmmph." The sound may have been a snort or simply a clearing of his throat. "Ah, yes, my granddaughter said you were one of the members of her scientific circle."

"Indeed," said her friend evenly. "You must be extremely proud of Kate's accomplishments in the field of botany. Her recent essays on the Spice Islands have earned accolades from some of the leading scholars here and abroad."

The duke's bushy brows drew together.

"If you will excuse us, sir, I should like to show Lady Fenimore to her quarters," said Kate hastily, hoping her friend caught the subtle hand signal to cease speaking of her intellectual achievements. For Cluyne, they were only further indication of her oddities. "And then take a quick turn of the conservatory and hothouses while the light is still good."

"Of course." He pursed his lips. "We dine promptly at seven. I ask that you be in the drawing room a half hour beforehand, in order to meet the other guests. Most of them arrived this afternoon, though a few will not be here until the morrow."

"As you wish, Your Grace," said Kate. Taking her friend's arm, she drew her toward the door. "Until then."

Chapter Seven

Muttering an oath as she glanced at the mantel clock, Kate scrubbed a smudge of dirt from her cheek and tugged at the tabs of her day gown. "Drat, why is it that time always seems to fly when you are engaged in something interesting?" As opposed to how slowly the seconds ticked by when you were listening to some boring aristocrat prattle on about his horses or his hounds.

"A good question," answered her maid. "But at the moment, it's not one that we are at leisure to examine." Alice helped Kate into her corset and quickly did up the laces. "Lift your arms."

The dark azure silk was as soft against her skin as the petals of the Javanese orchid she and Charlotte had been admiring. However, the flower's hue had been a pale, pastel shade of pink with ivory edges…

"Now turn around."

Still thinking about the rare bloom, Kate obeyed mechanically.

"You haven't heard a word I've said, have you?" asked Alice after another few pokes and prods.

Her head jerked up. "Sorry, my mind was elsewhere."

"Well, your body had better be in the drawing room in a quarter hour. Let us try not to antagonize your grandfather the first night we are here."

"Right," muttered Kate. She took a seat at the dressing table and folded her hands in her lap as her maid took up a brush and began to arrange her hair. "Thank God you are a dab hand when it comes to moving quickly."

"In my former line of work, speed was of the essence," said Alice dryly through a mouthful of hairpins. "Do sit still."

Heaving a sigh, Kate watched as her maid artfully threaded a ribbon through the twist of the topknot and loosened a few curls around her ears and the nape of her neck.

"There," announced Alice, stepping back to observe her handiwork. "That smoky shade of blue sets off the color of your hair quite nicely. And as a finishing touch, I suggest you wear the pearl earbobs and necklace."

Kate made a face but did not argue. The jewelry had been a birthday gift—a grudging one in her opinion—from her grandfather. The set had belonged to her late grandmother, and by all rights should have passed to her mother...

"Try not to look as if a sea monster is gnawing on your leg."

Kate's scowl quirked into a rueful smile. "I shall try to put my best foot forward tonight."

Alice chose a paisley shawl, figured in pastel swirls of ivory and cerulean. "Well, try not to trip over your own tongue."

"Thank you for the vote of confidence," murmured Kate. "If I fall on my face, it certainly won't be on account of your efforts." She took one last peek at the looking glass and then rose. "I swear, you are a magician to have tamed these unruly curls."

"Unfortunately, my powers do not include the ability to conjure up a magic carpet, so you had better start moving."

A knock on the door punctuated the warning.

"That will be Charlotte." Looping the shawl over her shoulders, Kate hurried into the corridor, wishing that Alice could cast a spell to make the hands of the clock spin like a whirling dervish and strike midnight.

"You look lovely, my dear," said Charlotte as they headed for the stairs.

Kate fingered her heirloom necklace, the smooth lustrous orbs feeling cold and clammy against her flesh. "I seem to remember an old adage about casting pearls before swine."

Choking back a chuckle, her friend waggled a finger. "I fear I have set a bad example for you. I'm allowed to be a sharp-tongued shrew at my age. But you—you ought not let yourself be so cynical."

"Don't blame yourself, Charlotte. I've seen enough of the world to make my own judgments."

"Still, you must guard against being overly harsh on Polite Society. As you well know, both Ciara and Alessandra were a trifle too quick in forming an opinion."

"In this case, three is *not* a charm." On that emphatic note, they entered the drawing room.

"Ah, there you are, Katharine." The duke stepped away from a group of gentlemen and came over to offer his arm. "Allow me to introduce you to my guests." A brief, belated nod acknowledged Charlotte. "And Lady Fenimore, of course."

Charlotte waved him off. "You two go on. I am sure that you would like to present your granddaughter to the others without my company, Your Grace. I shall make their acquaintance during the course of the evening."

Cluyne murmured a gruff thanks.

Stifling a sigh, Kate placed her gloved hand on her grandfather's sleeve. Going through the motions of such formalities seemed so stilted, and yet that was the way of the Polite World.

Lud, she might well have been in Kurdistan instead of Kent, for all that English manners still felt foreign to her.

"...our neighbor, Lord Tappan."

Realizing that the duke was speaking, Kate shook off her musings and tried to pay attention.

"As you know, Katharine, His Lordship is a minister with the Foreign Office."

"A very junior one," said Tappan with a self-deprecating quirk of his mouth.

His face did not seem at all familiar. But then again, thought Kate wryly, most of the fancy balls and soirees had passed by in a boring blur. Deciding the best response was none at all, she just smiled.

"Allow me to introduce several of my fellow diplomats from the Continent," continued Tappan. "Count Vronskov and Colonel Von Seilig."

"*Enchanté, mademoiselle,*" said Vronskov in a heavy Russian accent as he lifted her hand to his lips with a flourish. "Had I known that the *crème de la crème* of English womanhood was so beautiful, I would have made the journey from St. Petersburg long ago."

"*Merci,*" she murmured, echoing his use of French, the court language of the Russian nobility. There was no point in upsetting her grandfather by making mention of her American blood, she decided. They would soon enough have something to lock horns over.

The colonel clicked his heels and bowed. "It is a pleasure to meet you, Miss Woodbridge."

Kate appreciated the simple gesture, along with the fact that his chest was not clanking with row upon row of gaudy medals. "And you, sir. From your accent, I would guess that you are from the north of Prussia—perhaps near Danzig?"

"*Jawohl*, Miss Woodbridge." His face was not handsome, but with a flash of pleasure lighting his pale blue eyes, he was rather attractive. "I am indeed from that port city. You have an excellent ear for languages."

"A very pretty ear it is, too," said Vronskov with an effusive laugh.

She ignored him. "Have you been in London long, Colonel?"

"Just a few months. I have been assigned to serve as military attaché to our embassy here, though I will soon be joining our delegation for the peace conference in Vienna for several weeks."

"I should very much like to see that city," said Kate. "As well as the Danube and the Rhine."

"Have you traveled abroad?" asked Von Seilig.

"Yes, I..." Seeing her grandfather's mouth compress, she caught herself. "I visited some foreign places when my parents were alive."

Von Seilig seemed to sense her hesitation and tactfully let the subject drop.

"Gentlemen, if you will excuse us now, we must greet the others," said the duke.

The three men stepped aside, Vronskov adding another elaborate bow.

Kate and her grandfather proceeded to circle the room, repeating the polite formalities. There were, counted Kate, twenty guests, not including herself, the duke, and Charlotte. That meant that only one had not yet arrived, seeing as the duke's butler had informed her that the party would be an even two dozen people.

Yet another prosy diplomat, she thought to herself.

Several of the English gentlemen were accompanied by their wives, but most of the foreigners had come alone. However, Cluyne and Tappan had made an effort to ensure a feminine presence. Kate recognized an influential matron of the *ton* and her two unmarried daughters, along with the widowed Countess of Duxbury.

"Ah, here is the last member of our party. Conte Ghiradelli just arrived an hour ago, Katharine," intoned the duke. "Allow me to introduce you—"

"We've met," she said curtly.

"Indeed, I have had the pleasure of making your granddaughter's acquaintance in London," elaborated Marco.

She narrowed her gaze in warning. Surely the rogue wouldn't be so rag-mannered as to tell the story of their first encounter outside Angelo's fencing salon. Her grandfather would not be amused.

"My cousin is a member of Miss Woodbridge's scientific circle," he continued smoothly. "And recently married the Duke of Ledyard's youngest son. Your granddaughter and I attended the wedding in Oxfordshire."

"Ah yes, Lord James Pierson," replied Cluyne. "He is said to be an excellent fellow."

To Kate's ears, the statement carried a note of

reproach. No lordly suitors or military heroes were currently seeking *her* hand.

"Quite," she replied evenly.

"A most excellent fellow," agreed Marco. He slanted her a wink glittering with suppressed mirth. "His upstanding character puts most of us mere mortals to blush."

She pretended not to see it. Whatever might bring a tinge of red to the conte's face, it would *not* be contrition over his moral shortcomings. "Are you, like many of our other guests, heading on to the Continent after this gathering?" she inquired as her grandfather stepped away to speak with Tappan.

"Should I be?" he asked with feigned innocence.

Refusing to be provoked, Kate answered sweetly, "La, I wouldn't know, sir. Your affairs are none of my concern."

"Perhaps that will change," he murmured *sotto voce*.

The silky sound stirred a strange flutter inside her chest. Had she known Marco was to be one of the guests, she might have reconsidered her decision to come here. Dealing with Cluyne was going to be difficult enough without a darkly sensuous devil-in-the-flesh to torment her thoughts.

She wouldn't. Think about Marco, that is. With all the other guests around, it should be easy enough to avoid his company.

She was saved from having to make further conversation with Marco by the arrival of Andreas Vincenzi, who greeted his fellow Italian with effusive delight and drew him off to the far corner of the room.

The ordeal of introductions over, Kate was about to return to Charlotte when Jeremiah Ludlowe, an American from Philadelphia, requested that she join the group gathered by the hearth.

"Miss Woodbridge, might I ask you to help us settle a debate. Lady Gervin and I disagree on how many specimens your grandfather's conservatory is said to hold..."

"A glass of sherry would be lovely," said Charlotte to the liveried footman. After accepting the drink, she moved back into the shadows of the corner alcove and returned to her study of the botanical prints on the wall.

The delicate colored engravings looked to be from a medieval herbal. From southern Switzerland, she decided, judging by the spidery German script. Magnified by the lens of her quizzing glass, the alpine specimen of St. John's Wort looked to have somewhat longer leaves than the common English variety.

Lost in scholarly thought, she moved on to the next one.

"Fetch up another three bottles of champagne from the cellars. And be sure that Higgins has decanted the claret to serve with the roast beef."

"Yes, Your Grace."

Charlotte was suddenly aware of having company within the secluded alcove.

"Add the '78 Madeira to the selection of ports," continued Cluyne to his butler. "Better include a malt from Scotland—"

She didn't move quite quickly enough to dodge a collision with the ducal backside.

A grunt—or rather a growl—rumbled in his throat as Cluyne turned around. "I beg your pardon, madam," he said, sounding more irritated than apologetic. "I did not realize anyone was lurking in here."

Her opinion of him already colored by Kate's resentment, Charlotte found herself piqued by the duke's abrasive manner. *To hell with pandering to his imperious pride*, she decided. If he wanted to toss her out on her arse, he was welcome to do so.

Her bum was already bruised.

"Feel free to have your servants check under my garments," she replied, lifting the edge of her shawl. "To make sure I am not purloining any of your valuable art."

He had the grace to flush.

"They are also welcome to poke through my reticule after supper, to ensure that I haven't slipped in any of the heirloom silver."

"Perhaps 'lurking' was a poor choice of words," he said through gritted teeth. "I meant no offense."

Apologies did not come naturally to him, thought Charlotte. And why would they? A duke was never expected to express contrition for anything. Raising her quizzing glass, she regarded him with a cold stare.

As anticipated, his scowl grew more pronounced.

Repressing a smile, she turned back to the prints. "I was *looking*, not *lurking*. Have you any objection to my studying this display of prints? Which are, by the by, quite magnificent. They are Swiss, are they not?"

"Yes," he muttered.

"From Basle, I imagine," said Charlotte, noticing the printer's mark at the bottom of the page. Forgetting her initial ire, she subjected the image of the *Pastinaca sativa* to a more thorough scrutiny.

"Indeed." Cluyne joined her by the print. "From the workshop of Johann Froben, whose skill in printing was unrivaled."

"I would say that the Parisian atelier of Simon De Colines was equally adept at capturing the nuance of line," she replied. "Though I daresay you are right about the coloring. The artists employed by Froben achieved more subtlety in their shades."

"Hmmm." The duke cleared his throat and shuffled a step to his left. "This one of a *Monarda fistulosa* shows the brush technique more clearly."

"Yes, I see what you mean," said Charlotte after examining the print for a long moment. "Speaking of which, are you familiar with the work of Pietro Andrea Mattioli?"

"I have several examples hanging in my study." Another cough. "Not many people know of his work."

"No, but he is a great favorite of mine."

"You are welcome to view them," he said gruffly. "There are a number of illustrated volumes in the library that you might also find of interest. I shall have one of the servants put them out for you."

"Thank you," she murmured.

"Hmmph." Clasping his hands behind his back, Cluyne blew out his cheeks. "The last two prints of this series are hung on the other side of the curio cabinet. You ought not miss them." Moving back to rejoin his butler, Cluyne paused and then added, "Simpson, be sure to check under Lady Fenimore's shawl when she leaves."

Charlotte wondered whether the wink was merely a flicker of the candelabra. Or did the duke actually possess a sense of humor to go along with his hauteur?

"Yes, Your Grace," replied the butler without batting an eye.

Cluyne consulted his pocketwatch. "Have Frampton ring the dinner bell in twenty minutes."

Chapter Eight

Marco reined his stallion to a walk as the graveled drive crested the hill. In the pale half light of early morning, the colonnaded entrance of Cluyne Close appeared an oddly ethereal vision, rising from a sea of pearly mist like a vision from some fanciful dream.

"Hell," he muttered, wincing slightly as he adjusted the brim of his hat. His mind was half asleep. He had stayed up all night with Vincenzi, talking and drinking far too much brandy from the duke's excellent wine cellar. And while the ride had cleared most of the fogginess from his brain, the stale taste of spirits and tobacco still lingered in the back of his throat.

Inhaling a lungful of the cool, clean air, Marco swiveled in his saddle and surveyed the deserted grounds. Despite his muzzy state, the decision to ride out at dawn had been a good one. It was always important to know the lay of the land when beginning a mission, and he had been able to spend the last hour exploring the fields and woods of the estate, making a mental map of the area.

Despite the inauspicious start, Lynsley would have no reason to question his professionalism on this assignment.

With a flick of his reins, Marco turned his stallion for the stables. He needed a shave and a bath before appearing at breakfast. Rubbing his hand over his bristled jaw, he imagined that he looked like…

"Hell," he repeated, watching a horse and rider materialize from the swirling mists.

The flutter of dark-green skirts looked just like a bat winging out from the smoke and brimstone of the Underworld. Then, as the apparition came closer and closer, he could just make out a telltale curl of wheaten hair beneath the stylish shako.

Swearing another oath, Marco swung his mount around and dug his heels into the big stallion's muscular flanks. "*Andiamo*, Nero," he urged, tightening his grip on the reins. In his current condition, he didn't feel quite up to an encounter with Kate Woodbridge. "Let us fly!"

The horse responded with a foam-flecked snort and a leaping burst of speed.

Bending low, Marco galloped through a stone archway and angled for the open meadows, where silvery tendrils of fog floated up from the long grass. Wind whipping against his face, he headed for the far end of the field, where earlier he had spotted a bridle path that led down to the lake.

As the stallion's hooves cut through the swaying fescue, kicking up great clods of earth, he ventured a look behind him.

Sure enough, the lady was trying to match his pace but he was leaving her in the dust.

"*Va bene*, Nero." Marco shifted his hands and the stallion lengthened its stride. "We have our masculine honor to defend—we can't allow ourselves to be caught by Miss Woodbridge and her mare."

They thundered past a copse of beech trees, setting the leaves to dancing wildly in their wake. His blood was now heated, burning the last vestiges of haze from his head. A challenge always served as a spark.

Perhaps in a rowing race she would have a chance. But in riding, he had no doubt that he would claim an easy victory. Smiling to himself, Marco shot another glance over his shoulder.

Damn!

The bay mare was still racing over the turf but its saddle was now empty, its rider nowhere to be seen.

Marco pulled up in a flash and quickly reversed directions. Veering sharply, he cut off the other horse and snagged the dragging reins, aware that his heart was pounding hard enough to crack his ribs. He fisted his hand around the leather and tried to remain calm.

If Kate Woodbridge didn't know better than to gallop hell-for-leather over unfamiliar land, then she deserved to break her bloody neck, he told himself.

But as he stood in his stirrups and looked desperately around for any sign of movement, he felt fear seize his chest. *Dio Madre*, a fall from a fast-moving horse was always dangerous. Flying hooves could crush a skull or trample a body. Bones could snap like twigs....

A flutter of emerald wool suddenly stirred in the light greens and golds of the meadow grass.

He spurred forward.

"Ooof." Kate grimaced as she tried to stand.

"Don't try to move!" cried Marco as he vaulted out of his saddle.

She was already on her feet, though her legs were a little wobbly. The ostrich feather of her hat was bent in half and a streak of mud covered one side of her face, but otherwise she looked unharmed.

He released his pent-up breath in a roar. "*A diavolo!* You are bloody lucky to be alive!"

Kate plucked several stalks of straw from her disheveled curls. "No thanks to you."

"*Me?* That's just like a woman, to blame someone else for her own foolishness." He stalked to her side. "What in the name of Lucifer were you thinking, to ride after me like a she-devil?"

Her expression turned mulish. "Why did you run away?"

Marco ignored the question. Taking her arm—none too gently—he led her over to the winded horses. "I give thanks to the Almighty that there are no broken bones!"

Kate's frown softened. "I've just a few bumps and bruises—"

"I was speaking of your *horse*," he snapped.

She opened her mouth to retort but he cut her off with another harsh oath. "It would have been a great pity if an innocent animal had suffered for your recklessness. An inexperienced rider should never try to cross rough ground at a gallop."

"I..." Kate bit her lip. "I...didn't think. You are right. It was wrong and egregiously selfish of me to put my mare at risk. I saw your action as a challenge, and..."

"And you never back down from a challenge," he said roughly. Fear still had him on edge. "Next time you wish to match your physical prowess against mine, use your brain as well as your body."

She hugged her arms to her chest, her kidskin gloves chafing at the sleeves of her riding habit. "I have admitted my error, Lord Ghiradelli. It is not necessary to subject me to further scorn."

Her frank admission caught him by surprise.

"As you see, pride goeth before a fall," he muttered, unsettled by his own sudden impulse to gather her in his arms and whisper a comforting word in her ear. With her hat askew and her face covered with lopsided smudges, she looked oddly vulnerable.

A hot spark lit in her eyes, quickly dispelling the impression. "Well, if that is the case, *you* will no doubt be tumbling all the way to Hades."

"Not from a horse," he retorted. His first rush of relief had turned to righteous anger that she had put herself in such danger. "I know how to keep my arse in the saddle. Which is more than can be said for you, Miss Woodbridge. You may be an experienced rower, but you are a bloody awful rider!"

Rather than dignify his taunt with a reply, she turned away and grabbed up her crop from the ground.

"A moment," he growled. Taking a firm grasp of her shoulder, he slapped his hand back and forth across her backside. "Let me help you pat the dust from your bottom."

"Ass." Wrenching free, Kate swung around.

This time Marco was ready for her. He caught her wrist. "My strike is even quicker than yours."

"Yes—I've heard you are called *Il Serpenti*."

"It's not because of my hand, *cara*." He curled a mocking smile. "Care to guess what part of me gave rise to the moniker?"

A flush stole to her cheeks.

"My *soul*, sweetheart." He gave a sardonic laugh. "I have the morals of a snake."

Kate fixed him with a furious glare. "That is likely the least of your faults."

His smile slipped just a bit. *How much about his background had Alessandra told her close friends?* Surely she would not betray his painful, private past. "I would not have thought that the Circle of Sin engaged in girlish gossip. What tales has my cousin told you?"

"Of course Alessandra does not pass on any of the lurid details of your life. As if we would give a fig to hear them." Lifting her nose in the air, she moved to her horse. However, the air of imperious disdain was marred by a pronounced limp. He guessed that there were several large bruises on her bum.

"Who knows..." He came up close behind her and placed his hands on her waist. "You might find them intriguing."

Kate tried to pull away.

"Stop squirming. Unless you wish to walk all the way back to the stables, you are going to need my help to get back in the saddle." Marco couldn't resist adding, "But then, if your delicate parts are too sore to sit upon hard leather, I could carry you in my lap—"

"Lift me up," she said. "And do make it quick."

He was about to do as ordered when a loose strand of her hair brushed against his cheek. *Neroli* and wild thyme—the scent tickled his nostrils for an instant before wafting away in the breeze.

Damn. Whatever memory it stirred was equally elusive.

He felt her stiffen and realized his hands had stilled on the swell of her hips. The curves fit quite comfortably against his palms, and he let them linger, savoring her shape.

"Well?" Kate demanded. "What are you waiting for?"

The mare gave a whicker as Marco tossed her up and helped hook her leg on the sidesaddle's pommel. "Walk your mount back. It's still early enough that you shouldn't encounter anyone on the way up to your rooms," he advised. "I shall follow along later, unless you truly can't make it by yourself. You know how evil minds like to speculate, so it would be best if we are not spotted together without a chaperone."

"I'll manage," she said curtly.

He stepped back. "Next time, take a groom. They are usually expert riders and can offer helpful pointers on the basics of horsemanship."

As she rode off, Marco heard a few parting words slip from her lips. Including ones that sounded suspiciously like 'insufferable' and 'prick.'

"These books are indeed magnificent." Charlotte sighed as she closed the tooled leather covers. "I once owned a copy of the medieval herbal by Matthaeus Platearius. Until my late husband sold it to cover his gambling debts."

"Men," muttered Kate through gritted teeth. She

shifted her position on the library's window seat and bit back a wince. Lud, her bum must be turning a vile shade of bruised purple.

But the worst blow had been to her pride. She was usually dispassionate about judging her own capabilities—or lack of them. Which made the decision to go galloping in pursuit of Marco even more incomprehensible. Her brain knew it was imperative to stay as far away from the conte as possible.

But her body… She shifted slightly, uncomfortably aware that the sharp prickling of her flesh had nothing to do with her recent bruises. *Damn her body for responding to the rogue.* She wasn't a pirate any longer, a free spirit allowed to make her own rules. She must learn to behave like a gently reared lady, even though she was anything but.

Prim and proper, she reminded herself. But rebellion must run in her blood, for she couldn't seem to make her spirit give any heed to her conscious commands.

"*Men*," repeated Kate, a little more loudly. "To the devil with the lot of them." Setting aside the volume of floral engravings she had been perusing, she rose from the tufted cushions. "*Ouch*."

Charlotte looked up. "Are you all right, my dear? I noticed that you seem to be walking rather gingerly."

"It's nothing to speak of—I had just a slight accident on the bridle path this morning."

"Perhaps you ought to lie down for the rest of the day," said her friend in some concern. "A fall from a horse is nothing to be trifled with. Are you sure that you've suffered no broken bones?"

Kate rubbed at her rear. "For better or for worse, I landed on a spot that has ample padding."

"You haven't an ounce of protection, despite all the pastries you consume," replied Charlotte with a sympathetic grimace.

"A long soak in a hot tub after we have a look at the bromeliads in the conservatory and I will be fine."

"If you are sure..." Rising from the reading table, Charlotte carefully placed the rare books in a neat row. "I am looking forward to examining the specimens, of course, but I would be just as happy to spend the afternoon here with these marvelous works of art. I so rarely have a chance to study such valuable engravings." She gave a longing look at the cavernous room and the ornately carved floor-to-ceiling shelves of sherry-colored oak. "I can only imagine what other intellectual treasures are here."

"Feel free to explore. You are welcome to use the library whenever you wish," said Kate.

"I would imagine that the duke does not allow just anyone into his bailiwick—"

"You are correct, Lady Fenimore," said a gruff voice from behind the half-open paneled door. "My ancestors spent a great deal of time and blunt assembling this collection. It is my duty to preserve it and pass it on, undiminished, to future generations."

Kate watched Cluyne enter the room, his movements as stiff and precise as the starched folds of his cravat. His name ought to be the Duke of Duty, she thought rather sardonically. *Did he never unbend?* Like the Prince Regent, he always seemed to be wearing a corset—with stays made of steel instead of whalebone.

"As I said before, Your Grace, I am perfectly willing to submit to a search of my person, should you fear I am purloining your property," Charlotte didn't hesitate to answer with a tart retort. "That is, assuming I am granted the privilege of looking at your books."

The duke's nostrils flared as he inhaled sharply and then let out the air in an audible *hmmph*. "You are, as my guest, welcome to enjoy any of the amenities that Cluyne Close has to offer. Unlike many people who come here, you at least appear to appreciate books."

Kate caught her friend's eye and lifted a brow in apology. She wasn't quite sure why the duke seemed to be in an ill temper. But then, she didn't pretend to understand his moods or his motivations.

"The same cannot be said for your late husband," added Cluyne abruptly, "who sold several lovely volumes of rare French engravings to a print shop in the Pantheon Bazaar, so they could be cut up and sold as single pages. If you ask me, the fellow was a deuced loose screw."

"Yes, he was," said Charlotte, her voice remaining calm, though a flush of color ridged her cheekbones. "But if you are implying that *I* had any choice in the matter, that is grossly unfair. I didn't. As you know, well-bred females have no say in picking a husband. Fenimore was willing to accept my dowry, and as my family was anxious to fire me off, they didn't bother to ask themselves why."

Charlotte paused and lifted her chin. Despite her height, the duke's imposing bulk seemed to dwarf her presence. Unintimidated, she met his gaze. Kate could almost hear the clash of steel striking steel. "I should have told them to go to hell, but that is from an older, wiser perspective. As a green girl, with no experience, no idea of the harsh realities of what life would be like with a drunkard and gambler, I was too naïve to know any better."

The duke opened his mouth as if to reply and then shut it.

Kate blinked in surprise. She had never seen her grandfather rendered speechless.

"Live and learn," finished Charlotte. "And by the by, the books were mine, and I was devastated to lose them. But Fenimore needed money to pay a gambling debt, so artistic integrity wasn't overly important to him. He was, however, extremely stricken when I explained how much more he could have gotten from an antiquarian book dealer."

Cluyne coughed, and then, for a long moment, there was only an uneasy silence.

"Oh, look, the sun has broken through the clouds," said Kate brightly. "The light should be perfect for looking at the newly arrived *Heliconia rostrada* from the Antipodes. If you will excuse us, sir, we've plans to spend the rest of the afternoon in the conservatory."

Inclining a curt nod, the duke turned and walked off toward the far end of the room, his gleaming boots clicking loudly on the polished parquet.

"Men." Kate fixed her friend with a baleful glance. "Sorry. That was unspeakably rude of Cluyne. For all his faults, he is usually scrupulously polite. Good manners is yet another ducal duty."

"Don't fret about me, my dear," said Charlotte, the color still high on her face. "I can take care of myself."

"Ghiradelli."

Marco crossed through the open French doors and joined the trio of men out on the terrace.

"So, you finally got here. I was beginning to think

you had found more convivial company in Town," went on Lord Tappan with a grin. Turning to the two others, he explained, "The conte has no lack of invitations for intimate entertainment."

"So I have heard," said Von Seilig. "It seems you haven't changed much since your time in Berlin. Still the same ramshackle rake."

Marco perched a hip on the stone railing and lit a cheroot. "It seems you haven't changed much from those days either. Still the same stick-in-the-mud."

The Prussian responded with a tight-lipped smile. "From you, I take that as a compliment."

"You shouldn't," drawled Marco, though actually he rather liked the colonel. He was sober and serious, to be sure, but could converse intelligently on a number of diverse subjects. Which was more than could be said for the majority of the foreign diplomatic corps currently in England.

"Ha, ha, ha." Vronskov gave a loud guffaw. "The conte is right, Von Seilig. You work far too hard."

"Yes, Prussia has much to do in order to prepare for the upcoming peace conference in Vienna." The colonel paused a fraction. "You know what they say—the King of Prussia will think for everyone, the King of Bavaria will drink for everyone, the Emperor of Russia will make love for everyone, and the Emperor of Austria will pay for everyone."

Marco and Tappan chuckled at the witticism, while Vronskov looked somewhat miffed. "Tsar Alexander is a great and good ruler. Indeed, given that he has been blessed with divine intelligence and good looks, it is no wonder that the people of Russia call him The Angel."

"And the ladies of Europe call him the opposite,"

quipped Von Seilig. Like his grandmother, Catherine the Great, Tsar Alexander was known for his sexual appetite. "Now that he's helped conquer Napoleon, he is moving on to new, virgin territory."

"We Russians cannot help it if we have a way with women." The Russian turned and waggled a leer at Marco. "Speaking of which, I have heard that your knowledge of London's nocturnal haunts is unrivaled, Lord Ghiradelli. I'd like to get your recommendations for the best brothels in London."

"That depends on what you are interested in," replied Marco with a slow smile.

Vronskov wet his lips.

"I'll write down a few suggestions, and make a note of each establishment's specialties."

"Splendid, splendid!" The Russian clapped him on the back. "I knew I could count on you for an intimate description of London's pleasure spots!"

Tappan flicked a bit of ash from the tip of his cheroot. "I noticed last night that you are acquainted with Lord Vincenzi."

"*Si*, we went to school together," answered Marco. "And Rochambert and I know each other from Milano."

"They are out riding right now. The duke has some very fine-blooded hunters in his stables and has kindly made them available to us for the duration of our stay."

The duke was a generous host, thought Marco. Having already observed the selection of prime horseflesh in the stables, he knew that a small fortune was riding on the iron-shod hooves.

"I shall enjoy putting them through their paces," he murmured.

"As will I," announced Vronskov. "My equestrian skills are much admired in St. Petersburg."

The Russian nobleman was not only a braggart but a buffoon, decided Marco. Only a sapskull would make such an announcement to other men.

"I am sure that you look quite splendid mounted on a great black bear," he said with exaggerated innocence. "But here in England, we ride *horses.*"

Tappan and Von Seilig laughed.

Smoothing a hand over the drooping ends of his mustache, Vronskov tried to hide his irritation. "Ha, ha, ha. I see you have a quick wit, sir. I shall have to be careful around you."

"Me?" Marco gave a careless shrug as he lit up a cheroot. "Don't give it a thought if I annoy you. I annoy everyone."

"Save for the ladies, of course," said Tappan with a knowing wink.

With some exceptions. Marco exhaled a ring of smoke, recalling his recent encounters with Kate. She certainly showed no interest in encouraging his attentions. Not that he could blame her. His teasings had been deliberately flagrant.

"It doesn't appear as if Ghiradelli will have much chance to exercise his prowess with the opposite sex. The females here are all respectable ladies," said Von Seilig. "Isn't your English code of honor very precise about that sort of thing?"

"Come, come, as a diplomat you know that rules are never black and white. There are always a nuanced range of grays in between. And there is always room for negotiation," pointed out Tappan. "The Countess of Duxbury, who has accompanied her brother here, is a prime example. She is a widow, and so is allowed some latitude in her personal behavior, as long as she is discreet about it."

Stroking his whiskers, Vronskov narrowed his gaze to a speculative squint. "Ah, I am liking England more and more."

"But as for unmarried young ladies of genteel birth, you are right, Colonel. They are not considered fair game for a gentleman," went on Tappan. "I wouldn't advise anyone to trifle with the duke's granddaughter. To do so would be asking for grave trouble."

Trouble. As Marco took another puff on his cheroot, the tip flared to a red-hot glow. *That was putting it mildly.* Seeking any further contact with Kate Woodbridge would be playing with fire. Lynsley had been very clear—his mission here was one of simple observation.

But then again, he seemed to be inexorably drawn to fire. Like a moth to a flame.

"A pity," remarked Vronskov with a lascivious leer. "I wouldn't mind bedding the beauty."

Von Seilig frowned. "Keep a respectful tone when talking of Miss Woodbridge."

The Russian rolled his eyes. "Don't you Prussians ever unbend," he muttered.

"We don't behave like barbarians."

"Shall we have a game of billiards before it is time to dress for dinner?" suggested Tappan.

Marco waved them on. "You go ahead. I think I shall stroll to the stables and see if the riding party has returned." Tossing down the butt of tobacco, he ground it out beneath his boot, taking care to stamp out a sudden flare of irritation along with it. The Russian's comments about Kate might be crude, but they were none of his concern. He wasn't here to play the noble knight in shining armor—a role, he reminded himself, for which he was singularly ill-suited. Only the mission mattered.

Besides, she seemed perfectly confident of looking out for herself.

Chapter Nine

Candlelight flickered over the mahogany paneling and gilt-framed paintings. The click of crystal and the sounds of conversation were muted by the rich damask draperies and plush carpets. Kate drew a deep breath as she entered the main drawing room, feeling a little overpowered by its opulent elegance. Perhaps it sensed that she was an impostor, she thought wryly. Someone who didn't quite belong.

"Sherry, Miss Woodbridge?" offered one of the passing footmen.

"Champagne," she decided, hoping that the wine's effervescence might add a little sparkle to her spirits. They were a little flat tonight...no doubt because her self-esteem had been thoroughly squashed by the morning's debacle. Lud, she still couldn't believe what a fool she had made of herself. From now on, she would stick to walking.

"Katharine." Her grandfather's voice rose above the hushed tones of the guests. "Do come join me."

She crossed the room, trying not to limp.

A tiny frown pinched at the corners of his mouth. "Is something ailing you?"

"I'm just a bit sore from riding," she replied—and then instantly regretted the admission on seeing who was standing by Cluyne's side.

"One must be careful not to overdo a strenuous physical activity," said Marco. "Especially if one is unaccustomed to it."

He need *not* look so smug, thought Kate.

Marco seemed to read her mind, for his smile turned even more sardonic. "If you like, Miss Woodbridge, I would be happy to ride out with you and give you a few lessons."

"As would I." With a flourish, Vronskov appeared by her side and bowed over her hand.

"How kind," she said to both of them. "But you gentlemen need not bother. I shall be spending most of my time in the conservatory."

"Did I hear that you meet regularly to discuss science, Miss Woodbridge?" Von Seilig broke away from the group of guests by the hearth and came to join the duke's circle.

"Yes." Kate favored him with a smile, grateful for the opening to ignore both Marco and the Russian.

"I, too, have an interest in the subject, as does my superior, Wilhelm von Humboldt. He will be our ambassador to the Congress in Vienna, and I shall be serving on his staff."

"Humboldt?" Kate didn't have to feign interest. "The classical scholar and linguist who founded the University of Berlin?"

"*Ja*, Miss Woodbridge. And perhaps you have heard of his brother Alexander, who is a noted explorer and naturalist."

"Indeed I have," she replied enthusiastically. "His recent essay on ocean currents is quite fascinating!"

Marco cleared his throat with a cough. "Perhaps we ought to seek other company, Vronskov, before we find ourselves humbled by yet another paragon of manly virtue."

The Russian scowled, clearly loath to leave the field to the colonel. "Bah, don't bore Miss Woodbridge with talk of academics and books, Von Seilig. Ladies don't comprehend such stuffy subjects. Nor do they care to."

As he leaned in and smiled through his carefully curled mustache, Kate was forced to recoil. The man was as heavy-handed with his musky cologne as he was with his florid compliments. Both were equally obnoxious.

"Speaking of books..." Tappan paused in passing. "I heard you and Lady Fenimore talking about early engravings of Caribbean plant life as you came in. I have several very rare Spanish editions in my estate library that might interest you. My collection is, of course, quite paltry in comparison to Cluyne's treasures, but these particular volumes happen to be ones that he does not have."

"We should very much like to see them," replied Kate. "Are you interested in botany, sir?"

"A little, but I hardly claim to be as knowledgeable on the subject as you or your grandfather," he said. "I shall ride over to Hillcrest House first thing in the morning and fetch them."

"Thank you, sir. That's very kind of you."

"Come, come, let us change the subject," announced

Vronskov impatiently as Tappan moved on. "We gentlemen all know that ladies would much rather talk about the latest fashions or what balls they have attended. They are simply too polite to say so."

Kate heard Marco swallow a snort. For all his faults, at least the rogue wasn't a blathering idiot.

"You are obviously an expert on the feminine mind, as well as a good many other things," she replied coolly.

The Russian thrust out his chest. "I pride myself in being a cultivated man of the world."

"Pray, do tell me what your favorite color is, Miss Woodbridge," said Marco with an exaggerated flutter of his dark lashes. "And do you favor mutton sleeves for a day dress, or is your preference for the latest *a la greque* style from Paris?"

She bit her cheeks to keep from smiling. "Actually, I wouldn't know a mutton sleeve from a slab of roast beef."

Vronskov's expression was suddenly not so smug.

"Colonel Von Seilig, would you kindly offer me your arm for a stroll around the room." Flirting was not so onerous after all, Kate decided. The Prussian was a pleasant gentleman, and she found herself looking forward to discussing science with him. "I should very much like to hear more about von Humboldt and his discoveries."

"Don't stray too far," murmured Marco. As he turned away, he contrived to smooth his evening coat over his well-shaped…posterior. "I'm sure Vronskov would assure you that ladies would never dream of overexerting themselves in vigorous physical exercise."

Marco had a feeling the slight hitch in her gait was due more to injured pride than any bodily ache or pain.

He really ought to resist the temptation to tease her, no matter that her eyes sparked with such a beguiling blaze when she was annoyed. Not only would Alessandra be furious with him if he kept up his provocations, but Lord Lynsley expected him to perform his duty without allowing any distractions.

Wild. Careless. Losing his edge.

Lynsley's assessment of his recent performances—delivered with the marquess's usual analytical precision—had stung. Marco took a long swallow of champagne, trying to submerge the niggling little stirring of self-doubt. To hell with his saintly superior's lecture. The accusations were unfair. He never allowed his drinking or carousing to interfere with his duties. Scotland had been an aberration. His nerves and his judgment were as sharp as a razor.

"Lord Ghiradelli?"

Vronskov elbowed him in the ribs and whispered, "The duke is speaking to you."

"Forgive me, Your Grace," apologized Marco, forcing his gaze away from Kate's shapely silhouette moving in and out of the flickering light. "I was… admiring the magnificent painting on the far wall. It is by Tintoretto, is it not?"

Cluyne's eyes narrowed, as if guessing what he had really been observing. "Yes, it is," he replied gruffly. "I was asking whether you have a special interest in politics, sir."

"Not particularly," he responded casually. "I am far more interested in artistic pursuits."

"Have you no concern about what will happen to the Italian peninsula at the upcoming conference in Vienna?"

asked Vronskov. "Given your extensive landholdings and your title, I should think that you would have a great deal of interest in what decisions are made."

"I leave that to the diplomats, who are far more knowledgeable about the nuances of power than I am," said Marco, contriving to sound bored. "I should, of course, like to see the artistic treasures that Napoleon plundered from our cities be returned."

"I can vouch for the fact that international diplomacy is not one of Lord Ghiradelli's interests," quipped Tappan, who had drifted over to join the conversation. "He has managed to provoke two challenges to a duel in the last month. Or was it three?"

Vronskov snickered. "Napoleon is not the only man who has been helping himself to pretty things that do not rightfully belong to him."

Cluyne's expression appeared carved out of granite, making Marco wonder what the duke had been told about the true purpose of his presence here.

Not much, he decided. Lord Tappan had been the one to request that Marco's name be added to the guest list. But despite the baron's position in the Foreign Office, and his upcoming trip to Vienna as part of the English delegation, he was not privy to the real role that Marco played with Lord Lynsley's secret intelligence service within English government.

Lies and deception. By now they fit like a second skin, thought Marco as he smoothed a wrinkle from his sleeve. His cover as a rakish reprobate, interested in only the pleasures of the flesh, kept anyone from asking any serious questions about his presence in London.

"I daresay Ghiradelli will be on his best behavior

here," said Tappan lightly. "The duke's treasures are perfectly safe."

Cluyne tightened his jaw. "I should hope so."

"Tell me, Vronskov, is it true that your tsar is seeking Prussian support for the creation of an independent Poland?" asked Tappan, tactfully seeking to change the subject. "We hear that in return for giving up some of his coastal ports, he will agree to the annexation of Saxony."

"There are many rumors floating around," countered the Russian. "Tell me, does England view the idea with favor?"

"Ah, well, that would depend on a number of things...."

Marco listened to the discussion for a bit, then excused himself to go talk with the French envoy who was holding court on the other side of the room.

A cousin of Prince Talleyrand, the Foreign Minister of France, Rochambert was one of the lucky aristocrats whose family had managed to escape the terror of the Revolution's early years. Aided by his powerful relative, the Frenchman had risen to an influential post in the diplomatic service and would be representing the newly restored Bourbon monarchy in Vienna. Whether France saw Russia or Austria as its main ally was a key question.

Concentrate. Marco forced his gaze away from Kate as he made his way past several other groups of guests. It was going be hard enough keeping all the names and alliances straight in his head without adding a distraction. This gathering was a little like a chess game, with the international envoys jockeying for position on the board while using the countries of Europe as their pawns.

The balance of power rested on the outcome of the conference, and one errant move could prove costly for England.

He sipped his wine, feeling the tiny bubbles explode against his tongue. The prickling sensation somehow seeped through his throat and slid down his spine.

The actual war might be over, but Marco had a feeling that the battlefield was still as treacherous as ever.

"Miss Woodbridge, do come sit beside me." The Countess of Duxbury patted the plump pillows of the sofa. "I have heard much about you from my younger brother and am delighted to finally make your acquaintance."

Kate cast an apologetic look at Charlotte. "I suppose that we must make a stab at being social," she whispered.

The sumptuous supper finally over, the ladies had withdrawn from the dining room, leaving the gentlemen to linger over their port and cigars.

"The invitation did not include me," observed Charlotte under her breath. "You go on. I shall oversee the setting up of tea."

Repressing a sigh, Kate joined Lady Duxbury. Given the fact that she shunned most of Society's parties, she couldn't imagine what the countess had heard from her brother.

"Ah, finally a chance for a comfortable coze." The countess flashed a dimpled smile. A statuesque brunette, she wore a stylish gown cut to show off her flawless alabaster skin and well-endowed bosom. An expensive gold necklace, highlighted by diamonds and a large teardrop topaz, accentuated the creamy expanse of cleavage.

The widow did not appear to be mourning her marital

state, thought Kate with a touch of cynicism. Though she paid little attention to tittle-tattle, it was hard to avoid seeing the frequent mention of the lady's name in all the newspaper gossip columns.

"As I said, I've been quite anxious to meet you," added Lady Duxbury.

"I'm flattered," murmured Kate. "But perhaps your brother has me confused with someone else. I don't go out much in Society."

"Oh, make no mistake, he definitely knows who you are." A mischievous gleam lit the lady's brown eyes. Lowering her voice, she added, "Apparently you threatened to cut out his spleen in front of Angelo's fencing salon."

A flush rose to Kate's cheeks. "I fear that your brother may have misinterpreted my meaning. In any case, be assured he has greatly exaggerated the incident."

"It may have been his liver rather than his spleen." Lady Duxbury tapped her fan to Kate's wrist. "Still, I found the story rather delicious. I admire boldness in a lady." Lowering her voice to a conspiratorial whisper, she added, "Gilbert mentioned that you sent in a note which summoned a nearly naked Lord Ghiradelli into the middle of Bond Street." A throaty laugh. "Now *that* is a sight I should like to have seen."

"From what I understand, it is not such a difficult thing to arrange," replied Kate dryly. "The conte is apparently willing to shed his clothing at the slightest encouragement."

The countess laughed. "And from what I understand, that is not such an unpleasant experience. I imagine he's rather skilled at..." She finished with a knowing wink.

Kate found the lady's manner far too presumptuous for a stranger. Mimicking the duke's imperious look of hauteur, she drew back a touch. "I am not quite sure what you mean," she intoned, though she knew exactly what the other lady was implying.

"Oh, have I offended you, Miss Woodbridge?" The countess assumed a contrite expression. "It was meant as a little girlish teasing, so please do not take it amiss. Do say that you forgive me." She fluttered her lashes. "I have a feeling we could be very good friends."

"Really?" replied Kate coolly. The countess's over-friendly advances struck a false note. "Yet you don't know me at all."

"Oh, but we ladies have a natural camaraderie," said Lady Duxbury. "After all, don't we all love to gossip and share confidences?"

That was just the sort of behavior Kate loathed—spreading rumors and savaging one's so-called friends behind their backs. Polite Society was anything but.

"Actually, I find such frivolous pursuits a waste of time," she replied.

Lady Duxbury's eyes narrowed slightly at the obvious rebuff, but she forced a smile. "Yet you take pains to encourage the attention of Ghiradelli and Von Seilig."

Kate couldn't quite believe her ears. To be accused of blatant flirtation was absurd. "You misinterpret my actions. Von Seilig and I are conversing on scientific subjects. And Lord Ghiradelli is the cousin of one of my closest friends." She rose. "Now, if you will excuse me, I had best help Lady Fenimore prepare the tea service."

"Of course." The countess fixed her with a venomous look. "Please do not let me keep you."

Kate rose and returned to where Charlotte was arranging the gold-rimmed cups and saucers. "There will soon be another disparaging *ondit* about me making the rounds of the drawing rooms," she said under her breath. "In addition to being called a bluestocking and a recluse, I will also be called a rude and humorless harpy."

After hearing the gist of the exchange, Charlotte frowned. "You really should not go out of your way to make enemies."

"I didn't," she protested. "I just made it clear that we are not going to be friends."

Her friend arched a brow.

"Can you blame me?" asked Kate after a fraction of a pause.

"Not in the least. I just think it would be wise to be more subtle in your sarcasm. Especially with Lady Duxbury. I have heard that she's someone who likes to stir up trouble."

Kate shrugged. "What harm can she do me? I couldn't care less what is whispered about me by the tabbies."

Charlotte didn't answer right away, and when she did, there was a note of concern in her voice. "Don't underestimate the power of rumor and innuendo. We have seen how dangerous they can be. Look at what Ciara and Alessandra went through when a mistake from their past came back to haunt them."

Despite the steaming heat of the teapot, Kate felt her palms turn a touch cold. She carefully placed it down beside the cups and busied herself in arranging the silver spoons in a precise row.

"I... I can't imagine that happening to me. In my former life, I was a completely different person—there is no connection between Kate Woodbridge, the vagabond American adventurer, and Katharine Woodbridge, the English granddaughter of the Duke of Cluyne."

"You are no doubt right, my dear. But as scientists, we should always remember that one should never take anything for granted."

The arrival of the gentlemen forestalled any further discussion of the matter. Turning to the ritual of serving tea, Kate put the unpleasant encounter behind her. It had been yet another reminder of how the waters of Polite Society were fraught with hidden shoals.

And speaking of stormy seas... Out of the corner of her eye, she saw Marco saunter into the room, his handsome face alight with laughter at something that Lord Tappan was telling him.

Her insides clenched, and though she willed herself not to react, a slow spiraling heat rose up to her cheeks. She fumbled with the pot, hoping to cover her dismay in a cloud of steam. Lady Duxbury's nasty comment couldn't be further from the truth. She had *never* consciously encouraged Marco's attentions.

But her body seemed to have a mind of its own.

Chapter Ten

"Thank you, Miss Woodbridge." Von Seilig accepted a cup, but did not move away. "Would you care to sit down to a game of whist?"

"Actually, I'm not overly fond of playing cards."

"Neither am I." He smiled. "I much prefer conversation."

"As do I."

"Excellent. Then perhaps you would not mind if the colonel and I continue our discussion of the upcoming peace conference." Rochambert, the French envoy, came over to join them. "But if politics bore you—"

"Not at all," she assured him. "From what I have read, the delegates mean to address a fascinating array of issues. I am particularly interested in Mr. Cotta and Mr. Bertuch's ideas on intellectual property."

"Indeed," agreed Von Seilig. "It's a very important topic. Publishers from a number of countries are quite concerned about the piracy of ideas."

Rochambert nodded as he added a splash of cream to his cup. In contrast to the blond, heavyset Prussian, the dark-haired Frenchman was slender, with a narrow face and delicate features that bordered on the effeminate. The lace on his cuffs and cravat accentuated the impression, as did his burgundy swallowtail coat, velvet knee breeches, and gold-threaded silk waistcoat.

But Kate sensed that beneath the show of finery, he was not nearly as soft as he appeared.

"It promises to be a very intriguing few months, both for the politics and the parties," said Rochambert, after a sip of his tea. "Have you been to Vienna, Miss Woodbridge?"

"No, but I have heard it is a lovely city. I should like very much to visit it someday."

"Now that peace has come to the Continent, travel is no longer dangerous. So perhaps your grandfather would consider taking you for a visit," suggested Von Seilig. "It is a very historic place, with a picturesque medieval center, many beautiful parks, magnificent churches, and baroque mansions. Legend has it that the city walls surrounding the Old Town were built with the ransom money paid by King Richard the Lionhearted, who was captured while on his way home from the Holy Land."

"How fascinating." Kate closed her eyes for a moment, picturing the exotic setting. She missed the excitement of traveling—the sights, the sounds, the smells of a foreign land stimulated the senses.

"Emperor Francis of Austria will host several other monarchs at the Hofburg, his palace in the center of the city," said Rochambert. "That alone is worth the visit, for it houses many incredible treasures."

"One of the Emperor's hobbies is tending to his plants in the palace hothouses. He is also an expert in European geography," added Von Seilig. "His collection of rare maps and books is extraordinary."

"It sounds like exactly the sort of place that I would enjoy visiting," mused Kate.

"I doubt that Francis will have much time for his plants or his library when the conference begins. Metternich and Talleyrand will be playing cat and mouse, while the Russian tsar and the King of Prussia negotiate over the fate of Poland and Saxony..."

Kate listened with great interest as the two gentlemen began to discuss the nuances of European politics. They were both articulate and knowledgeable, and when she ventured a question, they did not brush her off but answered it with careful consideration.

Why, perhaps parties weren't so awful after all. It was pleasant to be treated as if she possessed a brain, to go along with the rest of her body, she thought to herself.

Ludlowe, the American envoy to London, and Villafranca, a Spanish government official, came over to join them and quickly offered their perspective on the jockeying for power in the wake of Napoleon's defeat.

Caught up in following the lively arguments, Kate was unaware of how much time had passed until the tall case clock in the corner chimed the hour. Suddenly aware that she had left Charlotte to fend for herself, she slanted a hurried look around the room, hoping that her friend was not sitting alone in the shadows with naught but a book for company.

A prick of guilt jabbed at her conscience. Had she actually been enjoying the evening so much as to forget about her fellow 'Sinner'? She owed Charlotte an abject apology for abandoning her to a crowd of strangers...

Hell. Spotting the reflection of her friend's silvery hair in one of the large glass-front curio cabinets, Kate swore a silent oath. Standing next to Charlotte was Cluyne, his face pinched in an all too familiar scowl.

"Excuse me, gentlemen." Without waiting for a reply, she backed up and quickly skirted around the card tables.

"...You are mistaken, sir. I am quite sure that it is not a *Somei Yoshino* but a *Shidarezakura* depicted on the vase." Charlotte's voice was as firm as the decorative ironwork framing the cabinet's glass doors. "Do take a closer look at the shape of the leaf."

Her grandfather grumbled something under his breath and reached into his pocket for a pair of spectacles. "Hmmph," he snorted, once they were perched on his nose. "You may—*may*, I say—be right."

"Forgive me, Charlotte," interrupted Kate in a rush. "I lost all track of time."

"That is quite all right, my dear. You looked to be enjoying a spirited discussion with the gentlemen."

"Yes, it is always interesting to hear different points of view..." Argument was stimulating. Only now was she aware that the debate had brought a touch of heat to her face. Strangely enough, Charlotte also seemed to have two hot spots of color on her cheeks.

Whether from anger or embarrassment was impossible to discern in the candlelight.

"Thank you for keeping Lady Fenimore company, Your Grace," said Kate in a rush. "But we need not impose on your hospitality any longer." Turning to Charlotte, she took her arm. "Come, I'm anxious to show you the book of botanical prints from America."

Cluyne's frown deepened for an instant before he stepped aside to let them pass.

"I apologize," whispered Kate as she led the way to a sofa near the crackling fire. "I hope you were not stuck there with Cluyne for long."

"Long enough to get into a disagreement on the species of cherry tree shown on his Ming Dynasty vase."

"Lud, I'm so sorry."

"Don't be." Her friend quirked a grin. "He was forced to concede his error."

"He ought to know better than to challenge a 'Sinner' on a question of science."

"I think that I shock him," said Charlotte cheerfully. "How nice to know that at my age I can still tweak a few noses."

Kate made a face. "I don't mean to disparage your accomplishment, but it doesn't take much to upset the duke. He has no sense of humor."

Charlotte looked thoughtful. "Actually, I think he does. He just hasn't been encouraged to show it."

"Perhaps you are right." Though she didn't think so.

"But let us leave off discussing Cluyne. Tell me about your conversation with the gentlemen."

"They were explaining some of the issues that shall be decided during the coming months in Vienna," said Kate. "Which, by the by, sounds like a fascinating city."

"So I have heard. It is a center of music and art, as well as learning." Charlotte paused. "And the pastries are said to be divine."

"Just imagine," she mused. "It will be an impressive gathering of people from all over the Continent…"

• • •

Marco watched Kate from over the top of his playing cards. The candles cast a ring of gilded light around her hair. A softly shimmering halo. Though God knows, the lady was no angel.

Not with her devil-be-damned defiance of Society's rules.

Her lips twitched in response to something her companion said, and he felt his own body stir with a sudden spasm of heat. A throaty laugh floated through the air, its salt-roughened sound leaving a wake of pebbled goose-flesh as it slid over his skin.

What was it about Kate Woodbridge that aroused such a visceral physical reaction in him?

Shadows played across her face. *Light and dark.* Innocence and experience. Aquamarine eyes, swirling with hints of sunbeams and storms. Beckoning him to strip naked and dive into their depths.

A surge of pure, primal lust welled up inside him. Oh, he was evil—*truly evil*—to be thinking of how luscious her honey-colored hair would look fanned out on a tangle of creamy white sheets, how sweet her bare breasts would taste against his tongue. How sensuous her sleek, sweat-sheened body would feel beneath his, rising and falling with the same inexorable rhythm as the ocean tides.

Evil. But then, he had never pretended to be a saint.

Hell, the list of his sins would stretch from here to Hades and back again. Still, bad as he was, he didn't usually sink so low as to fantasize about seducing a virgin. Tightening his grip on the cards, Marco fought down a twinge of guilt. He was debauched but not depraved. His bedmates were all equally jaded souls who understood the rules of their naughty games. *Expect nothing more than a moment of fleeting pleasure.*

Despite the strange rippling of darkness he sometimes saw in her gaze, Kate Woodbridge was not of his world. The hint of hidden secrets was just an illusion. She was a creature of the day and he was a creature of the night. Her passion was for living, growing things, while his own soul had long since shriveled to dust.

Causing a death, no matter if it was accidental, changed one's life forever.

A whispering of silk fanned the fire to a sudden blaze of burnt-gold flames. Kate rose along with her elderly friend and smoothed her skirts over her hips.

Marco imagined his hands tracing those same shapely contours and curves, and suddenly all his good intentions seemed to fall by the wayside. It wasn't as if he was actually going to deflower the lady, he rationalized. Just tease a touch or two over her lovely petals. She wasn't so innocent that she had never experienced a man's advances. As a connoisseur of female reactions, he knew she had been kissed before.

And enjoyed it, no matter that she tried to hide her reaction.

So surely there was no real harm in a little sporting flirtation...

A nudge brought him back to the game at hand. "Your turn to play, Ghiradelli."

Choosing a discard at random, he tossed it down.

His partner groaned and shot him a pained look.

Shoving himself back from the table, Marco stood up and relinquished his chair. Kate and her friend had just bade her grandfather good night and left the room. "If you don't mind, I think I shall step outside for a smoke."

He was not alone in abandoning the formality of the duke's drawing room. A set of French doors led out to the stone terrace, where a handful of other gentlemen were already lighting up cigars. The flare of the glowing coals dotted the deepening twilight, like oversized fireflies in the night. A cool breeze ruffled through the greenery bordering the balustrades, mingling the pungent tobacco smoke with the subtle fragrance of roses and hyacinth.

Someone had brought a bottle of brandy with him, and the soft splash of the spirits passed from glass to glass. The mood was always a bit reserved at the beginning of a large house party, as guests became acquainted and assessed whose company was worth keeping. It was particularly true for this gathering, thought Marco as he lounged against the railing and surveyed the others with an air of casual nonchalance.

It would not be easy to see beneath the diplomatic smiles, the practiced lies, to discern who were allies and who were enemies.

All the more reason to keep his mind on his work, Marco reminded himself. With Lynsley already thinking that he was slipping, he couldn't afford a misstep.

Russia in league with Prussia. Austria taking sides with the Kingdom of Saxony. France, in the form of the legendary Prince Charles-Maurice de Talleyrand, determined to have a say in how the new map of Europe would be drawn. Blowing out a mouthful of smoke, Marco made a mental review of the reports that he had read.

Lynsley must suspect that some intrigue was afoot here. The marquess did not waste time or resources on mere conjecture.

Vronskov and Von Seilig did not seem overly friendly, but appearances could, of course, be deceiving. Rochambert merited close observation, for France needed to forge an alliance with one of the other European powers in order to have a bargaining chip at the peace conference table. And then, the Spanish and Danish envoys were minor players . . . or were they?

As Marco surveyed the smiling faces, he couldn't help wondering what scheming was going on beneath the surface show of unity.

Deceit and deception. Politics was an ugly business, especially when the stakes were so high. So was espionage, he admitted. But at least he believed that he was toiling for a higher good. There wasn't much in his life that he was proud of. However, his work with Lynsley was the one exception.

"A pleasant evening, though a trifle dull compared to the delights of London." Lord Tappan crossed the tiles and paused to flick a bit of ash from his cigar. "No doubt things will become a bit livelier."

"So I would imagine," replied Marco blandly.

Tappan smoked in silence for a few moments. "As you heard, I plan to ride over to my estate tomorrow morning in order to fetch several books for Miss Woodbridge and her friend. Would you care to join me?"

"Why not?"

"Excellent. I shall meet you in the stables at eight." After another few puffs, Tappan drifted away.

Yet another relationship to sort out, thought Marco as

he resumed his study of the other guests. Tappan's exact role had not been spelled out by Lynsley. He might have been asked to share his ministry's information on the foreigners. Or he might have been asked to keep an eye on Marco's behavior and report any dereliction of duty. Espionage was a dirty business. No emotion, no rules, no remorse. Which was why it suited him to perfection.

Out of the corner of his eye, he saw Lord Allenham step out into the night, accompanied by his sister, the widowed Countess of Duxbury. In the light of the oil lamps flanking the doorway, the coppery gleam of his curling side whiskers clashed with his florid complexion. A big, beefy man, the baron had a look of well-fed complacency about him. And yet, there was a certain hungry light in his eyes.

Like a man looking to snap up a tasty morsel, no matter how full his ample stomach was.

From Lynsley's notes on the guest list, Marco knew that Allenham sat on the governing board of the Northern Mercantile Exchange, a highly profitable private trading company that dealt in shipbuilding supplies from the Baltic region. Timber, turpentine, pine tar—all were critical commodities for the British Admiralty, which maintained the most powerful navy in the world. And as the Empire spread to the far corners of the globe, new merchant fleets would be needed to carry the English way of life to the new colonies.

The baron looked around briefly, then headed straight for where Von Seilig stood sipping his wine.

Marco waited a moment before beginning a leisurely stroll along the length of the outer railing. Prussia controlled some of the most important commercial ports on the North Sea. But if the rumors were true, and a new state of Poland was created at the Congress in Vienna, then the trade agreements could change dramatically in the region. It would be interesting to overhear what the two gentlemen had to say to each other.

Edging closer, keeping to the shadows of the large decorative urns, he caught a glimpse of the Lady Duxbury's profile through the leafy twists of ivy. Unlike Kate Woodbridge, the countess was a lady whose innocence was not in question. According to the whispers he had heard, the buxom beauty was rather free with her favors. Not that he found anything wrong with that. He had always thought it absurdly hypocritical for men to judge women any differently than they judged themselves.

Bathed in the moonlight, her face had a pale pearlescent glow. And yet, oddly enough, the effect hardened rather than softened her features. The same could probably be said for his own jaded looks, reflected Marco. Cynicism polished to the smoothness of fine marble. Exquisitely sculpted. Impervious to emotion.

Perhaps he should consider bedding her, just to keep boredom at bay.

Lady Duxbury laughed at something her brother said, and for some reason the idea did not seem terribly appealing. Her voice had a brittleness to it—all jagged edges and sharp corners. As opposed to the lush, liquid sound of Kate Woodbridge's amusement.

Marco looked away to the mist-shrouded gardens and concentrated on what the gentlemen were saying. It was not hard to hear them, for the conversation was turning increasingly heated.

"*Nein*, my mind is made up on the matter, sir." Von

Seilig's words cut through the stillness. "And nothing you can say or do will change the advice I intend to give to von Humboldt and my king."

"We'll see about that," muttered Allenham. "We have more power and influence than you imagine." Taking his sister's arm, he pivoted for the door. "Come, Jocelyn."

As the countess turned, her gaze glided over the urn's foliage. She paused for a moment as her eyes found his, a half smile playing at the corners of her mouth. Despite the coolness of the evening, she snapped open her fan and fluttered it over her décolletage.

Tempting.

The lady knew her charms and was not afraid to flaunt them. Marco watched her go, but decided not to follow. Not tonight. He hadn't slept more than a few hours in the last several days and couldn't afford to have his wits clouded come morning. An empty bed wouldn't kill him.

The other guests were beginning to file inside and retire to the guest wing. He hesitated, feeling oddly restless despite his fatigue. Deciding a breath of country air might help clear his head, he took the terrace stairs down to the gardens.

Chapter Eleven

"Good night, my dear." Charlotte opened the door to her bed chamber. "Really, you need not have left the party early on my account. At my age, I find that I no longer have the stamina to stay up past midnight."

"I am fatigued myself," replied Kate. "All the activities of a house party are rather exhausting."

Her friend pursed her lips thoughtfully. "Yet you seem to be enjoying yourself."

"I suppose I am," admitted Kate. "The guests are more interesting than I expected."

"They are," agreed Charlotte. "It is always stimulating to hear a spirited exchange of ideas."

Thinking of her grandfather's earlier comments in the library, she made a face. "Certain opinions are best left unsaid. I apologize again for Cluyne's overbearing rudeness this afternoon."

"Oh, pish." Charlotte waved off the words. "Like most men, the duke clearly has a low regard for bluestocking females. It's rather fun to argue with him and see the look of shock on his face." Cupping her candle, she stifled a yawn. "I shall see you at breakfast. Are you sure you wish to spend the morning in the library looking at books instead of joining the others in the archery games? Colonel Von Seilig seems eager to offer instruction."

"Quite sure," said Kate. "I'd only be tempted to put an arrow in Vronskov's bum."

A chuckle stirred the shadows. "Let's have no blood spilled. A murder might upset the party."

She swallowed hard before forcing a laugh. "Right. I'll try to restrain my violent urges."

Charlotte withdrew, and Kate moved down the darkened corridor to her own rooms. But despite the late hour, she found her head was too unsettled for sleep. Maybe it was the champagne, or the effect of being in the company of so many new people.

Sighing, she hesitated at her door. She wasn't in the mood for any further encounters, but this part of the manor house appeared quiet. The party would likely last for another hour or two. Treading lightly over the Oriental runner, Kate made her way to the back stairwell and down to the one spot amidst all her grandfather's ducal splendor where she felt at home.

Clicking open the heavy brass-framed glass doors, she slipped into the conservatory.

All at once, she was in another world. In contrast to the dry formality of the drawing room, the air was alive and untamed—its wet warmth caressed her cheeks and tickled her nose with a riot of earthy, exotic scents. Kate sucked in a deep breath, savoring the swirling rush of sensations. She loved the wildness of nature, the heady sense of freedom inherent in its colors and shapes.

Lighting a pair of hanging lanterns, Kate watched their reflections flicker off the surrounding glass. In England, she so often felt that she was trapped in a gilded cage. She missed the sense of adventure in her life. Everyone around her was so predictable—save, of course, for the 'Sinners,' who shared her curiosity and desire to explore the unknown.

Their friendship was the one bright spot in her life. And yet…

She started down the mossy brick walkway, touching her hand to the swaying leaves. Marriage was subtly changing the Circle. The friendships weren't any less strong, they were simply…not quite the same.

Ciara, Alessandra, Ariel—they all now had a soulmate with whom to share their most intimate hopes and fears. A shoulder to lean on. A love to hold doubt at bay.

Kate rubbed at her arms, feeling an inner chill raise a pebbling of gooseflesh despite the enveloping warmth. The chances of her meeting a kindred spirit in civilized England were virtually nil. She was too different. *Too dark.* London ladies were all sweetness and light. While she was the opposite. The vagabond travels, the pressures of poverty had demanded a toughness in order to survive.

A palm frond brushed against her cheek, the points sharp against her skin. And survive she had, despite all the hardships. Hell, she didn't need anyone's help. She had learned to be smart, savvy, and ferociously independent. If at times she felt a little lonely, it was easy enough to shrug off. After all, what man would be attracted to a female who had committed the cardinal sin of…

Don't dwell on mistakes of the past, Kate told herself. As for men, what did it matter what they thought of her?

In the hazy glow of the lantern flames and the moonlight, Kate tried to distract her maudlin musings by studying the surrounding specimen plants. The collection offered a tantalizing array of textures and hues.

So why was the wild tangle suddenly taking the form of Conte Ghiradelli's sin-dark hair and sensuous face?

It must be the wine. Kate pressed her palms to her heated brow. It had nothing to do with the memory of his fleeting kiss or the strong, solid muscles of his arms lifting her into the saddle.

Her insides clenched as she recalled the subtle scent of his skin, a masculine mixture of leather, smoke, and midnight revelries.

Dear God, was she really attracted to the devil?

Much as she hated to admit it, the answer was yes. She couldn't help responding to his animal allure. He was beautiful—in body, if not in spirit. The very image of masculine grace and power.

Pushing past the silvery blades of an olive branch, Kate plunged deeper into the shadows. In some ways, they certainly shared some similarities. The man made no effort to follow the strictures of Polite Society. He was a rogue, a rakehell who lived by his own rules.

But a dislike of conformity was all they had in common. She cared about serious things, like science and intellectual ideas, while he was a sybarite who lived only for selfish pleasure.

Her steps quickened. She had no idea what had brought him here to her grandfather's staid house party.

But one thing was for sure—for her own peace of mind, she must try to stay far, far away from him.

In no real hurry to reach his empty bed, Marco wandered along the graveled pathways, choosing to meander around the back of the manor house to the side entrance near his rooms. From the grove of pear trees came the song of a nightingale. Crickets chirped in the freshly cut grass.

When was the last time he had listened to crickets, or lifted his eyes to gaze at the glittering stars overhead?

He slowed his steps, listening to the long-forgotten night music, so very different from the drunken laughter, the shuffling cards, the sultry murmurs that usually serenaded his nights. A breeze blew through the high boxwood hedge, and its scent, redolent with the clean, fresh tang of earth and leaves, suddenly stirred old memories of the past. Of boyish larks through wild meadows, of moonlit swims in forbidden lakes, of shared adventures with his brother.

Bloody hell. What maudlin mood had come over him? Marco forced a sardonic laugh through his clenched teeth. Thank God he was no longer a callow, naïve youth, besotted with childish dreams. He had made his own life, his own rules. The road to perdition was far more fun than trudging along the beaten path.

As he rounded the corner, he stopped short and felt his jaw drop.

Dappled in starlight, a soaring glass pavilion rose up like some black magic apparition. Its graceful form—unearthly planes of shimmering silver silhouetted against the dark trees—seemed to be floating on swirls of mist.

Marco blinked, unsure whether his eyes were playing tricks on him. Then he recalled hearing mention of the duke's famous conservatory and its exotic array of plants.

Curious, he stepped off the graveled path and approached the structure. It was as if a window had suddenly opened onto some enchanted world. Several brass lamps were lit, their softly flickering flames casting a mellow glow over a lush jungle of greenery. Potted palms swayed gently, their delicate fronds misted with beads of moisture. A profusion of colorful blooms that he couldn't identify spilled from the terra-cotta planters that lined a narrow brick walkway. The faint splash of an unseen fountain drifted through the blurred shadows. Marco inhaled deeply, almost sure he could smell the perfume of the plants.

On a whim, he pressed his cheek to the glass and closed his eyes. Its surface was both hot and cold, and the strange sensation sent a shiver skating down his spine. He stood as still as a statue, held by some inexplicable force.

"*Diavolo*," he murmured, the sound of his own voice finally breaking the spell. He raised his gaze—only to find himself eyeball to eyeball with another human form.

A wood spirit from the forest, or djinn from the smoky lamp?

Momentarily disoriented, he had to stare at the ghostly reflection for an instant longer before the face of Kate Woodbridge came into focus.

Her stance mirrored his—they stood facing each other, legs slightly spread, palm pressed to palm, with only a thin slice of glass between them. He could see the throb of pulse at her throat, the rise and fall of her chest as her breath slowly misted the window. His skin began to tingle. Somehow the effect was intensely erotic.

"What the devil are you doing out there?" Her muffled voice slapped down the thought. "Stand back. You are welcome to break your neck during your drunken stumblings, but I'd rather you didn't crack the glass."

He jerked upright.

"You had better come in, before you do yourself any harm." She motioned to an iron-framed door near the corner.

Marco did as she bade. The latch clicked open, and as he crossed the threshold, he was immediately aware of warm, humid air kissing against his cheeks. Its earthy sweetness filled at his nostrils, making him momentarily light-headed.

"Have a care," she warned. "These orchids just arrived from Madras, and my grandfather will have your head on a pikestaff if you knock them over."

"There is no need to shout," he replied. "Neither my wits nor my hearing are impaired. In fact, I've had very little to drink this evening."

"Ha! Sir Beesley was complaining that you couldn't seem to count to ten when you partnered with him at the card table."

"It was not the brandy; it was the company. I was bored playing whist with a bunch of stiff-rumped bureaucrats."

"Then why did you leave London?" demanded Kate.

"I was bored playing *vingt-et-un* with a bunch of debauched scoundrels."

"What does it take to excite your interest—" she began, then stopped with a snap. "No, on second thought, don't answer that. I don't want to know."

Marco laughed. "I thought scientists were supposed to be inquisitive by nature."

She sucked in a breath, but didn't reply.

He deliberately moved a little closer to her. "Afraid that you might learn something you don't know?"

In the low, flickering play of the lantern's flame, her face seemed to take on a slight burn.

"There's precious little I haven't..."

"Haven't what?" he demanded when she stopped abruptly.

Kate looked away from the light.

"Seen? Or done?" Marco curled a sarcastic smirk. "Somehow, I rather doubt you have any real idea of how depraved life can be."

Her eyes flared wide for an instant. But the look of vulnerability vanished just as quickly, leaving him to wonder whether he had merely imagined it.

"Think what you like," said Kate in a tight whisper. Picking up her skirts, she started to turn. "Since you claim to be sober, you should have no trouble finding the way out on your own."

"Wait." Marco seized her wrist. "Not so fast."

Hemmed in by the overhanging trees and potting benches stacked high with fragile seedlings, the narrow walkway allowed little room to maneuver. She tried to back away but bumped into a slab of solid oak.

A hiss of air escaped her lungs.

"Still a trifle sore, *bella*?" asked Marco, unable to keep from taunting her. Her face looked so lovely when it was on fire. "Let that be a lesson to keep a tighter rein on your impulses."

Her hand curled in a fist. "Has anyone ever told you what an obnoxious, arrogant ass you are?"

"More times than I can count."

"But you don't care to listen?"

"I don't care to change. There is a difference."

"Not a meaningful one," she countered. "Now, let me go, sir. Before I force you to do so."

"Oh, that sounds intriguing." With a casual flick of his fingers, he drew her close, so close that her breasts were pressed up against the front of his coat. Dropping his hands, he slid them lightly over her hips.

Heat thrummed through him as their thighs brushed. She gave a little gasp at the intimacy.

"There. I'm ready."

"You won't be grinning quite so smugly when my knee smashes into your *testicolos*."

She had a point. "A lady is not supposed to know such nasty little secrets."

"And who said I was a lady?"

Her chin rose a fraction, revealing a hairline scar on its tip. For one mad moment, Marco felt the urge to touch it with his tongue. A proper young lady didn't have the nick of a knife blade on her skin. A proper young lady didn't have a weathered weariness shading her expression. A proper young lady didn't have a hardened yet haunted look to her gaze.

Most females were simple to figure out, but Kate Woodbridge was different. An enigma. A puzzle whose pieces he could not quite fit together. She intrigued him.

Perhaps that was part of the challenge.

"What are you staring at, sir?" She turned her face to the trees, obscuring her features in the leafy shadows.

"You—you have a dusting of freckles across your nose, and a crinkling from the sun at the corners of your eyes." And a spicy scent to her skin that was bedeviling his memory.

"As you see, I am hardly a pattern card for the perfect young London miss." Kate tried to twist free. "Kindly release me. Or do I have to make good on my threat?"

"No, I should prefer to keep my manhood in full working order." And yet he was strangely loath to let her go. "Tell me something, though. Your perfume—it reminds me of southern Italy, with its orange blossoms, wild thyme—"

She shoved at his chest, knocking him back a step.

"*Dio Madre*, sheath your claws, you little hellcat." In catching her arm to steady himself, he pulled them both off-balance.

His hip hit the bench, rattling the terra-cotta pots. Mindful of destroying the duke's precious plants, he spun clear, using his body to shield Kate from a blow. They teetered along the brick path, falling deep into the jagged shadows before he found his footing.

"That was close," he said, exhaling softly. Her cheek was just a hairsbreadth from his, and the puff of air stirred the tendrils of hair around her ear. Despite the half light, its contour was distinctive—a perfectly proportioned curve, shaped like a seashell.

Bloody hell. *That shape. That scent.* No wonder they struck a familiar chord. He had encountered this lady before. Suddenly the details came flooding back.

Drawing back a touch, Marco bared his teeth in a

smile. "Well, well, well, so we meet again, *Bella*..." He paused a fraction. "*Donna*."

Fear flared in Kate's eyes, along with some other emotion. "I—I have no idea what you are talking about."

"Oh, but I think you do. The city of Napoli. A harbor brothel."

"A brothel?" Her voice was brittle as the surrounding glass. "You *must* be drunk. Or mad."

Yes, it was completely insane. For a moment he wavered, wondering whether his wits had finally cracked. And yet, he knew instinctively that he was right.

But in that heartbeat of hesitation, Kate had slipped free of his hold. The shadows swayed as she disappeared into the darkness, leaving only the *swoosh* of silk to echo the wildly waving palm fronds.

Chapter Twelve

The morning sunlight slanted through the glass panes, filling the corner of the conservatory with a tropical warmth. Rolling up her smudged sleeves, Charlotte took up a magnifying glass and spread the petals of a *Cymbidium rubrigemmum.* She and Kate had been working for over an hour, and they were both beginning to look a little bedraggled.

Worried that the heat and humidity might be a bit much for her friend, Kate rang for a pitcher of lemonade.

"Have a look at this—the pistils are quite unusual!" exclaimed Charlotte. "And would you kindly pass me my notebook? I would like to make a quick sketch."

Kate handed it over, along with a pencil. "Interesting," she agreed. "Let's make a note to ask Mr. Hopkins about it when we return to London. I wonder if he's seen a similar arrangement in the specimens from Ceylon."

Engrossed in her drawing, Charlotte gave a vague nod.

Kate returned to her own study of an orchid from

jungles of southern India. The color was a delicate shade of purple...or maybe puce...

"*Ouch!*" Sitting back on her heels drew an involuntary grunt of pain. As if she needed the constant reminder of her egregiously awful lapse in judgment.

How had she been so bloody, *bloody* stupid? Common sense had warned her to stay away from Marco. He might be a dissolute womanizer, but he was not a fool. In fact his wits were sharper than most.

Which begged the question of why she hadn't been smart enough to keep her face and her fragrance from dredging up a memory from the past.

"Really, my dear." Charlotte clucked in sympathy. "I insist that you go upstairs and lie down for a few hours of rest. Squatting in such a position cannot be...comfortable, given the nature of your injury."

"I've put up with far worse aboard a ship," muttered Kate. "Trust me, when there is a storm at sea, one suffers a good many hard knocks."

"Undoubtedly. But you are not at sea."

And yet a wave of uncertainty washed over her. *As if she needed any further complications in her life.* If Marco were to speak of a certain incident in public, the consequences would be terrible. A few whispered words and her reputation would be ruined, her grandfather humiliated.

He wouldn't. *Would he?*

Kate squeezed her eyes shut, trying not to think of Naples.

Normally, her family's ship would never have put into port there. The city was a notorious cesspool of crime and corruption. But both her parents were dangerously ill, so she had been left with little choice. They needed a skilled physician and medicines. Unfortunately, both cost money, and the Woodbridge purse had been suffering through one of its frequent dry spells.

But over the years Kate had honed her ingenuity and cleverness to a fine edge. She had learned how to improvise. A chance meeting with a harbor whore had allowed her to offer some business advice to the woman and her friends. Using her skills in arithmetic and accounting, Kate had drafted several charts showing profits in comparison to expenditures, resulting in an increase in pay from the brothel owner.

As a token of gratitude, the whores had invited Kate to use her other less savory skills—which included picking pockets and cutting purses with a quick slice of her knife—to rob the drunken patrons of the brothel. She was good at it. Good enough to earn the name of '*Belladonna*,' the beautiful but deadly efficient thief who easily eluded the authorities.

Marco had staggered in one night, a vision of drunken but divine masculine beauty. She had almost been tempted to tumble into his bed before robbing him blind. *Almost.* Thank God that reason had overruled lust on that occasion.

She made a wry face. No doubt her body was now exacting a measure of revenge.

"What was that, my dear?" asked Charlotte, looking up from her pots.

"Nothing. I was just having a little trouble dislodging the roots of this bougainvillea from its pot." Kate worked her trowel deeper into the soil. She was not proud of what she had done. But with the lives of her parents at stake, she felt no remorse over her decision.

Her only regret was that the money had not purchased any respite from the raging fever. Her mother and father had died within hours of each other, leaving her no family but the distant, disapproving Duke of Cluyne.

"Your lemonade, Miss Woodbridge." The footman set the silver tray down on a potting bench. "May I bring you anything else?"

Blotting her brow with her sleeve, Kate blew out her breath. "No, thank you, Jennings." Life was full of little ironies, like being waited on as if she were to the manor born.

"Put aside your sketchbook and come have a cool drink," she said to her friend.

Charlotte looked up with an owlish squint. "What? Oh, er, yes, I suppose it is a trifle warm."

"I think we ought to stop work in here for the day," said Kate, giving herself a mental kick for not noticing the ruddy flush coloring her friend's face. "I insist that you spend the afternoon after luncheon in the library."

Casting a wistful look at the row of still unsketched flowers from Jamaica, Charlotte bit her lip.

"They will still be here tomorrow," said Kate with a fond smile.

"Which might not be said for you, if you are too addlepated to sense that this heat is dangerous for a lady of your years." Cluyne's voice floated over them like a dark cloud.

Charlotte's color deepened. "I beg your pardon?" She rose with great dignity and lifted her nose in the air. The effect was only slightly marred by the dollop of mud on its tip.

The duke coughed. If it hadn't been Cluyne, Kate would have thought the sound was a smothered laugh.

"Allow me to rephrase the remark, Lady Fenimore.

As host, I am concerned with the safety and welfare of my guests. The sun is bright, creating an oppressive heat inside the glass, so I kindly request that you refrain from further use of the conservatory today."

"Well, put that way, it is a sensible, scientific reason." Charlotte fanned her cheeks. "Excuse me while I go make myself presentable for nuncheon." To Kate she added, "I shall see you on the terrace, my dear."

"I had better go change as well," murmured Kate, after her friend had marched off.

The duke seemed distracted by the swoosh of Charlotte's skirts. It took him a moment to reply. "I would like you to join in the archery game, if you please. We have few enough ladies to lighten the mood." He paused. "And Colonel Von Seilig voiced his hope that you would be present."

So far, her grandfather had made few requests. "Very well, sir. Though I do hope you will not press Lady Charlotte into joining the sport. She would much rather read."

"I didn't imagine she would care to play Robin Hood."

Kate wasn't keen on the idea either, but she had promised to take part in the activities, and the Prussian was a pleasant gentleman. "Well, then, if you will excuse me, I will see whether I have a Lincoln-green gown."

Still feeling a little disoriented by his encounter with Kate, Marco rose early, dressed himself, and made his way down to the stables.

"I was wondering whether you would actually manage to show up at this hour." Tappan was waiting with the saddled horses. "Did you sleep well?" he inquired.

"I am unused to the country," muttered Marco, aware that he looked like hell. "I was plagued by strange dreams."

Tappan laughed. "You probably miss the coal smoke and the racket of the carriages clattering over the streets."

"What I miss are the caresses of a luscious ladybird."

"What? The song of a morning dove was not an acceptable substitute?" bantered Tappan.

Marco muttered a curse.

"There is something to see at Hillcrest House that might put you in a better humor. Once we have fetched the books for the ladies, we shall take a look." As they set their mounts into a leisurely trot on the bridle path leading down past the lake, Tappan chatted about rare illustrated books in his estate library. "I appreciate their beauty, but since my father beggared the family coffers with his extravagant spending, I cannot afford to add to my collection. Of course, it doesn't begin to compare to the duke's vast holdings. But I do have a few things that he does not."

"I am sure the ladies will be grateful," said Marco.

"Yes, I've heard that Miss Woodbridge is a bluestocking and has quite an interest in plants. In fact, she seems to favor them over any interest in balls or beaus." He paused a fraction. "I've heard that she had a rather odd upbringing. She only came to live with the duke a year ago, when her parents died. Her father was an American sea captain. But then, she is a good friend of your cousin, so you would know better."

Tappan was clearly fishing for information but Marco was not in the mood to bite. He simply shrugged.

After waiting for a few more moments, Tappan tried another approach. "She's a rather strange young lady. She appears to shun Society. Seems shy, almost mousy in company."

There were many adjectives one could use to describe Kate Woodbridge, thought Marco. But 'mousy' was not one of them.

"Maybe she's just bored by the *ton*," he replied. Up ahead was a gate in the high hedgerow, giving entrance to Tappan's lands. "Is there a reason you wanted to meet with me in private?" he asked brusquely.

Tappan flicked his crop. "Nothing pressing. Just thought I'd inform you that I will be departing earlier than expected for Vienna. After tomorrow, you will be on your own here. I've written down instructions for how to contact Whitehall if anything urgent arises." As he dismounted to open the gate latch, he shot Marco a sidelong look. "By the by, what the devil does Lynsley do for the Secretary of State for War? He makes some very odd requests of my department, and yet they jump through hoops to comply."

Marco kept his expression bland. "Haven't a clue."

"Well, whatever it is, it can't be very serious, seeing as they have chosen *you* to be here."

He feigned a yawn. "Hell, I hope not. Being serious is way too fatiguing."

Tappan laughed.

"The truth is, Lynsley is an old friend of my father," lied Marco. "Knowing that I was acquainted with some of the diplomats here, he asked me to come take part in the party and keep my ears open for any interesting conversations that I overhear."

"Have you? Heard anything interesting, that is."

"Powietski wears a corset—the stays creak when he bends. And Ludlowe hates strawberry jam. No wonder you English think the Americans uncivilized."

"I doubt Lynsley will lose any sleep waiting for that

information." Swinging back into the saddle, Tappan spurred his mount for the rolling meadow. "Follow me. We'll take a shortcut up to the manor."

"Charlotte?" Catching her friend's reflection in the cheval glass, Kate turned around in alarm. In contrast to its earlier flushed color, Charlotte's face was now a queasy shade of white. "Is something amiss? You look like you have seen a ghost."

"I have...in a manner of speaking." She held up a large book, its tooled leather cover stamped with ornate gilt lettering. "This was on my dressing table, along with a copy of *Les Fleurs Alpines de Haute Savoie*."

"How odd. Have you any idea how they got there?" Her grandfather was very strict about letting valuable books out of the library. Kate suddenly felt her jaw tighten. "Don't worry. I won't allow Cluyne to blame you for any confusion on the part of his servants."

Charlotte made a strange little sound in her throat. "There doesn't seem to be any confusion." She passed over a sheet of crested stationery.

Kate skimmed the short note. There was no mistaking the writing—it was Cluyne's distinctive script.

Lady Fenimore,
I purchased these books because I could not bear to see them fall under the knife. Now that I am aware of their true owner, I cannot in good conscience keep them in my possession any longer.

It was signed with a sweeping *C*.

"Well, this is a surprise," murmured Kate.

"That is putting it mildly." Charlotte sat down rather heavily on the bed. "Damn the man."

"Don't you want them?" asked Kate.

A finger traced the lettering on the age-darkened leather. "For years I've said that I would give my eyeteeth to get these back. They are very special to me."

"Then what is the problem?"

"The problem is, I don't have anything *but* my teeth to offer in exchange. I can guess what Cluyne paid for these, and I cannot afford to pay him back." She laid the book on the counterpane. "I'll bring the other one in. Kindly return them to him."

"Charlotte, it is clear that he does not expect any recompense," said Kate softly. "He is just trying to... do the right thing."

"As am I." Her friend's mouth quivered ever so slightly. "The duke is not the only one who has his pride."

"If it makes you feel any better, Cluyne can well afford it."

"That is not the point," insisted Charlotte. "It is a matter of principle. I do not wish to be in his debt."

Kate understood the feeling all too well. An independent-minded female had to fight a constant battle to keep her spirit from being squashed. But perhaps pride and principle could once in a while bend without breaking.

"You don't owe him anything," she reasoned. "Look at it this way—he has a moral obligation to return stolen property. He is merely righting your husband's wrong."

The steel in Charlotte's eyes wavered just a little as she slanted a longing glance at the book. "I... I don't know what to say."

"Say thank you," murmured Kate, and then added her

own silent whisper of gratitude to her grandfather. She had the oddest feeling that he was acting not just out of duty, but also some other emotion. *Cluyne showing compassion?* The idea was hard to accept. And yet…

"Thank you." Charlotte's voice was tentative as she tested out the words. "I suppose that's not too hard to swallow." Her hand hovered above the book. "You are sure?"

"Quite," answered Kate firmly. "Now go finish dressing."

"Miss Woodbridge and her friend should enjoy studying these engravings." Tappan wrapped the rare books and placed them in a leather travel case. "But before we ride back, let me give you a look at something that we definitely won't be showing to the ladies."

He led the way outdoors and crossed through the back gardens to a large stone pavilion overlooking the lake. At first glance, it looked to be a copy of a classical Greek temple. But as they approached the colonnaded entrance, Marco noticed that the walls were solid marble, save for a single row of narrow diamond-paned windows set just below the lip of the roof.

Taking a key from his pocket, Tappan opened the lock. "This collection was purchased by my grandfather from a Turkish pasha, whose tastes ran to the…" The hinges groaned as he eased the heavy iron portal open. "Well, see for yourself, Ghiradelli."

Marco had been prepared for something exotic, but the sight that met his eyes made him blink. "Good God," he murmured.

"Yes, but only a pagan deity would have wrought such creations," quipped Tappan.

Indeed, the place was a paradise of…sculpted sin. Marco stepped inside the pleasure palace and looked around at the marble statues on display. The theme was the same—sexual gratification. But the variety of positions was highly creative.

Viewing pornography usually sparked only a mild amusement. But this was somehow different. Seeing things larger than life gave sex a new dimension. It was hard to remain entirely unmoved.

Tappan seemed to sense his reaction. "A man would have to be made of stone not to find this somewhat interesting. The sheer scale…"

"Is impressive," finished Marco.

Both men slowly grinned.

There was a stretch of silence as they wandered through the statues, stopping now and again to take in all the different angles.

"Interesting. Having done a great deal of experimenting in the matter, I am not quite sure that a flesh-and-blood body could bend into that position," murmured Marco. "But one might die happy for trying."

"My grandfather occasionally entertained his friends here," said Tappan as he strolled over to a pair of satyrs with monstrous erections who were wrestling over a flagon of wine. Bathed in sunlight, the stone seemed almost alive. "From what I have heard, the parties became rather wild."

It didn't require much imagination to picture the proceedings.

"So, it appears that the famed English stiff upper lip extended to other parts of the old baron's anatomy," quipped Marco.

"For the most part, he was a staid, sober fellow. But I daresay we all have some primal passions lurking inside us." Tappan gave a last look around. "We had better be going if we are to get back to Cluyne Close in time for nuncheon."

"I daresay the duke's party would grow more lively if we brought the guests here after the evening meal."

"Can you imagine the look on Cluyne's face? Lud, I'd give a monkey to see his reaction." Tappan gave a bark of laughter. "As for the ladies, they would likely swoon with shock."

Not all of them, thought Marco. Somehow he couldn't picture Kate falling into a fit of megrims. She would likely get out her magnifying glass and subject the statues to a thorough examination—and then afterward offer a critique on all the minute errors the artist had made.

"And I daresay the Prussian colonel would be terribly confused," went on Tappan with a snigger. "He seems so straightlaced, I have a feeling that he sleeps in his uniform."

"Some women find that braid and medals excite their imagination."

"I should think those rough edges would be awfully uncomfortable rubbing up against certain places."

"One man's pleasure is another's poison," remarked Marco.

Dust motes danced in the air as Tappan ran a hand over a nymph's lush buttocks. "Yes, that's true," he murmured. "To each his own."

What passions did Tappan have lurking inside his breast? wondered Marco idly. Outwardly, the fellow seemed to embody the perfect qualities for a diplomat—an affable temperament, polished manners, and a quick intelligence. Yet as the baron slowly stroked the smooth marble, Marco saw the tautness in the tiny muscles of his hand.

The pressures of the upcoming peace conference were enormous, he reminded himself. England and the other major powers would be responsible for remaking the map of Europe. The intrigue would be thicker than a London fog, swirling old enmities and sworn alliances into a haze of noxious shadows.

"Vienna will be an orgy of self-interest," mused Marco. *Subterfuge and secrets.* Suddenly curious, he asked, "Are you looking forward to the trip?"

Tappan held his palm still on the sculpted thigh. "It promises to be an interesting interlude," he replied slowly. "Though I shall be little more than a glorified clerk in Castlereagh's delegation, I hope I may have some influence on the outcome of things."

"A noble sentiment," drawled Marco. "I wish you luck."

"You don't care how the Continent is carved up?"

"Not particularly. You politicians are welcome to wield your blades, just as long as it doesn't upset my little world of brandy and boudoirs."

Chapter Thirteen

"Well done, Mr. Ludlowe," called Rochambert. "So far, your arrow has hit closest to the bull's-eye."

Lady Caroline Chitworth tittered. So far, observed Kate, the eldest daughter of the Countess of Hammond seemed incapable of coherent speech. She had heard nothing but giggles and sighs from the chit.

"Who is next?" asked the American, stepping back from the chalked line.

Von Seilig reached out for the bow. "I will take a try."

"I fear your military training gives you an unfair advantage over us," said Rochambert. "Perhaps you should be required to move back several paces."

"It has been over a century since we Prussians fought with arrows and clubs, monsieur."

Kate hid a smile. She hadn't expected to enjoy herself among strangers, but the colonel was proving to be very pleasant company. He had spent much of the nuncheon with her, much to Lady Duxbury's ire. Even now, the countess was glowering at her.

Ignoring the barbed looks, she turned her attention back to Von Seilig. His dry wit and inquisitive mind defied the preconceived notion that all Germans were dull and humorless. He was well-read and his knowledge of plants was particularly impressive. The harsh climate of the Baltic coast did not allow much latitude for fieldwork.

But the colonel's hidden facets were not the only surprise. Kate angled a glance around the lawns, looking for the bearish bulk of her grandfather among the other guests awaiting their turn to shoot. Oddly enough, he was nowhere to be seen. He had been conspicuously absent at the outdoor nuncheon as well.

It wasn't like Cluyne to duck his duty as a host.

Twang. An arrow whizzed through the air.

But perhaps it was her own judgments that were sailing wide of the mark.

"Bull's-eye!" called Marco from his perch atop the terrace railing. "Come Vronskov, can you match that?"

The Russian made a haughty face and waved off the challenge. "I am not a Cossack. Such sport is too primitive for me."

"I have no such qualms." Tappan removed his coat and stepped to the line.

"That is because you sturdy English yeomen are renowned for your prowess as archers," called Marco with a waggish grin. "Have a care, Rochambert—remember Agincourt!"

Lady Caroline's loud laugh provoked a tight-lipped glare from the Frenchman.

Kate refused to join in the laughter. *Lud, was the man*

always seeking to stir up trouble? What a foolish question. He seemed to seize every opportunity of getting under someone's skin.

Which begged the question of what he intended to do about Naples. A prickling teased at the nape of her neck, like tiny knifepoints teasing against her flesh. She didn't dare think of what damage he could do. A whisper or two was all it would take...

"Alas, I am afraid we may have to end our archery competition early." Tappan displayed the limp cord, which had slipped loose from the bow. "The notch has worn away on one of the ends," he explained after a closer inspection. "I don't think a new knot will hold."

"That should not be too difficult to repair." Kate automatically reached into the hidden pocket sewn into her skirts. Old habits died hard—she never went anywhere without her knife. It was crafted with a silver handle, semiprecious stones, and a blade of Toledo steel. Lovely, but lethal, the weapon had been a birthday gift from her father, who had also taught her how to use it. He believed that a female ought to be able to defend herself from any danger.

She rose. "May I have a look?"

Quirking a wry smile at the flash of steel, the baron handed it over. "I am not inclined to argue."

With a few quick strokes, she cut a groove into the wooden tip and shaved away the rough edges. "Try that."

"You are very adept at handling that blade," observed Tappan. "Most ladies wouldn't know one end of a dagger from the other."

Kate gave herself a mental kick. Such skills would

only stir up more gossip about her eccentricities. "I often sailed with my father, and on board a ship one learns to be handy with a number of tools."

"I commend you for your cleverness, Miss Woodbridge," said Tappan. "That is an unusual design. May I see it?"

"My father had it made for me in Spain," she murmured, reluctantly handing it over.

"It's quite lovely." Von Seilig came over to admire the workmanship. "The hilt is very distinctive. It is silver, is it not? And the stones look to be a very fine grade of turquoise."

"They are from Persia. Father found them in a bazaar in Barcelona and had a silversmith craft it from a sketch he made."

"Was your father an artist, Miss Woodbridge?" inquired the colonel.

Actually, he was more of a pirate, thought Kate with an inward grimace. But that wasn't something she was about to admit in polite company. "My father possessed a great many talents."

"So it would seem." Tappan hefted its weight, admiring the perfect balance before handing it back. "Do have a care. The blade is razor-sharp, and I'd hate to see any blood spilled."

Kate slipped the dagger into its leather sheath. "I know how to handle a weapon, and as you can see, I am very careful with it."

Inclining a gentlemanly bow of thanks, the baron tested the bowstring and then took his shot. The arrow nicked the outer circle, drawing a round of light applause from the ladies.

Marco's hoot of laughter rose above the patter. "Hardly a show of Anglo-Saxon superiority," he called. "Perhaps you had better ask the lady to make another adjustment to the bow."

"We have yet to see you step up to the mark, Lord Ghiradelli," called Vronskov. "Come and show us if your aim is anywhere near as sharp as your tongue."

Waving off the request with a flourish of a champagne bottle, Marco pointedly refilled his glass. "Thank you, but I think I shall pass." He winked at the ladies. "It's too hard to concentrate on martial arts when surrounded by so much pastoral beauty."

The dowager's daughter giggled while Lady Duxbury responded with a sultry smile.

The last few contestants took their turn, and then the party began to split up for the other afternoon activities. A carriage had been arranged to take the ladies into the nearby town, and the gentlemen had been invited to take a ride around the lake and inspect the grouse moor.

Kate withdrew from the shopping expedition, grateful for the chance to steal a bit of solitude. Charlotte had already retired to her room, announcing that she needed a nap to refresh her strength for the evening.

Arthritic knees had slowed her friend's step, but Kate suspected that what she really wanted was to spend some time with her newly restored books.

Ouch. As she escaped around the corner of the privet hedge, her own aching body protested the hurried pace. Pausing to massage her bruised bum, she realized she was cutting a very unladylike figure in the middle of the gardens.

Thank God the guests were all off enjoying the duke's hospitality.

As for her plans, they certainly didn't include getting anywhere near a dratted horse. Not with Marco, who raced like a centaur, waiting to enjoy another laugh at her expense.

Unfortunately there were precious few places at Cluyne Close where she could hide from his amused eyes.

Looking around, Kate squinted into the light reflecting off the conservatory glass. A sun-warmed breeze stirred and through one of the open doors wafted the pungent scent of the interior knot garden, with its heady assortment of medicinal, culinary, and ornamental herbs.

Her muscles twinged. Perhaps Charlotte was right and a long, hot soak would sooth the niggling pain. If only it might help assuage her mental distress. All throughout the midday meal she had surreptitiously tried to read in Marco's face some hint of his intentions.

But all she saw was a mask of merriment. A man who lived for the present moment. He laughed, he flirted, he drank. If at times a fleeting shadow seemed to shade his eyes, it was likely an illusion. Marco did not appear much given to introspection.

While she would sit in a steaming tub and stew over the consequences of their midnight encounter.

Heaving a sigh, Kate cut some rosemary and arnica flowers for the bath water with her knife, then wandered over to a potted arrangement of clove trees. The gardeners had left a small sack of the dried spice buds on the potting table and she added a handful to her basket. Fragrance was a balm for the spirit, and the exotic sweetness of the cloves reminded her of the lush, languid islands half a world away.

Lud, how her life had changed. The journey from vagabond sea merchant to a lady of privilege could not be measured in mere miles. The distance was far more profound. In the past, she had been free to shape her own self, while now she was expected to conform to a rigid set of rules.

To the devil with rules. Kate chose the pebbled pathway leading through the orangerie. There were times when she just wanted to pick up her skirts and run barefoot on a sandy beach.

A profusion of potted specimen trees lined the way, their lush greenery creating a canopy of swaying shadows overhead. The gardeners had just misted the leaves, and the humid air hung heavy with the sweet aroma of ripe fruit and wet earth. It reminded her of the jungles along the coast of Java…

A tingling suddenly snaked along her spine, causing her to stumble. Strange, but all at once she felt as if watchful eyes were on her. As if a hidden predator was stalking her every move.

Don't be foolish, she chided herself. She wasn't in the Molluccan Islands. She was in England, and there wasn't a more civilized place on earth—

"Need a hand to steady your step?"

Il Serpenti. Ah, no wonder she had the sensation of something slithering over her skin.

Before she could answer, Marco took hold of her arm.

Kate shook free of his grip. "Why aren't you out riding with the others?"

"I decided that I would rather enjoy the rare beauty of the flora…and fauna."

She swore under her breath. "I don't know what game

you have in mind, Lord Ghiradelli. But be assured that I don't intend to play it with you."

"No?" A blade of sunlight cut across his face, accentuating the supremely sensuous shape of his mocking smile. "And here I was under the impression that you quite enjoyed the challenge of going *mano a mano* against a male opponent."

Fear seized her throat.

"Come, don't tell me the infamous, insolent *Belladonna* is at a loss for words. As I recall, you had quite an active mouth in *Napoli*."

For an instant, she debated whether to deny the accusation, then dismissed the idea as pointless. Marco might be a wanton wastrel, but he was not stupid.

"I'm amazed you remember what country you were in that night, never mind what city," she shot back.

His long, lithe fingers wrapped around her wrist. "You are very hard to forget, *bella*." He leaned in closer, his long, dark hair dancing over his snowy white shirtpoints. A few drips of water spilled from the overhanging leaves, and as Kate watched them slide down the line of his freshly shaven jaw, she felt an insane urge to flick out her tongue and lick them away.

"Your eyes are remarkable. A man could drown in those ocean-blue depths," he said in a *sotto voce* growl.

"Y-you were already submerged in a sea of brandy," replied Kate, surprised that her voice sounded so unsteady.

"True. I was well in my cups, but certain details remain imprinted on my memory. Like the color of your gaze, the feel of your skin here..." He touched the hollow of her throat. "And here." His hand slid over the ridge of her shoulder.

She shivered in spite of herself.

"But it's your scent that truly marks you." His nostrils flared as he inhaled slowly, filling his lungs with the humid air. He held it for a long moment, savoring it like a fine wine, then let it out with a whisper-soft *whoosh*.

Kate felt her toes curl as the breath caressed her face.

"I would know it—and you—anywhere."

"Clearly, you have a knack for sniffing out trouble," she said. "Yes, I was another person in another life. But if you dare make mention of it to anyone, I vow, I shall... I shall..."

"Shall what? Cut off my tongue with that dainty little dagger of yours?"

She clutched at her basket to keep her hands from trembling. "For once in your life, try to behave like a proper gentleman."

"Why should I? You most certainly didn't act like a proper lady."

Jerking back, Kate tried to twist away, but Marco tightened his hold. The slap of the wet leaves was cold against her burning cheeks.

"You are a beast."

"And you are the infamous *Belladonna*, the bold-as-brass cutpurse thief who eluded Naples harbor authorities for a month before disappearing into thin air."

"You men make it laughably easy to avoid capture. With your brains pickled in wine and your trousers tangled around your ankles, you don't react very quickly." And yet, Kate was intimately aware of how easily his lean, muscled body moved to cut off her retreat. The stretch of his shoulders blocked the light, trapping her in a swirl of shadows.

"*Si*, you caught me off guard. Don't count on it happening again, *bella*. I very rarely make the same mistake twice."

She knew it was dangerous to taunt him, yet she couldn't help herself. "And that fact pricks your pride?"

Despite the shade, his tawny eyes seemed to blaze with a molten fire. "You fucked me, Kate."

"Actually I didn't. I merely stole your purse."

"And I intend to make you pay for it."

Her mouth opened and shut several times in silent outrage before Kate could manage to speak. "It was a paltry amount," she whispered. "But go ahead and name the price for your silence."

"Oh, it's not money I want from you." Marco inched closer. His thighs were now touching hers.

"Th-then w-what?" To her chagrin, her voice broke. The air around them seemed to crackle with tension, and she could sense the power coiled in his hard, masculine body. "If you think I have jewels or South Sea pearls, you are sadly mistaken."

"No? Then we'll have to think of some other forfeit."

"I cannot believe my ears. You would stoop to blackmail, sir?"

"A man like me is capable of anything."

Marco felt her recoil. Oh, she was right. It was evil to tease her. His cousin would ring a peal over his head. However, at this moment, the only sound he could hear was the heated thrum of his pulse.

Ta-tum. Ta-tum. Ta-tum.

As her lips parted in outrage, the pounding grew louder, and Lynsley's stern warnings to keep his mind on the mission fell on deaf ears.

"You owe me something, Kate."

Her eyes widened at the intimacy. Only a close friend or a lover was allowed the liberty of stripping away the formalities of Polite Society and using her pet name. He was neither, but he liked the feel of it—a rough-edged growl that started deep in his throat and then slid from his tongue in a short, sweet rasp of air.

"Kate," he repeated, savoring the sound.

"How dare you call me that!" Anger had ridged the sharp slant of her cheekbones with a slash of crimson. Like her flesh was on fire.

"Because I am a wicked, wanton wastrel." He traced the back of his hand along her jaw.

The tiny muscles twitched beneath his touch. "What do you want from me?" she demanded.

"Just a kiss." Planting himself in her path of escape, Marco slowly framed her face. "And don't tell me you haven't been kissed by another man before."

"Then take it, and be done with it, you cad," she said through clenched teeth.

"*Va bene*. Then with your permission..."

He had no intention of rushing the experience. His lips hovered for a moment, a whisper from hers. Heat radiated from her every pore, prickling sharp as her Spanish dagger against his skin. The scent of oranges and Mediterranean thyme teased at his senses. Closing his eyes, he could almost taste it—sweetness, spice, and the foam-flecked salt of the sea.

"W-what the devil are you waiting for?" she whispered.

Damn him for a fool. He ought to rein in this reckless need to crush his mouth to hers. But restraint was not part of his nature. Not anymore.

And so he gave way to desire. To lust. To something he couldn't begin to put a name to.

In answer to her tremulous question, Marco nipped the swell of her lower lip.

"Beast," she repeated, and then bit him back.

He gave a rough laugh. "Spitfire." He kissed her cheek, which seemed to surprise her. She stopped struggling and went very still. He kissed the shell of her ear, tracing its shape with his tongue.

She let out a little moan as the basket slipped from her grip.

A surge of fire shot through his blood. He might be doomed to burn in the eternal flames of Hell for his sins, but at this moment he didn't care.

"*Bella*," he murmured, teasing a trail of tiny caresses to the corner of her mouth.

Her hands came up, and all at once her slim fingers were tangling, twisting, twining in his hair. Kicking aside a terra-cotta pot, Marco braced her up against one of the fluted iron columns and possessed her with a hard, hungry kiss. The shards crunched under his boots as he hitched his hips, pinned her between the cold metal and his hot steel.

"Oh." She sucked in a breath as he slowly released her lips. His arousal was thrust up against her belly, an unyielding shaft of throbbing, engorged flesh. "You are a *very* wicked man."

Her body arched—not to seek escape but to meet his advances with a slow, sinuous slide of silk over the taut leather of his buckskins.

"And you," said Marco, trying to control the urge to fist her skirts and yank them up over her thighs, "are a *very* bad girl."

Her expression tightened, and for a fleeting instant she looked as vulnerable as a child. Unsure, and perhaps a little afraid. Then the sardonic mask was back in place.

"That shouldn't come as any surprise, Lord Ghiradelli..."

In contrast to the polished tones of a proper young lady, her voice was a little rough around the edges. Low and husky, the sound seemed weathered by wind and salt. Marco found it incredibly sexy.

"...now that you know my dirty little secret," finished Kate.

Secrets. He was about to ask what had made the granddaughter of an English duke turn to thieving in a seamy Italian brothel. But the trembling jut of her kiss-swollen lower lip was too great a distraction. Coherent thought gave way to desire. And then, against all reason, to a desperate need to taste her lush, lovely mouth.

With a primal groan, he coaxed her lips apart and delved inside her warmth, deepening the kiss until their tongues touched and twined together. Their movement set the slender trees to swaying. The leaves danced overhead, showering them with a fine mizzle of orange-scented mist. The sensation was intensely erotic.

Mindless of the glass walls, Marco slowly circled his palms over the swell of her breasts.

She shuddered. Her knees buckled and she clutched at the slope of his shoulders, her fingers digging into his knotted muscles.

Pushing away from the iron support, she found a path through a circle of unplanted palm trees and drew him into the shaded center.

Dark slivered shadows played over their bodies as

Kate stumbled back against an ancient marble column, one of the many antique sculptures decorating the conservatory. The long fronds were thick, the interlacing leaves weaving an emerald screen to hide them from prying eyes. Still, there was always a danger that someone might stumble upon the shocking scene.

Ah, but danger was all that made him feel truly alive, thought Marco as he slid her skirts up over her thighs.

Her breath was coming in ragged gasps. He paused for a fraction, giving her a chance to say no.

"*Si,*" she whispered, nipping at his neck.

The temptation was too great to resist. Finding the slit in her drawers, he thrust his fingers between the feminine folds of her flesh. She was warm and wickedly wet to his touch.

"*Dio mi aiut,*" groaned Marco; the sensuous shiverings of the leaves nearly drowning out his words.

God help me, he repeated to himself. But it was the devil himself who guided his hands to the flap of his breeches and wrenched the fastenings open. His shaft sprung free.

With a heated moan, Kate clasped her arms around his neck.

His hands found the taut curves of her bottom and lifted her up. Bracing her back against the stone, he thrust his body hard against her heat.

"Wrap your legs around me, *cara*," he urged. The earthy scent of damp soil and aroused sex swirled around them. This would have to be swift and savage. A rush of pure, animal passion amidst the jungle greenery.

Kate responded with equal abandon. Her knees clenched his hips as he drove himself deep inside her.

She gave a soft cry as he withdrew and thrust in again. And again.

Her hips rocked to his rhythm, and he felt her body tighten with tension.

"*Cara*," he rasped, feeling fire surge through his limbs. Hot with need, he pressed his mouth over hers, muffling her cry of climax as she came undone in his arms.

Somehow, he had the presence of mind to pull out just in time. High overhead, the sun glinted wildly off the glass as his seed spilled over the dark earth.

Dragging in a lungful of air, he eased her down until her feet touched the ground, and then he drew her into his arms. Her head came to rest on his shoulder, and he held her until her hitching breaths grew calmer.

Marco had kissed countless women over the years, but his response to Kate Woodbridge left him a little shaken. Conflicting impulses stirred strange sensations. *Dangerous sensations.*

He found himself feeling a little uncertain. A little confused.

The clatter of a water cart being wheeled over the brick walkway cut short any further reflections.

Kate heard it, too, and shook off her daze to straighten her bodice and smooth her skirts. Her hands were shaking. But when she looked up, her composure suddenly turned hard as cold steel.

"Satisfied, Lord Ghiradelli?" she asked. "I trust you will consider the debt paid in full."

Taken by surprise, Marco matched her sardonic edge. "The contents may have been paltry, but the purse itself was made of very expensive Florentine leather. By my reckoning, Kate, you still owe me something."

Her eyes widened. "And who is to decide the final tally?"

He tugged at his cuff. "Oh, I am sure we can come to a mutual agreement."

As the gardener's cheerful whistlings grew louder, Kate darted a look over her shoulder. "Don't count your pennies just yet," she muttered, pushing past him and ducking under the low-hanging leaves.

A moment later, she was lost in a sea of green.

Pails rattled. Water sloshed.

Stepping over the broken pot, Marco picked up the basket of herbs Kate had dropped and placed it on one of the potting benches before clicking open the side door and letting himself out.

Chapter Fourteen

Fool, fool, fool!

The angry tattoo of her heels on the polished parquet seemed to echo her self-loathing thoughts. Taking the stairs in an unladylike rush, Kate flung open her bedchamber door, and then kicked it shut behind her.

The thump, a noise loud enough to wake the dead, finally brought her back to her senses. Tentatively touching her lips, she smoothed her fingertips over the kiss-roughened flesh. She dared not venture a peek at the looking glass, sure she would see that a total stranger had stolen into her skin.

The real Kate Woodbridge would never dream of allowing a rapscallion rogue like Giovanni Marco Musto della Ghiradelli to make her whole body boneless with longing.

Would she?

Kate drifted to the bank of windows and stared out at the distant hills. She wasn't sure how to answer the question. For the longest time, she had felt lost in London.

Adrift without a compass. In the past, she had guided her family's ship through thunder and lightning, through hurricanes and typhoons with unerring confidence. She had navigated through the waters of poverty and creditors without running onto the rocks. But now she felt rudderless.

And it made her angry. Afraid.

Crossing her arms over her chest, Kate took a seat on the counterpane of her carved tester bed. This bastion of opulent wealth and ducal privilege ought to be a safe harbor, and yet the crosscurrents and hidden shoals of Polite Society seemed far more dangerous than the open sea. In truth, she would much rather sail through a raging monsoon than the mansions of Mayfair.

It was confusing, and at times she wished for...

Kate blinked the beads of salt from her lashes. *Hell's bells*. She *never* cried. The ever practical, ever pragmatic Katharine Kylie Woodbridge was tough as a marlinspike, strong as a steel-straight mainmast, resilient as a coil of whipcord rope.

Only a silly schoolgirl would yearn for a shoulder to lean on.

Sniff.

Only a hopeless romantic would delude herself into thinking that a rake's lovemaking offered any comfort.

Sniff.

"Are you coming down with a head cold?" Alice entered the room with a freshly pressed gown looped over her arm. "Shall I send to the kitchens for a tisane?"

"No, no, I'm perfectly fine." Kate rubbed at her nose. "The pollen from the *Adenium obesum* must have irritated my eyes."

Her maid squinted. "If ye asked me, missy," she

said after closing the door, "I'd say that the irritation comes from an entirely different species. One that ain't a plant."

"How—" began Kate before biting back her words.

"You had best dab a bit of beeswax balm on your lip," suggested Alice. "That ought to soothe the swelling by dinnertime."

"Oh, Lud, is it that obvious?" She couldn't help scrambling up and taking a peek in the glass.

"Not to most people," answered her maid. "However, I've seen enough of...*that* to recognize the telltale signs."

Kate quickly looked away. "*That* won't happen again."

A skeptical snort answered the assertion. "I wouldn't wager a ha'penny on it. There seems to be some force at work between the two of you." Alice carefully shook out the emerald-colored skirts and hung the gown in the armoire. "Ye know, like that scientific experiment ye showed me with a magnet, and all the little shavings of steel."

"You are saying that Lord Ghiradelli and I are attracted to each other?"

Alice nodded.

Sniff.

"I fear you are right." Returning to the bed, she lay back against the pillows and laced her hands behind her head. However, the loosened hairpins and tangled tendrils were an uncomfortable reminder of her less than laudable behavior, and so she assumed a more ladylike pose.

Stop sniveling, she scolded herself. It wasn't as if she had just surrendered her virginity. That had happened several years ago. She had been curious, and the young

American naval officer in Antigua had been charming. The affair hadn't lasted long, and there had been only one other time. Still, she considered herself a woman of the world, not a dewy-eyed schoolgirl.

Expelling a sigh, she rubbed at her nose. "Oh, would that I could sprout wings and soar away."

"To where?" asked Alice gently.

Kate didn't know how to answer. There wasn't really any place that she thought of as home. "Perhaps the moon," she joked halfheartedly. "I'm very fond of cheese, and I would imagine that the green variety is similar in taste to English Stilton."

Alice eyed her in silence for several moments. "Men can make you miserable," she observed. "I often wonder whether they are worth it."

"I'm not miserable," protested Kate. "And if I were, it would not be on account of an arrogant rakehell rogue." *Who had just made wild, passionate love to her.*

"Right," murmured her maid.

A clever retort came to mind, but somehow, when Kate opened her mouth, all that came out was a choked sob. "On second thought, I must be falling ill," she managed to say a moment later. "I never turn into a watering pot."

A handkerchief fluttered in front of her nose. "Here, blow your nose, Missy, and I'll order up a nice, hot bath. There's nothing like a long soak to soothe yer spirits. If ye want, I can send word to your grandfather that you are feeling under the weather and wish to cry off from the evening."

Behave like a craven coward? After a small sniff, Kate crumpled the linen in her fist, kneading it into a tight little wad. Katharine Kylie Woodbridge did *not* back away from a confrontation, no matter how daunting. She had fended off irate creditors, she had outmaneuvered Chinese pirates, she had stood firm against a knife-wielding Neapolitan brute.

She wasn't about to crawl under her coverlet and let Marco think she was too afraid to be in his company.

"No, I'll be just fine." Putting on a brave face was a trick that Kate had mastered long ago. By now it was like slipping into a second skin.

The gilt-edged card on his dressing table announced that the guests were expected in the drawing room for drinks promptly at seven. Marco gave a last little tweak to his cravat and dismissed his valet. No wonder he avoided these country gatherings like the plague, he thought. The duke had planned the daily routine with military precision, and while most of the guests enjoyed the regimented activities, he chafed at having to march in line with someone else's expectations.

But orders were orders.

Having accepted the assignment, he must discipline himself to perform it well.

The key was to keep his mind on the gentlemen. Entering the drawing room, Marco kept his gaze from seeking the gleam of wheat-gold hair. Teasing Kate Woodbridge had begun as a tantalizing distraction, but it was threatening to get out of control.

"Did you enjoy the ride around the lake, Lord Ghiradelli?" After murmuring something to one of the liveried footman, the duke turned and joined Marco by the one of the Elizabethan display cabinets flanking the entrance doors. A massive silver candelabra crowned its top, the candles gently flickering with the arrival of each guest. Light and shadows rippled over the polished patterns of the tiger's eye maple.

"I decided to take a stroll in your gardens instead," answered Marco. "I rode in the morning and have already had the pleasure of seeing the views across the water."

"Have you an interest in plants, sir?" asked Cluyne.

"No, Your Grace. But even for one who cannot discern beggarweed from Spanish lavender, it is hard not to admire the color and symmetry of the design."

The duke sipped his sherry. "Yet you recognized the shrubs bordering the orchard walk," he said dryly.

"My mother was an avid gardener. She enjoyed digging in the dirt," said Marco, surprised at the pinch of pain that the memory stirred. He suddenly thought of languid summer days, playing hide-and-seek with his brother among the ornamental grasses and flowering shrubs, the contessa laughingly warning them not to trample her precious blooms. Daniello had inherited her passion for coaxing life from the earth...

"But me, I find my pleasures elsewhere," he added with a hard smile.

Cluyne gave a grunt that made Marco wonder whether one of the workmen had seen him and Kate together in the conservatory.

"Of course," he hastened to add, "I am not seeking anything here at Cluyne Close but an interlude of restful relaxation and convivial conversation while enjoying the pastoral beauty of your lands."

"Hmmph." The grunt was more pronounced this time. "Apparently, Tappan had some reason for requesting that your name be added to the guest list."

Marco deflected the oblique question with a casual

shrug. "I am acquainted with several of the Continental guests, so I assume that he thought a familiar face would make them feel more at home."

Cluyne's silvery brows rose a notch. Up close, Marco could see the subtle similarities between Kate and her grandfather. The line of the jaw, the angle of the cheekbones, the imperious tilt of the nose—and, most of all, the watchfulness of the aquamarine eyes.

He would have to be on guard. The duke was no doddering fool. There was a sharp intelligence lurking beneath the scowl.

"Then allow me to let you go mingle with your friends." With a discreet gesture, the duke summoned the butler from his station just outside the oak-paneled doors. "While I have a look at the arrangement of flowers for the dining room."

Why, wondered Marco, would a man of such obvious intelligence allow his family to be torn asunder by pride? He looked up at a pair of unsmiling ducal ancestors peering down their painted noses at him from the gilded confines of their ornate frames.

But then, he was hardly one to comment on familial relationships. His own past was not a pretty picture.

Marco looked around to see Kate enter the drawing room just as her grandfather was going out. Her color was a touch flushed, and she appeared to be a little breathless.

"Sir." She stepped aside in a whisper of silk to let him pass.

Cluyne hesitated, and then fixed her companion with a gimlet gaze.

"What a marvelous collection of *Liliaceae* you have in the conservatory," said Von Seilig enthusiastically.

"Forgive us if we are a little late, Your Grace, but Miss Woodbridge was kind enough to give me a short tour of the new arrivals just now."

"We met on the stairs," said Kate. "And the colonel expressed such an interest that..." Her words trailed off, but a mutinous expression remained on her face. The colonel might not be aware of the nuances governing the rules of an English lady's behavior, but she clearly comprehended her transgression.

And didn't give a damn, observed Marco. He felt his lips thin to a wry grimace. Had she been enjoying another heated interlude among the tropical greenery? Perhaps Kate Woodbridge—the infamous *Belladonna*—was a harder female than she let on.

"Katharine," began Cluyne.

"Of course, I, too, was anxious to see them. So we all decided to have a look," announced Charlotte, who quickly appeared from the depths of the corridor. "I trust you don't mind, sir."

That the elderly scholar had come from the opposite direction of the conservatory did not escape Marco's notice. Nor did he think that the duke was fooled.

Cluyne's eyes narrowed, but Charlotte did not look the least bit intimidated by the ducal daggers.

Flicking open her fan, she gave a languid wave. "My, my, it was quite warm in there. I should very much like a glass of champagne."

Von Seilig, who to his credit sensed that some misstep had been made, kept his mouth shut and offered one arm to her and the other to Kate. "Allow me to be of service, ladies."

The trio moved away, leaving Cluyne standing in the doorway. The duke watched Kate's rigid retreat for a fraction of a moment before turning to the corridor, an inscrutable expression on his face.

Personal battles were none of his business, Marco reminded himself. Lynsley had sent him here as part of a far bigger war. Time to sharpen his sword—and his wits—and prove his mettle.

Spotting Lady Duxbury and her brother, Marco strolled over to join them. Allenham's greeting was friendly enough, but he seemed a little distracted, and his eyes kept darting around the room. "You missed a capital gallop this afternoon, Ghiradelli. The duke has some prime mounts in his stables."

"I decided to exercise my own legs instead," said Marco.

The countess ran her gaze up and then down the length of his trousers. "Ah, yes, I have heard that you have a great fondness for vigorous physical activity." Regarding him through her lashes, she murmured, "What a pity you didn't mention your intentions. The carriage ride into that dreary little town was a bore. I should have *much* preferred a walk in the woods."

Or a roll in the hay.

Marco grimly reminded himself to avoid the darkened corridors of the manor late at night. Lady Duxbury seemed intent on stalking her chosen prey with the ruthlessness of a hungry lioness.

"I took a tour of the gardens," he replied lightly. "They are magnificent. The duke has quite a passion for botany."

She made a face. "Eccentricity seems to run in the family. His granddaughter also seems to enjoy mucking in the mud. I saw her come out of the conservatory yesterday covered in filth."

He felt himself bristle. "She is a noted scholar of plant life, and her work demands careful observation of actual specimens."

"Work," repeated Lady Duxbury with a toss of her auburn curls. "Another oddity. If you ask me, Miss Woodbridge is aloof and arrogant. And abominably rude. Why, I tried to engage her in friendly conversation the other evening and was coldly rebuffed."

"Keep your voice down, Jocelyn," warned Allenham.

"Oh, pish." Crooking a finger, she signaled a footman to refill her glass. "Everyone knows that she is considered a frightful bluestocking by Polite Society."

"I think you have had enough champagne," growled her brother.

"I don't think you can *ever* have enough of a good thing." Lady Duxbury gave a provocative pout. "Don't you agree, Lord Ghiradelli?"

"Far be it from me to contradict a lady," said Marco.

"There, you see." She jabbed a triumphant finger into the starched folds of Allenham's cravat.

As the footman approached, her brother took the empty glass from her hand and ordered rattafia punch instead.

She made a moue of distaste. "I think I shall go speak with Ludlowe and Tappan. They are far more agreeable company than you are." Her words seemed to hang in the air, a challenge—or perhaps a taunt—to Marco. "*Ciao*."

Allenham expelled a sharp breath as she crossed the carpet. "Have you any siblings, Ghiradelli?"

"No." *Not since a fateful day long ago in the past.*

"Count yourself a lucky fellow." A tiny muscle twitched along the heavy line of the baron's jaw. "Between the bacon-brained escapades of my younger brother and the overt indiscretions of my sister, it is a wonder that I have any time to deal with my own affairs."

Seizing the opening, Marco casually asked, "I would imagine that the conference in Vienna could have great repercussions for trade through Europe, especially in the northern lands along the sea where your consortium does business."

The baron nodded. "The maps will be redrawn—it's simply a question of who will get what."

"Are you not afraid of being left out in the cold?" probed Marco.

"No. I am not."

An interesting response. He waited, but the baron did not elaborate.

Vronskov detached himself from a group of gentlemen by the hearth and drifted over to join them. "Rochambert may be a problem for us," he muttered through his teeth. "He is saying that the French will press hard to have a say in the Polish question—"

Allenham signaled him to silence with a quick frown.

Marco pretended not to notice. Flicking his gaze to the dowager's daughter, he made a show of flirting with smiles and winks.

The Russian hesitated a fraction and then Marco heard him continue in a low voice. "Bah, Ghiradelli isn't the least interested in our business. I think I've convinced the Austrian attaché to accept our offer, but we must bring Von Seilig around in order to be sure of our position."

"Ssshh." Allenham let out his breath in a sharp hiss. Angling his back to Marco, he added, "Let us discuss this after supper."

Fingering the heavy gold fobs on his watch chain, Marco uttered a soft oath. "Damn. I think these cursed things have snagged a thread on my new waistcoat." He fussed with the silk, smoothing a hand over the expensive embroidery. "I say, does it look to you as if it is ruined?"

Vronskov shook his head. "I don't see any damage."

The baron didn't bother with a glance. "It appears perfectly fine."

"Thank God." Marco exaggerated a sigh of relief. "The color and cut are quite special. I know the English tend to favor Weston and Stutz, but I have an excellent Italian tailor to recommend in London. In his backroom, he has an assortment of printed fabrics from India that feature some very interesting designs of naked ladies engaged in..." He gave a conspiratorial wink. "Let us just say, you won't be wearing them in Polite Society. But they certainly enliven the conversation at any establishment where gentlemen gather to enjoy themselves."

A wolfish grin flashed through the Russian's luxurious mustache. "Be so good as to add that establishment to the list you are making for me."

Marco chuckled. "With pleasure."

Deciding it was time to move on, he excused himself and sidled over to where the Frenchman was holding court with several of the Southern Europeans. His old friend from Italy was among them—and if ever a fellow could be pumped for information, it was Vincenzi.

He drew his countryman aside and after a quarter hour had no reason to revise his assessment. Vincenzi was still a garrulous gossip, but along with the lurid details of a prominent Milanese nobleman's sexual peccadilloes, he had also passed on some useful political tidbits. Lynsley would no doubt be interested to learn that Austrian officials in Milan were holding secret talks with an envoy from Saxony.

Satisfied with his progress so far, Marco allowed himself a moment to sip his wine. The seating chart for this evening's supper showed that he was placed between the two Spanish attachés. So perhaps he would be able to coax a few more bits of information out of the conversation.

Had he missed anyone important? Raising his glass, he surveyed the room through the cut crystal. The faces all looked a little blurred by the faceted glass and refracted light. Only one seemed to stand out in sharp relief.

Look away.

The inner voice of Reason resonated loud and clear. However, he had been turning a deaf ear to the sound for longer than he cared to remember. Why change now?

Marco watched as Kate edged into the shadows of an arched alcove. A gentleman ought to respect her wish for a moment of privacy.

But he was no gentleman.

Hearing Von Seilig laugh set his teeth on edge. *Had Kate allowed the colonel to make free with her favors?* Any lady who had dallied with not one but possibly two men in one day deserved to be tormented just a little.

Chapter Fifteen

Kate slid around the corner of the ornate carved bookcases, grateful that the dark wood provided a sliver of sanctuary from the party. Perhaps she ought to have taken her maid's suggestion and claimed to be feeling poorly.

She rubbed at her bare arms, feeling her flesh pebble beneath her touch. *Hot. Cold.* She couldn't quite decide.

"Maybe I *am* ill," she whispered, pressing her palms to her cheeks.

Encountering Von Seilig on the way down to the drawing room had only exacerbated her odd mood. The colonel was proving to be a very pleasant companion, and when he had asked if he might have a quick look at the newly arrived *Liliaceae*, she had not wished to put him off with platitudes about propriety.

The decision had been purely... intellectual. She admired his interest in botany, as well as his forthright demeanor. Unlike most military men she had met, he was not a strutting popinjay in love with his own glittering reflection of braid and brass.

As for any other interest...

Kate drew her brows together, wondering why she felt nothing but a warm friendship for the Prussian. Unlike the sparks of liquid fire that shot through her whenever Marco came near. Von Seilig was solid, steady. Marco was wild, wicked.

It made absolutely no sense. As a scientist, that bothered her. She set her teeth, slowly tightening the muscles of her jaw. She and her fellow 'Sinners' were used to solving complex conundrums. All one had to do was apply reason.

Yet when she was around Marco, reason seemed to go up in smoke.

Kate fanned her cheeks and listened to the clink of crystal and muted sounds of laughter. Much as she wished to linger in her refuge, she knew that she ought to return to the guests.

Gathering her skirts, she was about to step around the bookcase when a shadow fell across her path.

She hesitated, hearing the rasp of a ducal cough. "Ah, there you are. Why are you skulking in the shadows?"

For an instant, Kate thought Cluyne was talking to her, but then Charlotte answered.

"I am not *skulking*, sir. I was merely seeking a bit of space. I don't mingle well in a crowd."

Kate ventured a peek through the space between leather-bound spines. Cluyne and Charlotte were standing together in the recessed archway, half hidden from the rest of the guests by the fluted moldings. The duke's dark evening clothes were indistinguishable from the paneling, but a nearby candelabra painted his profile in a soft light.

He thinned his lips, as if annoyed by the tart remark. But when he spoke, it was to comment on a different subject. One that Kate hoped he had forgotten about. "You weren't in the conservatory with my granddaughter," he accused. "Why did you say you were?"

"To prevent you from ringing a peal over her head," replied Charlotte. "Why must you be such a martinet?"

"M-martinet?" sputtered Cluyne. "I am simply trying to ensure that Katharine does not...make the mistake of finding herself shunned by Society."

"Well, you are going about it all wrong," said Charlotte frankly. "Kate is a very independent young lady, and wise beyond her years."

"Too independent," growled Cluyne.

"Perhaps," countered Charlotte. "Be that as it may, she is trying to fit in. You might make it easier if you were to show her a little kindness and understanding, rather than always shout and scowl."

His mouth opened and then shut with a snap.

"It shouldn't be so difficult. I have a feeling that your bark is worse than your bite."

A ferocious frown tightened Cluyne's face for a moment. And then, to Kate's surprise, it relaxed into a wry grimace. "I'm not sure whether I have been complimented or castigated."

Charlotte quirked a tiny smile. "Perhaps a little of both."

After an awkward moment of silence, the duke shuffled his feet. "Is there any other criticism you care to voice before I return to my guests?" he asked.

"You might try calling your granddaughter Kate, rather than Katharine. It might help break the ice, so to speak."

"Hmmph." He gave a curt nod and started to turn away.

"Just one more thing, Your Grace."

Cluyne paused.

"It's about the books. I... well, I don't know quite what to say—and as you may have noticed, I am rarely rendered speechless." Charlotte drew in an unsteady gulp of air and went on in a rush. "So I'll simply say thank you. It was incredibly generous of you. And... thoughtful."

The duke cleared his throat with a gruff growl. "I was merely returning them to their rightful owner, Lady Fenimore. You, at least, appreciate them more than most people. I daresay you won't cut them up into pennyprints."

"No," said Charlotte, her voice a little breathless. "I won't cut them up."

Kate never heard her friend sound like a giddy schoolgirl. Angling a quick look at her grandfather, she saw that his expression had turned... odd.

Bashful?

Good Lord, the champagne must be affecting her head.

She blinked, and sure enough, her grandfather's craggy features had their usual sharp edge. "I am glad to hear it."

With that, he pivoted on his heel and walked away.

Charlotte slowly released the fisted fringe of her shawl and smoothed out the folds before following.

Kate leaned back against the books. Some mischievous ghost of Cluyne Close must have stirred up an ancient spell to plague this house party. She made a face. And whatever the black magic, it was awfully potent.

No scientific rationale could explain the mysterious force that was making opposites attract each other.

"Found a good book to read?"

Speak of the devil. Kate looked up at Marco. "I was actually looking for a volume on alchemy."

"You wish to transform base metals into gold?" His gaze held a glint of amusement. "I was under the impression that fancy baubles were not to your taste."

"I wish to transform plaguey rogues into perfect gentlemen."

His low laugh tickled against her cheek. "I'm afraid that may be beyond the powers of any magic, black or otherwise. But you are welcome to try."

The close confines of the alcove seemed to intensify his presence—his shoulders seemed even more muscular, his smile even more sensuous, his scent even more...

Masculine.

There was no other word for the heady mix of tobacco, brandy, and sandalwood shaving soap.

"As a scientist, I take pride in being a realist. Any experiment to change you would be a waste of time. I recognize a hopeless task when I see it."

Marco shifted his stance, and suddenly his thigh was touching hers. "I thought scientists were not supposed to jump to conclusions."

Her knees gave a little lurch.

"Aren't you supposed to gather empirical evidence to prove your assumptions?" he pressed. Somehow, his terrible, tempting mouth was now only inches from hers.

"I've observed enough to make a logical deduction,"

said Kate. "You are an incorrigible womanizer who hasn't a serious bone in his body."

"I'm not sure you explored my anatomy thoroughly enough to come to that conclusion."

She couldn't help but imagine what his lean, chiseled chest, stripped bare of wool and linen, would feel like against her hands. "You have just proved my point—"

His kiss was so swift that she wasn't quite sure whether she had simply imagined the touch of his lips. "All that I have proved is the fact that your cheeks turn a very beguiling shade of pink whenever I get under your skin."

A lick of heat teased up her spine. Kate told herself it was anger. And yet anger had never before stirred the strange sensation of butterflies beating their gossamer wings against her ribs.

"*Bella*," he murmured.

"D-don't call me that," she whispered.

"Why? Does it remind you of your wicked past?"

Oh yes, she was wicked.

"Or your wicked present?"

She felt a little woozy and her ears began to ring.

"Ah, there is the bell summoning us to supper. Shall I escort you to the dining room?"

"I..." For an instant she was tempted to take his arm and lean her head against the muscled stretch of his shoulder. But then there was a sinful little flicker in his eye, as if he guessed at her thoughts, and she regretted her momentary weakness.

"I would prefer to go there on my own." Gathering what remained of her dignity, Kate whisked her skirts free of his legs and hurried to join her grandfather's guests.

• • •

Discipline. Contrary to the prevailing perception, Marco could exert a modicum of self control when he chose to. So, although the meal seemed to go on interminably, Marco made polite conversation with the two Spaniards and listened patiently to their long-winded assessments of European politics.

But it wasn't easy.

His gaze kept stealing to the head of the long table, where Kate sat flanked by the Prussian colonel and Lord Tappan. A massive silver epergne filled with a profusion of exotic flowers obscured his view of her face. She appeared to be enjoying her supper partners, and yet, beneath her light smiles, Marco sensed lurking shadows. *Secrets and lies.* Not for the first time, he wondered about her past.

There was a mystery surrounding her, and for all his dissolute habits, Marco was very good at solving mysteries when he put his mind to it. Even Lynsley conceded that, when motivated, Marco was the best clandestine agent in Whitehall's secret network.

Lifting his wineglass to his lips, Marco watched Kate slice off a morsel of roasted duck with a deft flick of her knife. The blade flashed, and for one mad moment, he was reminded of the sunburned harbor of Naples, where a notorious pimp had been found stabbed to death in an alley. Strange that the timing coincided with the disappearance from town of the female cutpurse known as *Belladonna.*

No, impossible. However, in his profession, coincidence always stirred suspicions.

Be that as it may, duty demanded that he concentrate his attention on the European diplomats. Whatever sordid secrets lay in Kate Woodbridge's past, they were none of his concern. Leaning back in his chair, Marco saw that he was not the only one surreptitiously watching her. The duke's gaze flitted to his granddaughter, and his normally impassive face betrayed a flash of mingled consternation and concern.

So Cluyne found Kate a conundrum, too, thought Marco.

As the final savories were removed, the ladies rose in well-practiced union and left the room.

The duke surveyed the remaining gentlemen and fingered his chin. "What say you to enjoying our port and cigars out on the terrace this evening. The night is mild and the skies uncommonly clear, so I think that the ladies would enjoy joining us with their tea. The gardens appear especially fine in the light of the full moon."

A murmur of assent greeted the suggestion and the servants were dispatched to set up the tables and torchieres.

The party was soon reassembled outdoors and tea was served to the ladies while the gentlemen savored several excellent vintages brought up from the duke's cellars.

"I daresay there will be many a lavish gathering in Vienna," said Tappan. "It is said to be a city that loves a party."

"A city that loves to dance." Lady Duxbury looked up at the sky and heaved a theatrical sigh. "Imagine—moonlight swirling over the Danube and couples waltzing under the stars."

"Mama say the waltz is very risqué," murmured Lady Caroline.

"Pish." Lady Duxbury waved off the comment. "Even the dragonesses at Almack's now permit it."

"I—I have never seen it done," admitted Lady Caroline.

Rochambert smiled. "Come, there is plenty of space here on the terrace if we gentlemen shift a few of the urns. I should be happy to demonstrate the dance with Lady Duxbury, if His Grace does not object to an impromptu ball."

Cluyne gave a nod. "I see no reason to spoil the fun."

Even the dowager countess did not object, though she did summon her daughter to stand by her side. "You may watch Caro, but nothing more."

Clapping her hands in delight, Lady Duxbury looked around. "And if we open the doors to the music room... Perchance does anyone know how to play a waltz on the pianoforte?"

"As a matter of fact, I do," volunteered Charlotte. Catching Kate's quizzical look, she explained. "Remember, when I visited Helen Gosford at the beginning of the summer? She had a sheaf of sheet music sent to her by a friend in Vienna, and during the evenings we would take turns playing to entertain ourselves. I think I can remember one of the simpler tunes."

"*Merci, madame!*" Rochambert gave her a gracious bow. "Music will make the experience even more enjoyable."

He and several of the other gentlemen quickly slid the marble decorations to one side. Offering his hand to Lady Duxbury, the Frenchman led her to the center of the slates. Through the open doors of the music room floated the first lilting notes of the melody.

Marco had to admit the scene was wildly romantic. Flickering flames, a gentle breeze, the distant glimmer of the lake, its waters pale and pearlescent in the softly shimmering light.

Setting down his brandy glass, he cut across to where Kate was standing. "The more, the merrier." Before she could protest, he took hold of her arm and drew her onto the makeshift dance floor.

"I—I don't know the steps," she hissed in his ear.

"But I do," Marco replied. "Relax, and just follow my lead." He placed his hand on the small of her back, just where the gentle curve of her spine formed a slight hollow. She stiffened as his palm flattened against her gown. "Relax," he repeated. "The waltz is all about abandoning yourself to the rhythm of the music. A dancing couple must move as one."

"If you get any closer, we might as well be glued together," said Kate. Her voice sounded a little unsteady.

"Yes, the English find it shocks their sensibilities that a man and a woman are allowed to touch so intimately in public. What about you, Kate?"

"I—I..."

Before she could answer, Marco swept her to the first gliding steps of the dance. "Trust me," he murmured, twirling through a slow spin. Her slender body fit perfectly against his, and through the thin layers of fabric he could feel the quickening of her breath. His feet felt as if they were skimming over the stone in a blur.

Faster, faster. Kate looked up, a tentative smile on her face, and his heart began to race. *Or was it hers?* Marco wasn't quite sure he could separate the tattoo of tiny thuds against his skin.

Dio Madre, he was a jaded rake, a wanton wastrel. A chaste dance should not be making him lose control.

"Hold on tight, Kate," he whispered. "For the next few minutes let us fly."

Her feet were lifted from the ground, and suddenly Kate was whirling through the air, as if she were as light as a feather in his strong, sure hands. The breeze kissed her cheeks, and a laugh bubbled up inside her. For a giddy instant, she felt free as a seabird, soaring high over the ocean.

Even when her slippers touched back down to earth, the heady excitement stayed with her. Marco moved with a lithe, light grace and she instinctively sensed the subtle changes in his steps. His hand rested lightly near her hip, yet she was intimately aware of its heat searing straight to her core.

No wonder English society had been loath to allow the waltz to cross the Channel. It was wicked, indeed. And wonderful. She felt like a fairy princess, capering in the moonlight madness.

As they spun through a turn, Marco's long, dark hair brushed against her cheek. Kate wished she could strip off her gloves and twine her fingers through the silky tangle. And then pull his sensuous mouth close and taste the hot spice of brandy lingering on his lips.

Oh yes, the waltz was sinful. *Seductive.*

It took her an instant to realize the music had stopped and the guests were applauding. A little dazed, she stepped back to catch her breath.

"La, what fun!" exclaimed Lady Duxbury. She looked at Marco, her eyes overbright with champagne. "Now it's my turn to dance with you, sir!"

"I shall go sit with Charlotte," said Kate quickly. "I

don't want her to feel that she must sing for her supper, so to speak."

"Indeed," said Cluyne. "It is bit unfair that she must stay inside while the rest of us enjoy the evening. Perhaps instead of dancing, we should all take a stroll in the gardens."

"What an enchanting idea, Your Grace," exclaimed the dowager countess. "I wouldn't mind a bit of exercise myself, after such a splendid meal. And midnight is such a magical hour."

"I shall go inform Lady Fenimore of the change in plans," said the duke.

Rochambert gallantly offered his arm to the dowager's daughter. "Would you care to take a walk with me, *mademoiselle*?" He winked at the countess. "We shall, of course, not stray out of sight of your *maman*."

Kate saw Von Seilig glance her way, but suddenly Marco cut him off. "Miss Woodbridge, shall we continue our *pas de deux* and take a walk to the statuary garden?" he asked. "The view overlooking the lake promises to be quite lovely in starlight."

Kate shot him a quizzical look but did not voice an objection.

The Prussian politely offered to escort the dowager countess, and Tappan quickly followed with an invitation to Lady Duxbury. "An excellent idea, Your Grace," he said as Cluyne returned with Charlotte on his arm. "A last walk around these lovely grounds before duty calls me away will be most welcome."

"What? You are leaving us soon?" Lady Duxbury sounded surprised. "But the party isn't scheduled to end until next week."

"Alas, as I informed the duke several weeks ago, the Foreign Office requires me to leave for Vienna before the rest of you depart. I just received word that makes it necessary to depart on the morrow. Most of our delegation is already in place, and there is much work to be done during the preliminary negotiations." Tappan inclined a bow to the rest of the guests. "Allow me to take my leave of you now. I shall be returning to my own estate this evening, in order to oversee all the last-minute details for travel."

The lady made a face, but the rest of the company offered their good wishes for his journey.

"Indeed, I wish you and Lord Castlereagh good luck in creating a new Europe, now that Napoleon has been banished to Elba," added Cluyne. He raised his glass. "To peace and harmony among all nations."

"I couldn't agree more," said Tappan, returning the salute. The sentiment was seconded by all the other diplomats.

"Yes, and now let us finish with politics and cap off this lovely evening with a moonlit walk," said Rochambert. "Do all the ladies have escorts?"

Out of the corner of her eye, Kate saw the duke murmur something to Charlotte, who visibly hesitated before giving a curt nod.

"Your fellow 'Sinner' looks a little nervous at the prospect of finding herself alone in a dark place with your grandfather," murmured Marco as he led her down the steps to the gardens.

"I doubt that she fears he will try to take liberties with her person," replied Kate. "Whatever else his faults, the duke always behaves like a perfect gentleman."

"What makes you so sure that Lady Fenimore would be averse to his advances?" he countered.

"Don't be absurd."

"Is it so impossible that your friend would welcome a kiss or caress? She lives by herself, now that her sister has married. I would imagine there are times when she is lonely."

Kate's expression pinched. "I—I . . ." Gravel crunched underfoot. "I admit that the idea hadn't occurred to me." The furrow between her brows deepened. "But then, I haven't been thinking too clearly about anything of late."

Marco looked about to make a clever quip, then seemed to catch himself. "Any particular reason?" he asked softly.

The question took her by surprise. "W-why do you ask?"

For an instant she was tempted to confide in him, to share her doubts and fears. *Don't be a fool*, she chided herself. Men like Marco would only exploit a weakness.

"So that you may discover yet another sordid secret to hold over me?" she quickly added. "I am not quite sure why you take such delight in tormenting me, Lord Ghiradelli."

Marco turned their steps off the main walkway, choosing one of the smaller side paths that led along the walled rose garden. "My intention has been to tease you, not to torment you, Kate."

"Oh, is that so? Well, you do a damn good job at making the two seem one and the same." Beneath the bravado, she was dismayed to hear a tremor of uncertainty.

"If what happened this afternoon has upset you—"

"I'm not upset," she interrupted. "As you may have noticed, I wasn't a virgin, so you need not worry that I'm going to kick up a dust over the matter."

He didn't respond, save to fix her with a shadowed stare.

"Do me a great favor and just...just leave me alone." Snugging her shawl around her shoulders, she lengthened her stride and turned sharply through an opening in the boxwood hedge, heading away from the manor house.

Chapter Sixteen

In the pale wash of moonlight her slender silhouette looked very small and vulnerable as it was swallowed up by the darkness. After a moment of indecision, Marco followed at a discreet distance.

The path looped around to the far edge of the formal grounds. Through the branches of an espaliered pear tree, he saw the back side of the conservatory, its pearly glass rising like a fanciful mirage from the night shadows. An owl hooted from the nearby grove of oaks, the ghostly echo sounding strangely plaintive as it floated in the breeze.

He caught up with her at a small stone bench nestled within a screen of evergreens. Hands braced on the weathered granite, Kate was leaning back and staring up at the heavens. High overhead, the constellations glittered with the brilliance of faceted diamonds against a black velvet sky.

She didn't object when he sat down beside her.

"I imagine you are an expert at navigating by the stars," he murmured, after gazing in silence at the winking points of light.

"Given a chronometer and a sextant, I can find my way to any port from the most remote spot in the ocean," replied Kate in a small, unsteady voice. "It's just when I reach land that I seem to have trouble getting my bearings."

"Look there," said Marco, tilting his head back. "That's Orion just above us. Follow the line of his belt and it points to the North Star. *Ursus Major* is close by." He paused for a fraction. "So you see," he added softly, "wherever you are in the world, familiar friends are there to help guide you on your journey."

Kate didn't answer right away.

Marco sat very still, recalling with a pang the long-ago nights of youthful stargazing with his brother. *The heady excitement of wondering where life would take them.* Somehow he had strayed far, far from those times.

Could he ever find his way back?

"That's a very astute observation, sir." When finally she spoke, her voice was barely more than a whisper. "You're right—it should be easy. And yet, at times I can't help feeling a little lost."

"You are not alone in that, Kate." He slid his hand across the rough stone and found hers. "I think we all feel unsure of our place in the universe."

"Even you?"

"*Si*, even me."

"That is hard to imagine," she said wryly. "You always appear so self-confident, so supremely sure of yourself."

"As do you," he pointed out. "Perhaps we have more in common than you imagine."

Kate gave a mock grimace. "I find it hard to think so."

"Then don't. Think, that is. Sometimes it is good just to sit and savor the present moment."

Their fingers twined, and through the thin leather of her glove, the pulse of her heartbeat was warm and steady against his skin. The feeling was oddly comforting. Crickets chirped in the grass, and frogs croaked in the lily pond—the natural rhythms of the night in harmony with their own. A flutter of air wafted through the juniper needles, mingling the faint fragrance of pine with Kate's own sweet scent.

Strange how all he ever sought from women was a willing partner in physical pleasure, mused Marco. A fleeting joining of flesh. Yet Kate touched him in a way he couldn't quite explain.

Which was probably just as well.

Ye gods, that he, a practiced libertine and lecher, was turning sentimental over holding a lady's hand—a *gloved* hand—was a sign that he wasn't thinking straight this evening.

He rose abruptly, breaking the connection between them. "We had better return, before Cluyne sends out a search party. Or, rather, a hunting party, with orders to pepper my hide with buckshot."

She slowly squared the hem of her kidskin glove. "Quite right. My grandfather is already annoyed at my disregard for the rules of propriety. I shouldn't disappoint him again." A look of vulnerability once again shaded her expression.

"Kate," he began.

"You must stop calling me that. I don't recall giving you permission to address me by that name," she said coolly.

Their camaraderie was gone just as quickly as it had come.

"Formality seems a little absurd, given the intimacies we have shared, *bella*," he said, resuming his usual sardonic drawl. "You are welcome to call me Marco."

"I am sure you have plenty of women willing to utter their undying admiration, sir." She dusted her hands and got to her feet. "You don't need me to flatter your vanity."

"Alas, I feel it shriveling by the second."

Her lips twitched. "Good night, Lord Ghiradelli."

At least he had managed to make her smile again. "I'll walk with you back to the main walkway."

"There are no predators here in Kent," she pointed out. "I shall be perfectly safe traversing the ducal lawns."

"Call it an attack of gentlemanly scruples, but I prefer to escort you to within sight of the terrace," said Marco. "Tell your grandfather that I stayed behind to smoke a cheroot. It appears everyone has been enjoying a respite from the rules. I don't think he'll blister your ears with a scold."

"Ha," she said under her breath. "He doesn't need much of a reason to find fault with me."

His resolve to be distant and detached wavered on hearing the catch in her voice. Perhaps it was her damn perfume that was having such an unnerving effect on him.

Whatever the reason, he found himself saying, "It is hard to believe that the duke would judge you so harshly. What more could he wish for in a granddaughter? You are beautiful, intelligent, and fiercely loyal to your friends, as I can well attest to. And you share his passion for plants."

A spasm of emotion flitted across her face, but in the shifting patterns of light and dark, it was impossible to read. "His disapproval runs far deeper. He disowned my mother for marrying against his wishes." She drew in a deep breath, the tiny muscles tensing along the line of her jaw. "I am just a constant reminder of that rebellion."

"Perhaps he regrets his past actions. Have you tried talking about it with him—"

"The duke does not talk," she said quickly. "He pontificates. So the situation is rather hopeless. What's the point of reaching out when I'll only be rejected?"

"For someone who sees most subjects with sharp-eyed clarity, you may have a blind spot in this particular matter."

Her mouth quivered, then pinched to a hard line.

"People change," said Marco softly. *He was living proof of that.*

"You really think so?"

"Yes. I do."

For a moment, he thought he had overstepped his boundaries. Like him, Kate was a very private person and did not let anyone get too close. But after a step or two, she forced a tentative smile. "It's kind of you to offer advice, sir. No matter that it's for naught."

They walked along in companionable silence. Clouds were scudding in from the west, deepening the surrounding shadows. The breeze began to freshen and the rustle of the leaves muffled their steps. Mist rose in silvery tendrils from the tufts of ornamental grasses.

"Let us cut around the conservatory. It's quicker than following the perimeter path," murmured Kate.

As they passed close to the glass walls, a wink of light

appeared within the jungle of dark foliage. It was gone in a flash.

"That's odd." Kate stopped and tried to peer through the glass, but the moisture of the warm air inside had fogged the panes. "The place should be shut up for the night."

"Perhaps someone else is enjoying a private tryst," said Marco. "You have to admit it is a rather romantic setting."

Her frown deepened in concern. "It's not a playground for pleasure. There are a number of very delicate and very rare specimens in this section of the plantings."

"I'm sure no harm has been done. In all likelihood, it's just one of the servants, checking that all is well before he locks the doors."

"Perhaps," she answered. A swipe of her sleeve did nothing to clear the mist from the glass. "However, I will go check on it as soon as I return to the drawing room."

They were about to continue on when, up ahead, the latch to the side door opened with a soft *snick*. A figure emerged and moved swiftly for the cover of the rhododendron bushes.

"Who was that?" Kate craned her neck but the dark shape had already melded into the foliage.

"I am not sure. I didn't catch a glimpse of the face," replied Marco. "It might have been Tappan. And if it was, it isn't any mystery why he was moving so quickly. I, too, would be fleeing from the clutches of Lady Duxbury." He chuckled. "I doubt he escaped with his virtue intact."

She shot him a sour look. "Why is it that ever since the Original Sin in the Garden of Eden, men are always blaming women for their own weakness of the flesh?"

"It was Eve who offered Adam the apple," he replied.

"Have you conveniently forgotten that the serpent was Satan? Who was most definitely male," countered Kate.

"You have a point," conceded *Il Serpenti* with a grin.

Pinching back a smile, she led the way through the shrubbery and regained the graveled walkway. The terrace torchieres blazed brightly, sending up plumes of pale smoke. "Good night, Lord Ghiradelli," repeated Kate.

The tone of dismissal was unmistakable.

"Sweet dreams, Kate," he murmured.

Sweet dreams.

Ha! What with the way her thoughts were tossing and turning inside her head, Kate didn't expect to sleep a wink. She had always prided herself on being intelligent.

But maybe she wasn't so smart after all.

Lifting her gaze from the gravel, she saw her grandfather pacing along the terrace railing. He looked pensive, and in the flicker of the red-gold flames, the lines of age on his craggy face appeared more deeply etched than she had noticed before.

Had she been so sure of her own point of view that she had failed to see the full depth of his character? A stab of uncertainty caused her throat to constrict. Marco's oblique criticisms concerning both Cluyne and Charlotte had served to point out her own glaring faults.

She was so quick to anger, so quick to judge.

No wonder the duke thought her a headstrong hellion. And if he—or any of her friends—ever learned the real truth about her…

Thank God that Marco did not know the full story about her stay in Naples.

"Katharine."

"Sir!" she replied, the word sounding more shrill than she had intended. "Forgive me if I am late in returning. Lord Ghiradelli and I noticed a strange light in the conservatory, so we stopped to investigate. And then he wished to have a smoke by the lily pond, so I showed him the way."

His expression fell for just an instant. "I was not intending a rebuke."

"Oh." Kate couldn't quite meet his eyes.

"I was simply going to remark that it is a—a pleasant evening, is it not?"

"Yes. Indeed. Very pleasant," she stammered. A look around showed that the terrace was deserted, save for Von Seilig and the two Spaniard diplomats, who were quietly conversing over their brandies by the French doors. "Where is Charlotte?"

"Lady Fenimore said she was fatigued and decided to retire for the night," replied her grandfather.

"It *has* been a long day," said Kate, a little nervous at finding herself alone with him when her thoughts were so confused. "I think I shall do the same. But first I shall just check that the conservatory door has been properly locked."

Cluyne frowned. "Simpson does that every evening."

"I know, it's just that with moving the tea service and drinks table out to the terrace, it might have been overlooked." She didn't wish to mention seeing someone come out from the side door. It might only embarrass one—or two—of the guests. Not to speak of raising uncomfortable questions of why she and Marco had moved off the formal paths.

"I shall send one of the footmen," he offered.

"No, no, I'll do it." Anxious to be alone with her thoughts, Kate hastened for the door. "It is on my way, and won't take but a moment."

Her grandfather took several steps and then stopped. "Very well."

"I was just going inside as well, Miss Woodbridge." Von Seilig set down his empty glass. "Allow me to accompany you."

Kate gritted her teeth in frustration. "Thank you," she said curtly, brushing past him without slowing her stride.

The colonel was quick to catch up. "Have I done something to offend you?" he asked quietly.

"No!" Belatedly realizing that the two Spaniards were not far behind them, she lowered her voice. "Forgive me, sir. I assure you that it's not you. I am simply tired and unused to entertaining so many people."

Von Seilig smiled. "I understand. But would you mind if I come with you to look at the lock? Just in case there is a problem, I may be of some help." A twinkle lit his light-blue eyes. "I give you my word that I shall then leave you to your well-deserved solitude."

Feeling a bit churlish for snapping at him, Kate readily agreed. He really was a thoroughly nice gentleman. In fact, she had come to think of him as a friend. "Your company would be most welcome."

Passing the staircase to the guest wing, they turned down the corridor leading to the conservatory. Kate heard the click of steps on the marble treads as the two gentlemen started up to their rooms.

"You have not been called to Vienna early?" she asked, as the colonel paused to light an extra candle.

"No. I have one more meeting in London with the Admiralty next week before I take my leave."

"You must promise to write and give me an account of what it is like in Vienna. The newspapers say that the city will be a very exciting place for the next several months."

"I hope that you will have a chance to visit it yourself, Miss Woodbridge," he replied. "I know that you would find it fascinating."

"I'm sure I would." Perhaps Cluyne would consider a European trip. Inviting Charlotte might be something to think about.

But not at the moment.

The candlelight illuminated the burnished brass fittings of the conservatory doors.

Kate reached out and tested the latch. It held firm for the first jiggle, but then a click sounded and the catch released.

She tried to reengage the mechanism but it would not close properly.

"I think a screw has come loose," said Von Seilig. After passing her one of the candles, he knelt down and angled his own light for a better look. "Yes, that looks to be the problem. I could fix it with the proper tool."

Kate shook her head. "Oh, please, you need not bother. I really don't think there is any harm in letting it go for now. I'll have the head gardener take care of it first thing in the morning."

"You are sure?"

"Quite."

He rose and dusted the knees of his trousers. "I daresay the duke's abode shall be safe for the night."

"Yes." Stifling a yawn, she moved away from the door.

A loose screw was the least of her concerns, considering how unhinged her own emotions were feeling at the moment. "Again, thank you for taking the trouble to check, sir."

Von Seilig turned to retrace his steps, making way for her to continue on into the adjoining corridor. "*Schlafen Sie wohl*, Miss Woodbridge—that is, sleep well."

"*Auf weidersehen*," she answered in German. "I will see you in the morning."

Chapter Seventeen

Hearing a maid knock on Charlotte's door with her morning tea, Kate slipped on her wrapper and peeked into her friend's room.

"Do you mind if I join you?" She brushed back the snarl of curls falling around her face, knowing she must look a fright.

"Did you not sleep well, my dear?" asked Charlotte. "You look a little peaked."

"No, not well," she admitted. "I was... thinking."

Charlotte carefully added two cubes of sugar and a splash of cream to her cup before asking, "About what?"

How to put the tangle of doubts and questions into words? Kate was used to thinking of herself as strong. Tough. Fearless. But maybe her perceptions were not as sharp as she wished to believe.

"About me. And all the stupid mistakes I've made of late. I feel as though my whole world is turning topsy-turvy, and I can't really say why." She blinked. "For someone who is supposed to possess a brain, that doesn't sound very smart, does it?"

Setting down her cup, Charlotte patted the chair beside hers. "Come have a seat, my dear. Unlike a frog or a fruit of a *Mangifera indica*, emotions can't be dissected and studied under a microscope to see how they work. For the most part, feelings defy any attempt to impose rational order on them."

Kate smiled in spite of her jangled nerves. "Would that I could take my blade and slice them into neat little pieces."

"Is there anything in particular that is bothering you?"

"To begin with, there is Marco," she blurted out. "That is, Lord Ghiradelli. Against all reason I—I am very attracted to him. Or rather, a part of me is very attracted to him. The other part knows better." Shivers slithered over her flesh as she recalled their heated coupling. "Unfortunately my brain is dwarfed by the rest of me."

"He *is* handsome as sin," murmured Charlotte.

"Sin," repeated Kate with a grimace. "That is putting it mildly. The man is a rogue, a rake, a rascal." Her breath whooshed out in an audible sigh. "Hell, he ought to have the word 'dangerous' tattooed in black brimstone letters on his forehead."

"Which might scare away the prim and proper young ladies of the *ton*," observed Charlotte dryly. "However, I have a feeling such a sign would likely only make him more intriguing to you."

"Am I that bad?" Kate asked in a small voice.

"My dear, it was not meant as criticism. You have intelligence and imagination—no wonder you find him attractive. He is far more interesting than most men. Like you, he dares to be different."

Kate looked down at her hands, which were tied

together tighter than a bosun's knot in her lap. "Sometimes, I wish that I weren't different."

"Well, don't," said her friend firmly. "It may be difficult on occasion, but it is far better to be a unique individual than to be a pattern card of boring conformity."

The words stirred a fresh prickling of guilt against her already sensitive conscience. "Oh Lud, what I am is a self-absorbed *prima donna*. You have listened for months to my endless whining, always responding with wisdom and patience. While I have never stopped thinking long enough about *me* and my own petty problems to ever ask you about *your* feelings."

"Your friendship has been a great gift to me," said Charlotte.

"But I should have known about the loss of your books," insisted Kate. "I've never thought to ask whether you are happy. Or lonely."

For a moment, the only sound was the stirring of silver against porcelain. "What has agitated such strange thoughts?" asked her friend after blowing a tendril of steam from her cup.

"Marco," answered Kate. "He said a few things that opened my eyes to the fact that I've been looking only at myself lately."

"That is an unfair observation—"

A pelter of steps in the corridor cut off Charlotte's reply. One of the tweenies screamed.

"Good Lord." Kate shot out of her seat. "I wonder what's wrong?"

Before she could move for the door, her maid flung it open and announced the answer.

"Someone has been murdered!"

• • •

Reining his lathered stallion to a walk, Marco blew out his own breath and watched the heated vapor dissolve in the breeze. An early-morning gallop through the estate's vast meadows had put him in a slightly better frame of mind. Sweat loosened his muscles, helping to dispel the tautness of his mood.

"*Carpe diem*, Nero," he murmured, patting his mount's glistening neck.

The horse snorted.

"*Si*, I know you would prefer to fly hell for leather over the moors, but we have a job to do." A job that was getting harder and harder to concentrate on.

Not that it mattered much, he thought with a grimace. In this case, Lynsley's concerns seemed unwarranted. He had learned nothing of interest to report. Still, he was determined to remain alert and observant.

Perhaps it would keep his mind off Kate Woodbridge. Of all the guests, she was the dangerous one.

Dio Madre, the casual flirtations had been meant as a game. A distraction, a devil-may-care bit of teasing. But some perverse imp of Satan had turned the red-hot pitchfork and stuck it back in his own arse.

Marco gritted his teeth as the burn twisted through his gut. *Damn.* He had thought himself impervious to this sort of feeling. Emotional attachments were only asking for trouble. For pain.

What he needed was an assignment that called for dodging blades and bullets. Physical threats he could handle. This mental duel was leaving him cut to shreds.

Perhaps Lynsley was right—perhaps he was losing his edge.

A shout from near the stables roused him from such mordant reveries. Marco looked up to see one of the footmen pelting down the path from the manor house.

Spurring to a canter, he quickly covered the short distance and dismounted. "What's the trouble?" he asked, handing the reins to one of the stableboys.

"Murder, sir!" replied the lad, his eyes wide with excitement. "One of the gentry morts was found dead. Jem is to fetch the coroner right away. And the magistrate."

Murder?

The lad must have it garbled. Marco spotted the head groom and called him over. "I hear there has been a death in the manor house."

"Murder, sir," echoed the man. "Ain't never had such a scandal here. The duke will be most unhappy."

Not to speak of the victim. As he peeled off his riding gloves, Marco asked, "Any idea who?"

"No, sir. John the footman just said there's a gent's body in the conservatory with a fancy silver knife sticking out of his heart."

Slapping the leather softly against his palm, Marco drew his brows together. Like it or not, the duke was about to find his name once again caught up in a swirl of scandal.

And so was his granddaughter.

"Please calm yourself, Alice. There is no need for histrionics," ordered Kate. "I am sure there must be some mistake, and you are only frightening the poor girls by shouting such rumors."

"Trust me, there's no mistake, Miss Kate," replied Alice, once she had caught her breath. "I saw the body myself, and helped Simpson cover the poor soul with a sheet when the parlormaids panicked."

Kate's legs went a little wobbly and she sat back down rather quickly. "Who?" she managed to ask.

"That foreign military gent," answered her maid.

"*Colonel Von Seilig?*" she gasped.

"Aye, I think that's the name Simpson mentioned. He is—was—a sturdy fellow, with blond hair and a scar on his left cheek. His body was found in the conservatory."

"How terrible," exclaimed Charlotte. "But as to murder, surely that's impossible. It must be a tragic accident."

"Not unless he stuck a knife in his own heart," replied Alice.

"My God," whispered Kate.

"Aye, but that's not the worst of it," said her maid grimly. "The blade in question is yours, Miss Kate. That's why I rushed here to tell you."

"*Mine!*" Kate suddenly felt light-headed, as if all the air had been sucked from her lungs. "But that can't be."

"I'm afraid there is little doubt," said Alice. "What do you think the odds are that someone else here owns a silver-handled knife set with Persian turquoise?"

"High enough that we can dismiss the possibility," answered Charlotte. Ever practical, she leaned forward and braced her elbows on the table. "By the by, did you do it, my dear?"

"Y-you need ask?" replied Kate.

"Yes," replied her fellow 'Sinner.' "If you did stab the man, I imagine there would be a very good reason for it, and we would need to start marshalling the facts for your defense."

In spite of her shock, she felt a burble of laughter well up in her throat. "Oh, Charlotte, what would I ever do without your stalwart support and unshakable sense of humor? You are quite the most wonderful friend in the world."

Charlotte blinked several times in succession. Carefully removing her spectacles, she polished them on the sleeve of her wrapper. "You are very special to me, Kate. The Circle of Sin has been a blessing in my old age. But let us not get too sentimental."

"Aye," piped up Alice. "The magistrate will be arriving at any moment, so you had best come with me and get dressed, Miss Kate."

"I am sure we will all soon be summoned to face him," agreed Charlotte.

The speculation proved quite accurate. Within a half hour, word was sent to all the guests requesting their immediate presence in the drawing room.

Standing by the portal, rigid as a pillar of carved marble, the duke avoided meeting Kate's eye as she passed. His expression looked as though it had been sculpted in stone.

Once everyone was accounted for, Cluyne cleared his throat. "I regret to inform you all that an unfortunate incident has taken place here at Cluyne Close. Sometime during the night, Colonel Von Seilig was..." He hesitated, seeming to struggle with how to phrase the death.

The magistrate had no such qualms. "The gentleman was murdered," he announced loudly. "The coroner has not yet made an official pronouncement, but that is a mere formality. There is no question of it."

A collective gasp greeted the statement.

"Sir Reginald Becton, our local magistrate, will be conducting the investigation," said the duke, introducing the man by his side. "He will, of course, need to ask all of us some questions."

The other ladies in the room looked confused or frightened, noted Kate. Save Charlotte—and Lady Duxbury, who fixed her with a spiteful look.

Word must have already spread about the knife.

The gentlemen, though solemn, were quick to voice their own queries.

"Have you apprehended the perpetrator?" asked Rochambert.

"I thought England was a civilized country—how did a murderer gain entrance to a duke's abode?" demanded Vronskov.

"Do we have any idea why?" said Lord Allenham.

Sir Becton raised a hand to silence the murmurs. "Colonel Von Seilig's body was discovered early this morning in the conservatory with a knife pierced through his heart."

The dowager Countess of Hammond let out a little moan and began rummaging in her reticule for her smelling salts.

"As to who and why, that is my business to find out. And be assured that I will." He raked the group with a grim gaze. "To begin with, I shall speak with each of you individually about last evening. The duke has allowed me use of the morning room for that purpose, and I will begin with the ladies."

"Surely that is not necessary," said Vronskov. "The fairer sex should not be subjected to such an ordeal. They are far too delicate."

The magistrate's mouth curled in contempt. "I'll be the judge of that, sir. Perhaps in your country no female has ever committed a violent crime. But I rather doubt it."

The Russian looked affronted but had no retort.

"Lady Hammond, I shall begin with you, if you please."

Revived by a whiff of vinaigrette, the elderly matron rose from the sofa. The rustle of her dark-hued skirts and flapping shawl around her reminded Kate of a ship of the line setting sail into battle. Her two daughters dutifully followed in the mother's wake.

"Hmmph." Becton's eyes narrowed, but then he gave a grudging nod. "Very well, I'll see the three of you together."

An uneasy silence descended over the drawing room. Chairs had been arranged near the hearth, and one by one, the guests settled down to wait, scrupulously avoiding each other's eyes. Several servants quietly set up a table with refreshments, but no one appeared to have any appetite.

Kate chose to stand by the windows, while the duke began pacing the length of the room. Marco, she noted, was the only one who looked unaffected by the shocking news. If anything, he seemed bored by the proceedings. Hands clasped behind his back, he strolled from the curio cabinets to the display of rare engravings, casually studying the art.

Lud, was he actually whistling under his breath?

Forcing her thoughts away from Marco, she tried to concentrate on Von Seilig's murder. She had, in all likelihood, been the last one to see him alive. *Save for the person who had killed him.* It wouldn't take the magistrate long to uncover that fact. And if, in truth, her knife had been used as the murder weapon, what rational explanation could she offer?

Her mind was a blank.

"Miss Woodbridge." The duke's majordomo called Kate for her turn.

It proved to be a very perfunctory interview. Aside from asking her to identify the knife, the magistrate asked a few questions about her movements and when she had left Von Seilig to retire for the night. He wrote down her answers in a small notebook and then dismissed her with a curt nod.

After a lengthy time spent interrogating the other guests, Becton finally reappeared in the main drawing room. "Thank you all for your cooperation. Rest assured that I shall make every effort to resolve this heinous crime as quickly as possible," he announced. "However, due to the gravity of the situation, I cannot permit anyone to leave the estate grounds until further notice. The duke has been informed of this..." He fixed Cluyne with a chilly stare. "And His Grace has kindly extended his hospitality for as long as is required. I will take my leave now to pursue the matter."

However, the magistrate made no move to go. "But first, if I may, I have a few more questions for Miss Woodbridge."

Marco leaned a shoulder against the alcove archway, the subtle shift of position allowing him a better view of Kate's face.

Cluyne started to object to the request, but she quickly cut him off. "Yes, of course. Ask anything you wish."

"If Sir Reginald insists on interrogating you further, let us withdraw to the morning room," growled the duke, shooting a challenging look at Becton. "And this time, I shall come with you."

"There is no need, sir. I have nothing to hide."

The magistrate's small smile of triumph was almost imperceptible, but Marco didn't miss it. Nor did he miss the answering clench of Cluyne's jaw. There did not appear to be any love lost between the two men. And despite the difference of rank between them, Becton was, for the moment, the one who held the upper hand.

"Thank you, Miss Woodbridge," said the magistrate with exaggerated politeness. "I would just like to clarify a few things, now that I've heard statements from everyone." A pause. "You were the last person to see the colonel alive?"

"No, I was not," replied Kate without hesitation.

Becton's eyes narrowed. "Then can you tell me who was?"

"If I could do that, you would have your murderer."

Bravo, bella. Marco smiled at her *sangfroid.* Kate Woodbridge was not easily intimidated.

"Indeed." Becton did not looked pleased with her response. His lips pursed as he consulted his notebook. "Yet I see here in my notes that you were last seen with him. And that the two of you were engaged in a quarrel—"

"No!" exclaimed Kate.

"No?" repeated the magistrate.

The Spanish diplomat coughed. "I regret to say that I distinctly overheard you two disagreeing. Quite loudly."

His companion of the previous night nodded in agreement.

"What were you arguing about?" pressed the magistrate. He made a show of thumbing back through the pages. "A number of people have commented that Colonel Von Seilig was paying particular attention to you. Was he making unwanted advances?"

"We were simply *friends*," said Kate, her voice suddenly taking on a brittle edge.

Perhaps she was aware of how weak the reply sounded, thought Marco.

"Good God, man," interceded Cluyne. "You can't possibly think that my granddaughter—

The magistrate cut him off. "I am making no judgments, Your Grace. Not yet. My job is to find the truth, no matter who is involved."

Lady Duxbury leaned over to whisper in her brother's ear. Marco saw Allenham's gaze narrow. The man's hand slipped to his watch chain, and for several long moments he merely fingered the gold links, watching and waiting as the silence stretched out.

Then Allenham cleared his throat. "Much as it pains me to say it, Miss Woodbridge, I must speak the truth of what I know. Your father was Josiah Woodbridge of Boston, was he not? The owner and captain of the merchant vessel *Kestrel*?"

"Yes," she answered stiffly.

"The same Captain Woodbridge who was involved in a very unpleasant incident in Antwerp? The account I heard mentioned that he absconded without paying a hefty cooperage and repair bill."

"The chandlery shop had grossly overcharged us," muttered Kate.

"What of the disagreement in Lisbon?" pressed Allenham. "During that dispute, word has it that a female aboard the *Kestrel* fired shots at the pursuing longboat, forcing it to give up the chase."

"Shots?" repeated Becton. The word echoed sharply off the polished paneling.

Oh, cleverly done, thought Marco. With one sound, the magistrate had made the lady out to be a dangerous lunatic. Trying to maintain a sense of detachment as the confrontation escalated, he crossed one booted ankle over the other and continued to observe the nuances of word and gesture.

"And what of the time in Algeciras?" went on Allenham. He, too, seemed intent on casting her in an ugly light. "In that city, a merchant complained to the authorities that Captain Woodbridge's daughter had brandished a knife when he tried to come aboard ship to collect on an overdue bill."

"Yes, but..." Kate bit her lip. "You must understand, seaports can be very rough places, filled with unscrupulous people seeking to take advantage of foreigners. Sometimes one is forced to act...boldly in order to fend off danger."

"So, you are admitting that you resorted to force?" demanded Becton. "You fired a pistol? And threatened a respectable burgher with a knife?"

"He was *cheating* us," exclaimed Kate. "I simply scared him off. I never intended any harm."

The magistrate thumbed to a fresh page and touched his pencil to his tongue.

She looked like she wanted to ram it down his throat. "It's not what you think," she protested.

But despite her explanations, Kate Woodbridge was in hot water.

Scalding, really, amended Marco. Which was hardly any wonder, seeing as she was a tempest unto herself. But despite feeling a stab of sympathy, he warned himself to stay detached. Lynsley would expect a dispassionate report of the proceedings.

Kate finally seemed to realize that her words were only being used against her and remained silent. But the tilt of her chin was eloquent in her defiance.

His face ashen, the duke made no further attempt to speak up in defense of Kate. He looked fragile, a mere shell of his usual imperious self.

Thump. The notebook snapped shut. "That will be all for now," said Becton. "If anyone else remembers anything—*anything*—that may be relevant to the investigation, I will be returning here first thing in the morning."

On receiving their release, the guests quickly filed from the room.

Marco was the last to leave, and he took his time in walking toward the guest quarters.

Why, he wondered, was Kate Woodbridge being thrown to the sharks?

Did she kill the Prussian?

He didn't doubt that she had the temper and the courage to do the deed. But it made no sense. Von Seilig would never have forced himself on her. And even if he had, Kate could easily have escaped his clutches without resorting to murder. As for any other motive, he couldn't for the life of him come up with one.

Crossing the marble entryway, Marco saw that this wing of the house seemed deserted. He slowed by the stairs and then turned his steps for the rear of the house. The wall sconces were unlit, leaving the corridor wreathed in shadows. Halfway down its length, Marco flattened himself against the wainscoting as several servants came out of the conservatory, talking in hushed tones about arranging a cart to take the body to the coroner.

They headed off in the opposite direction and after a

moment, he continued on. The latch was unlocked and Becton had not thought it necessary to post a guard.

Might as well have a quick look for himself. His report should include all the gory details.

A sheet lay over the colonel. Marco lifted it gently, noting that the knife had been removed. He felt a twinge of pity on looking at Von Seilig's lifeless face. The Prussian had been a very decent man, upright and honorable to a fault. He did not deserve to have a sliver of steel shoved ruthlessly into his heart.

Did anyone?

Quelling his personal feelings, Marco quickly opened the man's bloodied coat and shirt for a look at the actual wound. The cut, a thin slice, perhaps two inches wide, was located just below the left breast. Leaning low, he carefully probed at the colonel's chest, inspecting the angle of the blade's entry. The flesh was cold to the touch.

Despite his own doubts about eternal salvation, he whispered a terse prayer for the dead man as he checked under the colonel's fingernails for evidence of a struggle. Moving on, he took a moment to look for bruises on the neck before gingerly feeling at Von Seilig's skull for any sign of a blow.

Hmmm. Sitting back on his haunches, Marco stared out at the swaying, shifting leaves. Here he was, in a bastion of civilized society, and yet the primitive laws of the jungle had proved stronger...

A gust rattled the glass panes overhead, reminding him that he ought not linger. Replacing the sheet over Von Seilig's corpse, Marco wiped his fingers on his handkerchief and quietly left the conservatory.

Chapter Eighteen

"I may murder the wretched man myself," muttered Charlotte darkly. "With my bare hands."

Kate closed the door to her rooms and took a seat on the bed. She felt as if she were disengaged from her own body and floating in a fog. When she spoke, her voice sounded very far away. "The magistrate was just doing his job."

"Ha! A magistrate is supposed to be fair-minded." Her friend was bristling with indignation. "How dare he encourage Allenham to tell such tales and then cast them in the worst possible light."

"Allenham only spoke what was true," said Kate, trying to bring herself back down to earth. It did no good to give in to despair. No one was going to fight her battles for her, so she must *think*. Trouble was no stranger, and in the past she had always been clever enough to elude its snapping teeth.

"But he deliberately twisted the truth to make you appear a bloodthirsty savage."

She set her jaw. "I've been called worse."

Alice gave a soft knock and poked her head into the room. "Will you be wanting to take your supper here?" she asked. "Most of the guests have decided to dine in their own quarters, rather than gather for a formal meal."

"No one wants to eat at the same table as a murderess," remarked Kate.

Charlotte snorted. "As if you could stick a knife in a man's ribs."

She felt the blood drain from her face.

"Just let anyone make a nasty remark," muttered her friend, "and I shall cram it back down his—or her—throat."

"Oh, they are far too well-bred to say anything rude to my face. As we know well, the *ton* prefers gossip and innuendo as the weapons to cut up a person's character," said Kate bitterly. "That way, you can't lift a finger to defend yourself."

"I vow, I shall not let some buffle-witted magistrate make a terrible blunder in this case," promised Charlotte. "We've solved far more complex conundrums. We shall get to the bottom of this before Sir Reginald can."

"No, you must *not* get involved, Charlotte!" exclaimed Kate, suddenly picturing Charlotte poking around the conservatory in the dead of night. "This isn't your laboratory or library. There is a ruthless murderer among us, and you must be very careful of what you say or do."

"Pfff, I'm not afraid." Light winked off her friend's spectacles.

"Well, you should be." Kate chafed at her arms, feeling the pebbling of gooseflesh. "Leave it to me. I've experience in navigating through dangerous shoals."

"So do I, my dear. Besides, people tend to underestimate an old lady. I can appear dotty when I want to..." Charlotte assumed a sweetly vacuous expression that Kate had never seen before. "And ask questions that seem quite innocent."

"Your acting skills are impressive," replied Kate. "But please, promise me that you won't do anything rash."

Charlotte gave a small sniff. "I won't do anything *stupid*," she amended.

Kate didn't press the point, knowing it was unlikely she could wring any further concession from her friend. "Lud, I wish I could say the same for myself," she whispered, tucking her legs up under her. "I...I must have made some egregious misstep to find myself in this mess."

"Don't say such a thing." Charlotte wagged an admonishing finger. "Why on earth would you think that?"

"Because..." Kate bit her lip. If Allenham knew about Lisbon and Antwerp, how much did he know about Naples?

A more chilling thought was, how much did Marco know?

He had put two and two together and figured out that she was the elusive cutpurse *Belladonna*. With a bit of simple addition, he might very well hit upon the full sum of her activities in that city.

She fisted the coverlet, feeling a blade of fear twist in her stomach. If he guessed it, would he betray her sordid secret? A tenuous friendship seemed to have formed between them. But Marco was, by his own admission, a man who was not bound by morality. He was driven by his own selfish desires.

Looking up, Kate saw that Charlotte was waiting for her to finish. "Because," she said slowly, "Th-there are things in my past that I am not proud of."

Her friend came and sat beside her. "My dear, we all have things that we regret. Things that we would have done differently. However, it is pointless to dwell on them. We must concentrate on the present, and how we are going to prove you are innocent of any wrongdoing." She tapped her chin. "To begin with, I suggest we go down to the conservatory and have a look at the body." To Alice she added, "Yes, we shall take our supper here in the rooms. I am sure that we will want to start writing up our notes."

Charlotte's enthusiasm was endearing, but it would have to be nipped in the bud. At the moment, however, Kate was too drained to argue. And ghoulish as the idea sounded, it was a good suggestion. Two sharp-eyed scientists, skilled in the art of empirical observation, might very well see something that others missed.

"Very well," agreed Kate. "I'll bring a sketchbook."

Whoever had come out of the conservatory last night had moved lightly and left no footsteps in the bedding of the bushes. Marco rose and brushed the bits of leaves from his trousers as he surveyed the surrounding grounds behind the conservatory. Following a straight line would only lead down to the lake. Any other direction begged the question of why the man did not use the graveled paths.

Likely there was an innocent explanation, he decided. After all, Von Seilig had still been alive at the time.

Marco was about to walk on when he heard the side

door to the conservatory open and shut with a hurried click as someone stepped out from the glass-paned structure.

"Sir, might I have a word with you?"

He turned slowly. "As long as you place your hands palms up and keep them where I can see them."

"That is *not* funny," said Kate.

"You are right." He offered his arm, though he couldn't resist adding, "I should be safe enough, seeing as your knife is in Sir Reginald's hands."

"A good thing, too, or I might be tempted to..." Her words trailed off. "Look, might you sheath your sarcasm for once? I'm not really in the mood for verbal fencing, and I don't have much time. Charlotte is examining the plantings around where Von Seilig was found, but I don't wish to leave her alone too long."

"I shall bite my tongue," he murmured. Turning through an opening in the privet hedge, he chose a more secluded path. "I take it you have sought me out for some specific reason?"

"Yes." She came to halt and crossed her arms over her chest. "I—I have a proposition to make."

"A proposition?" He lifted a brow. "How intriguing."

"A *business* proposition," she stressed. "I have a favor to ask, and as the daughter of a merchant, I am very aware that people rarely act out of altruism. Goods and services must be bought and paid for."

"Even more intriguing, Miss Woodbridge. You have my complete attention."

"I..." Sunlight glinted off her lashes as she looked away. "Drat, this is not going to be easy."

Marco quelled the urge to gather her in his arms and

kiss the look of bleak uncertainty from her face. "Do go on," he said. "I shall refrain from further comment until you are done."

She drew a ragged breath. "Oh, hell, I have nothing to lose." The whisper seemed more for herself than for him. "My life is already in tatters."

"Kate..." He took an involuntary step toward her.

"No. Please." She held up a hand. "You promised to let me finish."

He stopped.

"I have been thinking." Her face tightened, making her cheekbones look sharp as knife blades. Bruised shadows darkened the delicate skin beneath her eyes. "Your cousin Alessandra has hinted that you have experience in certain clandestine activities. On top of that, you are said to be skilled with a sword. And by my own observation, it is clear that you are clever, sir."

Her sidelong glance seemed to seek a reaction and so he nodded.

"So, to get straight to the point, I need your help to discover the killer," she said in a rush. "It's not myself that I am worried about. It's Charlotte. She is determined to help, and I fear she may put herself in danger by asking too many questions."

"I—"

"Wait! Hear me out," she exclaimed. "As I said, I'm not some dewy-eyed schoolgirl who dreams of a white knight riding to her rescue. So I'm willing to pay for your services." Her voice wavered just a touch. "Money does not seem to be important—you are said to be quite rich. Therefore, I had to think of what else you might want. And...and seeing as you demanded...physical contact for keeping silent about my cutpurse past, it seemed that...sex might be the right enticement."

A breeze whispered through the twined ivy, and for an instant, Marco was sure he had misheard her. "I beg your pardon?"

"Sex," she repeated. "I'm offering you my body again in return for your help." Her gaze rose to meet his. "Those are the terms. Do we have a deal?"

"Let me make sure that I understand," said Marco slowly. "You are offering yourself to me, to do with what I will, in return for my sleuthing skills?"

"I'm not expecting any declarations of affection, if that is what you are worried about," replied Kate coolly. The ice, however, did not quite reach her eyes. "And I won't fall into a fit of megrims when you come to collect your payment."

She looked so pale and vulnerable standing there, trying to appear a hard-bitten woman of the world. Guilt lanced through him at the thought that she believed life—and he—was so callous.

"Good God, I am a lecher and a libertine, Kate. But I am not Lucifer Incarnate," he said softly. "Only the Devil himself would take advantage of you in such a way."

The tiny muscles in her neck constricted in a swallow.

"I meant to help in any case," he went on. "I have my own reasons for wishing to learn who committed the crime."

Her expression remained wary, torn between hope and fear.

Kate Woodbridge might have experienced a great many things during her world travels, thought Marco.

But clearly she wasn't used to accepting help. Quickly he drawled, "So, you will have to think of another way of enticing me into your bed."

As he had intended, the teasing quip sparked a flash of indignation in her eyes. "*Me* beg *you* to make love?"

Gone was the look of bleak defeat. Ire now animated her features, bringing the color back to her cheeks. He held back a grin.

"Ha!" she exclaimed. "You may dream until Doomsday, but that will not happen."

"Don't be so sure of it," he murmured.

"Do you really think that every female in Christendom is lusting after you?"

"Well, judging by the number of *billet doux* that I receive..."

"Your arrogance is astounding," muttered Kate.

"Now, now, be nice, Kate." Marco reached out and tucked a wind-loosened curl behind her ear. "After all, we are now partners in crime, if not in bed, so don't you think that we ought to agree to a cordial working relationship?"

"Cordial." Her lips thinned, then slowly curled up at the corners. "Very well. I shall do my damnedest to be nice."

Kate willed her heart to stop hammering against her ribs. But somehow her body was blatantly ignoring the signals from her brain. From the roots of her hair to the tips of her toes, she seemed to be thrumming from the same strange vibrations.

Lud, were her knees really trembling? Only the silly heroines in a novel gave way to girlish emotion. Not tough-as-nails Kate Woodbridge, who had confronted some of the scurviest scoundrels in the world without batting an eye.

So what was she afraid of? Kate blinked, uncertain of the answer.

"Thank you. That is, no doubt, a great concession," said Marco dryly. "Now that we have established the ground rules, perhaps we ought to begin examining the facts of the case. I assume from your earlier statement that you didn't murder poor Von Seilig."

"No. I did not." She lifted her chin. "Do you believe me?"

He nodded gravely. "In fact, I do."

Kate was surprised at how relieved she felt on hearing him say so.

"You see, I had a chance to examine the body."

"Charlotte and I were hoping for a look, but he had already been taken away to the coroner." She hesitated. "Will an autopsy prove me innocent?"

"Not likely," replied Marco frankly. "There is nothing clear-cut, to use an unfortunate term. However, I happen to be familiar with violent death and all the subtle ways that one can commit murder. I saw a number of little things that make me quite sure it was not you who killed him."

"Really?" Scientific curiosity overcame her personal worries. "What sort of things?"

Marco gave a soft laugh. "Most females would be swooning in shock, rather than demanding the gory details."

"By now it should be obvious that I am not like most females."

"Quite." His expression was unreadable as his lazy, lidded gaze locked on her face.

She felt herself turning uncomfortably warm under the scrutiny. Which Kate Woodbridge did he see? The eccentric bluestocking? The hot-tempered hellion? The bold-as-brass thief?

The tawdry jade who had just offered herself on a platter?

To hell with what he thought. She lifted her chin. "And no doubt you find my behavior sinks me beneath contempt."

"Who am I to judge?" he said softly. "It seems to me that you have shown admirable resourcefulness and courage in dealing with some very difficult situations." His mouth twitched. "Considering my own flouting of Society's rules, it would be awfully hypocritical to condemn you for doing the same."

"Most gentlemen would not be so egalitarian," she said.

At that, a glint of amusement lit in his eyes, sun-flecked sparks dancing across the deep topaz hue. "By now it should be obvious that I am not like most gentlemen, Kate."

True—no other man had such beautiful brandy-hued eyes. Dark, sensuous. Mysterious.

"Speaking of observation," she finally managed to say, "I'm anxious to hear what you noticed. About Von Seilig, that is."

"To begin with, he was not killed by your knife."

She frowned. "But the magistrate said that the blade had pierced the colonel's heart. Surely he could not be mistaken about that."

"A sliver of steel was shoved between his ribs," agreed Marco. "But the wound did not bleed overly much.

I'm quite sure that he was already dead when he was stabbed."

Her consternation deepened. "Then why would someone go to the trouble of stealing my knife?"

"Actually, I believe you left it in the herb basket," answered Marco. "As for why someone would use it, I should think that would be obvious to someone of your intelligence."

"But *why*?" A numbness seized her, making it difficult to speak. "Why would someone want to frame me for murder?"

"A good question. Let us hope we can uncover the answer."

We. The simple word was like a lifeline thrown into a storm-tossed sea. And at the moment she felt a desperate need to cling to some strand of assurance that she wasn't alone.

"Thank you," she blurted out. "I confess, I am very grateful for your offer of help, Lord Ghiradelli. It's very... noble of you."

Marco leaned in close, and for the hitch of a heartbeat she thought he was going to kiss her.

But instead, his mouth remained hovering a hairsbreadth from hers. "Don't make the mistake of thinking me noble, *cara*. I am not." The earthy scent of him swirled around her, forcing the air from her lungs. "I'm an amoral scoundrel, and you must never forget that."

Kate touched the tips of her fingers to his cheek. He flinched but she didn't draw them away. "And yet, *Il Serpenti*, it seems to me that your fangs are not quite as sharp as you would have everyone believe."

"Serpents are cold-blooded creatures, ruled by a

primitive brain," he said in a rough whisper. "They strike without warning." With a flick of his hand, he thrust her away. "Don't get too close, Kate. I'm poison."

She slowly rubbed at her wrist.

"Go back inside and take Lady Charlotte up to her rooms. I'd like a little time to dig around in the conservatory, and it would probably be best if I did so alone." He didn't wait for a reply, but turned on his heel and cut across the swath of lawn.

Kate watched his wind-whipped hair dance around his shoulders, suddenly reminded of Medusa and her head of writhing snakes. *Dangerous, dangerous.* The very air seemed to hiss a warning.

Then the clouds scudded over the sun, and his shape was swallowed in shadows.

Chapter Nineteen

"What the devil do you think you are doing in here?"

Charlotte straightened with a start from the conservatory walkway, nearly dropping her brass-handed magnifying glass. "Really, sir!" she huffed, her face flushing in indignation. "Must you creep up on me like that?"

"I can hardly be accused of 'creeping' in my own residence, Lady Fenimore," said Cluyne stiffly.

"A residence that is now home to a murderer," she pointed out.

His nostrils flared as he drew in a sharp breath. "Which is all the more reason for you to be ensconced in the safety of your rooms, rather than wandering around alone, looking for trouble."

"*Trouble?*" she sputtered. "I am looking for any evidence that might help prove Kate innocent of the crime."

The duke pinched at the bridge of his nose. "You—you don't think she did it, then?"

"Of course she didn't! How could you think that?"

"Don't ring a peal over his head, Charlotte." Kate stepped out from the cluster of arica palm trees. "His Grace can't be blamed for thinking the worst. He doesn't know me."

Cluyne's expression crumpled as Charlotte scowled at him. "And whose fault is that?" she asked.

"I..." He hesitated, looking uncertain. But as she waggled her brows, he lurched forward and gathered Kate awkwardly in his arms. "Lady Fenimore is right to rail at me. I have only myself to blame," he murmured against her hair. "Forgive me, Kathar—Kate. This is all my fault."

Kate stiffened, then let herself soften in his embrace. "No, it isn't," she said weakly. "I haven't exactly been a pattern card of propriety. I'm sorry you had to hear such sordid things."

"I should have shielded you from the harshness of life earlier, but I was too deucedly proud." Remorse shaded his face. In the filtered light, the lines around his eyes looked as though they had been gouged with a chisel. "If you will let me, I will try to help now."

To her dismay, tears were coursing down her cheeks. She couldn't seem to stem the tide.

"Of course she will," said Charlotte, while Kate was still struggling to find her voice. "It's never too late for love to take root," she added decisively.

"I've turned into quite a watering pot of late," sniffed Kate. "The head gardener need not send his bucket brigade to this section of the plantings."

Cluyne offered her his handkerchief—after he had dabbed at own his eyes.

"Thank you." She blew her nose. "Sorry. I'm afraid that your cravat looks like it's been hit by a tidal wave, sir."

"You are welcome to dampen every starched length of linen in Cluyne Close," said the duke, his voice a little watery at the edges. He cleared his throat with a cough. "I hope . . . that is, perhaps one day you will consent to call me something other than 'sir' or 'Your Grace.' "

"Cluyne." It felt a little strange on her lips, but Kate decided she could get used to it. "Thank you, Cluyne."

His features softened in a tentative smile.

"Sentiment is all very well," said Charlotte briskly. She once again brandished her magnifying glass. "But we have a murder to solve."

"I'll send to Bow Street for the best Runner money can buy," began the duke.

"No!" exclaimed Kate. "That might only open Pandora's box. If he delves too deeply into the past . . ." She let her voice trail off. "I beg you, let me try to resolve this myself," she added, after taking a moment to order her thoughts. "I'm innocent, so there must be a way to prove it."

"My dear, I understand your concerns, but this is far too dangerous to undertake on your own. Your neck is more important than your reputation," said Charlotte. "We can weather any past scandal."

The duke nodded.

"No, you don't understand. And please don't ask me to explain." Some things were better left unsaid, thought Kate. "I am not unaware of the dangers. I have asked Lord Ghiradelli for his aid, and he has agreed to help uncover the truth."

Cluyne let out a low snort. "That does not make me rest any easier. The man appears to be interested in naught but wine and women. What possible help can he be?"

"Yes, Ghiradelli is a rake and a reprobate," agreed

Kate. "But our friend Alessandra, who is his cousin, has hinted that he has hidden facets to his character."

"True," corroborated Charlotte, her mouth pursing in thought. "I am under the impression that he is involved in some clandestine activities for the government, but it is all very secret."

The duke looked unconvinced. "Well, he does a deucedly good job of appearing an indolent fribble."

"He's already determined that Colonel Von Seilig was not killed by my knife." She went on to explain why.

"How very clever of him to have noticed such a thing," mused Charlotte.

"He appears to have a brain buried inside that pretty head," conceded Cluyne. "But clever or not, it still doesn't bring us any closer to the real culprit."

"I've not yet finished my search," said Charlotte.

"And I would rather that you didn't." Before her friend could protest, Kate went on. "There is an old adage about too many cooks spoiling the broth. If we are all tripping around Cluyne Close searching for clues, we will only alert the murderer of our suspicions. For now, I think it best to appear willing to let the magistrate handle the investigation."

Charlotte made a face, but the duke gave a grudging nod. "I suppose that makes sense. Though I have no great faith in Sir Reginald to see that justice is done in this case."

"It seemed obvious to me that there is no love lost between the two of you," said Charlotte. "Normally, one would expect a baronet to show some deference to a duke. Is there a reason for the animosity?"

"Yes, I'm afraid there is," admitted Cluyne. "A year ago, Sir Reginald asked me to appoint his nephew to the living of a lucrative parish on my lands in Derbyshire.

However, after meeting with the young man, and making inquiries about his character, I had enough reservations that I could not agree to the appointment. Sir Reginald has been bitterly resentful ever since, and I daresay he will use this opportunity to punish me and my family."

The duke passed a hand over his face and heaved a mournful sigh. "It is yet another way that my imperious actions have come back to hurt you, Kate."

"You did what you thought was best," she replied. "That is all any of us can do."

"Let us leave regrets and recriminations in the past, along with the old mistakes," added her friend. "We must concentrate our attention on the present. And the future."

"A wise suggestion, Lady Fenimore," said Cluyne. "Shall we move on to the library? If we are to sit back and wait for now, we might as well put the time to good use. I've found several books on Far Eastern medicinal herbs among the manuscript collection that I think both of you would find very interesting."

"Very well," agreed Kate, though she had no intention of abiding by the rules she had spelled out for the others. One of the first lessons she had learned after embarking on a life of seafaring adventure was that she had to look out for herself.

"You go on," said Charlotte. "I'll join you shortly."

Kate narrowed her eyes.

"No need to give me that basilisk look. I'm not up to any mischief. I'm just going to put my tools away and then fetch my sketchbook. I left it yesterday on the potting bench by the *Brassavola nodosa* specimens."

"Don't dally," admonished Cluyne. "If you don't come soon, I shall return and carry you bodily from this place."

Giving a huff of indignation, Charlotte shook her trowel at him. "Hmmph. I should like to see you try."

The exchange brought a ghost of a smile to Kate's lips. *Cluyne and Charlotte?* It seemed an odd mix. But as Ciara—her fellow "Sinner" and chemistry expert—had once said, when one combined volatile ingredients and then added a spark of heat, the results were often unpredictable.

"Come, Cluyne." Touching his sleeve, she urged him forward. "I am sure Charlotte will be quick about it."

"Hmmph," he echoed, but allowed himself to be led away.

Curious, Kate could not help remarking, "I hope you are not offended by Charlotte. She does not hesitate to speak her mind."

"So I have noticed."

"I know you do not approve of independent females, but she had to be strong. Her late husband ran through her money and his, leaving Charlotte with naught but a mountain of debts. It was only her own resourcefulness and refusal to be bullied by creditors that allowed her to keep her home."

His brows twitched together. "I don't disapprove of Lady Fenimore. She has a tart tongue, to be sure, but it is hard to find fault with her intelligence."

"Very hard," murmured Kate. "She is one of the smartest, most sensible people I know."

Perhaps it was merely the muted light in the corridor, but it seemed that a tinge of color had crept to the duke's cheeks. "Well, let us hope she is sensible enough not to linger in the conservatory for any length of time. I do not like it above half that we are leaving her alone in such a deserted place."

A finger of fear tickled at the back of Kate's neck. Perhaps he was right. She slowed her steps and looked back over her shoulder at the glass doors. In the deepening shadows, they appeared as opaque as polished obsidian. "Shall we wait for her here?"

The duke did not have a chance to reply before the brass-framed glass flew open and Charlotte hurried out, her work boots drumming a brusque tattoo on the polished parquet.

"Is something amiss?" demanded Cluyne.

"To be truthful, I am not entirely sure." Her friend's voice was a bit breathless and she was wearing a very strange expression. "It may be nothing, but one of the rare jungle plants from New Guinea has also been murdered."

Cupping his hands to his face, Marco pressed close to the glass and watched to make sure that the flicker of lamplight was not returning.

"Finally," he muttered under his breath, seeing no sign of movement through the thick foliage. He gave it a few more moments, just to be sure, before easing open the outer door and slipping inside.

The sky was shrouded by a thin scrim of clouds, dimming the glow from the crescent moon. The air was still, and aside from the sound of dripping water close by, the cavernous space was as silent as a grave.

An apt metaphor, he decided. Mist pooled around his ankles as he walked lightly along the mossy bricks, adding to the eerie atmosphere. He half expected to see the spectral figure of Charon glide out from the shadows, ferrying the dead across the silvery River Styx.

Stop seeing ghosts. Marco paused to get his bearings. A cluster of tropical trees loomed large in their terra-cotta pots, their jagged jungle shapes taking on a menacing cast in the gloom.

Phantoms. Figments of his imagination. For the space of several heartbeats, Marco lost track of why he was here.

Helping a damsel in distress?

His inner compass was behaving oddly, he thought ruefully, its needle swinging erratically from east to west, from north to south. No doubt Kate could explain in great detail how magnetic forces within the earth could play havoc with a delicate scientific instrument, he thought glumly.

He didn't need a technical treatise to define what hidden current was exerting an inexorable pull on him. Kate Woodbridge was a powerful force of nature unto herself, and much as he tried to resist the pull, it was becoming increasingly harder to hold firm.

If only, if only... The tiny back-and-forth ticking of the compass point seemed to mock his innermost feelings, the ones he kept locked deep inside. Be damned with foolish longings that would never be said aloud.

"Damn." The oath trailed off into the surrounding tangle of leaves. Reversing directions, Marco made his way back to the outer pathway. Moving around the perimeter of the octagonal sanctuary would bring him to the section where Von Seilig's body had been discovered.

"Murdered?" said Cluyne. "That is not humorous, Lady Fenimore."

"It wasn't meant to be." Charlotte frowned. "I noticed that it was missing and on closer inspection noted that it had been snipped at the roots."

"You must be mistaken. The head gardener always informs me if any plant dies. Especially a valuable specimen."

"I am quite certain," insisted Charlotte. "In fact, Kate and I were examining it just yesterday, and it was in perfect health."

"You mean to say the *Nerilida toxinsis* is missing?" she asked.

Charlotte nodded.

"Bloody hell," she exclaimed, then darted an apologetic look at her grandfather. "Forgive my language. But that is not only an extremely esoteric, exotic plant, it's an extremely dangerous one."

"Are you sure?" asked Cluyne in a low voice.

"Yes," replied Kate. "It's not common knowledge, but if the beans from the seed pods are boiled with any type of alcoholic liquid, the resulting syrup makes a very potent poison. The native tribes use fermented coconut milk, but brandy or port will also work." She gave an involuntary shudder. "It is used to coat arrowheads and is far more lethal than South American curare. It's harmless if ingested, but a tiny nick from a tainted tip or blade can kill a man within a minute. And it leaves no trace—it simply seems that the victim died of heart failure."

The duke paled. "But only an expert in botany would know that," he said slowly.

Charlotte looked pensive. "Von Seilig was very interested in plants, wasn't he?"

"I trust you aren't suggesting that he murdered himself," said Kate, more sharply than she intended.

"No, but..." Charlotte shook her head. "I am not quite sure what to think. It's simply a strange coincidence."

More than strange, thought Kate. It was sinister. Though, for the life of her, she couldn't figure out why the disappearance of an obscure plant would have any bearing on the colonel's murder. Feeling a pain begin to pulse against her temples, she turned away from the glare of the wall sconce.

"I confess, it's sinister. It was a young specimen, and there weren't many beans. But enough to make a small amount of poison."

The three of them stood in silence for several long moments before the duke spoke up. "I think we ought to send to Bow Street for a Runner."

"Please, Cluyne. I tell you that will only cause more trouble—" Spying a flutter of silk in the connecting corridor, Kate bit off her words. "Who's there?" she demanded.

"Oh, forgive me! I did not mean to intrude." Lady Duxbury stepped out from the shadows, the swish of her skirts amplified by the uneasy silence. "I felt in need of a breath of air and thought I would not be disturbing anyone if I took a walk through this part of the house."

"We were just doing the same," said the duke tersely. "I should not want any of my guests to feel that they are a prisoner in their rooms."

"How horribly upsetting this must be for you." Her tone was sympathetic, but Kate thought she detected a glint of malice in her gaze. "Let us hope that the magistrate finds the culprit quickly."

"Indeed," murmured Cluyne.

"Well, I am sure you wish to be alone." Excusing herself with a dimpled smile, Lady Duxbury turned and headed back the way she had come.

As the sound of her steps faded, Charlotte pursed her lips. "What mischief is afoot here?" she muttered.

"What do you mean?" asked Cluyne.

"The countess seems to enjoy playing nasty little games that stir up trouble."

The corridor seemed to grow colder. Kate rubbed at her arms, trying to dispel a sense of unease. "I can't imagine what harm she can do. As far as I can tell, wielding her feminine wiles and flirting with attractive men are her paramount concerns."

"Her brother was quick to offer up unsavory stories about your past," pointed out Charlotte. "I wonder how he knew such details."

So do I, thought Kate. But aloud she merely dismissed the comment with a small shrug. "In the scheme of things, Lady Duxbury is the least of my worries."

The duke shifted his stance uneasily, as if he were standing on dangerous ground. "Cluyne Close has become home to a nest of vipers."

A fresh chill slithered over her skin.

"Let us continue on to the library," he added when neither she nor Charlotte replied. "I think I am in need of brandy, to go along with the books."

"A glass of sherry would be most welcome," murmured Charlotte.

"You go on," said Kate abruptly, suddenly feeling the overwhelming need to find Marco and tell him about the missing plant. "I feel a headache coming on and think I shall retire for the evening."

"I'll come—" began her friend.

"No, please. I would rather be alone, if you don't mind."

Charlotte's expression betrayed a pinch of doubt, but after a moment she nodded. "Very well. If you are sure…"

"Quite. I shall see you both in the morning." She

squeezed her grandfather's arm and set off down the side corridor, intending to sneak back to the conservatory through another part of the house.

Common sense said that Marco should be told this new information as soon as possible, she reasoned. Yet at heart Kate knew that it was not logic's whisper that was stirring the odd little fluttering in her chest. She found herself craving his company, if only for a brief moment. A touch, a smile, even a sardonic word of teasing would help steady her spirit for the long, dark night ahead.

Lud, was she really turning into a helpless horrid novel heroine? A starry-eyed schoolgirl with dreams about fairy-tale heroes?

The arched window reflected her self-mocking grimace as she turned into the alcoved entryway. Pausing, she squeezed her eyes shut and pressed her brow to the glass, hoping the chill would help dispel such childish fantasies. In a moment, she would lift her lashes and see the real Kate Woodbridge.

But it was not her own hazy image that she saw through the breath-fogged panes. A quick swipe of her sleeve showed that someone was hurrying along the path leading down to the lake.

Without hesitation, Kate unlatched the side door and stepped out into the night.

Chapter Twenty

Keeping close to the mullioned panes, Marco followed the perimeter path of the conservatory, alert for any sign of movement. Satisfied that all was still inside, he ventured a glance out through the thick glass. Turning the corner of the octagon had brought him parallel with the trellised rose garden and the lawns leading down to the lake. The dark, thorny vines of the climbing bushes twined in and out of the slats, nearly obscuring the painted wood. A breeze tugged at the leaves, scattering a shower of pale petals over the grass.

He was just about to continue on when a movement behind the latticework caught his eye. He froze, waiting for the shape to emerge from behind the screen.

Interesting.

What was Kate Woodbridge doing prowling the grounds late at night? *Looking for another victim?* No, he was sure she was innocent of murder. But any other reason seemed just as implausible, unless…

Unless she was meeting a clandestine lover.

A lover, he repeated to himself. Given several of his encounters with the lady—the Naples brothel, the deserted conservatory—he knew that she had no qualms about defying the rules of Polite Society. And, after all, she had been quick to offer her body to him as payment for services.

Yet despite all her hard-edged bravado, Marco sensed that she didn't really have much experience with men. Not that a loss of virtue required much time or effort, he thought sardonically.

In and out...

The door shut noiselessly behind him. Treading lightly over the soft grass, he ducked into the shadows of the privet hedge and quickened his steps to keep her in sight. It was, of course, none of his business if she was heading to a midnight tryst. Revealing her private life, her secret passions, was not part of their bargain. But against all reason, some elemental force, some hidden magnetic current, seemed to pull him along.

The clench of his hands was merely for balance, not because of some primitive urge to thrash any man who dared touch her. Marco willed his fists to relax as the sloping lawns gave way to a grove of ancient oaks. The way here was wilder—an ideal place for a rendezvous.

Bloody hell. Marco was a little surprised by the vehemence of his reaction. Kate was perfectly free to take a lover. To slide her tongue into the man's mouth, to lift her skirts and open her shapely thighs to his touch...

A twig snapped under his errant step.

Up ahead, Kate spun into the gnarled shadow of a tree.

Marco took cover behind a thicket of brambles. From his vantage point he could now see that there was another figure on the path ahead of them. It was a lady who was moving none too quietly over the rough ground to a small clearing overlooking the lake. A faint wash of starlight reflected off the smooth waters, giving a fleeting glimpse of her face as she looked around her.

He hesitated for an instant, then made his move.

"Mmmph!"

His hand quickly smothered Kate's surprise. "Sssshh," he hissed, trapping her body against the rough trunk.

At her nod, he slowly released her mouth.

"What are you doing here?" she demanded in a whisper.

"I could ask the same of you," he replied.

Kate squirmed against his grip, trying to shift enough to keep her eyes on her quarry. "I should think that would be obvious. I'm curious as to why Lady Duxbury is sneaking around the grounds at night."

"Given the lady's reputation, I should think that would also be obvious," said Marco. "She's likely here for a tumble in the hay."

Lady Duxbury began pacing in a tight circle.

"A bed would be far more comfortable," muttered Kate under her breath. "And convenient."

"Some females like to make love outside the bedchamber." His groin was now pressing up against her bottom. His senses aroused by the unexpected stab of jealousy, he was acutely aware of her softly rounded shape. "They find an exotic setting adds to the excitement."

"Thank you for such enlightening information. But if I want a primer on prurient behavior, I shall read

Casanova's memoirs." Sarcasm laced her throaty whisper, yet a clenching shudder betrayed her body's reaction to the intimate contact.

"The book is very long and very boring." He slid his hands down her back, drawing a slow, teasing trail along her spine, and set them on the swell of her hips. As a frisson of fire laced through the layers of clothing, Marco realized that she was not quite so cool to his closeness. "I could give you a far more intriguing guide to the art of seduction."

"S-stop that," she said, her voice a little shaky. "It's... distracting."

A quick look confirmed that Lady Duxbury was still alone.

"I can't help it, Kate." Marco nuzzled her neck, breathing in the heady sweetness of her scent. By now, its essence had entwined itself in his consciousness. It felt a part of him. "You are a powerful distraction."

She gave a little gasp as he pulled her closer. "It's not me; it's the silks and satins that cause the effect," she stammered. "No doubt you would flirt with the scullery sink if it wore skirts."

"*Si*, I am attracted to women, but this is different, *cara*," said Marco. "Call me bewitched, call me bedeviled, but you—"

"Sssshh!"

He heard the scrape of boots on the pebbled path and fell silent, his senses on full alert. Facing the challenge of a mission always sharpened his awareness. A rush of anticipation, intoxicating as any brandy, bubbled through his blood. Beneath him, Kate tensed. She, too, was primed for action.

Branches crackled as a man appeared from behind a thicket of gorse. A long black coat muffled his silhouette while his upturned collar and broad-brimmed hat hid his face.

"Damn," muttered Marco, watching Lady Duxbury greet the newcomer with a voluble cry, only to be signaled to keep her voice down. "I don't think we'll be able to make out what they are saying."

"Perhaps if we moved closer." Kate tried to twist free.

He kept her pinned to the tree. "No, we can't risk giving ourselves away." Craning his neck, he tried to get a peek at the man's features.

Kate swore softly as the stranger suddenly shifted his stance, turning his back to them. "Did you recognize him?"

"No."

Lady Duxbury appeared agitated. Flinging up her hands, she fell back a step and shook her head.

A lover's quarrel? wondered Marco.

Whatever they were discussing, the conversation quickly came to an end. After calming her with a kiss, the man spoke, rapidly and without interruption, then gestured for her to return to the manor house. Lady Duxbury looked reluctant to leave, but a small shove urged her on. Clutching her skirts, she lingered for a last look before starting back up the steep path.

The stranger remained at the edge of the clearing until the sound of her steps died away. Turning to retrace his steps, he kicked viciously at a sliver of stone, sending it arcing into the water. The splash shattered the glassy calm, sending black waves rippling across the silvery surface.

"Our unknown paramour did not come here for a romantic encounter," murmured Kate. "Any idea who it was?"

"No." Marco unknotted his cravat and turned his lapels to cover his white linen shirt. "But I intend to find out."

"And so do I."

He pushed her back against the tree. "Don't be a bloody fool," he said roughly. "You'll only be in the way."

"I'm just as good as a man in moving silently through the night," she reminded him. "Maybe better."

"Look, we don't have time to argue."

"Please." A flicker of moonlight hung for an instant on her lashes, lighting the look in her eyes.

Marco forced himself to look away. "*A diavolo*—women!" he said through gritted teeth. "If you dare shed a tear I shall throw you into the lake."

"I'm a very good swimmer," she countered.

He bit back a harried laugh. He had never met any female as fearless as Kate. Her courage was fascinating. And frightening. It was one thing for a dissolute wastrel like himself to risk his worthless life. The thought of her charging into the unknown made him want to keep her wrapped in his arms, shielded from harm.

"It's too dangerous," he protested.

"I have faced danger for most of my life," she said softly. "It's my neck that is at stake, and I'd rather not trust it to anyone but myself."

Don't. The voice of reason warned Marco that it would be a grave mistake to give in to her demand.

"Please," she repeated.

Ah, but when had he ever listened to wisdom?

"Don't expect me to act like a gentleman. If we run into trouble, it is every man for himself."

Kate tied the ends of her shawl around her waist. "Well, then, it's a good thing that I am a female who can fend for herself."

"Watch where you place your foot." The whispered warning floated down from the top of the estate wall. "One of the stones is loose."

Squeezing her fingers into a rough crevasse, Kate climbed nimbly past the trouble spot.

"Try not to make so much noise," growled Marco. "It sounds as if a troop of Hussars is storming the gate."

"Skirts are a cursed nuisance," she replied through her teeth. "I should like to see you try to scale this height with silk flounces tangled around your ankles."

"I have done so." He caught her hand and pulled her up beside him. "On more than one occasion."

"I don't dare ask," replied Kate, though she would have liked to. She was growing more and more curious about his past life. The rakehell wenching, the dissolute drinking seemed like a suit of armor rather than his real skin. But whether it was shielding a sensitive nature or imprisoning it was still something of a mystery.

"You should," shot back Marco. "The stories are quite outrageous."

"Everything about you is outrageous." She met his taunting gaze with a level smile. "Or so you would have everyone believe."

"Don't let your imagination deceive you, *bella.* All women want men to be heroes, but I am exactly what I seem."

"You have no idea what I want," said Kate softly. How could he, when she herself wasn't sure how to define the sharpening sense of longing that was cutting at her resolve?

"At present, I hope it is to avoid making a muck-up of this night." Marco broke off eye contact. "Ready?"

"Lead the way."

Rolling onto his belly, Marco began slithering along the narrow ledge.

As she followed, Kate squinted into the gloom. The slate-roofed house rose up from behind the spiky silhouette of an unpruned boxwood hedge. It was an unattractive structure, its unbalanced lines and heavy facade smudged in darkness, save for a single flicker of light in one of the lower windows. The wall bordered the rear garden. A row of tall juniper bushes abutted the mortised stone, and Marco dropped down lightly into the shelter of their shadows. The grounds had an air of neglect about them. Clumps of weeds sprouted among the border plantings and the narrow swath of lawn had not been cut in some time.

"The Foreign Office ought to pay its diplomats better," murmured Kate.

"That, or Lord Tappan ought to curb whatever private appetites are eating away at his coffers."

"You are one to talk."

"I can afford my vices," answered Marco grimly. "The same cannot be said of the baron." He made a quick survey of the surroundings. "I saw only the front grounds when I was here before. Out there, he has managed to keep up appearances."

"What else is he hiding?" mused Kate.

"We shall see—metaphorically speaking, that is." He glanced down at the pooled hems of her skirts. "I don't suppose it would do any good to ask you to stay here. If we have to move fast, I fear you will fall flat on your face."

Twitching up the silk, Kate drew a knife from the small sheath strapped to her leg. With a few swift slices, she shortened her gown to midcalf length. "Satisfied?" she asked, shoving the scraps beneath the evergreen branches.

"I would have preferred another foot or two," he answered dryly. "Do you always walk around armed to the teeth?"

"A lady never knows when she might have to defend herself."

"Well, let us hope tonight is not one of those times. One dead body is enough to account for."

Kate flinched, but thankfully he didn't seem to notice.

"Do you mind if I take the blade for now?"

To her own surprise, Kate handed it over without argument. "Why would Tappan lie about having to leave for Vienna this morning? If he's engaged in an illicit affair with Lady Duxbury, it would be far easier to conduct it at Cluyne Close."

Marco didn't answer.

Questions, questions. Kate felt a little light-headed, confusion suddenly swirling her senses, thick as an ocean fog. It didn't help that her nose was just inches from his upturned collar and every ragged breath was filling her lungs with his thoroughly masculine musk. The heat rising from his whipcord muscles only intensified the effect.

She felt him flex his shoulders, and an animal awareness thrummed through her. All pretenses were stripped away by the subtle move—the indolent rake hardened to a lithe, lean predator, his sleek strength coiled and ready to spring at the jugular.

Her throat constricted as she swallowed a tiny sound.

He turned slightly, the needled shadows giving a menacing cast to his expression. And yet she knew she had nothing to fear from him.

"Wait here for my signal." With catlike quickness, Marco crossed the lawn in a low crouch. Creeping close to the leaded windows, he angled a peek over the sill.

Kate strained to see through the half-drawn draperies, but could make out only a vague blur of muddled shapes. From this perspective, the house looked even more forbidding. The weight of the gloom hung heavy in the air, and as the chill from the damp earth crept along her exposed ankles, she realized that she was glad not to be alone in the dark, deserted grounds.

A flash of steel cut off her mordant thoughts. Before Marco could wave the knife again, she raced across the grass and dropped to the ground beside him.

Pressing a finger to his lips, he cocked an ear to listen. Kate heard voices, but the window was shut, muffling the words.

Damn, she mouthed.

Switching the knife to his other hand, Marco inched up the wall and carefully pushed the point between the wooden casement and the iron-framed glass. A deft flick eased it open a crack.

"...I don't like complications, Lord Tappan." The voice was raspy and heavily accented. *Russian? German?*

Hungarian? Kate couldn't tell. "Murder was not part of our original negotiations."

"Oh, come, every diplomat knows it's often necessary to improvise," replied the baron.

Kate heard the clink of crystal and a splash of liquid.

"You are quite the cold-blooded bastard," said the stranger.

"As are you," countered Tappan, sounding unruffled. "Otherwise you would not have had any interest in the deal that I proposed to you."

A harsh laugh rattled the glass. "Touché."

Fisting her hands, Kate tried to squeeze away the icy prickling in her palms. The thought of Von Seilig lying lifeless in the morgue made her want to smash the panes into a thousand slivered shards.

Marco touched a boot to her knee and shook his head in warning. She blinked at him, feeling tears give way to righteous anger.

"But just out of curiosity, why was it necessary to kill the colonel?" continued the stranger. "Prussia's objection to my country's proposal would have been moot, once I used your little secret to eliminate the real opposition."

"He was simply in the wrong place at the wrong time," explained Tappan. "He came back to the conservatory in order to fix the broken door latch. Being the thorough Prussian that he was, he decided to make an inspection before locking up. I was well hidden, but he spotted the evidence of my digging. Given that his hobby was botany, I feared that he would realize what plant was missing and immediately report it to the duke."

"It was clever of you to kill him with the granddaughter's

knife," murmured the stranger. "How did you manage to have it with you?"

"I didn't," said Tappan smugly. "While Von Seilig was bending down to examine the soil, I crept up behind him and hit him with my hammer—just enough to stun him but not crack his skull. Pressure on the carotid artery finished the job without leaving any marks of a struggle."

A wave of nausea washed over Kate as she listened to his dispassionate account of the crime. He might have been describing what he had for breakfast or his valet's newest recipe for boot polish.

"Here is where the clever part comes into play," continued Tappan. "I had noticed Miss Woodbridge's knife in an herb basket beneath one of the potting benches. She must have forgotten it earlier in the day. Now, I make it my business to learn about the background of people who may be useful to me, and knowing I was going to be staying with the duke, I did some research on Miss Woodbridge and uncovered some very curious stories concerning the girl's family. And so I realized it was a perfect way to deflect suspicion from the plant."

Tappan paused, and Kate heard the scrape of a flint against steel. A moment later a plume of cigar smoke wafted out into the night. "Sticking the blade into Von Seilig's ribs was an easy matter. As was covering up the gap in the soil by rearranging the surrounding specimens and sweeping up the telltale dirt. As an added measure to cast suspicion on Miss Woodbridge, I passed the stories on to Lady Duxbury—and she told her brother."

"What role does Lady Duxbury have in this?" asked the stranger. "My spies tell me that she is your lover."

If the announcement was meant to shake Tappan's

composure, it did not succeed. The baron merely laughed. "Correct. I made her my lover several weeks ago, figuring it would prove useful during the house party. It wasn't hard to arrange. The slut will sleep with any man who unbuttons his trousers." Tappan slowly expelled a mouthful of air with an audible *whoosh*, clearly savoring the taste of the pungent smoke and his own cunning.

"As for her role," he went on, "she proved useful in gathering gossip and keeping an eye on the guests when I was searching the guest rooms for any embarrassing papers that I could use to extort hush money from the foreigners, nothing more. She likes playing games with people and finds it amusing to earn a bit of extra blunt from it. She has no idea that I have anything to do with Von Seilig's murder."

"You are sure?" The stranger did not sound happy. "You promised that no one would know of our deal. It's imperative that my involvement can never be traced to what is going to happen in Vienna."

"Trust me, your secret is safe," replied Tappan.

There was a long silence. "You have finished extracting the substance from the plant?"

"Yes," said Tappan. "And as I said, it's the perfect poison for what you have in mind. I've had a special leather carrying case made for the vial. The glass is wrapped in a square of chamois and—"

A thunderous barking from the front lawn interrupted his words.

"What is that?" demanded the stranger. Footsteps crossed the parquet and the window swung open. Kate got just a quick glimpse of the face before he withdrew his head back into the room.

"Nothing," assured Tappan, his voice sounding uncomfortably close. "I took the precaution of having several men patrol the grounds. But just to make sure all is in order, I shall go outside and check."

"*Diavolo.*" Marco let out a low hiss as the dog barked again.

"Look." Kate pointed to the stable pathway, where a man with a gun was struggling to control a huge mastiff.

Grabbing her hand, Marco yanked her to her feet. "This way," he whispered. "And hurry."

Chapter Twenty-one

Marco darted through an opening in the privet hedge. Hugging close to the leafy shadow, he turned away from the main house and hurried their steps for the knot of Norfolk pines at the far end of the lawns.

"Cluyne Close is in the opposite direction," rasped Kate.

"So is an armed guard and a vicious dog," he replied. "And the others may be anywhere. We can't risk getting caught, and not just to save our own skins."

"Where—"

"Trust me."

She didn't protest, but picked up her pace, following with sure-footed grace as he veered around a massive stone urn and broke into a run.

Marco ventured a quick glance back at her. No weeping, no sign of a swoon—Kate Woodbridge flew into the face of peril without betraying a blink of fear. His hand tightened, the feel of her slim fingers against his callused palm sending a stab of remorse through him. He shouldn't have allowed her to come. Once again, his own devil-may-care disregard for danger was coming back to haunt him.

Ghosts. Demons. Would he ever outrun his past?

Legs churning up the last steep rise of the path, he rounded the screen of trees. Pale and serene in the dappling of moonlight, a row of marble columns stood like silent sentinels, guarding the half-hidden door.

"What's that?" asked Kate as they skidded to a halt in front of the windowless building.

"Our sanctuary," said Marco a bit breathlessly. "At least, I pray it is." Thrusting the knife blade into the iron keyhole, he set to jiggling the tumblers. "Any sign of pursuit?"

Hiking up her skirts even higher, Kate wrapped her legs around one of the fluted columns and shimmied up its length. "They are checking the side terrace," she called softly. "Mastiffs aren't known for their nose. With any luck, they won't track us here."

"Better safe than sorry." Marco dug deeper and heard the last catch open with a satisfying click. "Come inside—and be quick about it."

She swung out and caught hold of the iron lantern ring hanging from the portico.

"Were you a circus acrobat in your past life?" he asked, watching her drop lightly down to the ground beside him.

"A ship's monkey," she replied. "I've been climbing masts and rigging since I was a small child."

"Well, no need for further gymnastics. Right now we are going to hole up in here." Marco pulled the door shut behind him and twisted the latch to reset the lock. "And stay quiet as church mice until we are sure they are gone. Make yourself comfortable. We may be a while."

Kate's eyes widened as they adjusted to dim light. "My God."

"Only if you worship Eros," replied Marco.

"Or Dionysus." She slowly circled a larger-than-life statue of an aroused satyr guzzling from a wineskin. "This is..."

"Sinful? Shocking?" he suggested.

"A number of adjectives come to mind," she said cryptically. "You have been here before?"

"Tappan gave me a tour when we came to fetch the botany books for you and Lady Fenimore. His grandfather bought the collection from a Turkish pasha and built this place as a personal pleasure retreat. Apparently the old fellow was considered the paragon of propriety by the *ton*, but occasionally indulged in his own private fantasies."

"So, hiding scandalous secrets seems to run in the family." Pausing before a naked woman entwined with a writhing serpent, Kate ran her knuckles along the smooth marble.

It might have been the play of light and shadow but it seemed that her hand was shaking.

Marco moved up behind her and took hold of her arms. Beneath the whisper-soft fabric, her skin was as cold as stone.

"You're shivering," he murmured. "Here, take my coat." Shrugging out of the garment, he draped it over her shoulders.

"*Grazie*."

"*Prego.*" Her hair had come loose, and a tangle of wind-snarled curls fell over her shoulders. Burying his fingers in their silky texture, he brushed them aside and pressed his lips to the back of her neck. "I am sorry."

The muscles tightened in her throat as she swallowed. "For what?"

"For… for a great many things. But mostly for putting you in danger. I should have anticipated that there might be trouble."

Kate turned into his arms, her face impassive, save for a tiny quivering at the corner of her mouth. "I'm responsible for my own decisions." Her lashes lifted in a flickering of burnished gold. "Besides, I thought you didn't have a conscience."

"I don't, *cara*. I'm an amoral cad." He slid a booted foot across the floor, forcing her back against the sculpted stone. "A wicked wastrel."

"A ruthless rake?"

Her arms looped around his neck and his pulse began to thud wildly against her soft skin. Through his own salty sweat, he could smell the heady sweetness of her scent.

"*Si*. The worst sort of rotter," he rasped.

Her breasts grazed his chest, leaving two singed spots of fire.

"Are you trying to convince me? Or yourself?"

Gritting his teeth, Marco held back a groan. "*Dio Madre*, you are playing a dangerous game, Kate."

The coat slipped to the floor.

"That's nothing new. I've been doing it so long it's become second nature." The sardonic smile didn't quite reach her eyes. Pooled in their aquamarine depths was a ripple of some elusive emotion.

He leaned in closer, and though she quickly looked away, he caught the fleeting glimpse of the vulnerable young lady she tried so hard to hide. Catching her chin, Marco pressed his fingers to the delicate flesh and felt her tremble.

"Kate—Katarina," he whispered, slowly framing her face between his palms. Against his sun-bronzed skin, she looked so pale and fragile that he feared she might shatter at any moment. "You don't have to pretend with me. You can just be yourself."

A tear pearled on her lashes, but she blinked it away. "Myself," she echoed. "Oh, you have no idea how wicked a person the real Kate Woodbridge is."

Kate wasn't quite sure what had come over her. She felt as if she had fallen overboard into a churning sea, and the only way to keep from drowning in doubts was to cling to something strong and solid.

She skimmed her hands along the slope of Marco's shoulders, reveling in the sculpted contours of muscle and sinew. But unlike the surrounding stone, he pulsed with an inner fire. His breath, still traced with brandy, warmed her cheek and a hard, masculine heat rose up from the slabbed planes of his chest, burning away the damp chill of the air between them.

"Oh, trust me, Kate. I have seen enough wickedness in my life to recognize its face. And you do not remotely resemble it."

"You are wrong," she whispered. Hearing Tappan talk so easily of murder had shaken her to the core. A decent man lay dead, his life snuffed out as if it were of no more consequence than a candle flame. And the shock waves stirred guilty memories, ones she had thought lay buried in her past. But perhaps such ghosts were never really laid to rest.

"I—I am not innocent of murder." The words slipped from her lips of their own accord. "Not Von Seilig, but another man."

A tomblike stillness gripped the moment. Clouds scudded overhead, shrouding Marco's face in a passing shadow. The distant bark of the dog was the only sound to penetrate the windowless walls.

Kate shifted in a soft rustle of silk, forcing herself to seek his eyes. She would not be so cowardly as to dodge the look of disgust. Marco might be an unprincipled rogue, but no man would view the confession with anything other than loathing.

"I imagine there was a good reason for it, Kate. No matter what you say, you are not a cold-blooded killer." The moon broke through the darkness, lighting the glimmer of sympathy on his features. "You are not alone. I, too, have taken a life. More than one, if it makes you feel any better." He leaned back and propped an elbow on the sculpture. "It was in Naples, I imagine."

She nodded, choking back a burble of desperate laughter at seeing him leaning on a monstrous marble phallus. The situation was wildly, madly absurd. Here they were talking about death while surrounded by a lusty, lascivious ode to life.

No one could accuse them of having a conventional relationship, she thought.

"Ghiradelli, you are lounging on a—"

"Prick," he finished, "Yes, and a rather handsome devil, don't you think?" He ran a hand over the smooth rim of the flanged head. "Not that I've ever been tempted to indulge in that sort of play. I find women far more fascinating."

Kate couldn't repress another soft laugh. "Aren't you ever serious?"

"Very rarely, *cara*." He shifted his hips, drawing her back into his arms. Only a few thin layers of linen and gossamer silks lay between them. Through the soft wool of his trousers, Kate was intimately aware of the chiseled shape of his thighs, solid and unyielding against hers.

The dog and danger outside their sanctuary suddenly seemed very far away.

"Tell me about Naples," he pressed.

It was a story she had never dared tell anyone, not even her fellow 'Sinners.' Yet, somehow the words came out. She haltingly described the humid night, the fetid alley, and the pimp's attack on the helpless whore.

"I heard her cries and couldn't just slink away. The brute had a cudgel and had bloodied her face. When he pulled a blade from his boot, I drew my own knife and tried to scare him off."

"If I recall, Luigi Bonnafusco was twice your size and weight," murmured Marco. "With bulging biceps and fists as big as Parma hams."

"Yes, well, I have often found that bullies tend to be cowards at heart," she replied. "He retreated at first, and I managed to help Magda to her feet. But then he came at us again, swearing and snarling that he would see us both dead. I fended him off until we reached the end of the alley. Seeing us close to escape, he charged like a bull. And tripped over a broken wine cask." She paused, reliving the horrid few seconds of his fall—the jarring impact of his heavy body tumbling against hers, the hot slice of steel sinking into flesh as she lost her footing.

The twisted grimace and soundless scream as he dropped to the ground.

"It was an accident, Kate. The brute forced your hand and suffered the consequences." Marco steadied her trembling shoulders. "You did the right thing, *cara*, the honorable thing, in rushing to help the woman. Sometimes it is necessary to take a life in order to defend another person or a noble principle."

A connection seemed to form between them, drawing them closer together. "Please hold me. Just for a little longer," whispered Kate. "I—I don't want to be alone."

His lips brushed against her cheek. "I won't leave you."

The husky murmur sent a shiver through her, a spark of ice-hot fire that left her limp with longing. She had never surrendered herself completely. Her only affair—the short-lived dalliance with the handsome American naval officer—had been more out of curiosity than any heartfelt passion. Marco ignited far more complex feelings, far more burning needs. His body seemed branded on hers, every hard, lean muscle scorched on her flesh.

Fire sparked deep in her core.

She sensed that Marco was a kindred spirit. Like her, he seemed to dwell in a strange sliver of twilight, a netherworld of sun and shadow. They both had a darkness deep within, a secret place locked to all others. Marco immersed himself in dissolute pleasures, but Kate had a feeling that some private pain was driving him to the brink of despair. He was a good man, an honorable man, though he refused to admit it.

Secrets and suffering. Yet another bond between them.

A bond of friendship—no, more than friendship. She feared she was falling in love with him.

Looking up, she saw him watching her intently, a tangle of dark, silky hair falling over his brow. His half-hidden eyes had a dangerous glitter, like pirate gold beckoning from beneath the waves.

Tantalizing. Tempting her to steal a touch.

Kate lifted a hand and traced the line of his jaw. Love was, of course, not a word he would ever say. Nor would she. For a brief, beautiful moment their bodies would couple and then they would come apart.

She would have to be satisfied with that.

"*Strega*," he said in a sin-soft voice. "I fear you are a wild sea witch come to drown me in desire." His head was framed in the skylight overhead. The glass shimmered in the pale light as wispy clouds floated over the moon, weaving silvery threads in the black velvet sky.

Kate boldly brought his hand to her breast. "I seem to be sinking in the same spell. The ocean currents are a force too powerful to tame."

His gaze began to burn with a smoky, seductive fire. "Be careful what you start," he rasped. "You've already experienced the fact that I'm not a gentleman. I won't stop, even if you tell me to."

Kate didn't believe that, but it didn't matter. She had no intention of begging him to stop. In answer, she lifted herself on tiptoes and ran her tongue along the curl of his lower lip.

"Then it's a good thing that I'm not a lady."

His mouth quivered and then opened to suck her into a

lush, liquid kiss. He tasted of hot spice and raw need, and as his teeth nipped her sensitive flesh, her breath melted to a moan.

Marco was right—there was nothing gentlemanly about his embrace. It was ruthless, ravaging, and the fierceness of his passion sent a lick of fire curling between her legs.

Oh, she was wicked to ache for his intimate touch. Yet somehow it felt so exquisitely right. Arching into his body, she pressed herself up against the hard ridge of his arousal.

A rough growl resonated deep in his throat.

Slipping her hand inside the placket of his shirt, Kate skimmed her palm over his chest, reveling in the masculine textures of coarse curling hair and smooth muscle. Marco tensed as her thumb stroked over the flat nub of his nipple with a slow, circling touch.

"*Dio Madre*." Releasing her mouth, he trailed a line of lapping kisses to the soft, sensitive spot below her ear.

She shuddered as his warm, moist breath tickled her flesh, teasing a trail to the throbbing pulse point of her neck. A purr of pure pleasure escaped her lips.

"*Cara*—Kate." His voice was a little unsteady, Italian and English tangling together in a heated rush of murmured words.

She felt a rush of intoxicating power that she could affect his self-control. The feeling of naked femininity bubbled through her like costly champagne. Emboldened, she brought her palm down to the front of his trousers and traced the steely shape of his arousal, feeling its pulsing heat straining to break free of the finespun wool.

His groan grew louder. Rougher. Hooking a finger in her bodice, Marco pulled it down, exposed a breast. He bent his head, the rasp of his stubbled cheek in contrast to the wet velvet heat of his mouth closing over her. A flick of his tongue sent a jolt of fire spiraling through her belly.

"Marco," Kate whispered in wonder as sweet sensation played over and over her nipple. Biting back a louder cry, she twisted hard against his hips.

He looked up for just a moment with a sensuous smile. "*Lentemente, bella.*"

Slowly. Slowly. He resumed his unhurried caresses, laving, suckling her peaked flesh to a point of rosy fire. As he kissed her, his hands leisurely explored the curve of her back, the contour of her hips, the shape of her derriere.

Kate couldn't still her impatience. The need to join herself with him was growing unbearable. She wanted him filling the void inside her, sharing his strength—and his weakness. Both of them had aching, empty places. Perhaps for a fleeting interlude they could make each other whole.

"Oh, please," she gasped. "*Prego.*"

A low laugh thrummed against her skin. But as he fisted her skirts, a tremor betrayed that his own self-control was fast unraveling. Fabric frothed over her knees and his long, lithe hands lifted her up to a seat on the statue.

The marble was cool against her legs, and it took an instant for her feverish brain to realize that her perch was an oversized penis. Kate knew she should be aghast at her position, but in truth it was madly, wantonly erotic.

A dream beyond her wildest fantasy.

"*Sei belissimo.*" Marco's fingers were like silk gliding up the inside of her thighs. "You are so beautiful."

And he was an ancient Roman god come to life. Chiseled perfection, thrumming with passion.

He untied her drawers and pulled them off. "Spread your legs, Kate."

She gasped as he skimmed through her damp curls and parted her feminine folds. A fingertip found her hidden pearl.

"*Belissimo,*" he repeated, his touch teasing, tantalizing. His voice sounded fuzzy. All she could hear was the surge of desire pounding in her ears, like the surf of an azure ocean washing over a tropical shore.

Her hand found the fastening of his trousers and quickly freed it, allowing his shaft to spring free. She curled her fingers around his length, and the feel of him—steel and velvet—took her breath away.

Marco murmured something—she knew not what. All rational thought dissolved in a moan as he eased closer and positioned himself at the entrance to her passage.

He nudged in a fraction, parting the honeyed flesh.

"Yes." Her need was beyond words. "Yes."

With a hoarse groan, Marco thrust deep into her, burying himself to the hilt.

Her body clenched.

He moved slowly, gently at first, allowing her passage to adjust to him. Then, unleashing his restraint, he quickened his tempo, filling her with hard, powerful strokes.

Kate felt the muscles of his back harden, and quickly matched his rhythm. The tension was mounting inside her, too. Seeking release, she arched her body, riding the crest of the wave higher and higher. Marco surged into her, and suddenly a shower of stars was washing over her.

Covering her mouth with his, Marco muffled her cry of climax. *Dio Madre.* The taste was unbearably sweet—spice and sunshine overpowered every last vestige of dissolute darkness from his soul. He felt innocent. An illusion, of course, but for the moment it filled him with joy. With hope.

With...

Lust. That's all it was—a primal animal attraction. There was no room in a rake's heart for any softer sentiment.

Kate bit his lip as she bucked beneath his body. Driving deeper, Marco lost himself in the last shivering waves of her pleasure. Her warmth flooded through him, like fire-kissed honey. A shudder spasmed through him, and his own liquid essence spilled into her.

Hell, he had meant to withdraw, but...

A dog's agitated bark shattered the sultry stillness of the gallery. The sound was close.

Too close, cursed Marco.

Boots thudded on the stone tiles.

He froze, their bodies still joined together, and pressed a palm over Kate's mouth.

The door latch rattled. "Just as I suspected. It's locked. The only key is here on my ring." Tappan's voice betrayed a note of irritation. "Damnation, silence the bloody hound and take him back to the kennels. He must have scented a fox or a badger."

Marco heard a sharp slap, followed by a low snarl. "Yes, m'lord." The retreating steps quickly faded away.

"Let us hope it was not some larger predator." It was the stranger who spoke up.

"I tell you, there is no cause for alarm," Tappan assured him. "Everyone, including the Foreign Office, thinks that I've left for Vienna. Our secret is quite safe."

There was a fraction of a pause. "What if the missing plant is noticed by the duke? Are you not worried that its disappearance might cause suspicion to fall on you?"

"No," replied Tappan. "The duke's expertise is English wildflowers. He knows nothing about esoteric plants. Miss Woodbridge might be a problem, but even if she noticed its absence, she's hardly in a position to raise the alarm." He gave a low laugh. "I tell you, the plan is a perfectly constructed puzzle—no one is capable of putting all the complex pieces together."

The stranger gave a grunt.

"As for the poison itself, I shall take pains to appear at another venue on the night that you plan to use it. Is the Carousel still scheduled to take place at the Spanish Riding School?"

Silence.

"Oh, come, no need to be coy," said Tappan. "It is in both of our interests for me to be fully informed. The chances of anyone connecting me to the death are minuscule, and I should like to keep them that way."

"Very well," came the curt reply. "The answer is yes."

"Oh, excellent. And what a delicious irony. The victim will succumb to the prick of a blade while watching a faux medieval joust."

"Quiet," snarled the stranger.

"Don't look so grim," replied Tappan. "Rest assured that the poison leaves no trace. Everyone will assume the fellow died of natural causes. Then, with the throne empty, you should have no problem controlling your country's delegation."

"My God," whispered Kate, her eyes widening. "They are planning to kill a king."

Nodding, Marco drew a taut breath and held it in his lungs.

"I trust that you are as diabolically clever as you claim to be," said the stranger. "If all goes as you say, my countrymen and I will have other work for you."

"I look forward to a long—and profitable—partnership," answered Tappan. "My price for this was high, but I am sure you will find the result well worth the cost."

"Let us hope so."

"You won't be disappointed." Leather scraped over stone as Tappan stepped down from the terraced walkway. "Shall we go back and finish our brandy? My carriage will be ready to leave in a quarter hour."

Marco waited several minutes more before easing himself away from Kate. Swiftly, silently, they fixed their disheveled clothing. Relieved that she appeared in no mood to talk, he retrieved the knife from the floor and signaled her to follow him to the door. A turn of the lever released the lock and allowed it to swing open.

They slipped out and made their way over the garden wall and back to the woodland path leading to the duke's estate.

Leaves crackled underfoot as they skirted the lake, echoing his own conflicted emotions. He had done his duty for Lynsley—that was not in question. Yet he couldn't help feeling that somehow he had taken shameless advantage of Kate in a moment of vulnerability. Danger was like a drug—it did strange things to the mind.

He knew that all too well. But did she?

"Kate," he said hesitantly. "I... that is, we—"

"We need to act on Tappan's treachery, and quickly," she cut in decisively. "Alessandra has hinted that you occasionally work with Lord Lynsley. Have you any idea how to contact him?"

"Yes. I've a way to send a message, in case of emergency," he replied. "It's just a short ride away."

"You shouldn't have any trouble sneaking into the stables at this hour." She deliberately avoided his eye. "There is a side entrance by the water troughs that is used by the grooms—"

"Thank you, but I'm familiar with the layout of the stables."

"Very professional." Kate quickened her pace as they reached the outer fringe of lawn. "I suspected that you were exaggerating your dissolute depravity."

"Kate," he began again. "What happened between us—"

"What happened between us is irrelevant at the moment," she interrupted. "We have far more important issues to deal with than personal ones." Her skirts swished around her exposed legs. "Good heavens, Ghiradelli. I am not some simpering innocent, about to sink into a swoon over sacrificing her virtue—again, I might add."

Marco supposed that her cynicism should have put him more at ease. Instead, it only compounded his confusion. "You are right, of course. The threat to the peace conference must take precedence for now." He caught her arm and spun her around to face him. A squall was blowing through and the first few raindrops began to slap against the ornamental plantings. In the awkward silence, they sounded loud as gunshots.

"But we *will* discuss this," added Marco in a low voice. "Of that you may be sure."

Her chin came up a fraction. "There really isn't all that much to say. The interlude was pleasant."

"Pleasant?" he echoed.

"Your reputation is well-deserved." Kate reached up and slowly peeled his fingers from her arm. Beads of water clung to her lashes, dark as India ink in the murky shadows. Her hands were cold as ice. "Surely you don't need to hear a paean to your sexual prowess."

"Not unless you would care to recite it somewhere warm and dry," he said, using sarcasm to shield his uncertainty.

"You have another assignation," she retorted. "And you'd best hurry." Pointing to one of the side paths, she added, "That's a shortcut to the stables, in case your reconnaissance didn't extend to the gardens."

He shifted his feet uncomfortably, loath to leave her alone. "You can make it to the manor house by yourself?"

"Of course." Kate turned away, a tangle of sodden hair hiding her expression. "I am a pirate captain's daughter, remember? I am perfectly capable of navigating through stormy seas on my own."

Chapter Twenty-two

Kate eased into her darkened room and quietly closed the door, hoping her muddied shoes hadn't left a telltale trail of mud in the corridor. She didn't bother lighting a candle to dispel the gloom. Outside, a gray, grainy dawn was hovering on the horizon. The coming day looked to be dreary, but she was too numb and exhausted to care.

The night seemed so unreal. Flashing back to the moonlit sculptures, the shadowed play of light on the lewd stone and impassioned flesh, she couldn't help feeling as if some dark narcotic had swirled up from the marble.

Plopping down on her bed, she crossed her shivering arms and contemplated her rumpled garments. *Sniff.* Her nostrils crinkled. The scent of sex must be hanging like a dark cloud over her head, thick and noxious as a London fog. But instead of a putrid yellow, hers was likely a depraved scarlet. Perhaps it was formed in the shape of an *A*.

Sniff. This time the sharp inhale was to hold back the sting of tears.

The door to the adjoining rooms opened a crack, admitting a flicker of candlelight. "Miss Kate?"

"Yes." She tried to sound composed, but barely recognized her own voice.

Her maid took a long look, her knowing eyes slowly moving up from the bedraggled skirts to the skewed bodice to the tangle of snarled hair hanging limply over one shoulder.

"I must look like a tupenny whore," said Kate, essaying a note of humor. Only a slight tremor at the last word ruined the effect.

Alice set down the light and enfolded her in a wordless hug.

Kate bit at her lip, only to wince. The kiss-swollen flesh was still tender to the touch.

"I shall order up a hot bath," murmured her maid. "And a steaming pot of tea."

"It's four in the morning," pointed out Kate.

"Your grandfather employs an army of servants. I won't have any trouble enlisting a few to do my bidding."

Kate didn't argue. The idea of a soothing soak suddenly seemed heavenly. "Bless you, Alice," she murmured.

"It's not me that's in need of divine intervention," said Alice with a wry grimace. "But barring the appearance of a guardian angel, you'll have to make do with your maid."

Working with her usual quiet efficiency, Alice marshaled her forces and soon had a tub set up behind the lacquered bathing screen.

Stripping off her chilled garments, Kate lowered herself into the lavender-scented water with a blissful sigh.

"I'll see about the tea," said Alice, tactfully withdrawing from the room.

Taking up a bar of soap, Kate set to scrubbing away the mud, intent on submerging all thoughts about Marco and their lovemaking, at least for the moment.

Hell, she was immersed in enough problems without worrying about *that*.

Despite her resolve, her chin slipped down into the suds and a watery sigh escaped from her lips. Drawing her knees up, she hugged them to her chest. The water stirred, and for an instant she caught a reflection of her face.

In the eyes of Polite Society, she had sunk beneath reproach, not that she gave a fig for the opinion of such pompous prigs. Yet for some reason, she felt tears welling up, and wasn't quite sure why.

How silly, really. Kate blinked. She was an experienced woman of the world. There was nothing shameful about admitting that she enjoyed the act of physical intimacy with a man. To put it bluntly, she found sex a pleasurable experience.

Did that make her evil or depraved?

Marco didn't seem too disgusted by her wanton behavior. In truth, he was awfully open-minded on the subject. Most men were hypocrites, refusing to extend their libertine notions to the opposite sex. Marco, on the other hand, cheerfully conceded his own shortcomings...

Not that 'short' or 'small' was in any way a fitting description of his person. He was, in a word, magnificent. An ethereally beautiful man, oozing with a rampant masculinity.

Closing her eyes, Kate blew out another bubbly sigh and let the heat soak into her. Broad shoulders. Lean waist. Corded thighs. Long legs. And all those intriguing textures and contours of male muscles. Thinking of the touch and feel of him, she felt a lurch in her belly that slowly spiraled down and became an ache between her legs. She was a little sore, but strangely enough, the overpowering sensation was one of emptiness. As if something essential was missing from her core.

Tendrils of steam rose up from the water, curling against her damp cheeks. *What would it be like to share his bed every night?*

Kate shook off the fantasy with a rueful grimace. Assuming Marco had a home—and a bed—to call his own, it was doubtful that he spent any time there. He was too restless, too bored with convention to live a predictable life. A man of his nature would never be satisfied with settling down.

What *did* he want? she wondered. She considered herself adept at reading men, but Marco was impossible to decipher. His expression was impenetrable, his eyes enigmatic. Sometimes she thought she saw a quicksilver flash of longing, but maybe she was just looking through her own prism of experience.

Perhaps she should ask Alessandra about his past life. *His past loves.* Had he suffered some crushing disappointment in his youth?

No, decided Kate, running the soft sponge back and forth along the ridge of her collarbone. That wasn't a good idea. Such questions might reveal too much about her own state of mind.

Tilting her head back against the edge of the tub, she stared up at the painted plaster ceiling, feeling oddly adrift in the world.

Her feelings for Marco would be another secret to hide, even from her closest friends.

Alice's return quickly doused any further musings. Wielding a towel and hairbrush, the maid soon had her dried and bundled into a flannel nightrail.

"Drink this," she commanded, adding a splash of whisky to the fragrant tea. "Then it's into bed with you, and I've given orders that you are not to be woken up until suppertime."

Kate yawned. "Maybe an hour or two of sleep," she said drowsily, allowing herself to be tucked under the covers.

But her dreams were soon interrupted by the early-morning arrival of the magistrate, who, despite the duke's vehement protests, demanded another session of questioning.

Exhausted, and unwilling to reveal any hint of the truth, Kate stumbled through the interview, knowing her terse answers did her case no good.

Cluyne's snappish temper only made things worse.

Sure enough, when Sir Reginald stood, he eyed them both with a look of supreme satisfaction. "I have to warn you, Miss Woodbridge. Things look bad—very bad—for you. Unless new evidence comes to light by the end of the day, I shall be forced to take you into custody and hold you for the next assizes."

"Bastard," muttered Cluyne, clenching his fists as the baronet left the study. "I don't give a damn about his orders that none of us are to leave the grounds. I intend to ride to London and find Lynsley—"

"No need for that, Your Grace." Marco entered the room and shut the door behind him. "The marquess should be arriving soon."

"Not soon enough," grumbled the duke.

"The meeting must be at a secret rendezvous spot," continued Marco. "But given the circumstances, I think you ought to be allowed to attend. The three of us—"

"The *four* of us," corrected Charlotte, as the door opened yet again.

Kate rubbed at her brow, feeling a little dizzy.

"My step may have slowed a bit in my old age, but that does not mean that you can outmaneuver me," went on Charlotte. "Whatever you are planning in order to help Kate, I demand to be part of it."

"Lady Fenimore, we cannot take a carriage. We have to go by horseback through the woods to a ramshackle inn off the beaten path," explained Marco. "It will be rough going."

"I can ride," she replied grimly.

"Charlotte," murmured Kate. "You haven't been in a saddle since the last century."

"A horse still has four legs, does it not?" she shot back.

"Don't bother arguing," said Cluyne in resignation. "You would have a better chance of shifting the Rock of Gibraltar than Lady Fenimore's mind when it is made up."

Charlotte looked as if she wasn't sure whether to be angry or amused.

"There is a very docile mare in the stables," conceded the duke. "But if you fall on your arse, we will have no choice but to leave you in the mud."

"Don't worry about me. I can dig myself out of trouble." Charlotte looked at Kate, her gaze clouded with anxiety. "It's Kate who we need be concerned about. An arrest must be avoided at all costs."

• • •

Slumping wearily against the tavern's sooty wall, Marco sighed and ran a hand through his disheveled locks. No rest for the wicked, he thought wryly, recalling the luxurious bed standing empty at Cluyne Close. But time enough for sleep later.

He had dispatched an urgent message to London, then returned to the duke's estate just after dawn. But any hope of closing his eyes for a few blessed hours was quickly dispelled by an early-morning visit from the magistrate. After yet another round of questioning, the baronet had made it clear that he was on the verge of having Kate taken into custody.

Marco's fingertips lingered at his temples as he mentally reviewed the wild twists and turns the night had taken. Things were moving with dizzying speed...a rogue assassin threatening to destroy the peace conference in Vienna...a traitorous British diplomat on the loose...a murder charge hanging over Kate's head.

It might take a miracle to keep the mission from spiraling out of control.

But then, the Marquess of Lynsley was the consummate magician.

"Where is he?" growled the duke as he eyed the squalid room with undisguised horror. Aiming an irritable swat at the oily cloud hanging over the single candle, he added, "Another five minutes in this hellhole, and I swear, I shall—"

The marquess moved like a wraith. One moment there was only smoke and shadows, the next, he was standing among them, silent save for the beads of rain dripping from his broad-brimmed hat.

"Ah, here he is," murmured Marco. "*Buongiorno.*"

"Hardly," replied Lynsley. "Kindly refrain from your usual humor, Ghiradelli. At the moment, my mood is about as foul as the weather."

"But not as stormy as mine." The rumble in the duke's voice hinted that thunder could erupt at any time.

"I regret that the situation has turned so ugly, Cluyne." Lynsley shrugged out of his sodden overcoat and peeled off his mud-spattered gloves. His usual well-tailored elegance was disguised by a soiled moleskin jacket and baggy canvas pants.

The odor emanating from the garments was not something Marco cared to identify.

"Under normal circumstances, it would not be a problem to clear up this murder," continued the marquess. "But unfortunately, right now I cannot bring any pressure to bear on the local magistrate. These are very sensitive times for the government, and I've been asked not to draw any attention to this crime. Not only can't we afford to reveal the truth about Lord Tappan's treachery, but the Circle of Scientific Sibyls—that, is the Circle of Sin—has done some services for me that I would rather not have come to light." He nodded at Kate and Charlotte. "My sincere apologies, ladies. Especially to you, Miss Woodbridge."

"You mean to say that government business takes precedence over my granddaughter?" sputtered Cluyne.

"Yes," replied Lynsley frankly. "I'm afraid it does."

"Goddamn it, man, you can't just sit there and twiddle your thumbs!" said the duke, his voice perilously close to a shout.

"Now, now, Cluyne." Charlotte reached over to touch

his sleeve. "It does no good to bellow. I am sure that Lord Lynsley is pulling every string that he can to extract Kate from trouble."

The duke snorted but did moderate his tone to a dull roar. "My granddaughter is not a cold-blooded murderess. I'll not see her left to hang in the air just because Lord Castlereagh is afraid of upsetting his precious peace conference."

Marco felt his gut twist in a knot. Surely the government would not let Kate march to the gallows to cover up their own guilt in the crime. But even an arrest would ruin her forever in Society. Destroy any chances of her finding a place to fit in.

"My hands may be tied at the moment, but be assured that I will find a way to undo this knot," said Lynsley gravely. In the guttering light of the cheap tallow candle, he looked tired and travelworn. "I would never have involved you and your family had I any inkling that there was any danger involved. I pride myself on knowing what is going on. But I do make mistakes."

He braced a leg on the rough planking of the tavern table and blew out a sigh. "This was supposed to be a simple surveillance mission, a way to keep an eye on any alliances that might be forming for the upcoming peace conference. I anticipated a straightforward report of who was friendly with whom, not treason and murder."

Kate, who had been unnaturally quiet all morning, leaned into the pool of light. "If the mystery man succeeds with his assassination plan in Vienna, it could plunge Europe back into war, could it not?"

Lynsley's expression was very grim. "Quite likely."

"Then it's imperative that we stop him, and without anyone being alerted to the plot."

"Yes. Any hint that a British official was conspiring to murder one of the sovereigns would ignite an explosive scandal. Our ability to influence the future of Europe would go up in smoke." Lynsley fingered his unshaven chin. "We must, at all costs, keep this a secret. But I'll be damned if I can figure out how. My men are on their way to apprehend Tappan, but by the time they find him and bring him back for interrogation, it may well be too late." He shot a look at Marco. "You have no idea who his contact was?"

Marco shook his head. "I didn't recognize the man's voice. And to be honest, it was muffled enough by the glass that I'm not sure that I would know it again if I heard it. Nor did I see his face."

The marquess looked to the window and appeared to be contemplating the layers of grime coating the glass.

"But I did," said Kate softly.

All eyes turned to her.

"When the dog barked," she explained. "He poked his head out the window for a look. It was just for a moment, and the angle was not the best, but I caught a glimpse of his profile."

"Describe him," said Lynsley quickly.

Kate gave a wry grimace. "Brown hair, neither long nor short. A neatly trimmed mustache. Regular features." She lifted her shoulders in oblique apology. "I couldn't make out the color of his eyes. My impression was that they were dark."

"I'm afraid that doesn't help narrow down the possible suspects to a manageable list," said Lynsley dryly. "I can't set my operatives to trailing half the men in Austria."

"I know. I'm sorry," she murmured. "It's a pity that I do not possess Lord James Pierson's talent for sketching. Words don't create a good picture, but there was something about the set of his mouth. I—I am quite sure I would know him again if I saw him."

Silence settled over the room, punctuated by the drip of the tallow and Cluyne's heavy breathing.

Kate looked down at her lap and studied her hands, trying not to think of what they had been doing a few short hours ago. She had known that the feeling of profound peace would be fleeting. Like the eye of a hurricane, the moment was an illusion, a tantalizing hope before the raging storm once again darkened the skies with its fury.

Marco finally cleared his throat. "Sir, I have a suggestion that might actually solve both of our problems."

"Well?" barked the duke.

"I am all ears," murmured Lynsley. "What do you propose?"

Kate, too, swiveled around to listen.

"Marriage," he replied bluntly. "Not to you of course, sir," he added in a joking tone. "But to Miss Woodbridge."

Too shocked to speak, she could only stare in open-mouthed wonder.

Why was the rogue trying to do the honorable thing?

Her first reaction was to laugh aloud. But somehow the burble seemed to catch as her throat constricted and her chest tightened, forcing the air from her lungs.

She suddenly felt a little woozy. Her sleep-deprived brain was simply fogged with exhaustion. As was his. They would both come to their senses shortly, and she would shake off the silly twinge of longing. Still, it was rather...touching that Marco felt obliged to make the offer.

However, the ominous rumble in Cluyne's throat did not bode well for her grandfather's opinion of the idea.

"Wait and hear me out," said Marco quickly. "It would kill two birds with one stone, so to speak."

"*That* is putting it mildly," said Kate under her breath.

He ignored the interruption. "To begin with, it would clear the cloud of suspicion from Miss Woodbridge. I'll request a private meeting with the magistrate and swear that she and I were together the night of the murder. The explanation can be that we had a secret engagement and were just waiting to get the duke's approval to make it public. It's embarrassing, yes, but not unheard of. Seeing as I am a titled gentleman, he'll have to take my word as a witness."

Charlotte pinched the bridge of her nose.

"We can marry by special license," continued Marco. "Today, as soon as you can arrange it."

Kate's heart gave a lurch.

"And then depart immediately for Vienna. My taste for revelry is well-known. No one will question why I have brought my bride to partake of its pleasures. What sybarite wouldn't want a romantic honeymoon amid the sumptuous splendor of the biggest party ever thrown in Europe?" he pointed out. "Once Miss Woodbridge identifies our quarry, I can eliminate the threat, as it were."

Lynsley pursed his lips. "I confess, it could work. And would solve our problems rather nicely. Though it seems a little hard-hearted to ask Miss Woodbridge to take such a drastic step."

Kate looked at her grandfather. He tried to look stoic but she saw the obvious pain in his eyes as he agonized over the difficult choices. He had been far more emotional of late, allowing his feelings to melt the mask of ducal reserve. Mistakes and misunderstandings had kept them apart for so long. Could their fragile friendship weather another family scandal?

The sting of salt and acrid smoke clouding her eyes, Kate darted a look at Marco. His expression was inscrutable, impossible to fathom. She wasn't sure that she would ever plumb the depths of his character. And yet, despite all the unknowns, she felt a compelling urge to say yes.

She couldn't help recalling his lovemaking, his gentleness, his sense of fun. Life would be exciting with him, a wild journey, spiced with the unexpected. He didn't love her, of course, and he wouldn't be faithful.

But that didn't matter, she told herself. Not if she didn't expect it.

"Kate," began Cluyne, his rough whisper finally stirring the air.

"It's quite all right," she said quickly. "It's actually an excellent plan. It makes perfect sense."

"My dear..." said Charlotte, echoing Cluyne's concern.

"Really, a marriage of convenience suits me very well," she said forcefully. "It is, after all, how most of the English aristocracy arrange the matter. The conte and I can lead separate lives. I can return to London and my friends, and Lord Ghiradelli can...go wherever he chooses." She shrugged, feeling a tiny tingle snake down her spine. "So, I'll do it. For King and for country—though God knows why. I'm half American."

Marco's lips quirked. "*Va bene*." He looked to Lynsley. "A special license?"

The marquess answered with a searching stare, but after a long moment, he seemed satisfied with what he saw. "I'll have it from the bishop within the hour. You two can be wed at Cluyne Close by teatime and on a boat for Ostend..." He quickly pulled out a battered pocketwatch and flipped open the case. "By midnight."

All eyes turned at Kate.

"That doesn't leave us much time to pack," she said evenly. "What are we waiting for?"

Lynsley placed his mud-stained hat back on his head. "Send one of your servants to wait for me here, Cluyne."

The duke hesitated, then gave a wordless nod.

The marquess's gaze shifted to her and then to Marco. "Allow me to wish you happy in advance. It would, of course, not be prudent for me to appear at Cluyne Close for the ceremony."

"Thank you, *amico*." In the smoky light, Marco's expression was naught but a blur of soot and shadows.

Lynsley looked for a moment as if he was going to say something else. Then he seemed to reconsider and he silently slid on his gloves. Tipping his battered brim low over his eyes, he backed off into the gloom, disappearing just as quickly as he had appeared.

No one moved until a gust rattled the windowpanes, finally breaking the strange spell.

Kate tightened her shawl around her shoulders.

Cluyne picked up the candle.

"*Andiamo, bella*." Marco offered her his hand.

"Yes, let's go, " she replied.

Chapter Twenty-three

Kate awoke with a jolt, the touch of the carriage windowpane cold as ice against her cheek. Pulling the fur-trimmed lap robe up a little higher, she angled her shoulders back to the leather squabs and closed her eyes, wondering if her body would ever recover from the bone-rattling descent from the snowy mountains. She massaged gingerly at the back of her neck. There wasn't an inch of her that didn't ache. Save for her feet, which were now numb with cold. The felt-wrapped bricks had long since lost their heat.

Oh, for the comforts of Cluyne Close. Her maid was right—there was something to be said for luxury.

The journey so far had been a hellish ordeal, a grueling ten days of near nonstop travel. The first leg, a rough Channel crossing over stormy waters, had been made even more unpleasant by the dank cabin reeking of urine and vomit. Marco had been seasick the entire time—hardly an auspicious start to their marriage. From there, they had rattled over rutted roads and treacherous mountain passes. Kate rubbed her bleary eyes. It had all passed in a blur of rackety coaches and dismal inns, though now she would almost welcome a musty, flea-ridden bed to stretch out on.

She slanted a look at the slumped form beside her. Only a tangle of Marco's dark hair was visible above the lumpy blanket, but the soft rasp of his snore indicated that he had fallen into a doze. Reaching across the seat, she smoothed the heavy wool around his knees. His long legs were bent at an awkward angle in the cramped coach. No wonder he had been in no mood for conversation during the brief stop for food and a change of horses sometime after midnight.

Sighing, Kate settled back against the worn leather, trying to get comfortable. She had made her own bed, she reminded herself. And now she must sleep in it...

"Wake up."

"Mmmm?" Her lids lifted a touch as she tried to squirm away from the shaking sensation.

"Come, open your eyes, Kate. You should not miss seeing your arrival in Vienna."

"Vienna?" she murmured. As the word sank in, she sat up straight and scrubbed at the misted glass. "Oh, look," she exclaimed softly, craning her neck as they rolled over the majestic stone bridge spanning the Danube River.

Kate was still wide-eyed as their coach lumbered past the Augarten, with its Baroque gardens, formal lawns, and shaded walkways. The horses made a sharp turn and then they were bumping through the narrow, twisting streets of the city center.

"That is St. Stephen's Cathedral." Marco pointed out

the soaring limestone cathedral with its Romanesque towers and intricately patterned tile roof. "Its main bell is one of the largest in Europe and was cast out of cannons captured from the Muslim invaders in 1711."

"Fascinating," she murmured.

"And there is The Hofburg, the emperor's palace," he continued. "In Vienna it is simply called the 'Burg.'"

Kate gasped. "Why, the place is as large as an ocean."

"To my knowledge there are no sailing ships inside," said Marco with a chuckle. "But the main courtyard was designed as a jousting field."

She half-expected to see a battalion of armored knights come charging through the massive wrought-iron gates.

"The original structure dates from the late 1200s, but the Hapsburg rulers have added to it over the centuries. This is the medieval section, known as the Schweitzerhof. The entrance is named 'The Gate of Virtue'—you can see the crowned Hapsburg eagle flanked by a pair of lions."

Kate suddenly felt very provincial staring at the imposing walls. The city was an august crossroads of history, a place where East had met West since the dawn of civilization. With his noble bloodlines, Marco shared a common bond with its rich cultural heritage. While she was reminded once again that she was an outsider.

A nobody, really. No real roots. No real family. No real identity.

She had never felt so alone.

After turning onto the busy *Kartnerstrasse*, Marco rapped on the trap and called out an address to the coachman. The horses turned down a narrow cobbled side street and came to a halt in front of a small café.

"Wait here," he said. "It's almost impossible to find rooms in the city, what with half of Europe here for the conference," said Marco. "But Lynsley said that somehow he would manage to get word to one of his operatives. Let us hope he has worked his usual magic."

"He would need some special spell to give his messenger wings. Otherwise, I don't know how anyone could arrive quicker than we did." Kate stifled a yawn. "Lud, I could sleep on the cobblestones and wouldn't care."

Marco winced as he unfolded his legs. "I hope that the accommodations are better than that."

They were. But only barely.

Lynsley's contact was expecting them and had arranged for lodging on a nearby street. Kate followed behind as he led the way up a darkened stairwell and unlocked a garret apartment. The candlelight showed a set of small rooms that were cramped but comfortable.

"Sorry, but it was the best I could do under the circumstances. The city is overflowing with visitors," said their contact. "I've arranged for a maid and valet, and will have them start tomorrow morning. They each have a small room on the floor below."

"I've stayed in far worse," said Marco dryly. "We shall make do for now."

"I shall help you bring up your trunks. After that, you won't see me again." Kate saw the man quickly pass a packet of papers to Marco. "You'll be dealing with someone else. I imagine the details of making contact are spelled out in one of these sealed letters."

Marco nodded. "I shall be back shortly, Kate."

Spotting a pitcher and washbasin atop a painted chest of drawers, Kate splashed some cold water on her face and then kicked off her shoes and stretched out on the bed. She wiggled her toes, blissfully thankful for the dreamy comfort of the eiderdown coverlet and plump pillows.

Lud, she was sure she would sleep for a week…

"Sorry, but we have no time to lose." The mattress shivered as Marco sat down on the edge of the bed. "We have invitations to attend the Duchess of Sagan's salon tonight. It's a regular gathering place for many of the most influential people in town, so we'd best go and see and be seen."

"Right." Kate scrubbed at her eyes, nodded mechanically. "Sagan," she mused, thinking over the background information she had studied during the long journey from England. "The duchess is rumored to be Prince Metternich's mistress, is she not?" The Austrian foreign minister was in charge of the conference. He was also a notorious womanizer.

"Yes," he replied. "As is Princess Bagration, the lovely widow of a Russian hero who fell at the battle of Borodino. The princess is also quartered at the Palm Palace, where she entertains the elite with her parties. The two ladies are great rivals, and there is no love lost between them. It is said to be amusing to watch the different dignitaries arrive and choose which stairs to take."

Kate leaned in to touch the dark stubbling on his jaw. "You had better shave."

He flinched ever so slightly. "Oh, I shall manage without cutting my throat," he joked. "I don't need assistance in dressing. But I am sorry that you must fend for yourself tonight."

Though she longed for a hot bath and a chance to stretch her stiff muscles, she shrugged. "I am fine."

A tight smile tweaked his lips. "You have real bottom, Kate. Most females would be complaining bitterly at all the discomforts of the journey."

"I'm used to it," she replied. "I have endured many uncomfortable moments aboard a ship. There was the sudden storm where we nearly sank off the coast of Turkey, and the time the Barbary pirates chased us through the Straits of Gibraltar..." She let her words trail off. "But we must think of the present, not the past."

His expression was inscrutable. "Correct," he said in a clipped tone. "We have a job to do."

A job, she repeated to herself. She must not forget that this was just another job for him.

"Congratulations on your nuptials, Lord Ghiradelli." Prince Klemens von Metternich observed Kate with an appreciative gaze. "Your taste for beautiful women is well-known, so it's no surprise that your bride is an English Diamond of the First Water."

Marco took a sip of champagne to keep from snapping a warning to keep his hands—and his ogling eyes—aimed elsewhere. The Austrian foreign minister's reputation as a rake was legendary.

"Yes, she is a rare jewel," agreed Marco softly.

Seeming to read his thoughts, Metternich chuckled. "And you intend to guard your treasure carefully?" A well-groomed brow waggled. "Then you have come to the wrong city for your wedding trip. Vienna is a city of sybaritic pleasures, especially now. The sovereigns and diplomats of Europe have come here to make love as well as to make peace."

Marco quaffed another swallow of wine.

"Territories will be traded, borders shifted," added Metternich with a sly smile. "It is all part of the game."

"Of course," answered Marco with a careless shrug. He must remember to play along with the other rakes and roués, no matter that his first impulse was to bloody the prince's aristocratic nose. *So much for peace and harmony.*

"I have no intention of initiating hostilities over a trifling trespass of boundaries," he finished.

"Excellent. I see you already have a good grasp of basic diplomacy. I am sure you will have no trouble in learning all the nuances." Spotting the Duchess of Sagan across the room, Metternich gave a graceful bow. "Excuse me. I must go greet our hostess. You are, of course, invited to the Emperor's ball tomorrow evening at the Spanish Riding School," he added, along with a lazy wink. "And naturally, so is your wife."

Taking up a fresh glass of wine, Marco moved through the crowd, trying to quell his irritation. Myriad candles glittered in the crystal chandeliers, the smoke adding a dark undertone to the lush perfumes and spicy colognes swirling through the fleshy air. Gleaming jewelry, swooshing silks, predatory smiles—the room reeked of wealth. Of privilege. Of sex.

Suddenly feeling that he couldn't breathe, Marco stepped into a shadowed nook and tried to clear his lungs.

"What brings you to Vienna, *Il Serpenti*?"

Marco looked around to find that an old crony from Milan had sidled up beside him.

"Pleasure?" continued Nacchioni as he brushed a bit of Ostrava caviar from his mustache. "If your snake is looking for a nice warm hole, you've come to the right city." He waved his ivory spoon at the crush of colorful plumage, artfully arranged to show off every provocative detail of the feminine form. "Take your choice. The ladies are open to any suggestion."

Fisting his glass, Marco replied, "Interesting."

His erstwhile friend gave a slurred smile. "You have no idea *how* interesting. The problem is deciding which one to swive for the night." A flash of teeth gleamed in the flare of the wall scone. "Though sometimes you can simply take two."

Covering his disgust with a harsh laugh, Marco drained the rest of his drink. He felt dirty and depressed by the conversation. Had he really sounded as disgusting as that when his own wits were sloshed in brandy and lust?

The answer did not lighten his mood.

"Oh, look, here is Talleyrand," said his friend, pointing to an elegant Frenchman, resplendent in the sumptuous satin, lace, and velvet formality of the last century. "You know what Napoleon called him? Shit in silk stockings."

As the legendary foreign minister from Paris kissed the hand of a buxom blonde, Nacchioni guffawed. "Mathilde is casting out her lures in the wrong waters. She'll never land such a big fish as Talleyrand. He is only here to keep an eye on whom Metternich and Humboldt are speaking with. For warming his old bones, he has the Countess of Sagan's delectable younger sister, Dorothee de Talleyrand-Perigord."

Marco thought for a moment, trying to remember the dizzying list of names he had studied. It seemed as if every titled lady and gentleman in Europe, from exalted sovereign to local *landesknecht*, had come to Vienna.

"She is the widow of Talleyrand's nephew and has come here to serve as her uncle's official hostess." His friend's smirk stretched wider. "Though her other duties no doubt included offering herself on a silver platter."

Sick of the lewd remarks, Marco set his empty glass on a bust of Venus. "Excuse me. I must go find my wife."

"*Wife!*" Nacchioni dissolved in sputtering mirth. "*Santa Cielo*, you must be joking."

Marco didn't reply. Stalking away, he searched the side parlor for a sight of Kate.

Up to this moment, he hadn't realized just how difficult the mission was going to be. Oh, his brain had comprehended the assignment and its challenges well enough. But the full force of its emotional impact had not hit home until now. He felt as if he had been punched in the gut.

With a sickening lurch, he paused and leaned a shoulder to the carved corner molding, listening to the clinking crystal, the seductive laughter, the polished lies. Deceit and deception whispered in every flutter of the tailored finery. This was his world, not Kate's, and he suddenly loathed himself for exposing her to such debauched dissolution. Like the waves and wind of the open ocean, she was unpolluted by the drawing room perversions.

Her scent was sun-kissed citrus and fresh-cut herbs. In contrast, the cloying perfumes and oily colognes seemed to clog his nostrils, making it hard to move his lungs.

"Ah, there you are." The light sweetness of *neroli* and wild thyme was like a breath of fresh air. "I thought I'd lost you," murmured Kate.

Forcing a deep inhale, Marco reminded himself that he couldn't give way to sentiment. He must guard Kate as best he could. Later, there would be time to sort through his conflicted emotions.

"I was just making a survey of the surroundings," he replied. "And greeting a few old friends."

"I imagine you are acquainted with quite a few of the guests."

"Yes," he said tightly.

Kate's expression was unreadable. "Well, that will certainly make our job easier."

He didn't reply right away. Across the room he saw a trio of men observing Kate with sharp, speculative gazes. And no wonder. She was wearing a low-cut gown of twilight-blue silk. The deep, smoky hue accentuated the golden highlights of her hair and creamy color of her bare arms, while the simple styling set off her shapely bosom and slender waist.

One of the oglers said something and the others leered.

Gritting back an oath, Marco took her arm a little roughly and turned for the main salon. "I need a drink," he growled.

Kate's lips thinned but she said nothing.

Grabbing two glasses of champagne from a passing footman, he passed one to her and took a quick gulp of wine. "Enjoying the evening?" he asked, once the liquid had loosened his throat. A friend of Kate's grandfather, a senior member of the English delegation, had spotted her earlier and insisted on introducing her to his wife.

"It is different from London," replied Kate thoughtfully. "Lady Repton was talking with her friends about the shocking boldness of the ladies here. The Countess of Sagan is called the 'Cleopatra of the North,' and her rival,

Princess Bagration, is known as the 'beautiful naked angel,' as she wears only low-cut white dresses made out of thin India muslin."

She ran a finger along the rim of the faceted crystal. "And then there is Anna Protassoff, who supposedly served as the 'tester' for the guardsmen whom Catherine the Great chose for her bedroom." She made a wry face. "I confess, I can't help but admire such boldness in flaunting their individuality. No one can accuse them of being boring pattern cards of propriety."

Marco took another swallow of champagne.

Seemingly oblivious to his brooding, Kate continued to share what she had heard from the London contingent. "Both ladies are reputed to have slept with Prince Metternich. Of late, however, the Tsar of Russia is said to be pursuing the princess."

"Alexander chases anyone wearing skirts," muttered Marco.

"Isn't that rather like the pot calling the kettle black?" she remarked dryly.

He quelled the urge to crush the glass in his fist.

"Everyone is betting on how long it will take for him to slip between her sheets," she went on. "The men are equally outrageous. Lord Stewart of the English delegation has been dubbed 'Lord Pumpernickel' for his bright yellow boots and his penchant for instigating drunken brawls. The King of Denmark is smitten with a flower girl..." Kate shook her head. "How is anything serious supposed to be accomplished here when it seems that all people are thinking about is drinking, dining, and swiving?"

"That is not our problem," snapped Marco. He tugged

at the knot of his cravat, impatient to escape the overheated rooms. "I trust that you haven't forgotten that our reason for being here is to spot a certain face."

"I'm well aware of our duty," she answered coolly. "When I see him, you will be the first to know."

Any further exchange of sarcasm was silenced by the approach of the English diplomat and his wife.

"Congratulations on your recent nuptials, Lord Ghiradelli," said Repton politely. "Miss Woodbridge—that is, Lady Ghiradelli—was just telling us how romantic it was that you suggested Vienna for a wedding trip."

"Romantic, indeed," echoed his wife. "I can't imagine a more perfect place to celebrate. The city is known for its dancing and dining. And the opulence of the parties puts London to blush."

"Opulence is not the only reason for blushes," commented Repton. "The Continentals are gluttons for pleasure in any form—" He cut off his words with a grimace. "No offense meant, Ghiradelli."

"None taken," replied Marco.

"You must be sure to come around to Lord Castlereagh's quarters on the Minoritenplatz," piped up his wife. "Lady Emily holds a weekly soiree every Tuesday evening."

"We shall," said Marco.

"Monday is Metternich's night," said Repton. "And of course Friday belongs to our hostess and her rival across the courtyard. As for the other evenings, there is no lack of entertainment, but I daresay you will discover that for yourselves."

"Yes. Do be sure to visit the Apollo Saal. You can waltz all night in the indoor gardens, which are decorated with faux stones and fairy-tale grottos." Lady Repton clearly considered herself a fount of knowledge on Viennese life. "And don't miss the ballet *Flore et Zephire*."

"Thank you," replied Marco. "Now if you will excuse us, we shall be taking our leave. We are tired from traveling and wish to be rested for the Emperor's ball tomorrow night."

"Oh, that is definitely an evening not to be missed," exclaimed Lady Repton. "It is said that the state dinner will include three hundred hams, two hundred partridges, and two hundred pigeons, not to speak of three hundred liters of olla soup."

His head aching from a surfeit of wine, Marco cut off any further details with a curt nod. "Until tomorrow, then."

Kate said nothing until they reached the courtyard of the Palm Palace. "I'm surprised you are in such a hurry to leave. I thought rakehell rogues partied until dawn."

He didn't answer.

She paused to tuck the ends of her silk shawl around her bare arms. A breath of breeze stirred the loose tendrils of her upswept hair. They looked like silvery moonbeams dancing around her shadowed profile.

It was a mild night, with the stars glittering in the heavens like candlelit diamonds stitched onto black velvet. The high arched windows of the opposite wing were open, and the sound of gaiety drifted down from the brightly lit rooms. The lilting notes of a violin, the sinuous melody of a lady's laugh, the soft pop of champagne corks.

"It seems that Princess Bagration and her admirers are not to be outdone by the Countess of Sagan." Kate glanced up, watching the silhouette of two people wrapped in a passionate kiss. "Perhaps we ought to have a look for our elusive quarry up there."

She started to cross the cobblestones, but Marco caught her arm. "You've seen enough for your first night. I'm taking you back to our rooms."

Her arm stiffened beneath his grip. "And you?"

"As you so aptly observed, *cara*, rakes party until dawn," he drawled. "Once I have dropped you off, I have a few other places to visit."

Kate began to quiver—with suppressed fury. "I am not a soiled evening coat or a broken watch chain to be tossed aside at your whim. We are *partners,* in case you had forgotten."

He schooled all hint of emotion from his face. "Trust me, that fact has not slipped my mind."

She recoiled as if the whispered words had been a slap.

"Look, I need to visit several taverns where the presence of a woman will draw unwanted notice," he explained tersely. "There are contacts to be established with Lynsley's local agents, in order to set up a channel of communication. Tomorrow will be soon enough to start stalking our quarry in earnest."

"I see," replied Kate.

"For the mission to succeed, you need to be alert and well-rested," he added.

"Put that way, it is a perfectly practical suggestion." The blaze of the torchieres did not quite reach her face. "Let us find a hackney to take us back to our rooms."

Marco merely nodded, feeling too exhausted to risk starting another argument.

"*Si, andiamo*."

Chapter Twenty-four

Trumpets blared, the brassy fanfare echoing the rattle of sabers and stomp of boots on the polished marble tiles. Resplendent in their fancy uniforms, the soldiers flanking the entrance portico of the Amalienburg wing of the palace snapped a welcoming salute.

"The King of Bavaria," murmured Marco, identifying the rotund figure who waddled up the red-carpeted stairs.

"Is there a Queen of Bavaria?" asked Kate, craning her neck to observe the procession of gilded carriages lined up to enter the cobbled courtyard.

"Yes, of course. She attended the opening masked ball last week. But for the most part, the monarchs attend the parties without their wives," he replied. "They prefer being free to flirt with all the beautiful women who come to such regal gatherings as these."

Among other things, thought Kate rather acidly. No doubt Marco was regretting the encumbrance of her presence. A bride was simply extra baggage. An added weight, a dragging ball and chain to slow his footloose romping through the crowds of willing women.

Was it any wonder that English men referred to marriage as "getting legshackled"?

"Ready?" He slanted a questioning look.

Kate forced aside her brooding thoughts and lifted her chin. The Hofburg, with all its labyrinthine corridors and interconnected palaces, was an imposing sight in the twilight. But she had learned not to be intimidated.

"Yes, of course."

Passing through the ornate portals, they made their way to the main ballroom, which was already crowded with guests. Her eyes flared wide and she sucked in a sharp breath, trying not to be overwhelmed by the sheer scale of grandeur. High overhead, immense chandeliers cast a brilliant light over the shining white and gilt paneling. Kate stared up at the sea of fire—she had been skeptical on hearing that it took over eight thousand candles to fill the tiered crystal, but now she could well believe it.

Gold, glitter, and glamour. Everything in Vienna was done to sumptuous excess.

Lowering her gaze did nothing to dispel the impression. The flutter of all the fancy plumage made her feel a little like a drab English sparrow flitting among a flock of regal birds of paradise. Her gowns were considered quite *à la mode* in London, but Continental fashions cast her in the shade.

She slanted a look at a trio of ladies to her left. Lud, if the décolletage of their dresses dropped any deeper, they would be in China, she thought. But despite the flagrant flaunting of flesh, there was no denying that the styles were elegant in the extreme. The colorful crepe outer dresses were complemented by a whisper of pastel satin underneath. Sleeves were long and edged with lace, or short poufs of silk paired with long white gloves.

Kate fingered her simple strand of pearls. All around, precious stones shone in the candlelight, their predatory gleam a mocking reminder of how much of an outsider she was.

"The Count de Ligne has described the ladies as looking like brilliant meteors when the dancing begins," murmured Marco, eyeing the feminine fashions with obvious approval.

Seeing that jewels and ribbons threaded from the topknots of curling hair to the flounced hemlines, Kate could well imagine it to be true. "Yes, they must spin by in a blinding blur of light."

"You need not worry about focusing on them," he said dryly. "You need to be keeping your gaze on the men."

"They are little better," she pointed out. "Look at all the gold braid and gaudy medals. Lud, if they all were such magnificent warriors, why wasn't Napoleon exiled to Elba years ago?"

Marco chuckled. "A good question."

As the orchestra began to tune their instruments, he took her hand and headed for the large central staircase that led to the upper galleries. "The opening dance is a polonaise. We'll have a better vantage point from the balconies," he said.

Recalling their moonlit waltz on her grandfather's terrace, she looked down a little wistfully at the ballroom's parquet floor. "Will we not be joining in the dancing?"

"The polonaise is a slow, stately procession," he

explained. "Protocol demands that only those of royal blood take part." He twitched a sardonic smile as he accepted two glasses of champagne from a liveried waiter. "While the rest of us observe them in awestruck admiration."

"It's hard not be slightly impressed," admitted Kate, feeling even more like an impostor. The wine prickled against her tongue. *Champagne, silks, and jewels.* Surely everyone around her could see through the thin disguise and tell she was naught but an uncivilized savage.

A trumpet blast announced the arrival of yet another sovereign. "Is that the Tsar of Russia?" she asked, watching a tall, blond gentleman dressed in dark-green military splendor enter the ballroom.

"Yes, behold Alexander the Angel."

"He does look rather divine in his uniform," she said.

Marco waggled a brow. "It's said he gained so much weight partying on the way to the conference that he had to send to St. Petersburg for a whole new wardrobe."

"Is everyone here as vain as a peacock?"

"Vanity is the least of the sins here in Vienna," said Marco. "Come along." He lowered his voice. "And remember to keep your eyes on the crowd rather than on the monarchs."

Despite the admonition, Kate found it hard to focus on the faces. The opulent surroundings were a powerful distraction. Feeling as if she had been transported to a fanciful fairy-tale castle, she followed Marco up a magnificent carved staircase festooned with exotic flowers, trying not to gawk at the sumptuous red and gold velvet draperies hanging from the balconies.

Marco nudged an elbow to her side. "The *men*," he murmured in a not so gentle reminder.

"Right," she replied under her breath. Blinking back her schoolgirl wonder, Kate sharpened her stare.

Like the ladies, the gentlemen were dressed in a shimmering show of peacock finery. Swallowtailed coats, lacey cravats, and snug-cut trousers vied for attention with the martial display of medals and gold-braided dress uniforms. Already her eyes were beginning to ache from the glare of brass buttons and jeweled stickpins.

Concentrate, she chided, feeling a little light-headed from the cloying swirl of masculine scents. *Macassar oil, musky colognes, perfumed hair pomades and waxes*— females weren't the only ones who spent hours preening before a looking glass. She had never seen such an elaborate display of facial hair. From pointed beards and muttonchop side whiskers to glossy mustaches whose curled tips defied the laws of gravity...

"Astounding, isn't it?" said Marco dryly, following her gaze to a Russian nobleman. "To what lengths we will go to attract the attention of the opposite sex."

Kate nodded, noting that he had no need to resort to such wiles. The simple elegance of his stark black and white evening attire only accentuated his handsome face and lean physique. He was a sleek panther prowling through a gilded jungle of colorful creatures.

But there was another predator on the loose, she reminded herself.

"La, Maaarcooo!" A trilling call came from one of the side galleries, the feminine voice mouthing his name as if it were melted toffee. "You naughty man! I heard you had arrived in town." A tall, slender lady squeezed through the crowd and took hold of his lapel. Her raven-dark hair tumbled in artful curls from a topknot circled with a set of large rubies. The rich red color was mirrored in a stunning gown of crimson satin, which set off her ivory skin to perfection.

Pursing her rosebud lips in a provocative pout, the lady pulled him close and kissed his cheek. "Why have you not come to see me?"

Marco coughed. "Ursula, allow me to introduce my new bride. Katharine and I were married recently in England and have come to Vienna on our wedding trip."

"Married!"

"Kate, this is Baroness Ursula Von Augsberg. An old friend."

"Married," repeated the baroness. There was a perceptible pause. "My poor darling!" Waggling a bejeweled finger, she added, "How many times have I warned you of the dangers of dallying with an innocent." She gave Kate a cursory glance and then lifted her elegant brows in a dismissive arch. "I did tell you that the English take that sort of thing so very seriously."

Kate knew that she should respond to the barb with a cool smile. However, she couldn't help but shoot back with a sharp retort. "I am American."

Another pause. "How quaint." After subjecting her to a more lengthy scrutiny, the baroness heaved an audible sigh. "Tell me, what does your father do, seeing as Americans are all so tedious as to insist on working for a living?"

"Actually, he was a pirate."

For an instant, the baroness's mask of sardonic superiority slipped. But she quickly recovered. "Then you won't mind if I steal your husband away for a short while." The baroness tapped her ivory-handled fan to

Marco's sleeve. "Come, *schatze*. There are some other old friends who wish to see you."

Schatze? Kate tried not to scowl as she silently repeated the endearment. Marco was no kitten—but the lady was certainly wearing a cat-in-the-creampot smile.

He offered his arm. "But of course. Kate is quite capable of amusing herself while I am gone."

"Of course," she muttered, watching them move away through the crowd. Spearing another glass of champagne, she took a long swallow, hoping to drown the tiny tongue of fire licking up in her belly.

Don't. Don't be a fool. Their marriage vows were a mere formality—Marco had never promised to be faithful.

"How very churlish of your escort to abandon such a beautiful lady, even for a moment."

Kate whirled around as a touch of soft leather brushed along her bare arm. "Allow me to keep you company, Madame..." The gentleman's voice trailed off in question.

"Wood—" she began, then quickly corrected herself. "I am Contessa della Ghiradelli," she replied, finding that saying the fancy name helped steady her self-esteem. Determined to appear as smooth and sophisticated as the swishing silks around her, Kate flashed what she hoped was a brilliant smile.

"*Enchanté, contessa. C'est vraiment un plaisir de faire votre connaissance.*" The gentleman lifted her hand to his lips. He spoke flawless French, yet Kate's keen ear detected a slight Slavic accent. "Andrei Jackowski at your service." At the last moment, he turned her wrist and feathered a kiss just above the hem of her glove.

"You are Polish, sir?" she asked.

He shrugged a well-tailored shoulder and switched to English. "That is difficult to say these days. What with so many countries intent on carving up the country of my birth into tiny slices, I feel more like a morsel of pigeon, baked in a tasty pie."

Kate immediately warmed to his tart sense of humor. "Do not the English support an independent Duchy of Warsaw?"

"Good Heavens!" exclaimed Jackowski with mock amazement. "A lady who actually has an interest in the politics of this conference, not just the gossip and dalliances?"

"I do have a brain as well as a bosom," murmured Kate.

"And it appears to be just as well-developed," he replied, letting his gaze drop to her décolletage.

She felt herself growing a little warm. Her gown was not nearly as revealing as that of the baroness, nor were her charms as prominent. But nonetheless, it was nice to be admired.

"I am not sure that is quite a proper comment for a gentleman to make."

"Neither am I," he replied, gold-flecked sparks of amusement lighting his chocolate-brown eyes. He signaled for a waiter to refill her champagne glass, along with his own. "However, I hope that you won't hold my words against me. I should very much like to entice you to take a stroll with me while your friend is otherwise occupied."

Despite all the distractions, Kate had not lost sight of her mission. A walk through the galleries was exactly what she had in mind, and Jackowski might prove useful in identifying the different delegations.

"I should like that very much," she said slowly, setting her hand on his sleeve.

"Excellent." He pressed a little closer, his thigh kissing hers as they crossed through an arched alcove. "*Pardon*," he murmured. "It is, as you English say, quite a crush."

Kate didn't bother to point out that they had the narrow space all to themselves. If flirtation was part of the game, she would play it to the hilt. "Might we take a peek at the ballroom?" she asked, edging toward one of the balconies. "I have never seen such pomp and pageantry."

"Is this your first time in Vienna?" asked Jackowski politely.

"Yes," she said, staring intently at the dancers on the floor below.

"Ah, no wonder you appear fascinated by it all." He fell silent as the stately procession made its way around the polished parquet. "Trust me, it soon loses it allure."

"Like eating too many sweets?" murmured Kate. "At first, it seems utterly delicious, but then your teeth begin to ache and your stomach turns a little queasy."

"Precisely." A humorless laugh rumbled low in his throat. "You soon begin to crave something more than spun sugar and colored marzipan." He looked at her a little hungrily.

"It sounds as if you are bored, sir."

"A steady diet of decadent parties turns stale rather quickly," said Jackowski slowly. "The ladies are all alike and the pleasures are too predictable." He fingered his neatly trimmed goatee, and as the velvet swags stirred overhead, the rippling shadows made his slanted cheekbones look as sharp as knife blades. "You seem different."

Keeping her eyes on the dancing figures, Kate considered her next move. Perhaps it was the champagne making her a little reckless—she waved to a nearby footman for more—but she decided to encourage Jackowski's advances. *For now.*

"I am," she agreed. "This may be familiar to you, yet it is all so foreign to me. Will you escort me through the other galleries and point out the notables who are here tonight?" She lowered her lashes. "As you see, my husband is sadly neglecting his duties."

"Tsk, tsk." Jackowski sidled closer. "Be assured that I shall be delighted to serve as a surrogate, *cherie*."

"You must know many of these people," she said casually, as they started to meander through the galleries. The notes of a waltz drifted up from the ballroom, drawing some of the guests to the stairs, but the rooms were still crowded.

"Yes." He made a wry face. "Having spent the good part of the last year negotiating with the Russian and the various German states over the fate of my homeland, I am more intimately acquainted with the participants of this peace conference than I care to be."

"Who is the tall, bearded Viking?" she asked, turning just enough to dislodge his roving hand from the curve of her hip.

"The Sulky Swede." Jackowski chuckled. "He's constantly threatening to slit his throat over the fickleness of his latest lover. Seeing as he expresses his sorrows in terrible poetry, he would be doing the rest of us a favor by putting himself out of his misery."

"And the red-haired gentleman to his left?" asked Kate.

"Oh, that is Hertzfeld, head of the Pomeranian contingent…" Jackowski proved to be an interesting commentator, keeping up a steady stream of amusing anecdotes.

Kate kept a close eye on the faces, watching carefully for the would-be assassin from Tappan's estate as she tried to keep track of all the different factions and delegations that her escort mentioned. *Saxons, Prussians, Poles, Latvians, Russians*—with so many volatile elements crammed into a small space, it was no wonder that the Baltic was a powder keg, ready to explode at the touch of a single errant spark.

Feeling her own nerves growing a little singed, she took another sip of wine. The heat of the rooms, heavy with the scent of flowers and lush perfumes, was growing oppressive. The laughter was too loud, the jostling touch of flesh against flesh too intimate.

For an instant, she longed to escape the stifling splendor and seek a cold, cleansing breath of fresh air.

"Enjoying yourself?" Jackowski's hot breath tickled against her ear.

"Yes, quite." Clenching the crystal stem of her glass, Kate forced a false smile.

"Come this way," he murmured. "The rooms off the main galleries are less crowded and afford a chance for quiet conversation."

Kate doubted that his intention was to talk, but she followed along without protest. The glittering chandeliers gave way to flickering wall sconces and dark wood paneling as they made their way through a series of connecting rooms. Ancient tapestries decorated the walls and thick Oriental carpets cushioned their steps. The guests here were gathered in more intimate groups, and from what Kate could overhear, the discussions were not about politics.

She angled yet another quick look around. *Still no*

sign of her quarry—or of her husband. But then, the connecting corridors offered plenty of darkened nooks for a private tryst. Already they had passed several couples in the clench of a passionate embrace. It took little imagination to picture the baroness and Marco rekindling an old flame.

"Your glass is empty, Lady Ghiradelli." Jackowski took a bottle from a silver tray. "More champagne?"

Kate nodded, despite feeling a little flushed. "The bubbles tickle," she murmured, raising the glass to her lips and letting the effervescence tease against her tongue.

Setting a hand on the curve of her hip, Jackowski urged her into the shadowed corridor. "I can think of even more pleasant ways to bring the same sensation to your flesh."

"Really?" she said coyly. It would serve Marco right if she let a stranger kiss her. Not that he cared what she did with other men.

Turning for the last set of rooms, Kate suddenly spotted a familiar shock of silky black hair amid the lush velvet draperies of the stairwell up ahead. The baroness was curling a lock of it around her slim fingers.

"Excuse me, but I must withdraw for a moment." Thrusting her glass at Jackowski, Kate backed up a step.

"Allow me to come with you."

"Thank you, sir, but a lady really does not wish to have a gentleman accompany her on such a mundane mission," she said meaningfully. "The room is not far from here."

He looked loath to let her go, but could hardly argue the point. "I shall wait for you in here," he said, indicating a dimly lit side chamber paneled in mahogany. "Don't be long, *cherie*."

Gathering her skirts, Kate quickly turned down one

of the many corridors, grateful that the low light hid her flaming face.

How dare Marco flaunt his infidelity so soon after their marriage?

Fury bubbled through her, fueled by the wine. A part of her was tempted to turn around and accost him. Oh, how she itched to slap the seductive smile from his wanton mouth. Her palms prickled, even as she realized how naïve her reaction would appear to the jaded aristocrats.

Sex was just a game for them. As for love…

Love was a laughable notion.

Kate slowed her steps and ducked into the shelter of the colonnaded archway leading back to the main gallery. The marble was cool and calming against her skin. Pressing her cheek to the fluted stone, she sucked in a deep breath, willing her heartbeat to come under control. How absurd that she had actually fallen in love with her husband. She must not let anyone know her pathetic secret. *Discipline and detachment.* Her years of vagabond adventures had taught her how to survive adversity.

After taking a moment more to collect herself, Kate was about to step away from the columns when a pair of gentlemen turned into the corridor. Heads bent together, they were talking in low, rushed tones. Something about their manner made her stay hidden in the shadows.

They paused, and one of them looked back over his shoulder.

"Relax. You're as nervous as a virgin on her wedding night," growled his companion.

"This is my first time engaging in…" The other man let his voice trail off.

"You've nothing to do, save to make sure the papers I gave you are placed on his desk."

"Don't worry. I shall play my part without fail."

"I suggest you do."

The voice was soft but menacing. And unmistakably familiar. The tiny hairs on the back of Kate's neck stood on end as she inched forward, trying to catch a glimpse of the speaker's face. Light from the adjoining gallery reflected off the pale marble archway, catching close-cropped brown hair and a long, thin nose in sharp silhouette.

It was him.

"Let us not dawdle," went on the man she had seen at Lord Tappan's estate. "Ellendorff is waiting for us in the refreshment salon."

"Excuse me, *schatze.*" Kate touched Marco's sleeve "But I must drag you away from your friend."

He looked around, surprised. "*Cara—*"

"Do forgive me, Baroness." Her grip tightened on his arm. "I'm sure you'll understand."

Marco slowly unwound himself from the baroness's hand.

"I've seen him," she whispered.

His senses came instantly alert. "Where?"

"He just entered the refreshment salon." She quickened her step. "This way."

As they slipped into the room, Marco immediately headed for the punch table and grabbed up two glasses of champagne. "Laugh," he ordered, making a show of nuzzling her neck. "And look a little wobbly."

No one paid them much heed as they staggered in a dizzy spin. Propping her against the wall, he asked, "Which one?"

"The brown-haired man in the group by the display of medieval swords," she replied. "High forehead, angular nose, thin mustache. Dressed in the dark burgundy coat."

"I see him."

"Do you know who he is?" she asked, masking the question beneath a giggling laugh.

"No, but that should be easy enough to find out."

Weaving his way back to the punch table, he sidled up to an officer of the Emperor's House Guards. "The gentleman with the mustache, standing by the swords—is that Von Buehlen, the Bavarian minister?" he asked, exaggerating a squint.

"*Nein*," replied the officer. "That is Count Grunwald, of the Saxon delegation."

"Hmmph." He let out a loud belch. "Need to find Von Buehlen. I'm told he knows the best brothels in town."

The officer shrugged and walked off.

Marco made a show of draining a glass of punch before returning to Kate. "You are sure that is the man you saw at Lord Tappan's estate?" They couldn't afford to make a mistake.

"Positive," she answered.

He slumped a shoulder to the wall and looked up at the painted plaster ceiling, where a classical scene of cavorting nymphs and naked putti leered down on the modern-day revelry. A gilded reminder that beneath the artful smiles, the guests here were all in pursuit of their own selfish desires.

If Kate was wrong, a king would die.

Dropping his gaze, Marco stole a quick look at her profile. Fatigue smudged her features, yet it could not dim her luminous strength. She had been thrown to the wolves, but rather than swoon with fear, she had faced the snapping jaws without batting her lovely golden lashes.

Light hung for an instant on the curled fringe, a pure pale glimmer of clarity among all the excess. Kate was no innocent, but she had been true to herself. He wanted to lean over and press his lips to her cheek. Somehow, she had lived her life in a tough world without being sullied by its sordidness. It made him feel a little ashamed of his own cowardice. Perhaps one day he would find the courage to face his inner demons.

But that day would have to wait.

"Well done, *cara*," he said softly.

"You believe me?" It might have been the brittle clink of the crystal, but her voice seemed to have an odd edge.

"Without a doubt." Marco twined his fingers in the fringe of her shawl. "Let's take our leave. I'll explain in the carriage."

It wasn't until the wheels began clattering over the cobbles that he spoke again. "It's all beginning to make perfect sense. In the wake of Napoleon's wars, the biggest controversy facing Europe is how to divide the Baltic states. Russia, Austria, and England each has its own agenda, and the Kingdom of Saxony is key to the matter. The king is adamantly opposed to giving up any territory to Prussia. If he were eliminated..." He went on to explain the details that Lynsley had given him on the politics of the region.

"Our sources tell us that Grunwald favors the Russian claim—and he holds great influence over the heir to the throne. If the present king is assassinated, he stands to profit immensely, both in prestige, and no doubt in gold. Tsar Alexander is quite generous when it comes to buying alliances."

"I see," said Kate. The window draperies were drawn, leaving the interior of the carriage wreathed in darkness. The gloom seemed to add a certain coolness to her tone. "We are very fortunate that you are so observant." She gave a curt laugh.

Marco drew his brows together. Her nerves seemed strung taut, but then, given all the stresses on her of late, it was a wonder that she hadn't snapped.

"We're also lucky that you are so resilient, Kate. I'm sorry that your life has been turned topsy-turvy by forces out of your control."

The whisper of silk slid across the soft leather. "I've survived by knowing how to land on my feet."

Marco remained silent, unsure how to respond. He had not been nearly as successful in uncovering useful information. The baroness, who usually knew of every bit of gossip between Lisbon and Moscow, had nothing to offer on Lord Tappan. She had been much more interested in turning the talk to a more personal level.

It had taken a very firm hand to keep her lithe little fingers out of his trousers.

He shot a regretful glance in Kate's direction, wishing he could see a hint of her expression. He longed to wrap himself in her smoky laughter, to taste the heat of her mouth, her skin.

The scent of *her*—the fragrance of sun and sea—wafted through the blackness. *Sweet, elusive.*

And then it was gone as the carriage lurched to a halt and Kate flung open the door to let herself out.

Chapter Twenty-five

Woozy with wine, Kate slowly climbed the narrow stairs to their rooms, glad that she had told her maid not to wait up. Her body ached all over. The rigors of traveling and the tension of hunting an elusive quarry had taken a toll, but the pain was more than physical. Her spirit—always her stalwart strength—felt shaken. Bruised.

She should feel elated with tonight's work. Instead, the evening had left her feeling awkward. Unsure.

Aside from a fleeting kiss on signing the marriage lines, Marco had made no effort to exercise his conjugal rights. Oh, he had been anxious enough to toss up her skirts when the act was immoral, she thought with an inward grimace. But now that it was perfectly proper to take her to bed, he seemed to have lost interest in her.

It should come as no shock. She had always heard that the chase was what attracted a rake. Illicit trysts were far more titillating than conventional arrangements.

The heavy tread of his steps in the gloom sounded like a

funeral dirge. No doubt he was already mourning the death of his devil-may-care bachelorhood. She had seen the way his gaze had been riveted on the baroness's half-bared bosom. *Lust. Longing.* The taut stretch of gossamer silk had left little to the imagination regarding the other half.

Kate glanced down at her own chest. Compared to the elegant, worldly women gathered here in Vienna, she didn't measure up. They wore brilliant baubles, dazzling mere mortals with their glittering jewels, opulent gowns, and sophisticated charm. While she was as skinny as a boy and blunt to a fault in voicing her opinions. Men didn't like that. Or so it seemed.

As they started up the last flight, Kate slanted a surreptitious look at her husband. In the guttering flame of the tallow candle, Marco's face was drawn tight, the beautiful bones smudged by brooding shadows. He looked miserable, and who could blame him?

Her foot caught on the rough planking and she stumbled.

"Steady, *cara*." Catching her around the waist, Marco drew her close, his solid, muscular body steadying her trembling legs.

It was, she knew, revoltingly romantic, but he reminded her of the knight in armor who had greeted the Emperor's guests on his snowy white charger. A shining hero.

Only a silly schoolgirl would entertain such dreams.

"Just a few more steps and we are there," murmured Marco.

So close. And yet the distance between them seemed to stretch like a great black chasm.

His key scraped in the lock and the iron hinges creaked open.

Hot tears welled up against her eyelids as the door fell shut behind them. How ridiculous to be pining after her own husband. She knew he didn't care for her. This was a job. And she was an inconvenience, nothing more.

"*Dio Madre*." Muttering an oath, Marco shrugged out of his coat and struck a flint to the oil lamp. A spark flared to life, casting a pool of light over his torso. Pale as Carrera marble in the soft glow, the crisp linen shirt accentuated the sculptured lines of his shoulders. "Thank God that is over. If I had to taste another morsel of *foie gras,* I might expire on the spot."

He set the lamp on a side table and turned, silhouetting how the burgundy embroidered waistcoat tapered to his lean waist.

"Excellent work, Kate. Without you, this mission would be impossible," said Marco, reaching out to take her shawl.

Kate pulled away and hurried into the bedchamber. Yanking off a satin slipper, she threw it down. It skittered across the planked floor.

He raised a brow.

Damn him. She would *not* let him see her snivel or beg for his affection. The other slipper hit the wall with a satisfying slap.

"Is something wrong, *cara*?"

"No." Untying the tabs, she stepped out of her gown and kicked it across the woven rug.

Taking up a candle, he came to stand in the doorway. "Did I say something to upset you?"

"No." Awkwardly yanking at the strings of her corset, Kate wriggled free of the stays. A crack of whalebone warned that she wasn't being very ladylike about her actions, but she was too furious to care. Muttering an oath, she flung the garment at the dressing table chair.

"Do you always destroy your clothing after a fancy dress ball?" Marco carefully picked up the squashed silk gown and shook it out. "I had no idea I'd wed such an expensive wife."

"You had no idea because you never had any intention of taking a wife." At the sight of his bemused smile curling in the candlelight, all her simmering fears and frustrations exploded. "Well, now you can bloody well pay for it."

Jerking around, Kate meant to march for the wash-basin, but her thin shift snagged on the armoire latch. A sharp rip rent the shadowed silence, and a flap of delicate lawn cotton fell away, baring her breast.

She felt ridiculous. Humiliated. She knew she looked absurd, standing half naked, shrieking like a fishwife.

If he laughed, she would kill him.

"Kate." There was no amusement in his voice.

Bloody hell. A tear trickled down her cheek.

"Ah, *bella*."

"Don't. Call. Me. That," she choked out.

"Why?" He took a step closer.

She shrank away, hating how vulnerable she felt. She had spent all her life being strong and sure of herself. This sharp, painful need, twisting like a steel blade inside her, was a new and unsettling emotion.

"I can't help calling you that, Kate." Through the sin-black fringe of his lashes glimmered a flicker of jewel-tone blue. "It was la *Belladonna* who stole my affection," he murmured.

"I stole your purse," she whispered. "Your heart is untouchable."

"You wouldn't want it. It's far too black and shriveled to be of any appeal." He reached out and touched her lightly on the cheek. "But as for the rest of me, *cara*, I am yours."

"Oh, *si*. You belong to me—and any other lady who bats her lashes at you," she blurted out.

"Are you jealous?" he asked softly.

"No," she said through a trickle of tears. "I am furious. You . . . you . . ."

Before she could think of something suitably scathing to say, Marco swept her into his arms and in two quick strides was at the bed.

"Put me down!" she demanded, thumping her fists to his chest.

"As you wish."

Her bum bounced against the mattress and then sank into the plump eiderdown coverlet with a feathery sigh.

"Go away," muttered Kate, hugging a pillow to her chest.

Marco made no move to comply. Instead, he calmly unfastened his shirt and started to draw it over his head.

Whooph. The missile caught him smack in the chest.

Marco stepped back and waved the white sleeve of his shirt. "Might we cease hostilities for a moment and try to negotiate a truce?"

"To hell with peace conferences," she cried. "Go draw up terms of surrender with the Baroness of Bare-Breasts." Groping for more ammunition, she caught hold of the second pillow.

"A declaration of war?" He dodged the flying feathers. "Then I shall have to go on the offensive to defend myself."

Her blood was up now, anger sizzling away her self-pity. The next thing she grabbed was a book from the bedside chest.

"*Diavolo!*" He flung up an arm to deflect the blow.

"Lucifer doesn't have a prayer in hell of fighting back," she retorted.

"A woman scorned is a dangerous thing."

"Scorned!" scoffed Kate. "As if I want you in my bed." The next book was a weighty volume of Byron's poetry, perfect for doing some damage.

Let the wretch try to flirt with a blackened eye.

As if reading her mind, Marco swore a low oath and ducked just as she hurled the new missile. Flinging his shirt to the floor, he spun closer and pounced, fire-gold light rippling over the taut stretch of bronzed muscle.

The air whooshed from her lungs as his body pinned her to the mattress. Momentarily robbed of breath, she twisted in wordless fury, trying to squirm free of his enveloping heat.

"Oh, no," he growled, catching her wrists and dragging them up over her head. "A husbandly prerogative is to demand that my wife cease trying to pummel me to a pulp."

"You don't want to be a husband," said Kate in a fierce whisper.

His eyes glittered through the tangle of dark hair. "And what of you, Kate? Do you want to be a wife?"

She ceased struggling, and for a long moment the only sound between them was the ragged rasp of their breathing. The air swirled, hot and heavy with unseen sparks.

"Are you regretting Fate?" His tongue traced the swell of her lower lip. "The vagary of life that forced you to accept a wanton wastrel as your spouse?"

"I..."

Her flesh was now between his teeth. The nip sent a lick of fire through her limbs.

"I can think of only a few worse things," she mumbled thickly, trying to hold on to her anger. Any other emotion would leave her too naked to need.

"Such as?" he asked, moving his wicked mouth along the ridge of her cheekbone.

"Being tied to the mast and left for the seagulls to pick out my eyeballs," she murmured, as he kissed the salt from her lashes.

"Torture," he agreed. "Stuck up against a long, hard post sounds like a fate worse than death."

Kate couldn't help it. A low laugh vibrated in her throat. "You impossible man."

"*Si*. Incorrigible."

One wide, strong hand kept her wrists imprisoned while the other found the folds of cotton bunched at her hips. Slowly, slowly he inched the sheer fabric up the length of her thighs, its touch dancing over her flesh like the flutter of a butterfly's wing. Oh, but there was nothing whispery about the press of his broad palm. His stroke was firm. Possessive.

"Ohhh." Her laugh deepened to a darker sound.

Marco slid his fingers through the curls between her legs. "You think I don't want my wife, *cara*? I had better move to correct that impression right away." Parting her feminine folds, he teased his touch into her wet passage and then drew it out, gliding a slick fingertip over her hidden pearl.

Kate gasped as a wave of honeyed heat washed over her.

"I wouldn't want you to start questioning my manhood," he said a little roughly. A hitch of his hips thrust his throbbing erection against the inside of her thigh.

"Then show me," she demanded.

"Ahh." A wicked gleam lit in his eyes. "Now you want me in your bed?"

"Yes," answered Kate, wanting him desperately. "Yes."

He lowered his lips, letting them hover a hairsbreadth from hers. Shadows skittered over his chiseled features, dark over light, swirling around a wink of blue.

Her pulse began to quicken.

"*Va bene*." The wet warmth of his mouth was on her, searing and sensual. Yielding with a shivering sigh, she opened herself fully to his kiss.

The room began to spin, the age-dark beams and whitewashed plaster turning to a blur of hazy shapes. Was it the wine? Or the wildly wanton things he was doing to her body?

His tongue was gliding in and out of her, setting a shocking rhythm matched by his finger in her most feminine spot. The sensations were exquisite.

Explosive.

Surrendering to the searing fire, Kate came apart in a burst of pleasure.

"Ah, *cara, cara*," he crooned, once her cries had subsided. "Now, we are going to do it again, but with both of us entirely naked. And with my cock inside you."

It took every shred of self-control to keep from tearing her shift into a thousand tiny pieces and thrusting himself into her like a slabbering primitive beast. Slowly releasing her wrists, Marco slid the shift up over her head. Her loosened hair shimmered like a halo on the rumpled pillows, suffusing her face with a molten gold glow. Curling strands caressed her shoulders. Beneath the gilded flickers, her glorious body stretched out in sinuous splendor.

His beautiful naked wife.

"Undress me, *cara.*" His voice was a little shaky as he guided her hands to his trousers. "Please. I need to lie with you, nothing between us."

"Oh, I should make you beg," she murmured. "I should make you squirm." She dragged the wool down his legs a little roughly.

His response was immediate.

"I've been tortured quite enough," he rasped as she took his hardening shaft into her velvety grip. "Riding day and night in a closed carriage with your beguiling body rubbing up against mine. *Dio Madre*, it was enough to drive any man mad."

Circling her thumb and forefinger around his girth, Kate feathered a stroke along his length. Her mouth curled in a sublime smile. "Why haven't you touched me since our wedding?"

"I was..." Afraid. Dare he admit it? To care was to make himself vulnerable to pain.

"Unsure," he finished haltingly. "Unsure how you felt about being forced into marriage."

She turned on her side, the spill of her hair curtaining her face. "I didn't have to say yes."

"The other alternatives were even less appealing than I," he said.

"Ah, but you are forgetting..."

His mind went a little hazy as the heat of her palm curled around his cock. Liquid fire flooded his belly.

"I'm rather clever at getting myself out of sticky situations," continued Kate. "I wasn't in any real danger."

Ah, but he was in grave danger of losing himself altogether. As her touch played over his swollen manhood, he squeezed his eyes shut, savoring for the first time in ages a lightness untainted by dark, desperate fear.

Kate. His wild sea sprite, his beguiling, bedeviling Nereid. Conjuring up some secret science, she made the dead, black coal of his heart flare to life. A mad, hot, scarlet flame that warmed him to his very core. He found an indescribable comfort in her presence, some bone-shuddering force far more powerful than lust.

And yet, the feeling also kindled a sense of dread. *Love?* He couldn't give way to it. He feared that he would only disappoint her. Hurt her. Let her ask for the sun and the moon, but not his heart.

It wasn't worthy of her.

Her strokes quickened, her sweet mouth tracing the jut of his shoulder. Oh, she was a passionate creature, and wanted him here and now, despite his faults. He couldn't resist the selfish urge to respond. His hand slid up her creamy white thighs to where his fingers found her slick and ready for him. At the touch of honeyed warmth, a desperate growl welled up in his throat. There was no holding back.

With trembling hands, he rolled her over and spread her legs. A nudge pushed his ruddy cock closer, closer.

Squeezing his eyes shut, Marco thrust himself inside her with a shuddering groan. No more thoughts. No more regrets. Just this moment.

Her hands played over his back, tracing the contours, skimming over his ribs. "No man should be so perfect," she murmured, nipping at his earlobe. "A beautiful bronzed Roman god."

"Matched with a hellion angel."

She arched up to meet his thrust, clenching her knees around his hips. "Oh Lud, what a pair we make."

He laughed, feeling the rumble vibrate against her salty skin. "What a pair," he whispered, driving himself deeper. The slick, smooth warmth of her sheath held him tight. *Two as one.*

Rocking together, their bodies glistened in the candlelight, their rhythm mounting to a crescendo.

"*Ti amo*," she whispered, and came undone in his arms.

Ti amo—I love you.

The words made him want to weep.

Heart thudding wildly against his ribs, Marco felt a fierce joy pulse through him. A hot rush of happiness that he had thought was long gone from his life.

Muffling a shout in her sweet-scented hair, he convulsed in a surge of liquid silver rain.

For a long, languid interlude they lay still and silent, entwined in each other. Marco couldn't remember passion ever leaving him with such a profound feeling of peace. Overhead, the ancient beams groaned, and outside a gust rattled the leaded-glass windowpanes. But for the moment, the world seemed very distant. Nothing could intrude on their togetherness.

But all too soon, Kate stirred and gave a drowsy sigh. "I'm sorry..." she began.

Sorry? His insides clenched.

"For what I said," she added slowly. "I am well aware that love was not part of our bargain, Marco. I'm not a naïve schoolgirl. I don't expect any ardent declarations of the heart in return."

"If I had a heart, it would be yours, Kate. But there is nothing worthwhile of it to give."

She nestled her cheek against his chest. "Why?"

A simple question, but how to answer? He spun a lock of her hair between his fingers, watching the glints of gold spark in the dying light. "Has Alessandra said nothing to you about my past?"

"I told you, your cousin does not engage in idle gossip," replied Kate.

"Unlike most women," he said wryly. "But then, it's no surprise that the 'Sinners' have a special code of honor."

"You are changing the subject," she murmured.

"I am good at evading things," he replied.

"Why do you wish to avoid telling me?" she asked.

"Because it makes me vulnerable," he blurted out.

"Ah." She skimmed her palm in a slow, soft circle just beneath his breastbone. "I suppose it does. But sharing a sordid secret can also make the burden easier to bear."

Marco hesitated, unsure of just how close he dared to let her come to his innermost self.

Her hand stilled, and she started to pull away.

Catching her wrist, he kept her warmth pressed to his skin. "I've always been free-spirited, even as a boy. My older brother was of a more scholarly nature, yet we were the best of friends." Marco forced himself to go on, despite the tightness in his throat. "Daniello always followed my lead, saying he admired my sense of daring. One adventure—I had a notion to free a neighbor's old horse slated for the slaughterhouse—required climbing down a steep cliff."

He paused as the casement rattled in the gloom. "Daniello stopped halfway down. He wasn't as agile as I was, and wanted to back off. I jeered at him. Called him a coward. Questioned his manhood." Drawing in a ragged breath, he went on in a rush. "I imagine you can guess what happened. He fell to his death, and I became the heir to the Como title and fortune."

Kate moved her hand to his cheek and forced his gaze to meet hers. "And so you mean to spend your life punishing yourself for a youthful accident?"

"Put that way, you make it sound childish."

"We all make mistakes. We all have done things we wish we had not," she said.

"You did not kill someone you loved." Marco closed his eyes. "It pierced my heart."

"I am sorry." Her lips feathered along the line of his jaw. "Perhaps one day the wound will heal."

"I don't know if it is possible," he said bleakly.

"I think only you can decide that."

She didn't whine or cajole. But then, Kate knew how hard it was to battle personal demons. The choice to fight or flee she was leaving to him, and him alone.

Marco lifted her fingertips to his lips, grateful for her understanding. Grateful for *her*—the salt-sweet scent of orange and wild thyme, the silky-soft heat of her skin, the steel-tough strength of her spirit. "I can't promise what sort of future we shall have, but..."

"But we will deal with that when the time comes," she finished quickly. "Right now, we can think only of why we are here." Edging away, she rolled on her back and pulled the rumpled sheet over her body. "I assume that we shall want to move as quickly as possible, now that we have identified our quarry."

"Correct." The draft licked over his bare flesh, chilling the length where she had just lain. "We shall aim for the day after tomorrow. That evening, Prince Metternich is holding a lavish outdoor fete at his villa after the peace celebration in the Augarten. The festivities and fireworks should provide a perfect cover for our plan."

Chapter Twenty-six

Kate checked that the slim dagger was strapped securely to her leg.

"I don't expect you to need that," said Marco tersely.

"I've found that it's best to be prepared for any contingency," she replied, smoothing the blue skirts back in place. "No matter how well-conceived, plans can go awry."

"Which is why I would rather you didn't come along tonight," he muttered. "It could be dangerous."

Ignoring his words, Kate calmly took up her white shawl. All of the ladies had been asked to wear blue or white, the colors of peace, to Prince Metternich's gala party. Celebrating the first anniversary of the Allied victory at the Battle of Leipzig, the Peace Ball had all of Vienna abuzz over the extravagant preparations. A special domed building, graced with classical pillars and walnut parquet floors, had been constructed for the occasion at his summer villa on the Rennweg. Colorful lights and scarlet Turkish tents festooned the lobby—one diplomat had likened it to a scene from *The Arabian Nights*.

"We've already discussed that," she replied, making one last adjustment to the pearl-studded ribbon threaded in her hair. "I refuse to be wrapped in cotton wool and stashed in a cupboard just when things are getting interesting."

"You have a strange notion of 'interesting,'" growled Marco.

"Yes, I suppose I do." She watched a grudging grin tug at his mouth and smiled in return. "You had better get used to it."

He threaded a hand through his dark locks. "If you insist on taking such risks, my hair shall soon be turning gray."

"Perhaps that will discourage the ladies from flirting so shamelessly with you."

"You had better get used to it." Marco chuckled, but his expression quickly sobered. "Promise me that you will stand aside when the time comes to close in on our quarry."

"You are confident the plan will work?" she asked. Earlier that afternoon, Marco had outlined the strategy that he and Lynsley's Austrian operatives had come up with. The local men would be stationed around the grounds, disguised as waiters. At Marco's signal, they would all close in on the would-be assassin and carry him away to a waiting carriage.

He nodded. "Metternich's ball is going to be a spectacular affair. There's no question that Grunwald will attend—none of the dignitaries would dream of missing the event. And the scheduled entertainment should suit our purposes perfectly. Much of the festivities will take place outside. What with the display of fireworks over his gardens, and the excitement of a hot-air balloon ascension, no one will notice a guest being taken away, even if he does not go quietly. There will be a great many people drinking an excess of spirits."

"I am surprised that the marquess wishes to take Grunwald into custody, rather than simply eliminate him," she mused.

"Lynsley prefers that lethal force be used only as a last resort," explained Marco. "He believes there are much more effective ways to counter enemy plots. By using intelligence and subterfuge, the marquess is often able to turn a foe's strength into a weakness."

"From what little work that the Circle of Sin has done for him, it appears he is a very interesting man."

"'Interesting' does not do him justice. Perhaps 'unique' is a better word." Marco checked the priming on his Italian turn-on pocket pistol and tucked it into his coat. "Ready?"

"Yes." She couldn't resist adding, "I hope that we may have a chance to waltz together before duty calls."

He touched her hand, sending a tiny thrill dancing up her arm. "I imagine that will be easy to arrange. The Prince has several orchestras planted within his garden hedges so that the guests may spin along under the stars."

"You are joking."

"Not at all. He's also built several mock-classical temples to honor Mars, Athena, and Apollo—and hired Emilia Bigottini, the famous ballerina, to stage a special performance around them."

Kate blew out a long breath, trying to imagine the spectacle.

"Vienna is a city known for its decadent parties, but this one promises to be truly memorable," finished Marco.

"Yes, well, let us hope that our quarry has not changed plans and decided to add the murder of a monarch to the pageantry," she murmured.

The remark didn't elicit a smile. She had never seen him look so deadly serious.

Marco added a folded knife to his pocket, then suddenly turned and pulled her into a fierce hug. "From here on in, we must set personal feeling aside, *cara*," he said after crushing his mouth to hers in a swift kiss. "We have a job to do."

A parade of fancy carriages filled the streets, the gleam of their gilded trappings near blinding in the setting sun.

"Let's get out and walk," said Marco. "I'd like to make a last survey of the side streets." The vast gardens of Prince Metternich's villa were screened from the street by high walls and hedges, but he made careful mental note of the various gates, just in case the primary plan went awry.

"Where will you have a vehicle waiting to transport Grunwald to a safe house?" asked Kate softly.

"Actually, I've arranged for two—one at each end of the grounds. We can't be too careful, Kate. He must not be allowed to assassinate the king."

He quickened his step, feeling restless and on edge. To his relief, Kate seemed to sense his need to stay focused on the mission and didn't try to distract him with conversation.

The line of guests waiting to enter the villa snaked down the Rennweg, the white and blue ballgowns punctuated by the martial splendor of the various uniforms. Even the men in plain evening dress sparkled with medals and silver-threaded sashes. Precious jewels glittered all around—it looked as if the stars from the heavens had fallen to earth for one magical night.

He caught Kate's expression as she surveyed the crowd. "Behold the crème de la crème of the Continent," he murmured. "How does it feel to be part of the elite, Lady Ghiradelli?"

She muttered a rude word under her breath. "I'm not, and never shall be. If you wanted a wife to display in a gilded cage, you made the wrong choice."

Choices, choices. His heart began to pound against his ribs. Was he wrong to let her dance into danger with him? He had been part of enough missions to know that Fate could take an ugly turn at any moment.

The thought of losing his bold, free-spirited bride sent a blade of fear knifing through his gut.

Shading his eyes to hide his doubts, Marco surveyed the festive lawns. Colored lanterns burned brightly along the graveled paths, and the strains of lilting music wafted through the evening breeze. The lush plantings were echoed in the look of the ladies, many of whom had a profusion of olive and laurel leaves—the symbols of peace—woven into their hair.

"It's like a fairy tale come to life," breathed Kate, watching the elegant guests stroll among the strutting peacocks.

"This way," said Marco gruffly, turning down the central walkway. "Let us see if we can spot Grunwald."

The constant blare of trumpets from the main gate announced the steady arrival of sovereigns—emperors and kings rubbing shoulders with princes and archdukes. Never before had there been such an impressive gathering of titled aristocrats in one place. And yet, from what he could see, security was lax.

Which suited his purposes, thought Marco grimly.

Twilight colored the sky with streaks of orange and pinks that darkened to purple as it dipped into the shadows of the trees. Refreshment tents dotted the manicured grounds, the white damask walls billowing in the breeze. Champagne flowed, along with Mosel and Tokay wines. Toasts to peace rang out, punctuating the general mood of merriment and good cheer.

Tightening his hold on Kate's hand, Marco abruptly veered off the path and cut across the grass.

"Trouble?" she asked in a taut whisper.

In answer, he drew her into his arms. "Waltz with me, Kate." His fingers entwined hers as he spun into the first figures of the dance. "Before it grows too late."

He looped his other arm around her waist, reveling in the warmth of her body beneath the azure silk. Their feet skimmed silently over the freshly mown grass, twirling in harmony with each other. The music floated through the leaves, soft and lilting as the first pale dapplings of moonlight.

Her skirts flared as they whirled through a turn, and to his eyes she looked like an ethereal ocean wave washing over the soft earth.

Ti amo, he thought, pressing his cheek to the golden strands of her hair. He knew he should say it aloud, but somehow his tongue seemed to trip over the words. For now, the unspoken understanding connecting them would have to be enough.

Longing to hold the enchantment for more than a few magical moments, Marco closed his eyes and lost himself in her sweet scent. His palm traced the inward curve of her back, drawing her closer so that he might imprint every nuanced curve of her body to memory.

The violins rose in crescendo, then the notes died away, leaving only the twittering of the nightingales to serenade the night.

"Thank you." Kate lifted her face and smiled. "That was lovely."

"*Si, bella*," he whispered.

Her lashes flickered in the lanternlight as she averted her gaze. "I—"

Marco heard her breath catch in her throat.

"I see him."

He went very still. "Where?"

"There. Three paces to the left of Apollo's Temple."

Turning slowly, Marco saw Grunwald standing with several other men. They were smoking cigars and watching the ballet dancers.

"Stay here," he ordered. "And, Kate, be patient. I can't say how long this will take."

Kate watched Marco slip away into the shadows. *Patience.* It was not a virtue that came naturally to her, she thought wryly. Her first impulse was to follow along, but for his sake, she would try to rein in her hellion spirit. She understood that any distraction could put him in mortal danger.

Marco was dealing with a deadly adversary. A man who would kill without compunction.

Her hands smoothed over her skirts, feeling the lingering warmth of his presence. *Il Serpenti* could take care of himself, she told herself. Still, a frisson of fear snaked down her spine.

Forcing aside her worries, Kate turned away from the blazing lights and walked along the tall boxwood hedge leading to the outer fringes of the grounds. The laughter and the music grew fainter....

Oh, if only she could quiet her trepidation.

At the far end of the formal garden, she spotted a strange shape looming up in the shadows. It swayed gently in the breeze and then slowly started to grow larger and larger, a blaze of blue and white stripes rising above the dark leaves.

Recalling that a hot-air balloon was to be part of the evening's festivities, she edged closer, curious to see the contraption close up. Peering through the hedge, she watched two men carefully adjust the brass burner inside the passenger basket, slowly inflating the colorful silk.

Thick ropes tethered the balloon to the ground. Seemingly satisfied that all was in order, the men climbed out of the basket, which was now hovering several feet off the ground, and began draping silver bunting over the sides of dark woven wicker.

Kate lingered for another moment, then started to retrace her steps. The evening was certainly going to end on a high note, she mused. The prince had hired the famed Herr Stuwer, Vienna's master of pyrotechnics, to create a special show of fireworks. To highlight the awesome display, the orchestra was to play Handel's "Music for the Royal Fireworks."

Sparks and fire would light up the heavens—a fitting salute to the Allied victory over Napoleon.

Looking away from the starry sky, Kate saw the wink

and flash of the honor guard as they stood at attention among the white columns of the domed pavilion. Supper for the sovereigns was ending, and the dignitaries were starting to stroll out to partake in the outdoor festivities.

She tried to relax, but her nerves were stretched as taut as the balloon's tethers. So much could go wrong for Marco. What if the local agents had betrayed him to the Saxon conspirators? Everything was for sale in Vienna—state secrets, fleshly pleasures, princely kingdoms...

An involuntary shudder raced through her limbs.

Seeing an arched opening in the hedge, Kate slipped into its shelter and pressed her gloved hands to her cheeks, hoping to keep her imagination from running wild.

She was, after all, *Belladonna* of Naples, the steel-nerved cutpurse who had outwitted the authorities at every turn. She knew the importance of keeping a cool head when all hell broke loose.

A ripple of laughter drifted out from the nearby faux temple, and then suddenly the mellow sound was overridden by snapping branches and skittering feet on the rough gravel. Kate instinctively flattened into the shadows as she ventured a peek at the two onrushing figures.

The man in pursuit lunged and caught the coattails of his quarry. Both hit the ground hard, tangled in a welter of thrashing kicks and punches. As one of them rolled free and scrambled to his feet, a flicker of light fell over his features.

Face contorted in rage, Grunwald whipped a long stiletto from his boot and slashed at Marco's outstretched hand.

Kate bit her lip to keep from crying out as the blade grazed his fingertips.

Marco spun away. Dropping low, he aimed a hard kick

at Grunwald's knee, which sent the Saxon sprawling. But moving with catlike agility, Grunwald quickly recovered and shot up with the blade still in his grasp. His other fist clenched a rock, and in the same scrabbling motion, he hurled it at Marco's head.

The missile struck Marco flush on the temple, knocking him to the ground. Grunwald whirled, his breath coming in ragged gasps as he spotted two dark shapes round the far end of the hedge and come racing toward him. Cut off from the main gardens, he charged past Kate's hiding place and sprinted into the gloom.

Crawling to his knees, Marco exhorted his men to give chase.

But they were still a good distance away, noted Kate. And Marco was still groggy from the blow…

Without hesitation, she set off in pursuit.

Twisting, turning, through the darkness, Kate matched the Saxon's pounding pace as he cut through the ornamental plantings. A holly bush snagged her shawl and she flung it aside, ignoring the branches tearing at her skirts. *Faster, faster.* The looming garden walls had the Saxon trapped in a gateless corner. There was only one way for him to elude capture.

And just as she feared, the clever dastard was heading for the lone blaze of light.

Hurtling the stack of supplies lining the small clearing, Grunwald waved his blade, frightening off the balloon's tenders. With three quick slashes he cut the restraining lines, then climbed into the basket.

The billowing silk sphere began to float upward.

Kate scrambled over the crates, a moment too late. The wicker was way out of reach. But a gust of wind caught one of the trailing ropes, swirling it close. For an experienced sailor, it was an easy grab. Catching the end, she felt herself lifted off her feet. Hand over hand, she began climbing up its length.

The balloon was now just above the trees.

A last quick heave brought her over the lip of the basket. Hunched over the brass burner, Grunwald was busy adjusting the flame and the fuel to steady the flight. He didn't realize that he had company until Kate spoke.

"Step away from the fire, Herr Grunwald," she ordered, drawing her knife from beneath her gown.

"*Verdammt noch mal!*" Grunwald's look of astonishment thinned to a sneer. "Meddlesome bitch," he snarled. "Who the devil are you?"

"An avenging angel," she answered. "I don't intend to let you and Tappan get away with murder."

"*Miss Woodbridge?*"

"Yes," she replied, balancing lightly on her toes. The rocking motion was very much like the sway of a ship, so she felt right at home.

Grunwald did not appear quite so comfortable. He stumbled slightly as he rose and edged sideways. "Say your prayers. No female has the brains or brawn to fight me."

"You are not the first man to think that," she retorted. "Give it up. The game is over."

"Surrender to a *frau*?" Grunwald gave a nasty laugh and raised his stiletto. "Not bloody likely."

Shifting her feet, Kate was ready when he suddenly stabbed at her heart. Steel clashed on steel as she parried his blade. He lunged again, but the rocking basket threw him off-balance and he fell back against the big brazier.

Grunwald screamed as sparks flared and the spilled oil ignited in a whoosh of flames.

"*Kate!*" Marco's hoarse shout rose from the ground below.

Fire crackled as the wicker and bunting came alight. A rope snapped, and the balloon gave a sickening lurch. In another few moments the flames would shoot up the cording and ignite the silk.

"*Kate!*" cried Marco again.

Before she could respond, a small explosion rocked the basket, nearly knocking her off her feet. Looking around, she saw its force had stunned Grunwald. He lay slumped over the side, soot blackening his face and sparks singeing his coat.

Another line gave way in a shower of ashes.

Grabbing the dangling rope, Kate quickly wrenched the unconscious Grunwald upright and lashed their bodies together with a snug bosun's knot.

If her luck held, the balloon would stay aloft long enough to anchor a swing to safety. It was a dangerous move—but there wasn't much choice. With the roar of burning silk echoing in her ears, she took an instant to gauge the distance to the nearest tree and then jumped over the edge.

Clinging tightly to her prisoner, Kate sailed through the night air. *Watch the arc, watch the angle.* This was no different from swinging from the mast of her father's ship, she reminded herself. Using her feet to absorb the impact, she bounced off the tree trunk and twisted down through the branches until the tangled rope halted their fall.

A swift tug freed the knot at her waist. Grunwald was

still unresponsive, but by clutching the collar of his coat, she managed to lower him down to Marco and his men.

"Take him," ordered Marco. "You know where."

Lynsley's agents wasted no time in hustling the Saxon away.

"Hurry, *cara*!" Marco turned his attention back to her.

Kate slid down to earth just as the balloon exploded in a fiery shower of sparks.

At the other end of the gardens, the crowd erupted in delighted cheers, thinking the spectacle was the start of the fireworks display. As if on cue, rockets shot up, filling the sky with a brilliant burst of colors.

Amid the flash and thunder, Marco grabbed her and ran alongside a stretch of the wall until they reached a small gate hidden in the ivy.

Turning, he framed her smoke-streaked face between his quivering palms. Anger seemed to pulse from every pore. "Don't *ever* do anything that bloody reckless again!"

So much for a tender reunion.

Kate drew back a touch. "I couldn't just stand by and let him escape, could I?"

"*Dio Madre*." His lips traced over her brow. "I know you would fight Lucifer and all his legions to right a wrong, *cara*. Your courage puts me to blush." The kiss was now feathered over her cheek. "But damn it, I thought my heart would shatter into a thousand shards when I saw you grab hold of that rope and rise into the darkness."

"I—I thought you didn't have a heart," she said softly.

"Neither did I. Somehow you have brought a withered husk back to life."

Was it too much to hope that love might take root and blossom between them?

A brilliant burst of blue and white sparks filled the sky. The soaring notes of Handel's symphony trumpeted through the trees.

"Well, you certainly know how to orchestrate a dramatic moment," said Kate, hardly daring to think her wish might come true.

He hugged her, a fierce, hard clench that forced the air from her lungs. "I was afraid that I had lost you. Please promise me that you will never, ever scare me like that again."

Kate slipped her hand beneath his shirt. Through the shredded leather of her glove, she felt the steady thud reverberating against his ribs. "I know what you are thinking, but the past is the past and you cannot live in fear of its shadow. Life is fraught with risks."

His hold tightened.

"We can't guard ourselves against pain, but we can forge our own future," she added softly. "One full of joy if we dare to try."

"*Ti amo*," he whispered. "I am willing to try if you are."

"*Ti amo*." Kate smiled. "You know, I am looking forward to becoming fluent in Italian. I think it's the most beautiful language in the world."

"*Bella*." There was a long interlude before he spoke again. "Be assured, we shall have a lot of time to practice on the journey home."

Epilogue

"Now that you have returned safely to London, a celebration is in order." Lord Lynsley raised his wineglass and saluted the four other people seated at the Duke of Cluyne's magnificent dining table. "Allow me to offer a belated toast to your nuptials, Lord and Lady Ghiradelli."

"Hear, hear," murmured Charlotte.

"And to a successful mission," added the marquess dryly.

"All thanks to Kate," said Marco, seconding the toast. His words were soft, but his glance sent a shiver of heat through her.

"*Hmmph.*" Cluyne cleared his throat. "It's a good thing she is so deucedly clever and capable, you young rapscallion. Had you allowed any harm to come to her, I would have sliced your guts into garters."

Charlotte patted his arm. "Now, Cluyne, there is no cause to raise your voice. Unlike most mortals, none of us is intimidated by the ducal bellow."

"*Hmmph.*" Her grandfather tried to maintain a stern visage, but his mouth tweaked up at the corners. "Least of all you."

The peal of Charlotte's laugh had Kate wondering whether yet another set of wedding bells might soon be ringing for the Circle of Sin. The bantering exchanges between her eccentric friend and her starchy grandfather were becoming increasingly intimate. For all their outward differences, they seemed to be very much at home in each other's company.

Home.

Strange how the word had suddenly taken on a new resonance. For the first time in her life, Kate felt anchored in the world. *Friends. Family. Love.* She no longer felt like a vagabond soul, adrift on an ocean of uncertainty.

As her grandfather and Charlotte continued their verbal sparring, she looked down the table. The reflections of the massive silver epergne, its bowl filled with hothouse flowers, cast a pattern of cheery color on the polished pearwood. Her grandfather's London townhouse no longer seemed so forbidding. Laughter had softened the sharp edges of the carved marble and gilded wood. Happiness had infused the ornate furnishings with life.

Kate smiled as the champagne bubbled down her tongue, filling her with its sweet effervescence.

"Come, come, my dear. We are all anxious to hear the details of how you vanquished a dastardly enemy," said Charlotte, waving the duke to silence. "Not to speak of getting a full report on the Viennese pastries and the waltz."

She forced her thoughts back to the last few harrowing weeks and shook her head. "I don't deserve all the credit. I would say that the mission was a joint effort."

Marco swallowed a snort.

"All of us were instrumental in seeing that the plot was foiled," went on Kate, ignoring the risqué waggle of his brow. "If Cluyne had not consented to host the house party in the first place, if Charlotte had not spotted the missing plant, if Lord Lynsley had not marshaled his network of agents to arrange our stay in Vienna…"

It all still seemed a little unreal. "Tappan was right," she went on. "His plan was diabolically clever. Had I been a normal young lady of the *ton*, it would have worked to perfection."

"I, for one, am extremely grateful that you are… yourself," said Marco, just loud enough for her to hear.

"Tappan certainly did not count on you or Lady Fenimore being so knowledgeable about botany," said Lynsley. "Like most people, he underestimated the intelligence of a lady."

"And paid for his hubris," declared Charlotte.

"Indeed," agreed Lynsley. "Because of your information, we were able to apprehend him before his ship sailed from Dover. After intensive interrogation, he has revealed all the names of those who hired him. Coupled with the information we were able to extract from Grunwald, the whole group of conspirators has been exposed. Whitehall has passed the information to the King of Saxony—without revealing how we learned of the plot. Thanks to you, the volatile situation in the Baltic will be settled through diplomatic channels, not violence."

"And Von Seilig's murder?" asked Kate.

"Tappan confessed to that as well." Lynsley ran a hand over his brow. "The truth is, he was up to his neck in sordid schemes. He was working with Allenham, trying to bribe certain members of the Prussian ministry to grant the Northern Mercantile Exchange Company exclusive rights to the Baltic trade in shipbuilding materials. It would have been an extremely lucrative deal, and would have made Tappan a very rich man."

"No doubt that explained his affair with Lady Duxbury," said Marco cynically.

"Yes," agreed the marquess. "She was unaware of his involvement in treason and murder, but was a willing participant in trying to further the Baltic deal. She has expensive tastes, and having a wealthy lover and brother was to her advantage. Her role was to try to seduce Von Seilig...."

Lynsley looked to Kate, his expression turning grim. "But when he rejected her advances in favor of spending time with you, she was only too happy to help set you up for the crime. It was she who spread the stories of your past to her brother and the Spaniards. Tappan had done research on all the guests, just in case any old scandal could prove useful for his own plans."

"What will happen to him?" asked the duke.

"He will be charged with the murder of Von Seilig. In return for his cooperation, I've agreed to a sentence of life imprisonment rather than hanging. That way, both his family and the government are spared the terrible public scandal of treason. The true nature of the plot will remain a closely guarded secret."

"And Lady Duxbury and Lord Allenham?" demanded Charlotte, a martial light flashing off her spectacles. "It seems unfair that they escape any punishment."

"They do not get off lightly," replied the marquess. "Allenham has been forced to resign from his position with the Northern Mercantile Exchange Company, and it has been strongly suggested that he and his sister start a new life in India. They should be boarding a ship for Bombay just about now."

The duke gave a low growl. "To think that my own neighbor, whom I have known for years, would turn out to be such a despicable villain." He pursed his lips and frowned. "It's one thing that he fooled me, but damnation, Lynsley, you of all people should have known better."

The marquess accepted the set-down with his usual show of equanimity. "I do my best, Cluyne. But depravity is everywhere, and unfortunately it is often well-hidden beneath a polished veneer of nobility."

Just as nobility could lurk beneath a show of dissolute debauchery.

Kate ventured a look at her new husband across the table. The dancing flames of the candelabra illuminated his face, golden light gilding the bronze skin, the chiseled cheekbones, and sensuous curl of his smile. Their gazes met for an instant and she felt a warm rush of joy well up inside her.

Yes, appearances could be deceiving. They had both hidden their true selves behind an outer shell of toughness to survive. But thankfully love had proved a more powerful force than cynicism.

Marco winked, sparks tipping the fringe of his dark lashes. "*Si, amico*," he replied to Lynsley. "It is often hard to discern between black and white, eh? Sometimes the two blur together, creating a smudged shade of gray. Rather like me. Though of late, I find the darkness is clearing from the crevasses of my soul and my life is lightening."

"Gray?" Charlotte arched a silvery brow. "I would never describe you as colorless," she remarked, much to the amusement of Cluyne and Lynsley. "You have quite a colorful past, from what I have heard. However, I trust that you will try to temper your more outrageous exploits."

"I will try," said Marco, flashing her an angelic look. "But Kate would be bored if I become *too* good. I'm afraid we both have a weakness for adventure. And so…"

The marquess suddenly seemed extremely interested in polishing the single fob hanging from his watchchain.

"And so it should come as no surprise that we have agreed to help Lynsley look into another small diplomatic problem," he finished.

Cluyne's face clouded with concern, but Kate interrupted him before he could speak. "Yes, there is a matter of a missing Imperial medallion in St. Petersburg."

"Tsar Alexander was apparently a little careless during one of his sexual trysts," explained Marco. "The bauble in question is apparently one of great historical significance for the Russian people. If he doesn't wear it during the upcoming Orthodox Easter celebration, it will be considered a very ill omen for the Romanov Dynasty."

"The lady's husband is using that fact to force the tsar to rescind some of his social reforms," said Lynsley. "If our government can help him out of this embarrassing predicament, he would be extremely grateful."

"I don't see why my granddaughter must be drawn into another dangerous mission," growled the duke.

"Actually, I asked to be part of it," said Kate softly. "I know you disapprove, but I would be bored to perdition living the life of a proper London lady. I detest drawing room gossip and have two left feet when it comes to ballroom etiquette." She paused and crooked a smile. "On the other hand, with my seafaring pirate background, I'm awfully good at navigating tight spaces and climbing to precarious heights—not to speak of purloining carefully guarded valuables."

"After all, she stole my heart," quipped Marco.

Charlotte stifled a chuckle. "You are fortunate she didn't toss it away. A sensible female would have feared singeing her fingers on a red-hot coal from Hell."

"Kate is not afraid of a little heat." He waggled his brows suggestively. "Are you, *cara*?"

She felt her face flame.

After another little laugh, her friend turned serious. "Come, Cluyne. Much as we wish to protect the ones we love from harm, we must allow them freedom to choose their own lives. We cannot wrap them in cotton wool and lock them away in a chest like a precious piece of porcelain."

The duke gave her a baleful look and then blew out a harried sigh. "I wish you were not *always* right—but unfortunately you are, Charlotte."

"How very wise of you to admit it, Edwin," she said with a fond smile. "There is hope for you yet."

"Aye, well, perhaps that is because I was such a fool in the past, letting my pride take precedence over my feelings. I wish you would not take such risks, Kate. But if it makes you happy, I shall learn to live with it." He drew a handkerchief from his coat pocket and discreetly blew his nose. "If there is one lesson I have learned over my numerous years, it is that you must follow your heart."

Charlotte smoothed his sleeve. "Well said."

"You can trust me to look out for your granddaughter," said Marco softly, his voice far more solemn than usual. Brushing back the long, dark strands of hair from his brow, he looked at Kate through the flickering flames. "I won't allow anything to happen to her. She is the sun and I am the moon—without her, my life would be plunged back into darkness."

Charlotte gave a little sniff. "How very romantic."

"Speaking of romantic, I cannot help noticing that Cluyne calls you Charlotte and you call him Edwin," murmured Kate. "Has something been blooming in the conservatory beside these hothouse tulips?"

Her friend turned a very beguiling shade of pink.

Cluyne coughed.

"Well?" pressed Kate.

"We old people are not as impetuous as you young ones," answered the duke. "But by the time you return from Russia, I hope that I will have an interesting announcement to make."

The pink now turned to poppy red.

"Assuming that she decides it's not too late to start a new chapter in her life," he added.

"After the last few weeks of murder and mayhem, perhaps it's time to turn the page," said Charlotte.

Repressing a smile, Lynsley refilled their glasses.

"At least we all survived the dangers." Thinking over how much had changed in all of their lives, Kate murmured, "As the Bard would say, 'all's well that ends well.'"

"Ah, but it's not the end, *cara*." Marco's topaz eyes glittered with the devil's own mischief. "I would say that it's just the beginning."

An enchanting new historical romance series from the author who brought you the scandalous Circle of Sin trilogy.
Please turn this page for a preview of
Cara Elliott's
next sizzling Regency romance!
Too Wicked to Wed
Available in November 2011.

Chapter One

"So *this* is what a brothel looks like. It is not at all what I expected."

"Dear Lord," muttered Captain Harley Stiles as he blotted the sheen of sweat from his brow. "I would hope that you haven't given the matter a great deal of thought."

"Not a *great* deal," replied Lady Alexa Hendrie. She turned for a closer look at the colored etching hanging above the curio cabinet. "But one can't help being mildly curious, seeing as you gentlemen take such delight in discussing such places among yourselves."

Her brother's friend quickly edged himself between her and the offending print. "How the devil do *you* know *that*?" he demanded.

Despite the gravity of their mission, Alexa felt her mouth twitch in momentary amusement. "I take it you don't have any sisters, Captain Stiles. Otherwise, you would not be asking such a naïve question."

"No, by the grace of God, I do not." Though a decorated veteran of the Peninsular Wars, he was still looking a little shell-shocked over the fact that she had outmaneuvered his objections to her accompanying him into the stews of Southwark. "Otherwise, I might have known better than to offer my help to Sebastian, no matter how dire the threat to his family."

Alexa bit her lip....

"I, too, am curious." A deep growl, as dark and smoky as the dimly lit corridor, broke the awkward silence. "Just what *did* you expect?"

She spun around. Within an instant of entering The Wolf's Lair, she and Stiles had been sequestered in a small side parlor to await an answer to the captain's whispered message. The door had now reopened, and though shadows obscured the figure who was leaning against its molding, the flickering wall sconce illuminated the highlights in his carelessly curling hair.

Steel on steel.

Alexa froze as a prickling, as sharp as dagger points, danced down her spine. "Oh, something a bit less... subtle," she replied, somehow mustering a show of outward composure. She would not—could not—allow herself to be intimidated. After taking a moment to study the muted colors and rather tasteful furnishings of the room, she returned her gaze to the etching on the wall. "By the by, is this a Frangelli?"

"Yes." Straightening from his slouch, the man slowly sauntered into the room. "Do you find his style to your liking?"

She leaned in closer. "His technique is flawless." After regarding the graphic twining of naked bodies and oversized erections for another few heartbeats, she lifted her chin. "As for the subject matter, it's a trifle repetitive, don't you think?"

A low bark of laughter sounded, and then tightened to a gruff snarl as the man turned to her companion. "Are your brains in your bum, Stiles? What the devil do you mean by bringing a respectable young lady here? Your message mentioned Becton, not—"

"It's not the captain's fault. I gave him no choice," she interrupted. "I am Alexa Hendrie, Lord Becton's sister. And you are?"

"This isn't a damn dowager's drawing room, Lady Alexa Hendrie. We don't observe the formalities of polite introductions here." The sardonic sneer grew more pronounced. "Most of our patrons would rather remain anonymous. But if you wish a name, I am called the Irish Wolfhound."

"Ah." Alexa refused to be cowed by his deliberate rudeness. "And this is your Lair?"

"You could say that."

"Excellent. Then I imagine you can tell me straight off whether Sebastian is here. It is very important that I find him."

"I can." His lip curled up to bare a flash of teeth. "But whether I will is quite another matter. The place would not remain in business very long were I to freely dispense such information to every outraged wife or sister who happens to barge through the door."

"Is it profitable?" she asked after a fraction of a pause.

"The business?" The question seemed to take him aback, but only for an instant. "I manage to make ends meet. So to speak."

"Now see here, Wolf—" sputtered Stiles.

"How very clever of you," went on Alexa, ignoring her companion's effort to cut off any more risqué innuendoes. Smiling sweetly, she shot a long, lingering glance at the Wolfhound's gray-flecked hair. "I do hope the effort isn't too taxing on your stamina."

"I assure you," he replied softly, "I am quite up to the task."

"Bloody hell." Stiles added another oath through his gritted teeth. "Need I remind you that the lady is a gently bred female?"

The quicksilver eyes swung around and fixed Stiles with an unblinking stare. "Need I remind you that *I* am not the arse who brought her here?"

"Would that I could forget this whole cursed nightmare of an evening." The captain grimaced. "Trust me, neither of us would be trespassing on your hospitality if it were not a matter of the utmost urgency to find Becton—"

"Our younger brother is in grave danger," interrupted Alexa. "I *must* find Sebastian."

"We have reason to think he might be coming to see you," continued Stiles. "Is he here?"

The Wolfhound merely shrugged.

Alexa refused to accept the beastly man's silence. Not with her younger brother's life hanging in the balance. "You heard what the Wolfhound said, Captain Stiles. He is running a business and doesn't give away his precious information for free."

Sensing that neither tears nor appeals to his better nature—if he had one—would have any effect, she took pains to match his sarcasm. "So, how much will the information cost me?" she asked. "And be forewarned that I don't have much blunt, so don't bother trying to claw an exorbitant sum out of me."

"I am willing to negotiate the price." Despite the drawl, a tiny tic of his jaw marred his mask of jaded cynicism. "Kindly step outside, Stiles, so that the lady and I may have some privacy in which to strike a deal."

"I'm not sure, er, that is..."

"What do you think? That I intend to toss up her skirts and feast on her virginity?" The Wolfhound looked back at her with a sardonic smile. "You are, I presume, a virgin?"

"Presume whatever you wish," she replied evenly. "I don't give a damn what some flea-bitten cur chooses to think, as long as I get the information I need."

"Ye gods, Lady Alexa, bite your tongue," warned Stiles in a low whisper. "You are not dealing with some lapdog. It's dangerous to goad the Irish Wolfhound into baring his fangs."

Dangerous. Another touch of ice-cold steel tickled against her flesh. Or was it fire? Something about the lean, lithe Wolfhound had her feeling both hot and cold.

Stiles tried to take her arm, but she slipped out of reach.

"I really must insist—" began the captain.

"Out, Stiles," ordered the Wolfhound as he moved a step closer to her.

Alexa stood firm in the face of his approach. Oh, yes, beneath the finely tailored evening clothes was a dangerous predator, all sleek muscle and coiled power. And ready to pounce. But she was not afraid.

"You may do as he says, Captain. I am quite capable of fending for myself."

Stiles hesitated, and then reluctantly turned for the hallway. "Very well. But I will be right outside, in case you need me," he muttered. "You have five minutes. Then, come hell or high water, we are leaving."

"Do you always ignore sensible advice, Lady Alexa?" asked the Wolfhound, once the door latch had clicked shut.

"I often ignore what *men* consider to be sensible advice." The gray-flecked hair was deceiving, she decided. Up close, it was plain that the Wolfhound was a man not much above thirty. "There is a difference between the two, though someone as arrogant as you would undoubtedly fail to recognize it."

"I may be arrogant but I'm not a naïve little fool," he retorted with a menacing snarl. "At the risk of further offending your maidenly sensibilities, allow me to point out that when trying to strike a bargain with someone, it is not overly wise to begin by hurling insults at his head."

Alexa felt a flush of heat creep across her cheekbones. "Actually, I am well aware of that. Just as I am well aware that any attempt at negotiations with you is probably a waste of breath. It is quite clear you have a low opinion of females and aren't going to consider my request seriously."

Beneath his obvious irritation, Alexa detected a glimmer of curiosity. "Then why did you agree to see me alone?" he asked.

"To show you that not everyone turns tail and runs whenever you flash your fangs." She squared her shoulders. "By the by, why is everyone so afraid of your bark?"

"Because I am accorded to be a vicious, unpredictable beast," he replied. "You see, I tend to bite when I get annoyed. And my teeth are sharper than most."

Lamplight played over the erotic etching, its flickering gleam mirroring the devilish spark in his quicksilver eyes. It seemed to tease her. *Taunt her.*

Alexa wasn't about to back away from the challenge. "Do you chew up the unfortunate young women who work here, then spit them out when they are no longer of any use to you?"

For an instant, it appeared she had gone a step too far in baiting him. His jaw tightened and as the Wolfhound leaned forward, anger bristled from every pore of his long, lean face.

But just as quickly, he seemed to get a leash on his emotion and replied with a cynical sneer. "You know nothing of real life, so do not presume to think you understand what goes on under my roof," he snapped.

"Perhaps you would care to explain it to me."

The Wolfhound gave a harsh laugh. "Nosy little kitten, aren't you? Seb ought to lock you in your room, before you stray into real trouble."

Alexa fisted her hands and set them on her hips. "Ha! Let him try."

"You have spirit. I'll grant you that." He paused for a moment. "Still interested in making a deal?"

"What is your price?"

"A kiss."

Her face must have betrayed her surprise, for he flashed a rakish smile. "Haven't you ever been kissed before?"

She sucked in a sharp breath. "O-of course I have."

"Oh, I think not," drawled the Wolfhound. "I'd be willing to wager a fortune that no man has ever slid his tongue deep into your mouth and made you moan with pleasure."

"Why, you impudent whelp—"

Her words were cut off by the ruthless press of his mouth. He tasted of smoke and spirits—and a raw, randy need that singed her to her very core. She swayed and suddenly the Wolfhound swept her into his arms. With several swift strides, he crossed the carpet and pinned her up against the wall, setting off a wicked whisper of crushed silk and flame-kissed flesh.

Alexa meant to cry out, but as he urged her lips apart and delved inside her, outrage gave way to a strange, shivering heat. Her protest melted, turning to naught but a whispered sigh. As did her body. Against all reason, it yielded to his touch, molding to every contour of his muscled frame. Broad shoulders, lean waist, corded thighs—Alexa was acutely aware of his overpowering masculinity. The scent of brandy and bay rum filled her lungs, and the rasp of his stubbled jaw was like a lick of fire against her cheek.

She knew that she should push him away. Bite, scratch, scream for help.

And yet. And yet…

And yet, as his hands moved boldly over her bodice and cupped her breasts, she could not resist threading her fingers through his silky gray-threaded hair. Like the rest of him, the sensation was sinfully sensuous.

A moment later—or was it far, far longer?—the Wolfhound finally ceased his shameless embrace and leaned back.

"A man could do far worse on the marriage mart than to choose you," he said softly. "For at least he will likely not be bored in bed. Indeed, I might even be tempted to swive you myself, if innocence was at all to my taste."

The crude comment finally roused Alexa from the seductive spell that had held her in thrall. Gasping through kiss-swollen lips, she jerked free of his hold and all of her wordless, nameless, girlish longings took force in a lashing slap. It connected with a resounding crack.

His head snapped back, the angry red imprint of her palm quickly darkening his cheek.

"*That* was for such an unspeakably rude insult." She raised her hand again. "And *this*, you arrogant hellhound, is for—"

He caught her wrist. "Is for what? The fact that for the first—and likely only—time in your life, you have tasted a bit of real passion?"

She went very still. "Do you really take pleasure in causing pain?"

The Wolfhound allowed her hand to fall away, and then turned from the light, his austere profile unreadable in the flicker of the oil lamps. "Most people think so," he said evenly as he moved noiselessly to the sideboard.

"I—I don't understand," she began.

"Don't bother trying," he snapped. "All that should matter to you is the fact that I am a man of my word. You paid your forfeit, so in answer to your other question, your brother is not at present in The Wolf's Lair. And if he were, it would not be for the usual reasons that gentlemen come here." Glass clinked against glass. "Like you, he is seeking information and I've heard word that he thinks I may be able to help him. Should he come by tonight, I will inform him of your quest, and how desperate you are to find him."

Alexa turned for the door, yet hesitated, awkward, unsure.

Taking up one of the bottles, the Wolfhound poured himself some brandy and tossed it back in one gulp. "Now get out of here, before one of my patrons recognizes you. Trust me, the tabbies of this Town are quick to pounce on any transgression. And their claws are far sharper than mine."

"Th-thank you," she said, hoping to show that her pride, if not her dignity, was still intact. "For showing a shred of decency in honoring our bargain."

"Don't wager on it happening again."

Alexa stiffened her spine. "I am not afraid to take a gamble when the stakes are high." She could not resist a parting shot. "And I'll have you know, I am *very* good at cards."

"Here at Wolf's Lair, we play a far different game than drawing room whist. You have tempted the odds once—I would advise you not to do it again."

"How very kind of you to offer more counsel."

The Wolfhound's laugh was a brandy-roughened growl. "You mistake my sentiments, Lady Alexa. I am not being kind. I am simply trying to stack the deck in my favor. If I am lucky, the cards will fall in a way to ensure that our paths never cross again."

THE DISH

Where authors give you the inside scoop!

♥ ♥ ♥ ♥ ♥ ♥ ♥ ♥ ♥ ♥ ♥ ♥ ♥ ♥ ♥

From the desk of Jane Graves

Dear Reader,

Have you ever visited one website, seen an interesting link to another website, and clicked it? Probably. But have you ever done that about fifty times and ended up in a place you never intended to? As a writer, I'm already on a "what if" journey inside my own head, so web hopping is just one more flight of fancy that's *so* easy to get caught up in.

For instance, while researching a scene for BLACK TIES AND LULLABIES that takes place in a childbirth class, I saw a link for "hypnosis during birth." Of course I had to click that, right? From there I ended up on a site where people post their birth stories. And then...

Don't ask me how, but a dozen clicks later, my web-hopping adventure led me to a site about celebrities and baby names. This immediately had me wondering: *What* were these people thinking? Check out the names these famous people have given their children that virtually guarantee they'll be tormented for the rest of their lives:

Apple	Actress Gwyneth Paltrow
Diva Muffin	Singer Frank Zappa
Moxie Crimefighter	Entertainer Penn Jillette
Petal Blossom Rainbow	Chef Jamie Oliver
Zowie	Singer David Bowie
Pilot Inspektor	Actor Jason Lee
Sage Moonblood	Actor Sylvester Stallone
Fifi Trixibell	Singer Bob Geldof
Reignbeau	Actor Ving Rhames
Jermajesty	Singer Jermaine Jackson

No, a trip around the Internet does *not* get my books written, but sometimes it's worth the laugh. Of course, the hero and heroine of BLACK TIES AND LULLABIES would *never* give their child a name like one of these…

I hope you enjoy BLACK TIES AND LULLABIES. And look for my next book, HEARTSTRINGS AND DIAMOND RINGS, coming August 2011.

Happy Reading!

Jane Graves

www.janegraves.com

♥ ♥

From the desk of Cynthia Eden

Dear Reader,

I love strong heroes. When I write my romantic suspense novels, I try to create heroes who can save the day while barely breaking a sweat. Men who aren't afraid to face danger. Men who are comfortable taking out the bad guys—even while these heroes successfully romance their heroines. Oh, yes, I'm all about an alpha male.

And when it comes to my heroines, well, my response is the same. *Give me a strong heroine.* I don't want to write about a heroine who needs rescuing 24/7. I want a woman who is strong enough to defend herself (and her man, if need be).

When I began writing DEADLY HEAT, I knew that my heroine would have to be a strong match for FBI Special Agent Kenton Lake. Since Kenton appeared in my previous "Deadly" book, DEADLY FEAR, I already knew just how powerful and capable he was. Kenton hunts serial killers for a living, so weakness isn't exactly a concept he understands.

I didn't want Kenton to dominate his heroine, so I made sure that I created a very strong lady for him... and firefighter Lora Spade was born. Lora is a woman who fights fire each day. She's not afraid of the flames, but she is afraid of the way that Kenton makes her feel.

Physically and mentally, my characters are strong.

But emotionally? When it comes to emotions, both Kenton and Lora are in for a big shock.

After all...love doesn't always make a person weak. Sometimes, it just makes you stronger.

Since Kenton and Lora are about to track an arsonist who enjoys trapping his victims in the flames, they sure will need all the strength they can get!

Thanks for checking out my Dish. If you'd like to learn more about my books, please visit my website at www.cynthiaeden.com.

Happy reading!

Cynthia Eden

♥ ♥ ♥ ♥ ♥ ♥ ♥ ♥ ♥ ♥ ♥ ♥ ♥ ♥ ♥

From the desk of Cara Elliott

Dear Readers,

Yes, yes, your eyes do not deceive you. Just when the brouhaha in Bath had calmed down a touch, a new scandal popped up. The Circle of Sin is spinning into action again. Alas, trouble seems to follow our intrepid heroines, when all they really want is a life of quiet scholarly study.... Actually, I take that back. They do realize that there is more to life than books (a handsome rogue...but we'll get to that later).

As you probably suspect, this time it's Kate, the feisty, free spirit of the "Sinners", who has landed in hot water. She's spent most of her life gallivanting the world with her American sea captain father—some high sticklers may call him a pirate—so it's really no surprise that her life in London, where she's come to live with her imperious grandfather, the Duke of Cluyne, is not sailing along very smoothly.

But honestly, it's really not *all* her fault. That rascally rake, the Conte of Como—Marco to his more intimate friends—is the one making waves. He's an unexpected guest at her grandfather's staid country house party, and when one thing leads to another...all hell breaks loose.

Trouble takes Kate and Marco from London to Vienna, where the various rulers of Europe are gathering to discuss politics now that Napoleon has been exiled to Elba. Now, now, don't roll your eyes. It so happens that Vienna was THE ultimate party town at the time. Anybody who was anybody wanted to be there, to rub shoulders (and other unmentionable body parts) with the kings, princes, emperors, and other high profile celebrities.

The Emperor of Austria hosted many of the dignitaries at his magnificent castle, and his poor aides spent countless hours trying to figure out the room assignments, taking into account who was sleeping with whom, so that late night tiptoeing through the corridors wouldn't result in any embarrassing trip-ups.

Glittering balls, sumptuous banquets, fanciful medieval jousts, spectacular fireworks—the daily list of extravagant entertainments was mind-boggling. Party girls Princess Bagration and the Duchess of Sagan vied with each other to see who could attract the most influential men to their soirees. As for other pleasures, well, let's just say they all were intent on having a good time. In fact, the Tsar of Russia—a notorious skirt-chaser—had to have a whole new wardrobe sent from St. Petersburg because he gained so much weight partying every night!

But why, you might ask, is Kate plunging into the midst of such frivolous festivities? And how is a rake like Marco going to help her get out of hot water? Well, you'll just have to read TO TEMPT A RAKE to find out!

Cara Elliott

www.caraelliott.com

♥ ♥ ♥ ♥ ♥ ♥ ♥ ♥ ♥ ♥ ♥ ♥ ♥ ♥ ♥

From the desk of Amanda Scott

Dear Reader,

Most books grow from the seeds of isolated ideas. One reads about an unusual historical incident, or finds an odd phrase that triggers a string of thoughts, or overhears a comment on a bus or plane that stirs an idea for a situation or a character.

I was seeking such seeds as I began to plot HIGHLAND MASTER. I'd started with a vague notion of Romeo and Juliet, simply because I always want to create a basic conflict between the hero and heroine. But I did not want the simple "Capulets think Montagues are dreadful and vice-versa". When I found myself wondering what would happen if a Montague were dropped into a nest of Capulets with a mission to accomplish, the gray cells began churning. That is the moment when a writer begins asking herself, "What if?"

What if my Scottish Romeo had sworn to kill Juliet's father? In medieval Scotland, blood oaths and blood feuds were common. What if someone in authority over that Scottish Romeo, knowing nothing about his oath or the feud, sends him on a vital diplomatic mission to the Scottish Capulets?

Then, since one also seeks to raise the stakes, what if Romeo has somehow managed to swear a second oath in direct conflict with his oath to kill Juliet's father? What if he cannot keep either oath without breaking the other?

What if he meets his Juliet and falls for her without realizing that her father is the man he has sworn to kill?

Research soon drew me to the great Clan Battle of Perth in 1396, which was to all intents and purposes a trial by combat between Clan Chattan and Clan Cameron, the two largest, most powerful Highland clan confederations. Thirty "champions" from each clan fought on the North Inch of Perth before the King of Scots and his court. When I read that only one (unknown) Cameron had survived, and did so by flinging himself into the river Tay, which swept him into the Firth of Tay and most likely on into the North Sea, I knew that I had found my hero.

In my story, Scotland's finest swordsman, Sir Finlagh "Fin" Cameron, the last man of his clan standing against eleven men of Clan Cameron, escapes from the great clan battle, manages to avoid being swept out to sea and—calling himself simply "Fin of the Battles"—joins the service of Davy Stewart, the bedeviled heir to the Scottish throne. Seeking to ally himself with the Lord of the North and the Lord of the Isles against his scheming uncle, the Duke of Albany, Davy sends Fin of the Battles back into the Highlands to arrange for a secret meeting with the great lords, hosted by the powerful Captain of Clan Chattan, known to all and sundry as "the Mackintosh."

Entering Clan Chattan territory, Fin is felled by a mysterious arrow and rescued by the lady Catriona Mackintosh, granddaughter of Clan Chattan's captain and, yes, also daughter of the clan's war leader, Shaw Mackintosh, the very man whom Fin swore to his dying father on the battlefield that he would kill.

I hope you enjoy HIGHLAND MASTER. In the meantime, *Suas Alba!*

Sincerely,

Amanda Scott

www.amandascottauthor.com

Want to know more about romances at Grand Central Publishing and Forever? Get the scoop online!

GRAND CENTRAL PUBLISHING'S ROMANCE HOMEPAGE

Visit us at www.hachettebookgroup.com/romance for all the latest news, reviews, and chapter excerpts!

NEW AND UPCOMING TITLES

Each month we feature our new titles and reader favorites.

CONTESTS AND GIVEAWAYS

We give away galleys, autographed copies, and all kinds of fun stuff.

AUTHOR INFO

You'll find bios, articles, and links to personal websites for all your favorite authors—and so much more!

THE BUZZ

Sign up for our monthly romance newsletter, and be the first to read all about it!